Secrets in Ice

KENNEDY PLUMB

For my sisters— by blood, by marriage, and by choice.

AUTHOR NOTE | CONTENT GUIDANCE

Although this book is written and recommended for ages 13-17, it contains content that may still be triggering or disturbing for certain audiences, including: scenes with diabetes-related complications, car accidents, depictions of murder, suspense, gun violence, death, mentions of drug use, mentions of extramarital affair, and mentions of adult activities (not depicted on page).

Please note - the dog is always okay.

LISTEN TO THE PODCAST AS YOU READ

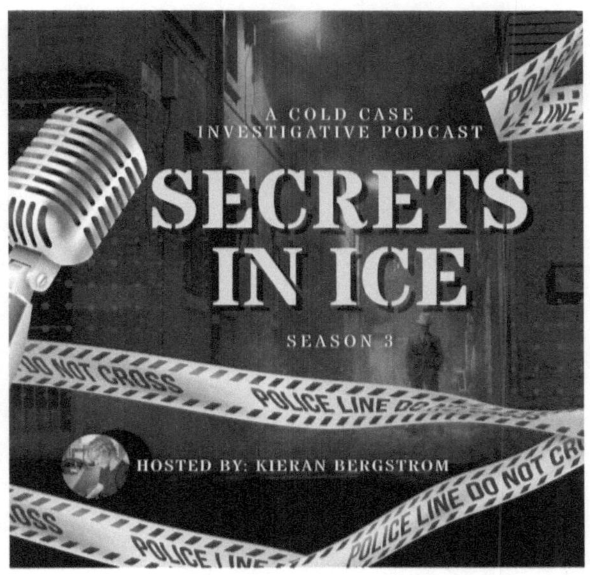

kennedyplumb.com/secrets-in-ice

PODCAST TRANSCRIPT
Secrets in Ice Season 3, Episode 1: The Girl Left Behind

[Secrets in Ice opening theme music plays]

KIERAN BERGSTROM:

On Saturday, October 17th, 2015, Gunnar and Ingrid Sinclair left their sprawling estate in the hills of Sapphire Pines, Oregon to take their eleven-year-old daughter Lizzy to a figure skating competition in a neighboring town.

Not only did they never arrive at the competition... they were never seen again. Alive *or* dead.

This tragic case was ruled a triple homicide, yet still remains unsolved ten years later, leaving much to wonder about what happened in the Sinclairs' final hours, especially considering what they left behind:

    1. A wrecked, abandoned car that showed signs of a struggle, ballistic evidence, and significant blood matching all three of the victims. But no bodies.

    2. An enviable manor up in the hills of Sapphire Pines with a sizeable estate to be inherited.

    3. A second daughter left behind at home with a babysitter.

Nikki Sinclair, tragically orphaned at only age seven and without answers even after all this time, has never been given the closure she deserves.

Come along with us on this season of *Secrets in Ice* as we reopen this ten-year old cold case and seek the truth.

What happened to the Sinclairs that day? Were they simply in the wrong place at the wrong time, or was this a premeditated attack?

And what everyone wants to know... why were their bodies never found?

Looking for answers among the shadows of the iciest cold cases, I'm your host Kieran Bergstrom, and you're listening to *Secrets in Ice.* This is episode 1, "The Girl Left Behind."

[Secrets in Ice opening theme music finishes playing]

1

———

NIKKI

REGULAR GIRL, REGULAR MURDERED FAMILY

It really could be a psychological study how obsessed I am with murder. I know there's some PhD student somewhere who'd love to analyze me, diagnose me. Probably write an entire dissertation about the effects of childhood trauma on shaping teenage hyper-fixations. I can see it now: the girl with the murdered family who can't get enough murder. Yeah. I'm a walking, talking, psychological phenomenon.

It would shock psychologists and regular humans alike how unfazed I am listening to the gruesome details of a small-town murder across the country while I eat a snack or give myself a manicure. Completely unbothered. But it's not as creepy as it sounds. Luckily for society, I'm not interested in the *practice* of murder. I'm not a serial killer or anything. I'm not a psycho. Just a regular girl who listens to true crime without even blinking but cries at the mere thought of a baby animal. A regular girl with regular hobbies and a regular murdered family.

Unfortunately, no podcast is interested in investigating

said murdered family—I know because I've harassed all of them to a humiliating degree about it—but I try not to hold it against them. They're busy. I get it. I'll continue to cling to the hope that one day someone with resources and know-how will take an interest in the case. But until then, I cope by listening to other people's families get murdered instead.

"Miss Nikki," Arrick's voice at the door of my suite startles me, and I rip my earbud out, which pauses the current murder I've been listening to.

"Sorry to scare you," he apologizes with a scolding glint in his eye, knowing what he's caught me listening to. He doesn't approve of my violent interests. "Your Aunt would like to speak to you."

There's a weight to those last words, and it hangs in the air for an extra second like it always does. Lingering.

"Has she taken her meds?"

Arrick's face pinches slightly, deepening the wrinkles around his eyes, which tells me all I need to know. He smooths down the fabric of his black suit jacket. "Come downstairs when you can."

He turns on his heel to leave, and his dress shoes echo down the staircase.

I roll out of my bed, dig around for my phone in the bundle of my Hermès throw blanket, and shut the door behind me to keep the warmth from my fireplace burrowed inside.

I wave hello to Bea—the other staff member who helps Arrick keep this ridiculous mausoleum of a house running —as I pass her on the spiral of the staircase, the pale oak of the railing cool and smooth under my palm.

"Are you done with your snack, dear?" she asks breathlessly, winded from the many steps of the staircase. She's getting much too old for these stairs, but she refuses to be let go or accept help.

"Not quite," I tell her, "but I'll bring it down when I'm done. Don't trouble yourself, Bee."

"Pah," she chides with a stern finger, and then carries on making her way slowly up the stairs, shuffling carefully on the wooden steps.

I've learned over the years that Lady Beatrice (which I call her sometimes affectionately) is impossible to argue with, so it's best to not even try. Old age and losing my older sister has made her especially stubborn and particular about my care. I adore her for it.

When I reach the bottom of the staircase, I step carefully across the beige and white checkerboard marble tile of the foyer that Bea has just mopped. Aunt Wren's suite door is ajar, spilling out the muffled sounds of her TV and the hacking of her cough.

Arrick lingers, pretending to dust a vase on the other side of the foyer so he has an excuse to stay nearby. He's been worried about her; both of them have been, but him especially, though he tries to be nonchalant about it. Sometimes I'll find him adjusting her pillows, or pulling the covers up over her shoulders when it's chilly, or filling up her water bottle with ice in the kitchen. Much to my dismay—because I will ship them together until the day I die—they're just good friends, but it's been hard for him nonetheless to see her like this.

I blow out a breath before stepping into my aunt's suite, knowing she needs me to stay positive. I straighten my shoulders and paste on the smile I've constructed just for her.

"Hi, Aunt Wren," I say cheerily, taking a careful seat on

the edge of her bed. "Hey Kayla," I add to her day nurse, who props up her pillows behind her back to help her sit upright.

I'm grateful at least she's here in her own colorful suite at home, surrounded by the bright colors of her art she's decorated the walls with over the years, and not the drab sterile gray of a hospital room.

Nurse Kayla, hidden from my aunt's view, pointedly eyes the unopened bottle of pills sitting on her side table and sends me an unspoken message with her eyes, *"Maybe you can talk some sense into her."*

My aunt tries to scold us between coughs. "Now don't you two... start...telecommunicating behind my back... again. I may be only a few feet away... from hell's gates, but...I ain't dead yet."

Kayla chuckles as she steps out of the room. "I don't know what you're talking about." She mouths to me before shutting the door, *"Good luck."*

I whip back around to my aunt with a stern eyebrow. "Why aren't you taking your medication? You want to leave me all alone in this giant empty house?"

"We both know the medication ain't doin' jack anyway." She waves it off.

I'm determined to out-stubborn her. "I beg to differ! The doctors said you had three months left to live" —I pretend to check the date on my watch even though I'm very aware of how many months it's been since then— "six months ago now?"

She rolls her eyes, and that's how I know I've won. I take her hand, fingers which were once always crusted in colorful dried paint but are now just frail and bony. I squeeze her hand gently. "What did the pulmonologist say about the surgery this morning? Did he get you all scheduled?"

She pats my hand, sighing as if she's taking a moment to think about what to say and how to say it, which makes me uneasy.

"What, will it be on a school day or something? I'm only virtual, so I'm totally fine missing a Zoom lect—"

"Annika," she interrupts, and I straighten at the use of my legal name she knows I hate. She meets my eye, and I'm knocked nearly breathless by the sudden sadness in her rheumy eyes. It's like they've turned to muddied ice. "They won't cover the pneumonectomy, sweetheart."

"What?" I breathe. "That can't be right, you have insurance. I'll go tell them—"

She shushes me gently. "You were there during the consult. You know there was a very small chance of the treatment working anyway."

I pull my hand away from hers and leap to my feet. "What, so we don't even try at all? Give up? No. We'll pay for the surgery. Who cares if insurance won't?"

"There's no chance I'm going to let you waste your inheritance on a 'maybe'." The added vigor thrusts her into another coughing fit.

I rub her back and reach for her water bottle to have on standby for when the fit passes.

When my parents and older sister died ten years ago, my aunt stepped in for me when no one else cared. If I have to, I'll shake down every piggy bank in this house to pay for whatever she needs.

Luckily, I'll be eighteen in four months anyway and will no longer need her permission to use my trust. I'll inherit the fortune my parents left behind, and stubborn aunts will get any life-saving measures available.

In the meantime, I'm going to give our family lawyer a

call. Maybe he can help me stand up to the insurance company with some teeth. Michael is great. He has personally checked in every few years since my family died to see how I'm holding up, and even sends Aunt Wren and I sparkling cider and a charcuterie board every New Year's Eve. I think it's just his client retention strategy, but hey, it works. Send me snacks, and you'll have my business for life.

I shake two capsules out of the pill bottle while Aunt Wren is sipping from her water bottle, a heavy wheeze coming from her lungs as she breaths.

I give her a meaningful look as I pass her the pills. "No self-sabotage on my watch."

Her icy eyes glaze with sentimentality for the quickest fraction of a second. "You remind me so much of her sometimes." And it's gone in a blink, the regular her returning quickly. "Both such a pain in the ass."

I chuckle, but part of me wishes she would talk more about her, no matter how much it may hurt. Her niece. My mother.

I was so young when she, my dad, and Lizzy died, that my own memories of them get dimmer by the second. I'm terrified that one day, the few blurry memories I have left will fade completely, taking my family with them for good.

Nurse Kayla comes back and announces that my aunt needs to rest, just as a text notification buzzes on my watch.

HUNTER

guess where my dad has to be for business tomorrow

I grin at the notification, my day instantly brighter seeing his name. We've been family friends for forever. Our dads were best friends back in the day.

We used to see their family all the time, even though they live all the way in Canada. We'd get together for school breaks or holidays or boating trips on the lake, but that all ended when my family died. It was probably too sad for them to bring only me along on vacations with them. The ghosts of my family's memory like hulking invisible elephants in the room you can't quite see but are impossible to ignore.

I haven't seen Hunter in a while, but we've been texting almost constantly after reconnecting on social media a few years ago. Apart from my aunt and the staff paid to care about me, he's the one keeping me upright on a daily basis.

I give Aunt Wren a kiss on the head. "No Jeopardy. Actual rest."

She shoots me a death glare. "You live your whole miserable sixty years, just for your great-niece to boss you around in the end."

I blow her a kiss. "Sleep well, Sleeping Beauty."

She grumbles something that sounds suspiciously like an expletive as I leave the room and pull out my phone to text Hunter back.

NIKKI

cat island?

HUNTER

that sounds like a made up place

NIKKI

take a geography lesson, canada

HUNTER

how many countries have you travelled to miss red, white, and blue? how many languages can you speak?

NIKKI

> fair. ok spill. rub it in. tell me what magical journey you get to go on next while I have to rot away in this coffin of a house

HUNTER

> how about I give you some company?

A photo comes through next, and I shriek so loudly it echoes off the beams of the ceiling overhead. Arrick runs out of a nearby hallway with a duster and a look of alarm.

"Miss Nikki, are you alright?"

I can barely formulate the response. "Yes, fine, *Hunter*, he's—"

I reach the top of the stairs, and I involuntarily break into a chaotic mixture of a victory dance and the Macarena.

"He's coming *here*!"

The photo is of a boarding pass and passport in his hand. The boarding pass says clear as day: *"ARRIVAL: PORTLAND, OREGON."*

I run into my room, throw myself onto my bed, and happy scream into my pillow.

But then I freeze in horror.

Not only will I be seeing Hunter for the first time in years... he will be seeing *me*.

Oh no.

I slowly put my earbuds into my ears and crank up the volume of my podcast. No better way to ease the stress of an unexpected visitor like audio murder. Time to panic clean.

2

KIERAN

YOU WANT ME DEAD? WAIT IN LINE

I groan as the sharp morning sunlight cuts through the curtain of my front windshield and right onto my eyelid. Keeping my eyes squeezed shut, I flip onto my other side, only to be sun slashed by the back windshield instead. At my movement, Vinnie rustles under my bed in the nook I built for him. I freeze, hoping he'll go back to—

Nope.

He shakes out immediately, his ears and collar flapping together and creating the absolute most noise possible. He hops onto my bed and lick-assaults my face. I pretend to be asleep, thinking maybe he'll take the hint and give me a minute to wake up at my own pace.

Also, nope.

He rests his snout on my chest and whines until I relent with a sigh.

"Good morning to you too," I say with no shortage of grouchiness, but it doesn't faze him one bit.

He leaps off the bed and spins in circles in front of the sliding door of the van, forgetting, as he does every morning, that he is in fact still a sixty-pound Husky and not the Chihuahua he thinks he is. His tail whips around, knocking everything off the counter. Including my laptop.

"Agh, easy!" I scold. I pull my boots over my sweatpants and thank yesterday-me for putting them near the heater last night before I went to bed. The warmth on my feet is a nice distraction from the dread that my laptop could now be broken and cracked.

Vinnie sits, trying to be obedient, but his wiggling butt has a mind of its own and scoots him across the vinyl flooring of the van. He couldn't sit still even if he wanted to.

My head nearly brushes the ceiling of the van as I stand, the boots giving me an extra inch or so. I pull my coat off the hook in the small closet I installed with the cabinets and drape it around my shoulders, taking a second in the cozy indoor warmth before facing the morning winter outside.

Vinnie howls impatiently.

"Yeah, yeah." I unlock the door when an alarm from the app that keeps me alive beeps. I groan when I read the notification.

"Error! Calibration of CGM needed. Urgent! Blood sugar reading may be inaccurate."

I hate pricking my finger.

Eh, I feel fine, and Vinnie doesn't seem to sense anything off. I'll do it later.

The second the door slides open just enough for him to wedge his body through, he leaps out of the van and straight into the pile of snow outside, disappearing into it momentarily as it swallows him whole. He emerges from the other side of the mound like a huge prairie dog, fur coated in white powder before he dives right into the next one.

I chuckle. There is nothing that makes him happier than

snow, and although I love a good snow day myself, it's nearly March. The snow is getting old. I'm ready for warmer temperatures. I slide the van door shut and click the button twice on the key fob to lock it.

"Don't talk to strangers," I yell as I walk over to the rest stop bathrooms. A phone notification buzzes in my coat pocket. I open to a string of text bubbles crowding my lock screen. Some hate comments from strangers mixed in with a few nice ones, some spam messages, a death threat or two probably. I swipe them away and try to focus on spending the least amount of time possible in this pungent bathroom. Oh good, someone left a fresh pee spot right next to the urinal. Lovely.

I wash my hands vigorously in the sink and try to tame the unruly mop of blonde hair that almost covers my eyes, before splashing some water on my cheeks. I welcome the refreshing chill that helps wake my brain up the rest of the way.

Outside Vinnie rolls around happily in the snow across the parking lot, next to a line of parked semi-trucks. The rest stop is otherwise empty, and I acknowledge the peaceful quiet. The hum of cars speeding down the nearby freeway. The soft crunching of my boots on the snow.

"Breakfast," I call over to Vinnie, the van beeping as I unlock it.

He speeds over as if I've announced that his genetics have miraculously changed, and he's finally allowed to try chocolate cake for the first time.

"Uh-uh." I wag a finger at him as he tries to hop into the van without shaking off the snow all over his coat. He obeys.

I kick my own snow-covered boots on the van exterior, slipping them off and setting my coat and boots on the doormat next to the heater under the passenger seat to dry.

I open the cabinet with Vinnie's food and pour a scoop of it into his bowl, which he devours right away like it's not the same exact thing he eats every single day.

While my electric kettle whirs to life, I weigh a pile of coffee beans on my scale, measuring carefully. When I have the perfect amount, I dump them into my grinder, taking a deep inhale at the aroma. I grind the beans finely and scoop them into my French press with the hot water. I'll give that exactly four minutes to steep, and then I'll have a perfect espresso. It's the best way to start the day.

Vinnie nudges my leg with an unpeeled banana in his teeth. I take it from him and peel it, popping it into my mouth to satisfy the furry busybody who is of the opinion that coffee doesn't count as breakfast.

I get the finger-prick out of the way, bolus my carbs for breakfast, and then swivel my driver seat around. The counter of the kitchenette I built doubles as my desk. I'm relieved to find that my laptop is crack-free from this morning's tail-induced tumble.

Once my laptop connects to my satellite internet pod, I scroll through my emails, mostly spam or promotions from various websites, but two emails in particular catch my eye.

The first email is from a private investigator friend who helped me on season one of my podcast. Wow, I can't believe that was over two years ago now. That season, we miraculously uncovered new evidence that led law enforcement to a murderer who had gone free for nearly twelve years. The victim was six-year-old Maycie Evans, who went missing out of her backyard. Her remains were found in the woods behind her home, but they could never find enough evidence to arrest any of the suspects.

The perpetrator was her uncle. He's rotting in prison now like he deserves. I won't even give him the satisfaction of naming him.

I open the PI's email.

GEORGE.MARSHALL@MAIL.COM

Subject: Your Neck of the Woods

Hey kid, hope you're doing well. Loved listening to season 2. You should be so proud. I'm sure that family is so grateful. I'm traveling for work and will have a layover in Portland tomorrow. Isn't that your neck of the woods? Anyway, would love to meet for lunch if you will be around. Let me know.

-George Marshall, Private Investigator

I snort. I love when people from the East Coast forget how big states are over here. Portland is nearly three hours away.

I click reply.

KIERAN@SECRETSINICE.COM

RE: Your Neck of the Woods

George, glad you enjoyed season 2. I've been taking a much-needed breather out in the woods ever since the finale premiered. Would love to meet for lunch, been wanting to pick your brain about season three ideas. There's a place downtown that makes a mean Reuben. Would noon work?

See you then, Kieran.

Honestly, even if it were ten hours way, I'd make the trip in a heartbeat for George. Without his help, the podcast never would have taken off, and I'd never be able to live out on the road on my own. I owe him my entire livelihood.

I hesitate before clicking the next email that I very well could have missed completely if it hadn't been right next to George's. It says it's from someone named "Ciphered Voyager." Odd, but okay. The subject line is what catches my attention, though: *"Roger Mackenzie Will Die."*

Roger Mackenzie was a key witness in the case for season two, which I just wrapped up. Roger, after pressure from my podcast and the community, came forward with information he had previously withheld of the murder of his coworker, Albert Jimenez, eight years ago. This information completely discredited the alibi of a suspect in the case— Frank Holt—and led to his arrest and subsequent confession, giving Albert's wife and children long-awaited closure. Frank Holt murdered Albert in cold blood, and Roger Mackenzie helped cover it up.

I usually ignore emails like this, but I'll give it a chance while I sip my fresh coffee. I give myself a second to savor the first steaming sip before I open the email.

CIPHEREDVOYAGERANON@MAIL.COM

Subject: Roger Mackenzie Will Die

Roger Mackenzie will die tonight unless you take down your podcast and cease further investigations. This is a promise.

-Ciphered Voyager

Well, somebody's bold.

I'm used to digital threats in my line of work; emails, messages, voicemail, but almost every single time, it's just some rando on the internet messing with me. You learn how to brush things off. Hate comment? Whatever. Death threat again? Eh. Join the club.

But this one? It makes a feeling churn in my gut that I can't shake off for some reason.

Roger Mackenzie is scheduled to testify in trial in a few months. I would hope that the county law enforcement is keeping a close eye on him, considering the case was so multi-layered and left cold for so long, but you can never be sure with under-resourced county governments.

I consider forgetting about the email entirely, since that season is already wrapped up, and I've done more than any regular citizen would be ethically obligated to do.

But I can't let it go. What is it about this guy that has me so rattled?

I pull out my phone, clicking the X on the bubbles of notifications from YouTube telling me I have new comments on my latest video. I type the name of the deputy I've been in contact with from that county. He's not a big fan of the podcast, or me for that matter, but we're cordial.

He doesn't answer, so I leave a voicemail instead.

"...and anyway, it could be nothing but just wanted to give you a heads-up just in case. Let me know if you have any questions. Ok, thanks. Bye." I end the message.

Because I'm, unfortunately, used to law enforcement not taking me seriously until it goes viral on the internet, I take a microphone out of the cabinet that holds my podcasting equipment and plug it in to my computer. I won't let this "Ciphered Voyager" lurk in his murky shadowed corner of the internet, hidden and unaccountable. You want to make threats? You don't like my podcast? Hi, welcome to the show.

I open YouTube and set my real self aside, layering my internet persona on like a heavy winter coat. I clear my throat and shove down any insecurity or doubt I've ever had and force myself to sound smooth and confident like the Kieran Bergstrom I've created is.

I take a final swig of my coffee and then press record.

"Welcome back Icers," I say into the microphone. "I wasn't planning to go live today, but I have an important request. If anyone happens to have any information about an internet account named 'Ciphered Voyager' in connection to Albert Jimenez's case, please alert Hood River County law enforcement immediately. Let me tell you about this crazy email I just got…"

PODCAST TRANSCRIPT
Season 3, Episode 1: The Girl Left Behind, Cont.

[a variety of soundbites from different people plays over suspenseful music]

A MALE VOICE:

Nice family. Real sad what happened.

NEWS REPORTER *[archival recording]*:

The disappearance of the Sinclair family this last weekend has sent shockwaves through the prominent community of Sapphire Pines, a tight-knit neighborhood where the wealthiest of the West call home. It's a case that continues to leave investigators and Oregonians baffled.

A FEMALE VOICE:

It's a well-circulated rumor among the kids in town that their mansion is haunted. It's a bit of a local attraction, especially around Halloween, since it was around that time they died. Poor girl. We don't see much of her.

A MALE VOICE:

From what I understand, the police always thought it was some kind of murder-suicide. They just could never prove it. They say the older sister had lots of psychological problems. Maybe they wanted to get rid of her.

ANOTHER MALE VOICE:

If you ask me, anytime a billionaire dies, a fairy somewhere gets its wings.

[a beat, as suspenseful music plays]

KIERAN BERGSTROM:

If you're from the Pacific Northwest, you have probably heard of the Sinclair family. Maybe you've seen a photo of their family, smiling on the cover of *Portland Society,* or you've seen their legendary estate nestled in the hills of Sapphire Pines, or maybe you've heard about the day they disappeared on the news. There aren't many who haven't heard the name Sinclair.

In my research, everything led to the fact that the Sinclairs were perfect. Perfect life, perfect home, perfect family.

42-year-old Gunnar Sinclair was the CEO of TrueNorth, an industry leader for oil and gas services, with an estimated annual revenue of $22 billion. Most of his employees, apart from a few disgruntled workers, which is to be expected in such a large company, described him as fair and easy-going. He and Ingrid got married young, but they were seemingly happy to those around them.

35-year-old Ingrid Sinclair was a renowned former professional ballerina for the New York City Ballet, turned philanthropist and advocate. She managed a nonprofit women's coalition focused on violence against women. She frequently hosted charity events that would raise upwards of one hundred thousand dollars at a time. She was active in her community and well-liked by those around her.

What I found unusual is how such a high-profile, admired couple and their daughter could be murdered, and the case could go cold. That everyone would accept that no answers were ever found? And especially that Nikki would be left without answers, without closure, all that time? I didn't understand it.

KIERAN BERGSTROM:

How did you know Nikki Sinclair? What can you tell me about her?

GRETA HALLOWAY:

I'm Greta Halloway, I was her soccer coach before it all happened. Very sweet girl, very bright. Tenacious on the field. She would get so competitive. When she loved something, she put her whole heart into it. It was a shame she wasn't allowed to come back to the team. I heard her new guardian wouldn't allow it.

KIERAN BERGSTROM:

What do you know about her guardian, Wren Delaney?

GRETA HALLOWAY:

I believe she is Nikki's great aunt. I've never met her personally, but a few of my friends have had run-ins with her around town over the years. They say she is foul-mouthed and grouchy. Keeps Nikki basically locked up in that huge house. Pulled her out of school, out of sports and activities, fired almost all of the staff, we pretty much never see them anymore.

KIERAN BERGSTROM:

What do you think happened to the Sinclairs?

GRETA HALLOWAY:

Mr. Sinclair was very well connected, *very* wealthy. It's not too far-fetched to believe that he made one misstep with the wrong person. Or maybe someone wanted what was his. I don't know. But I will say this. All alone in that big house? Shut out from the world? That poor girl may as well have died along with them.

3

NIKKI

THIS ISN'T A HALLMARK MOVIE

The next morning, I wake up to an absolutely spotless room. Yesterday I stress dusted every single brass light fixture and every inch of my sage green walls. Cleaned every fingerprint off the huge antique gold-trimmed mirror that takes up a whole corner of my room. I vacuumed *under* my jute rug, which I usually tell Bea not to worry about. My plants are freshly watered and perky. My sheer curtains are even steamed. It's lively and bright just the way I like it.

But even so, unfortunately the immaculate room still doesn't take away the raging anxiety that Hunter will be here today.

As excited as I am to see him, I'm also heart-stoppingly nervous. Over text, I've never had to be worried about my own awkwardness. No uncomfortable silences I don't know how to fill, no unspoken social norms I don't know about, no pressure to act a certain way or to look a certain way. We can just be ourselves, with nothing else to worry about.

And there's another thing... While, yes, he's my best

friend *only*, I do have eyes, so I won't sugarcoat this here: Hunter is objectively hot.

Every photo of him is perfect, even the unfiltered, candid ones. Someone could catch him off-guard at an odd angle eating barbecue ribs or something, and he'd still look perfect.

Me on the other hand? With the right angles, the right lighting, the perfect formula of just the right amount of concealer and mascara that doesn't look like I'm trying too hard, I can manage to pull off a decent selfie.

But real life?

He'll know in a second that I'm an awkward weirdo with *pores*.

I roll out of bed and sleepily cross the tile of my ensuite bathroom and scream at the sight of myself in the mirror, immediately wide awake.

A ZIT?! Right in the middle of my forehead?!

This must be my karma for what I've done to Arrick all these years. All the times I've hidden in shadowed corners because I love how he jumps when I scare him. The times he's had to buy me pads at the store in emergencies. Driving me all the way across town at the crack of dawn so I can buy a newly released book before it sells out. I know. He's an angel.

Oh, universe, you can be so crafty.

I have an entire dead family; doesn't that give me some kind of get-out-of-jail-free card? A karmic free pass?

Guess not.

After nearly an hour of scrubbing, dabbing, brightening, brushing, and smoothing, I sigh hopelessly in the mirror. Well, this is as good as it's going to get. For my copper-colored hair, I've opted for half of it up and slicked back, the other half down and wavy. I've perfected my minimal, glowy makeup with a pretty pink blush that makes my blue eyes look extra vibrant. Light gloss on my lips.

There is a knock on my bedroom door, followed by Arrick's muffled voice. "Are you ready to go, Miss Nikki?"

I sling my crossbody bag around my shoulder and slip my phone and wallet inside. I've scheduled a meeting with our family lawyer for this morning, which will fortunately keep my mind occupied until Hunter gets here.

I shut the door to my walk-in closet to hide the piles of clothes I discarded in frenzy before I was finally able to settle on this pair of wide leg jeans with cute patches of butterflies on them and a baby pink cropped sweater that matches my blush. Hunter won't see in my closet, it's fine if it looks like a tornado struck.

Bea intercepts Arrick and I at the foot of the staircase with a homemade muffin and my coat in hand.

"You should be making time for a better breakfast," she tuts but gives me a knowing smile. "You look beautiful, sweetheart."

I take the muffin gratefully with a laugh. "What do you mean? This is how I always look, absolutely nothing out of the ordinary here." I give her a one-armed hug, her wrinkled cheek pressing to mine. "Thanks, Bee."

I follow Arrick to the car, clutching my coat tightly as the freezing outside air engulfs me. He opens the back door, which always makes me feel more like a celebrity rather than a pathetic seventeen-year-old who still doesn't know how to drive.

Warm air from inside the car wraps me up like a hug, and I'm grateful Arrick thought to heat the car up ahead of time, so I'd be more comfortable. I don't deserve him.

He slides into the driver's seat, and I lock in place as a familiar deep voice blares from the speakers.

"And then he dismembered his body, strewing pieces of him all across—"

Arrick's head whips back to me, mouth agape. I fumble with the zipper of my crossbody in horror, trying desperately to get to my phone, which has connected to the Bluetooth in the car, automatically playing what I had listened to last.

After what feels like a lifetime, I finally manage to turn off the graphic podcast, disconnect Bluetooth, and strongly consider throwing the whole phone out the window as well. A blazing fire spreads across my cheeks.

I laugh sheepishly, wishing these leather seats could swallow me. "Oops."

He wordlessly shakes his head in judgment and drives down the cobbled drive of our estate, the huge trees creating a snowy canopy overhead. The fresh powder across the lawn and on the bricks of the manor looks so delicately and strategically placed that it's almost like my mother must have known we'd have visitors today and made nature act accordingly.

I smile. The thought of that distracts me a little from my embarrassment.

Driving into town, I'm struck by the charm of it all. Fresh snow always makes me see it in a new light. The expensive boutiques, luxury spas, dainty coffee shops. Pines all around as far as you can see, vast, white-tipped mountains in the distance. Sapphire Pines is the kind of place you'd fall in love in if you were the heroine of a Hallmark movie.

Before my family died, I remember snow days from school where the whole town would set aside family rivalries, small-town gossip, wealthy snobbishness, and bring out their sleds instead. The great equalizers. Lizzy and I would race down those hills without any fear. No one was worried about money, or drama, or competition for just a few hours.

Maybe they still do that.

But I don't. Not anymore.

Arrick pulls into the parking lot of Montgomery Law Group and helps me out of the car, reminding me to be careful crossing the slippery pavement.

"Do you want me to come in there with you?" he offers, his kind brown eyes containing no shortage of their usual sparkle.

Part of me wants to say yes, to accept any help he's willing to give. But he's already done too much for me, and I should do this on my own anyway. I decline his help with a grateful smile.

Carefully, as I promised, I step into the offices of our family lawyer.

"Miss Sinclair, so good to see you," Michael greets me as I walk in. Wow, I haven't seen him in person for years. I can't even remember when the last time was.

Was the last time when everything happened?

Is that why my body feels so queasy?

I follow him to his office and sit in the chair in front of his desk. His smile is bright and friendly as he lowers into his chair on the other side of the desk. He's grayer than I remember, but the smile is the same.

It brings back a memory of a time when he sat across from me with that very same smile and attempted to translate legal jargon to a grieving and confused seven-year-old.

"Okay, so I've looked into the insurance policy," he starts. "And I think I may be able to put some pressure on them. I'll start by sending a letter on our letterhead, and then we'll go from there."

"Great," I exhale in relief. "I hope that's all it'll take. I think I should have some backup options prepared just in case, though."

He clasps his hands together on the desk. "Sure, what did you have in mind?"

I steel myself, knowing I'll need to be assertive here.

"What would we need to do to sell some of my dad's cars?"

Michael's smile falters. His eyes fill with pity. "Are you sure you want to do that? You know how much those cars meant to him."

A guilty jab pierces my gut. My father's biggest joy was racing. Going as a family to watch his races are some of my favorite memories. The sports cars in the garage were his pride and joy, but they died with him ten years ago.

"I know. It's not an easy choice. Either that or I need to make a sizeable withdrawal from my trust." I keep it short and sweet, forcing my voice to stay steady and confident, even though I'm shaking a bit. Maybe it's being back here after all this time, the memories this office is stirring up.

"Why is that?" he asks.

I wring my hands in my lap, which are luckily hidden by the desk. "Like I explained on the phone, my aunt is very sick, so if her insurance won't cover the treatment, I'd like to pay for it out of pocket."

He looks like there is so much he wants to say but doesn't quite know how to without shutting me down completely. "From the experiences I've had with your aunt, I can tell you she'd probably prefer settling her affairs herself," he says carefully.

I'm getting discouraged, but I raise my chin. "I'd like to know my next steps, please."

Michael's hands move a lot as he explains, "Your aunt, as your caregiver, has been given a certain amount of discretion over the use of these funds as they pertain to your care. But as a minor, without her permission I'm afraid there's not much we can do, and I assume she doesn't know you're here today."

"Well, I turn eighteen in June, so when I—"

Michael's uncomfortable expression makes me stop.

"What?" I ask, almost afraid to know now. I dig my fingernails into the palm of my hand anxiously.

He hesitates. "Miss Sinclair, your parents... well, they were concerned about your ability to handle such a big responsibility. A trust of this size so young... They wanted you and your sister to have to work hard in school, get good grades. Earn your way into a good college. Not rely on money to get you there." He's speaking as if my parents themselves will regenerate into this office at the very mention of their deaths. "They couldn't have known what was going to happen to them... I looked it over when they passed, trying to see if there were alternate instructions in the case of their... early demise... but the terms of the will were the same either way."

I don't like where this is going, and by the look of him, neither does he.

"Which means...?"

"Your trust doesn't free up until you reach the age of twenty-one."

I gawk at him. "Twenty-*one*?"

He nods, his lips pressed together.

He must see the involuntary tears gathering in my eyes

as I process this. My parents' money is useless. My aunt won't survive four more years without the surgery.

My throat tightens. "What if my aunt gives her permission for the withdrawal?"

He rubs the back of his neck to deliver more bad news. "I'm afraid the money she can withdraw has very specific conditions for its use. Unless it's specifically for your care, it wouldn't be allowed."

A tear slides down my cheek against my will. I'm a Cancer; it just happens whether I approve it or not. "There's really nothing you can do?"

"Legally, no. The terms were very clear. You had to be twenty-one, or—" He stops himself.

I perk up. "Or?"

"Or married."

What? My throat is so dry I can't even summon a verbal response as the earth itself crumbles around me.

Michael's eyes soften. "I'm so sorry, Annika. The cars are also part of the estate and within your aunt's charge, too, but let's start by finding the titles. Find those, then we'll go from there. Maybe there's something we can figure out."

4

———

NIKKI

CRAZY FEELS LESS CRAZY WHEN YOU'RE DESPERATE

I sit in the back of Arrick's car, and like the saint he is, he simply gives me a quiet minute to cry without interruption. He pulls out of the snowy parking lot and wordlessly drives to my next destination.

From the corner of my eye, I catch him looking back at me in the rear-view mirror, checking on me but not pressing, allowing me the time I need.

I update him on what the attorney told me once I can take a full breath.

"Did you know?" I finish, hating how pathetic and snively I sound.

His long pause compounds the silence in the car, the click of the turn signal extra loud in contrast.

"Your parents always had a very unique way of doing things," he finally answers. Did his knuckles just tighten on the steering wheel ever so slightly?

"While I didn't know about this particular caveat, I can't say I'm surprised." He stops at a red light. "I'm sorry this news has come as a shock. Are you going to be alright?"

"I can't let her die, Arrick." My voice cracks. "I'll have to find some other way to get the money, inheritance or not."

He doesn't respond, but he passes me a tissue. I blow my nose as we pass under the archway of the country club and make our slow ascent up the hill to the clubhouse. The golf course is closed for winter, and it's kind of serene, looking out at the sprawling lawns coated in even snow, undisturbed by human life.

"Um," I say through the tissue, "do you happen to know where my dad would've kept all the titles for his cars?"

Arrick's eyes flick around as he thinks about it, lips turning downwards. "Hm. I don't think so. I can look around in the garage, but I don't know if I've ever seen those."

I nod, because of course he hasn't. I should've known it wouldn't be that easy. Why would anything be easy? As we approach the valet loop, I hurriedly fix my face with the front camera of my phone, groaning that the work I put into my makeup was ruined with only a couple minutes of human emotion.

A text bubble pops up at the top of my phone screen from Hunter. Thank goodness he's coming. I need this distraction more than oxygen right now.

HUNTER

running 10 min late, can you get us a table?

NIKKI

you're lucky I tolerate you, canada

HUNTER

I'll make it up to you in bread

NIKKI

the bread that comes for free with the meal? no, you can make it up to me in chocolate cake

HUNTER

at 10am? you're a monster

NIKKI

welcome to america where we have chocolate cake and dr pepper at all hours of the day

HUNTER

let freedom ring I guess

Arrick pulls the car to a park at the curb and helps me get to the door without slipping on the slick sidewalk.

"What time would you like me to return?"

My teeth chatter, a particularly brutal gust of freezing wind slapping across my cheek. "I'm not sure what his plans are. Can I text you?"

He opens the door to the restaurant, and I'm nearly hypnotized by the warm air coaxing me inside.

"Of course, Miss Nikki. I'm—" He hesitates, and it makes me pause at the door, looking back at him over my shoulder.

"You're what?"

He clears his throat. "I'm glad you're getting to spend some time with someone your age for a change."

I grin. "Look at me, meeting a friend for lunch like a normal teenager."

"Have fun." And he closes the door behind me.

The hostess is a proper-looking woman in her late forties, who smiles when I ask for a table for two, but it doesn't quite reach her eyes. I'm sure she's used to dealing with a lot of entitled people working in a place like this. I'm sometimes embarrassed to visit local places in my town, knowing that the snobs who live here also go to the same places. I always wish I could tell the workers, "Don't worry, I'm not like them."

I've always been in a different category completely in this town. My address is here, but I'm not *here*. A resident, but not really a member. I've never been one of them.

After my family died, and most of the staff was let go, Aunt Wren insisted I needed to get back to friends, be around the community again, do things normal kids do. She didn't want me to be isolated. She thought going back to my school and extracurriculars quickly would be good for me, that I'd be surrounded by love and support.

Well, big surprise, something about having a murdered family makes you a complete social pariah. No one wanted to be friends with the creepy orphan girl. Even the soccer team I'd played on for years shunned me. It was a hard lesson to learn so young, that I'd always be different than them. Other.

It's lonely sometimes, but one day I'll get out of this town.

One day that I thought was a whole lot closer.

I shake it off, clinging instead to the prickle of nerves at seeing Hunter, needing this distraction to keep me from spiraling into complete despair.

The hostess walks me over to a table close by, so Hunter can easily find me when he gets here, and she gives me the brunch menu. I thank her and greedily flip through the pages as if I could devour the pictures of the food alone.

I'm in the middle of trying to decide between eggs benedict or strawberry French toast, when a tap on my shoulder takes every ounce of nerves out with it, completely melting away any worry or anxiousness.

Because it's him. He's here.

I shriek happily, startling most of the old people in this dining room. I jump up out of my seat and throw my arms around his shoulders.

Hunter hugs me tightly, and I try not to cry, not realizing until now how much I needed a hug from a friend.

"And here I wondered if you'd be happy to see me," he laughs.

"You know you're not allowed to leave now, right?" I say into his sweater, my voice squished and muffled. "I will absolutely be holding you hostage and sending your father a ransom note with impossible demands for your safe return."

"I'd expect nothing less out of a trip to the States."

I step back to look at him. His real-life smile is just as runway model white as his pictures, his eyes just as bright green. His dark hair has been recently cut, so the fade on the sides is fresh and clean, the longer top section gelled to look strategically messy. He's wearing a subtly wealthy outfit—a hoodie that looks normal enough, but I recognize the discreet Balenciaga logo on the arm. And just casually wearing brown leather Prada boots that probably cost two thousand dollars.

He's stunning.

But I don't feel shy like I thought I would. Because my soul knows his soul, whether we're texting or talking. This is the same Hunter I've known digitally all this time. My best friend.

We sit at the table and immediately put our heads together and snicker about the old snobs all around us, deciding what each of them must be talking about.

I make up a very pretentious accent for the man in the gray wool sweater in the corner who is speaking to someone on the phone in hushed tones. "I can't leave my wife until after this campaign ends Susan, we've talked about this. I can only see you in private for now."

He laughs and nods over to two men behind me. I sneak a peek as I'm pretending to fish something out of my cross-body across the back of the chair. They are both sipping on a drink from a clear glass as they look longingly out the window to the snow-covered greens below.

Hunter makes his pretend voice gruff and low. "So ridiculous the club can't do anything about this snow considering how much I donated to their remodel last year."

I mimic what I envision the other man to sound like. "Customer service isn't what it used to be. One call to my team, and they'd be out there shoveling the snow themselves."

He straightens his shoulders to shoot back a snobbish reply, but he's interrupted by the waiter asking us what we'd like to order.

We snort into our menus, as if she's a teacher scolding us for talking during an exam. He smiles at me over the top of his menu, and I think I die a little inside at how much I've missed him.

To my delight, he orders the eggs benedict, so I order the strawberry French toast, knowing full well I'll be stealing some off his plate.

The waiter leaves us, and I take an eager sip of the coffee she set down in front of me, relishing the warmth of the mug on my palms.

Hunter's lips turn downward, and I immediately know what's coming. I fidget with my cutlery in awkward anticipation. So much for this visit distracting me from reality.

"How's your aunt?"

His eyes are so genuine and concerned that I swallow the shallow reply I was tempted to make to keep the tone light. I flip over the fork on my napkin a few times. As much as I want to gloss over the sad and the scary, to keep things carefree and easy, I can acknowledge that there's another part of me that longs to talk about it with someone who cares.

"She's..." I pause, collecting the years of testing, ups and downs, diagnoses, treatments, and trying to condense it down into a single thought, a single feeling. I bite the inside of my cheek. *Don't cry, don't cry.* "She's starting to give up."

He doesn't answer, but not in a way like he doesn't know what to say, but like he's giving me the opportunity to elaborate, knowing it could take me a second.

"She hasn't been taking her medication and insurance denied coverage of the pneumonectomy that she needs. It could cost up to a hundred thousand dollars," I spill, the words tumbling out of me like they've been caged in too tightly and are finally unlocked. "I've been trying to withdraw what she needs from my trust." I stab the napkin with the fork now, anger bubbling to the surface. "But it apparently has really fun extra limitations, because my parents going off and dying wasn't enough, but they had to also curse me from the grave, too."

He cocks his head. "Limitations? I can get pretty much whatever I want from mine."

"You're 18," I remind him. "Which I thought would be the solution for me too in a few months, but like I said. Cursed. My parents wanted me to be humble. Well, consider me humbled, Mom and Dad!"

"You won't get access when you're 18?" He looks baffled.

"21." I stab the napkin again to punctuate it. "Or, get this! *Married.*" I bark a sarcastic laugh. "Apparently if I were to get married it would magically make me more responsible and capable of handling my parents' money."

His perfect lips quirk into a smirk.

"What?" I ask, shrinking a little.

"Well, isn't it obvious?" His eyes shine with mischief and adventure and other dangerous things. "Let's get married then."

He says it as if it's not the most insane thing to ever be thought of, let alone uttered aloud.

"I think I must have had a stroke or something. What?"

He chuckles in a 'Oh there's Nikki being Nikki again' way and reaches for my hand. "I'm serious, Nik. Why don't we get married in June when you turn 18? Wouldn't that solve everything? You'd be able to pay for her surgery?"

I can't manage to get my vocal cords to function properly, so I splutter a string of unintelligible syllables instead. "Wha — you — my?"

Hunter jumps to his feet, smile so bright it knocks me nearly unconscious. To my shock and horror, he steps around the table right in front of me and then drops down on a knee. Right here. In the middle of the restaurant.

"Annika Marie Sinclair," he says, and I can't pick up my jaw off the ground. "Marry me?"

"You're serious? Like be so serious right now. Is this a joke?"

He takes my hands. "I'm not joking. Let's save your aunt. Marry me, Nikki."

The whole restaurant is watching us, even the server nearby has paused to watch with bated breath.

My brain whirrs in hyper-speed as it processes the choice before me.

For years I've felt so helpless to Life. Like I'm not a true driver, only a passenger along for the ride, locked in and forced to watch as Life happens all around me. My family taken too soon, but I'm left behind. No way to get answers about what happened to them, so I'm stuck with the unknown. And now my aunt... with no way to help her.

But what if there *is* a way I can help her, a choice *I* can make, something *I* can put in motion myself? Something I can take control of for once?

It's a crazy, absurd choice that anyone sane would never even consider.

But no one's ever considered me sane.

"Okay," I say with a disbelieving laugh, and he laughs too. "This is absolutely crazy. But I want to *do* something for a change instead of waiting for something to happen. So, YES. Yes, I'll marry you."

We celebrate with chocolate cake. A lot of chocolate cake.

Move over, Life. I'm taking the keys this time.

5

———

KIERAN

DO I ACTUALLY HATE THE CITY, OR AM I JUST HANGRY?

Vinnie howls dramatically from his nook as we make our way up the I-5 northbound, the noise so loud it nearly rattles the windows.

"Kevin Loki Bergstrom!" I yell at him over my shoulder. "You howl in here again, and I'm not sharing my lunch with you!"

He flops down with a theatric pouting whine, and I instantly feel bad for yelling. I admit that, like his, my patience is also short after being on the road for over three hours at this point. But fortunately, my phone GPS says we're almost there.

I glance at him in the rearview mirror. "I'm tired of the van too," I say with a softer apologetic tone, patting the passenger seat next to me. "C'mere."

He perks up right away and hops on it happily, taking full advantage of his new window view.

Fortunately, the highways around here are plowed often, so although I keep my speed a little slower than I normally like as an extra precaution, last night's snowfall has had little impact on our drive so far. It's been surprisingly nice to drive through the scenic snow-capped canyons and freshly powdered valleys. When I woke up to it all this morning, I expected a much worse drive.

As a full-time van-lifer, I'm more familiar than most on how brutal winters can be, especially since the places I prefer to decompress from work are in the more remote areas. It's cold, for sure. It's wet, absolutely. Some would even say miserable. But I'm much more familiar with the beauty of winter than most. Rather than only observing it from the top of a corporate office as it slowly melts, I get to live in it, become one with it. So yes, it does make life a little harder sometimes but getting an experience with nature not many other people get makes it worth it.

But I'm definitely not one to complain when summer arrives.

As we inch our way closer and closer to the city, the more buildings and people that come into view, the grouchier I become. It's like population count has a direct correlation with my overall mental state. It's only been a few hours, but I already miss the quiet seclusion of all the truck stops and campgrounds that most people avoid this time of year.

I had hoped I'd have a little more time to isolate myself before diving back into such an annoyingly *social*—but too undeniably lucrative to quit— profession, but I'm happy to cut my time off short to see George again.

Vinnie whines with excited anticipation as we cross over the river on the busy bridge and enter the downtown area. Hardly any snow remains this far into the city, only big hulking piles of it shoved into corners of parking lots, but the temperature is just as cold this close to the water.

I exit the freeway and follow the directions from my GPS

to the place George and I agreed to meet. I'm still almost twenty minutes early, but I'm glad I can take my time after such a long drive.

I switch off the gas, and Vinnie's entire attention snaps over to me. Within seconds, he's shed off the impatient enthusiasm at our potential adventure, and he steps into new fur entirely as he gets to work.

He barks at me when I stand up too quickly, and when stars glimmer behind my eyelids, I have to admit he's right. I sit back down to steady myself, realizing what Vinnie has already smelled on me— that I haven't eaten in too long, and my blood sugar is low.

Sure enough, my CGM beeps at me with a signal that my levels have gotten too low, and I grumble that everyone's making too much of a fuss.

Vinnie uses his snout to open the mini fridge like he's trained to do, and grabs an apple juice carton with his teeth, closing the door behind him with his hind leg before bringing me the juice.

I pet his head in gratitude. "Thanks, but we're about to eat, dude, I'm fine."

He drops the juice in my lap and stares at me in an almost humanly-stubborn way like this is non-negotiable.

I chuckle. "Fine. I will drink the juice *only* so you stop looking at me like that. I'm okay. Go get your stuff. Vest. Leash."

He scurries off to retrieve his items, his enthusiasm returning now that he's done his job. I keep my end of the deal and chug the juice.

He brings over his leash and the bright yellow vest I make him wear to new places, which he hates, but whenever I can avoid awkward conversations about why I'm bringing a sixty-pound hairball into a nice establishment, I'd much rather opt for a vest that unmistakably answers that question for me.

When he was a puppy, I was newly diagnosed as a type one diabetic, and I was overwhelmed with keeping myself alive. When nowhere would train him because "Huskies don't make good service dogs", I decided to do it myself, if not simply out of spite to prove them wrong. Training him while I trained myself made sense anyway. Two birds, one stone.

When the podcast took off a couple years ago, I could finally afford to get myself an insulin pump and continuous glucose monitor, which make Vinnie a little less of a necessity, but he still likes to notify me when I'm low before the monitor does, as a matter of principle, trying to remind me that he's still important.

He's important all right, but that's not why.

Truth is, we're all each other's got. And it's been that way for pretty much as long as I can remember.

The only parking spot I could find that would fit my bulky van was in an alley of sorts about a block away, but I don't mind the walk too much. The stark chill that hits me after leaving the warmth of the van makes me shiver. I pop the collar of my coat up closer to my ears as a breeze from the river slides down my back.

I give Vinnie extra length on the leash and allow him a couple moments behind the stores to take care of business, and he ultimately decides on a rusty dumpster.

We make our way down the alley toward the front and Vinnie sniffs and pees on basically every square inch as we go.

I roll my eyes at him. "It's the back door of a salon, really? You needed that in your territory?"

He carries on.

Wheels of a vehicle behind us crunch on the loose pebbles of the alley. I pull his leash tighter to give the car room to pass us, pulling myself in closer to the wall too, but the car doesn't pass.

It's a white cargo van kind of like mine, but with no windows. The kind usually used for work instead of passengers.

It slows down, barely creeping through the alley. I stop and wave at it insistently, so it knows it can pass.

It doesn't. In fact, it stops all together.

Okay, I guess.

We keep walking, passing by a particularly stinky dumpster as we go.

But then the van inches slowly again.

I'm annoyed at this point. I wave it past again, a little more aggressively this time.

It finally moves to pass me, and I grumble under my breath about how much people suck sometimes.

But then it stops again.

Right next to me.

I stalk up to the window, ready to ask the guy what the hell his problem is, when the back door slides open and suddenly arms are reaching for me, grabbing me before I can even think.

Strong hands yank me forward. I stumble, my knees whacking the side bar under the door. Vinnie barks and spits, trying to pull me back from his end of the leash.

I rip myself away. The faces attached to the strong hands are covered by unnerving masks.

One of them holds out a knife, and before I even comprehend that fact, he has already cut Vinnie's taut leash, severing the tether between us. Vinnie stumbles back.

"Vinnie!"

They yank me into the van and cover my mouth, wrestling me to secure my arms behind my back despite my flailing. The door is nearly closed, but Vinnie manages to wedge himself inside, causing the door to fall all the way open again with a *clank*.

Like back in the van, his whole demeanor shifts—he sheds off himself and gets to work. He gives a menacing growl before pouncing onto the ones holding me, like a tiger. Their grip loosens in surprise, and I take advantage of that, ripping my arms away and kicking the hand with the knife until it clatters to the ground.

Vinnie snarls and snaps and barks as I dole out punches and kicks in every direction until I'm close enough to the door to tumble out onto the ground.

Vinnie leaps out of the van just before it squeals off down the alley and onto the main road, speeding off in the other direction.

We both stay frozen for a moment, catching our breath and wondering if that really happened.

"Are you ok?" I reach out and pat him down, still lying in the road breathlessly.

He licks my hand, and apart from a scrape on his vest that very well could have drawn blood if the vest weren't there, he's fine.

What just happened?

I stand up on shaking legs, still processing it all. Was this just a random attack? Did they know who I was somehow? Did they follow us from somewhere?

My mind is still reeling as we finally reach the restaurant.

Should I call the police? George will know what to do.

But we wait at the restaurant for an hour.

George never shows up.

PODCAST TRANSCRIPT
Secrets in Ice Season 3, Episode 1: The Girl Left Behind,
Cont.

[suspenseful music plays]

KIERAN BERGSTROM:

I wanted to understand the dynamics in the Sinclair family. They seemed like a normal, happy family. But what were they really like behind closed doors? I reached out to the staff that was employed there at the time to get some insight.

Not many wanted to speak to me.

[sound bites play of doors slamming, phone calls disconnecting]

A VOICE, DISTORTED TO CONCEAL IDENTITY:

Never contact me again *[censored] [censored].* I want nothing to do with your 'investigation.'

ANOTHER VOICE, DISTORTED TO CONCEAL INDENTITY:

Leave that poor girl alone, she's been through enough.

KIERAN BERGSTROM:

And some wanted to speak to me a little too much...

SEAN BROCKMAN WITH DAZZLE WINDOW CO.:

Oh, my name? Yeah, it's Sean Brockman. I used to clean their windows, so I usually had a clear view of the girls' bedrooms. I probably still have some pictures on my computer somewhere. If you want them for your podcast. I'd be happy to share them. For a price.

KIERAN BERGSTROM:

A tip has already been passed along to Portland PD, but to be perfectly clear, I never encourage predators. I only expose them. So in case you missed that, it was Sean, S-E-A-N, Brockman employed at Dazzle Window Co. in Portland. Oregon.

[a beat, as suspenseful music plays]

Luckily after sifting through the slime, I was able to find a few who could give me real insight, both former and current members of staff, including Patricia Horne, who was a private tutor for the girls at the time of the disappearance.

[sound of a phone dialing]

KIERAN BERGSTROM:

Thank you for speaking with me today, Patricia. What can you tell me about the sisters?

PATRICIA HORNE:

Oh, I miss those girls. Nikki was the cutest thing. So playful and silly, always getting into mischief, but she could smile her way out of it in a heartbeat. She was very outgoing. Would talk anyone's head off. Lizzy was a beautiful girl. The more guarded and reserved one, but so kind to everyone. Very talented figure skater. We all assumed she'd go on to the Olympics one day. Such potential.

KIERAN BERGSTROM:

What was their dynamic like with each other?

PATRICIA HORNE:

They fought like sisters do, but they loved each other. They were best friends. Nikki absolutely adored her sister, she wanted to do everything just like her. Lizzy was very protective of her. Sometimes a little too much.

KIERAN BERGSTROM:

In what way?

PATRICIA HORNE:

I mostly worked with the girls during summers when they were off from school. I remember we had gone on a science outing to the aquarium once. We were all looking at the exhibit, and a little boy playfully tugged on one of Nikki's braids. She wasn't hurt, but Lizzy stepped in right away and pushed the boy down, sent him off crying. I always got the feeling there was nothing Lizzy wouldn't do to protect her sister.

KIERAN BERGSTROM to ANOTHER:

Okay, we're recording. Can you tell the listeners about yourself, Mrs. Hanover?

BEATRICE HANOVER:

I've worked for the Sinclairs for about... twenty-two years? Twenty-three? They brought me on shortly after they got married, even before Lizzy came along. There's not a day that goes by where I don't miss them, Lizzy especially. I cooked for that girl as early as six months old, making every pureed baby food for her you could imagine. I used to work entirely in the kitchen back then. I cooked all their meals, ran the kitchen, helped plan parties. Sometimes even helped with homework while the girls snacked after school, although I wasn't much help there. When they passed, the housekeeping staff was let go and so I took up those duties as well.

KIERAN BERGSTROM:

Twenty years is a long time. What made you stay so long? After everything happened, did you ever consider leaving when the rest of the staff was let go?

BEATRICE HANOVER:

They weren't just employers to me. They were like a second family. Mr. and Mrs. Sinclair were always very kind and grateful for the help, and with my grandkids all grown up, the girls were bonus kids I got to spoil. And leave? No, I'll never leave Nikki until I'm taken from this earth.

KIERAN BERGSTROM:

What do you remember about the day they disappeared?

BEATRICE HANOVER:

I wasn't here that day. Most of the staff had the weekends off. But I think about the Friday before a lot... what I would have done differently if I'd known... *[begins to cry]* if I had known I'd never see Lizzy again... I wish I could hug her just one more time.

[a beat as suspenseful music plays]

KIERAN BERGSTROM:

The more people I spoke to, the most confused I got. It seemed no one had a bad word to say about the Sinclair family and despite the wealth, they appeared to be a normal family. No enemies, no scandals.

No reason to vanish.

But they did.

6

———

NIKKI

A GAME OF TAG, LIKE THE MATURE AND SOPHISTICATED NEAR-ADULT I AM

My knee bounces with a new kind of energy as Hunter and I giggle and chatter in the backseat, Arrick at the wheel, looking back at us every so often as he drives us back to my house.

We haven't told Arrick the news yet.

Of our engagement.

Which is insane to even think. Me? Engaged? What??

We think it's best if we don't mention it until we have more of a solid plan, that way no one can try to interfere; namely, a certain stubborn aunt with a crazy agenda to die sooner than she needs to.

"What do you think your dad is going to say when he finds out?" I whisper so Arrick doesn't hear.

Hunter's smile stretches bigger and his green eyes shimmer, making my insides turn to jelly. "Honestly he'll probably be pissed, and I can't wait."

I click my tongue scoldingly. "He's still your dad."

"Yeah officially, I guess." He shrugs. "If he had it his way, I'd be an employee he could fire whenever I was done serving my purpose. But unfortunately for him, he's stuck with me."

"Do you think your mom will like me?" I'm afraid to even ask.

"Nik, she's known you your entire life." Hunter laughs. "She already loves you."

"She loved little kid me. Summer vacation me. Years ago me. But will she like *me* me? Today me, your fiancée me?"

"Of course she will." He nudges me with his shoulder. "We're getting married whether she likes it or not, so she better."

"Does it feel weird to say it?"

"Married," he repeats, testing it out. "Annika Marie *Vanderwaal.*"

I get butterflies hearing his last name at the end of my name.

He thinks about it for a second. "Nope. Not weird at all."

I smile at him, staring a little longer at him than I'd normally be bold enough to do. He's so impossibly beautiful.

"What? I have something on my face, don't I?" He swipes at his cheeks and lips.

"I just wish you could be here all the time." I avert my eyes out the window. "It's so lonely here."

He puts his arm around my shoulder. "I wish I could too. I hate it at home too."

I put my head on his shoulder and try to relish this closeness before he's gone.

My best friend. My fiancé. He's mine. And most of all, he's *here.*

We pull into the driveway right as the snow comes down again, growing in intensity as the sky darkens.

Arrick jogs around the parked car to open the door for

us, and we thank him over our shoulders as we run for cover and shuck off our shoes at the door.

"Wow," he says with a breath, leaning his head back to look up at the high bright ceiling in the foyer. "It's just like I remember it. Those are new though," he nods to Aunt Wren's colorful canvases that decorate the walls now, giving more vibrancy to the white interior than the last time he was here.

"Tag, you're it!"

He's surprised for a second at my sudden shriek, but he laughs as I take off running across the house.

"You've never won before Annika Sinclair, haven't you learned?" he calls from behind, not even moving, knowing he doesn't have to hurry. He'll beat me anyway, no matter how hard I try.

I scurry up the staircase and down a hallway, giggling as the booming of his feet come after me. My only advantage is to hide. His footsteps are dangerously close, so I fumble with the doorknob of the closest door and hurry in, closing it behind me as quietly and quickly as I can.

I try to catch my breath on the other side of the door discreetly, so my truly pathetic panting doesn't give away my position entirely.

That's before the breath gets knocked completely out of me when I realize which room I'm in.

My father's study.

My whole body stills to a reverent hush. Even my breaths and heartbeat slow to a respectful pace.

I haven't been in here in years.

Bea must keep up with the cleaning in here, though, because it still looks pristine.

Three of the four walls are lined with ornate built-in

walnut bookshelves that are filled with books, antique knick-knacks, towering golden trophies from his racing days lit by brass light fixtures. The wood-paneled walls and crown molding are a dark sophisticated burgundy I always loved. Not a speck of dust on any inch of the room.

His desk in the middle of the herringbone wood floor is the same walnut as the shelves, huge and daunting. As a child, I used to hide under there when I didn't want to go to bed. Dad would act like he didn't know I was there as he sat down in his chair, pretending to work, with his feet right next to my snickering face as I waited for him to notice me. Then he'd tickle me until I couldn't breathe.

I approach the desk with caution, as if my father's very spirit will rise from his grave and tell me it's bedtime or something. The leather of the chair is smooth to the touch, and it swivels into my touch. All the papers that usually covered every inch of the desk have been carefully cleaned up and set elsewhere, leaving an empty surface apart from a framed photo of our smiling family that nearly hypnotizes me.

I move the chair to sit in it, feeling almost like I can *smell him* here somehow, or at least the combination of smells that made him *him*. Leather, paper, wood, late nights.

I breathe it in, and oh how it hurts. The absence of him hurts bad in this moment. But despite the pain, being in here is giving me a little piece of him back that I didn't realize I needed so much, a sliver I can cling to now that the memories of him are fading with each day. Why don't I come in here more often?

As soon as my legs make contact with the cool leather of the chair, my phone vibrates twice in my pocket, setting my nerves ablaze. Obviously, it's not actually my father's ghost telling me to leave his stuff alone, so why do I feel like I'm in trouble?

As I lean back in the chair, I pull my phone out, expecting to see a text from Hunter asking me where I am.

But it's not from Hunter.

A freezing chill runs through my bloodstream.

It's from an unknown number.

UNKNOWN

Kiki, I need your help. It's me.

There is only one person who has ever called me "Kiki."

My sister Lizzy.

All the oxygen is completely sucked out of the room as I stare at the text, reading it over and over again.

With shaking hands, I text back right away.

NIKKI

who is this?

The message delivers. No response. I try calling the number, but an automated message tells me the phone number I'm trying to reach is unavailable.

I set my phone down on the desk, my head spinning.

I reason with myself to calm my heart rate. It's obviously not her. My sister has been dead for ten years. Someone is clearly playing a cruel joke on me. Anyone with access to the internet can find out about my family's case. I'm sure it wouldn't be that hard to find my contact information some-where online. There, a perfectly reasonable explanation. Internet trolls.

I leap to my feet at the knock on the door.

Hunter pokes his head in through the door I left cracked.

"You're it—" He cuts himself off at the sight of me. "Are you okay?"

I must look as shaken up as I feel.

I show him the text.

"But it obviously can't be her," I finish, more to myself than to him, as he reads it again. Maybe saying that aloud a few more times will knock some sense into me. *It obviously can't be her. She's dead.*

He gives my phone back to me, brows pulled together. "You should probably block that number. I don't like the thought of any creeps texting you."

I nudge his shoulder playfully. "Oh, engagement has made you a little protective I see."

"Protective or not" —he leans down to whisper in my ear, so closely that my insides completely rearrange themselves — "you're still it."

And he darts out of the room.

Just as I'm about to run off after him as if we're kids again, another vibration of my phone reminds me of the sobering reality that I'm not a child anymore.

Another text from Unknown.

> UNKNOWN
>
> I'm alive. I need your help.

THE QUIET IS DEAFENING with Hunter gone, and it's causing me to spiral a bit. I've been tossing and turning in bed now for hours, my brain refusing to turn off.

After Hunter's driver picked him up to take him back to his hotel, I had gone right to Aunt Wren's suite, charging in there to show her the text messages, since she's an adult and therefore would know exactly what to do to fix everything.

But she was lying there, resting so peacefully, Wheel of Fortune playing softly on the TV. I knew I couldn't disturb her. Arrick and Bea had already gone home for the night, back to their real homes. To their real lives.

So, I went back to my room, alone. As usual.

I didn't show Hunter the second text. I don't know why. Maybe it's because I knew what he'd say, how he'd remind me to block the number and not let strangers get in my head.

The thing is, he's absolutely right. It's stupid to let this dumb prank take up any more headspace.

But those two words send chills down my spine every time I reread them, morphing them into a wild, ferocious, *stupid* hope. Delusion. "*I'm alive.*"

If there's even a sliver, a molecule, of a possibility this could truly be her—it sounds so stupid even thinking it— shouldn't I take it seriously? When your dead sister texts you "*I need help,*" don't you drop everything, sanity included, and help like a good sister should?

As it gets later and later, the night taking any shreds of my remaining common sense with it into the dark, I've begun to think something I haven't allowed in a long time: *What if?*

What if she's actually alive?

I mean they never found her body, after all.

I was so young when they left and never came back. At seven years old, I never understood the gravity of what had happened, in part because the investigators always explained the case to me with so many euphemisms and sugar-coated everything to soften the delivery. No one ever flat-out told me, "Your family was killed." It was always: "They're gone," or "They're in a better place now."

So, I always believed they'd eventually be back, that one day they'd walk right through the front door as if nothing ever happened, bringing expensive gifts from out of town as an apology and all would be forgiven and laughed about in years to come. But as I got older, that hope hardened into sharp-edged reality when I confronted the facts that had been hiding in plain sight in front of me all along: *Foul play. Signs of a struggle. Blood. Murder. Dead. Forever.*

That's how it's been for years. I've gotten used to that.

But now? I've been completely transformed back into that seven-year-old girl all over again. The games with Hunter, the smell of my father's office, the *hope* that takes on a life of its own the longer I'm awake. I'm a little child again, waiting by the front door for her dead family to return.

Could Lizzy be alive?

And if Lizzy is alive... could my parents be too?

No. Nope. I reject that thought immediately. I refuse to believe my parents would ever willingly leave me here alone all this time. If they were out there somewhere, they'd find a way back to me. I know they would. They were strict, sure, but never cruel. They loved us. Mistakes aside, I know in every fiber of my bones that they loved us. They'd never do this to me.

I throw my blankets off in anxious frustration. This is going to be the thing that finally drives me to insanity. Not being orphaned and alone, not a dying guardian, not my only friend being in a completely different country, nope. Awaiting a text from an internet troll will be what does me in.

I need a snack.

I'm about to brave the creaky and creepy darkness of my near-empty estate when my phone vibrates again with another text.

With a conflicting amount of both dread and hope, I pull out my phone to read it.

UNKNOWN

My room. Floorboard under the window seat.

7

KIERAN

IT'S ONLY PARANOIA IF THEY'RE NOT REALLY OUT TO GET YOU

It's late. Very late.

But that's common for me. Comes with my line of work.

Digging into the very dark details of tragic events, trying to see into the minds of monsters to peel out any clues or evidence, the paranoia of putting dangerous people in the public eye when they don't want to be... Yeah, it makes for some sleepless nights.

Especially on days when you have an exciting run-in with a van full of masked men trying to abduct you in broad daylight.

Yep, that'll do it.

Vinnie snoozes enviably unbothered in his nook, his deep breathing almost as loud as the generator working overtime to keep this van warm inside as the temperature dips outside.

I still haven't heard from George since he blew me off this afternoon, and I'm equal parts frustrated that I drove all this way for him to ghost me, and also worried. It's very unlike him not to show up. Did the van men go after him too?

I roll over to my side and reach for my phone, which has been plugged into its charger while I've been unsuccessfully trying to fall asleep for the last couple hours. The brightness of the screen nearly blinds me when I tap it to open. I pale at the number of notifications on my lockscreen. I always have a lot, but this is too many.

That's never good.

I scroll past hundreds of DMs from social media on the lockscreen, so many that I'm not even computing what the previews say as I scroll, trying to find something concrete that makes sense in the mass.

I finally reach the green bubbles of seven missed calls. They are from my contact Jason at the Hood River County sheriff's office. I called him yesterday to let him know about that random threat against Roger Mackenzie...

Oh no.

That's when my brain finally registers the common theme of all the previews.

Roger Mackenzie.

The key witness in the trial for season two.

"He will be taken care of tonight," that anonymous email had said.

The last missed call from Jason was only nine minutes ago, so I don't feel bad about calling back at this late hour. I hold my breath, sending silent prayers to the universe that this feeling in my gut is wrong, that it's only a paranoia.

Please.

He picks up on the first ring. "Kieran?"

"Jason, what's going on?"

It's the sigh on the other line that confirms my worst fear.

"I'm going to need you to forward me that email you received."

"Is he ok?"

Another sigh.

"Jason?"

"He's been shot. A drive-by shooting that appears targeted. He's on life support. He probably won't make it through the night."

No, no, no.

I dig my fingernails into the inside of my palm to keep myself from screaming at Jason. I force a level tone, though my fury unavoidably breaks through. "Was he not being provided with police *protection*?" I ask through gritted teeth. "He was the *key witness*. What will this do to the case?"

Jason spits a curse on the other line. "I don't need you to lecture me about this case, Kieran. Send me the email you got immediately. And take down anything where you mention Siphon whatever his name is."

And then the line disconnects.

I throw my phone across the van with a furious shout. Vinnie is at my side right away, wide-eyed and alarmed to be woken out of a dead sleep so abruptly. I shove my head in my hands.

If Roger Mackenzie can't testify, Albert's killer could go free.

I punch my pillows in fury as if they are Roger's shooter themselves.

It's not fair. This poor family thought they were finally close to justice, only to have it ripped away again. And it's my fault for giving them that false hope. At least before I got involved, it was a killer without a face that could haunt them. Someone unknown for so long they could almost wonder if it had even happened at all, if he even existed. Now they have a face they can visualize, that will be in every shadow, every corner, every passing glance.

A face that will likely go free because I had to open my big mouth on YouTube about an anonymous threat I didn't take seriously enough.

I let out another yell, thinking maybe the more I shout, the less pressure I'll feel in my chest trying to claw itself out.

The only hope is if the judge allows Roger's deposition to be used in place of his testimony on the stand.

I slide on the closest pair of sweatpants and throw on some running shoes and a coat haphazardly, grabbing Vinnie's leash off the hook. He's confused but down for anything, his tail wagging at the unexpected adventure.

Fortunately, we're already parked in the parking lot of one of the twenty-four-hour gyms I pay a monthly membership to, one with locations all across the state, because I have a sudden and very urgent need to run, hit something, get in a fight, anything. I desperately need to blow off some steam before I break something in the van I rely on for survival.

With shaking hands, I throw my toiletry bag, fresh clothes, and a towel into my gym bag, and before I know it, I'm running as fast as I can on the treadmill inside. I know my blood sugar will make me regret the spontaneous run later, but I turn off my pump all together and click the speed on the treadmill faster, *faster*, hoping to push the guilt, the very thought, of Albert's case out with every step.

Just go faster, and it'll leave. Faster.

But I can't push out what cuts down deep in my bones. It's ingrained there now.

The fact that this is my fault.

I blasted Ciphered Voyager on my channel. I gave him the audience, the balls, to do this.

Roger Mackenzie is far from innocent. He claimed he didn't know how vital his witness was until I shed light on it in the podcast, but the information he chose to withhold from police allowed Albert's murderer to walk free for eight years. But Roger still didn't deserve this, not when he was trying to do the right thing.

And Albert's wife and kids sure as hell don't deserve this either. The last thing they need is this case being dismissed because Roger can't testify.

And it's all my fault.

Too fast.

I miss a step on the treadmill belt and nearly fall on my face. I stand on the sides, clutching the handrails, as the belt speeds on without me. My lungs are burning, my sides cramping, but I don't care. I deserve the pain. Vinnie eyes me with judgement at my near miss, but then he sniffs through my bag and pulls out my baggie of my 'Athletic Beans' (just a fancy term for jellybeans with electrolytes in them). I take the bag from his teeth and pop a handful in my mouth, feeling my knees start to shake from my sugars dropping. This always happens. I don't know why I keep thinking I can do cardio like a regular person.

I'm still trying to catch my breath when there's an eerie tickle on the back of my neck. That unexplainable unease you feel when someone is watching you.

You'd think I would be more careful, more observant, considering the van of dangerous men I barely evaded mere hours ago, but I came into the gym in such a cloud of rage that I hardly took any notice of anyone else around. I just assumed no one else would be here at this hour.

A discreet look around while I try to stretch out the cramp under my rib confirms two buff guys on the other side of the room working arms at the benches, a woman with headphones playing a game on her tablet as she bounces on an elliptical in front of me, and an older gentleman watching the news quietly playing on a TV in the lobby. None of them are paying me much mind.

With several million subscribers on YouTube, it's not uncommon for someone to recognize me from my channel. I post a lot of behind the scenes as I investigate for my podcast, many of which have gone viral on numerous occasions. Viewers enjoy feeling like they're a part of the process. And although I hate having such a public presence online, it's good money, and the more reach, the better when I need information or witnesses.

I shake off the uneasy feeling and walk with Vinnie to the locker room. When I chose this parking lot to camp the van in for the night, I had planned to come in here in the morning to shower anyway, so I guess thanks insomnia for clearing up my morning schedule for me.

I choose a shower and turn the temperature hot enough to appropriately melt all my skin off and wait for it to heat up. While I wait, I shuck my clothes off, peel all adhesives off my skin, and plug in my insulin pump to charge.

"If anyone tries to come in here to carry me off into the night, tell them to at least wait until I'm not naked," I say to Vinnie jokingly, but he straightens with authority, posting himself right in front of the curtain. I chuckle endearingly.

The steam of the shower helps ease some of my tangled-up brain, and for a moment, there's no guilt, no stress, no pressure, only the relaxing burn of the water on my skin.

Until Vinnie growls quietly on the other side of the curtain.

I wipe the water from my eyes and peek out.

There's no one there, but his ears are pricked and attentive. He's staring at the door, a low growl rumbling from his throat again.

"Really?" I ask him, waving to the empty room.

His eyes stay glued to the door.

Well, I'm officially freaked out now.

I finish my shower in a rush, hating that I'm so exposed and vulnerable as my skin tingles in anticipation again.

Even as I'm getting dressed and plugged back into the devices that keep me alive, I keep glancing over my shoulder, sure I'll see a group of masked men behind me ready to pounce, or a stranger staring, but there's no one.

Vinnie isn't helping the tension. He's as on-edge as I am. Growling at nothing, ears alert. He must feel that prickle too.

By the time we're walking out of the gym and into the freezing parking lot, I'm nearly nauseous from the anxiety, and I speedwalk to my van as fast as the slippery asphalt will allow, clutching Vinnie's leash tightly.

My fingers are stiff, and I fumble with the keys for a second before I manage to unlock it. Once we're safely locked inside, I feel ridiculous, panting heavily as if we were just chased with a knife, but there still isn't anyone around.

I click the lock again three more times to be sure and sit on my bed to take off my shoes with a heavy exhale, my pulse thrumming. Vinnie shakes out in his nook. I switch on the generator, and everything inside whirs to life, the line of blue strip lights on the ceiling casting an icy glow on the van interior.

The clock on my stovetop says 3:18 AM, and I sigh,

knowing I'll regret staying up this late in the morning, but there's too much adrenaline in my veins to allow sleep, and my blood sugar will spike any minute now (always does after cardio; thanks, useless pancreas). Might as well make the most of an even longer night to come, so I prop up my pillow and power on my Xbox.

The feeling of being watched, even locked in here, still lingers along my spine.

An email notification buzzes on my phone.

CIPHEREDVOYAGERANON@MAIL.COM

Subject: I Keep My Promises

I'll tell you one final time. Take down your podcast and cease further investigations, or you and everyone you love will be next.

-Ciphered Voyager

8

———

NIKKI

NIGHTMARE IN THE DOLLHOUSE

I don't know how long I've been sitting here on the edge of my bed, reading the texts from Unknown over and over like they're an echo in a canyon.

My room.

Floorboard under the window seat.

I've sent back at least twenty texts and have called over ten times, but no answer.

I'm being ridiculous. The room is right down the hall. I can simply go over there at any time and look. Check that there's nothing there—because of course there's nothing there—and that will confirm that these texts are nonsense. The solution is so easy...

But the truth is, I haven't been in Lizzy's room since before she died.

Ten years.

Back then, I didn't want touch anything, didn't even want to *breathe* in her room, because I was so sure she'd be back any day, and she'd know I was in there, like big sisters do somehow, and she'd be mad at me for being in her room.

Then years went by. And more years. And now it's been ten.

Bea keeps it clean from what I understand, but at this point, I'd prefer not to go in there at all. I even avoid walking by it whenever possible. It's creepy to me now, the thought of everything that used to be hers, forever frozen in there like some freakish dollhouse. It's a permanent, painful reminder of what used to be and never will be again.

But I push myself off the bed with a determined breath. It's so late that my eyelids beg me to put them out of their misery, but my brain won't let me sleep if I don't put this to rest. Then I can block Unknown, move on with my life, and re-accept that my sister is really dead.

My fuzzy sherpa-lined slippers pad softly across the wood floors and instead of taking a right down the hallway like I always do to go down the staircase, I go left instead, for the first time in years.

A quick left down the hallway is all it's ever been, although it's easier to pretend like it's not even there at all.

If I had made habit of dwelling on the loss of her, of my parents, I would never be able to function. Life would go on around me, and I'd be one extra casualty to the tragedy. It's the only way I can cope living in this morgue of a house: denial.

I stand in front of her door for a moment, my heart pounding. My fingers tremble as I reach for the doorknob, as if it might turn to dust as soon as I touch it. I half-expect the door to creak open with the melodramatic groan of a horror movie, but it swings silently, almost reverently, granting me access to a part of the past I really don't want to be in.

I'm struck by the strong floral scent inside the room from a plug-in air freshener, courtesy of Bea. Who doesn't love the smell of lavender and loss in the evening? I don't switch on the light, preferring to leave the room as undisturbed as possible. Moonlight filters through the sheer curtains, throwing shadowed patterns across the floor.

It's just a room; it's just a room.

The brass canopy bed is made pristinely, Lizzy's mountain of stuffies neatly stacked on top of pastel pink bedding that looks to be recently washed. There are still craft supplies—markers and bracelet beads—and unfinished homework assignments on her desk, though piled tidily. The light pink floral wallpaper I was always so jealous of wraps the walls decoratively. Her sparkling figure skating costumes hang neatly in her huge walk-in closet like glittering ghosts. Even a pink towel is still hanging frozen in her bathroom, as if she'll step out of the tiled shower at any moment. My throat swells at the evidence of a childhood cut short all around me.

Lizzy's childhood.

I remind myself to focus before I completely unravel.

Focus, focus.

Floorboard under the window seat.

I kneel on the hardwood and pat around for loose boards, trying to set aside the guilt of being here at all, tearing apart Lizzy's room, invading her privacy because an anonymous troll told me to. This is so silly and so wrong.

I'm about to give up entirely when there is a give in one of the boards. My pulse pauses completely to wait in suspense as I ease the board up.

There is a hidden cavity beneath, and it's hard to make out what's inside in the dimness. I flick on my phone's flashlight to reveal a few trinkets, a faded photograph of her and I as kids that brings burning tears to my eyes, and there, nestled underneath them is an old leather-bound journal.

Even my own breath feels too loud, too invasive, in the deathly quiet of this room as I pull out the journal. How could Unknown have possibly known this was here?

I flip through the pages, finding it halfway-filled with entries. I lower myself onto the floor and crisscross my legs to flip through it.

Seeing my sister's handwriting right in front of me is surreal and nostalgic and heartbreaking. The way she dotted her I's and J's with a full circle instead of a dot, the unmistakable loops and curls of her Y's and A's. This is really hers.

The first entry is dated March 15th, 2013. I do the math in my head. So, she was... nine years old then?

I find with a smile that her entries definitely reflect the inner workings of a nine-year-old girl. Drama with friends and crushes at school, complaints about parents and teachers, and I chuckle at the mentions of me, the grievances any nine-year-old would have about her annoying little sister.

"Kiki kept following us around when we were trying to play. Kiki stole my lip gloss and squirted it all over the couch and I had to clean it up. Kiki is such a crybaby and always gets me in trouble."

A tear trails down my cheek as I read on, feeling closer to her than I have in years as I hold this little piece of her in my hands, memories I've long suppressed coming to back to life.

I read every entry, finding nothing out of the ordinary. I flip through the second half of the journal, which is blank, wondering why Unknown would even tell me to look for this, until something catches my eye. It's a hastily scrawled paragraph nestled in the middle of a bunch of blank pages, an entry so short I almost miss it entirely. A scrap of paper falls onto my lap.

It's dated the day before she died—October 16th, 2015. Age eleven. It says:

I don't know what to do. They know I know. I'm scared.

The journal trembles in my hands as I read it over and over and over in the moonlight, hoping the more I read it, the more sense I'll find in the spaces between words. But no answers come. Every page after this one is blank.

I examine the scrap of paper that fell from between the pages, using the flashlight of my phone see it better. It was torn out of a children's book or something, the fragment of a colorful picture at its torn edges. Written on it in colorful pink glitter ink are four numbers.

3 - 7 - 0 - 5

I slide it back into the crack of the spine before closing the journal, unable to shake off the dread that is closing in on me.

She writes a hurried entry in her journal that she's scared and then the very next day, she and my parents are killed? What could she, a *child*, have possibly known that made her so scared? And of who?

Nausea bubbles up inside my stomach, these sentences shattering the naive peace I had made with my dead family. Cracking apart the quiet acceptance I've had—that due to the lack of evidence, and lack of bodies, it was likely an unfortunate but impromptu killing. That whoever was responsible didn't seek them out specifically, that my family was just in the wrong place at the wrong time.

But this changes everything.

Why else would she have been scared?

All I have now are more questions than I've ever had, questions that make me feel sick to even think. But can I continue to blindly accept what I've always been told after reading this entry?

Lizzy was scared, and then she was never seen again.

These texts from Unknown, claiming to be her, somehow knowing this journal with this entry was here. Texts asking for help from someone I've always blindly accepted was dead because *everyone told me she was dead*. Someone that everyone stopped looking for the second it became too inconvenient or started taking too long. Someone everyone has long since forgotten about.

Even my own subconscious has pushed her away, shoving my memories of her deep down and making them all but fade away entirely.

Unknown, whoever it may be, for good or bad, knows there may more to my sister's death than everyone has made me believe.

And I'm no longer okay simply accepting we don't know what happened. I'm no longer okay with forgetting her. Denial is no longer an option.

If my sister was scared in her final days, I will never stop until I find out why and of whom. And if the police won't help me, I'll do it myself.

～

EVEN AS THE warm tinges of morning peek in through the curtains of Lizzy's bedroom, I'm still awake, and though my body begs for sleep, I can't set aside the restless anxiety buzzing through me.

My family's murders could have been premeditated, and I'm supposed to be able to get a good night's sleep? Right.

I've been sitting here at her desk for a couple hours now, fiddling with the leather edges of the journal, my brain going a thousand miles an hour. I keep my phone close in case another text from Unknown comes in, feeling more unsettled than ever. Could they really be from Lizzy? How else could Unknown have known there was something worth seeing in this journal?

And if it's her... the urgency in the texts claws at me.

"I need help."

It's setting every unhealthy obsession I have with true crime absolutely ablaze. Every true-crime podcast and documentary I've consumed like oxygen over the years makes my brain whir with theories and questions. I know it's the equivalent of someone watching Grey's Anatomy and thinking they can now perform surgery, but is it that delusional to think I can finally put my glimmer of know-how to good use?

The killer was never caught, after all. They are still out there. What if they've hurt someone else now too?

What if they come for me next?

I've been racking my brain for hours trying to remember what I can about the case, trying to wade through the sugar-coated details given to a child, but I don't know much. I remember them saying their car had crashed into a tree on the side of a remote highway, which isn't so unbelievable on a cold October morning, but they said there was something different about the blood inside the car that made them believe there was a struggle of some kind.

Because if they simply died in the car accident, why weren't their bodies found?

I thought for a second that maybe they got out of the car to go find help after the accident and simply got lost. But you could never make me believe that my protective father would have allowed his wife and daughter to get out of the car in the cold to walk aimlessly in the wilderness. He would've gone for help himself.

But they could never find *any* of their bodies, not just his.

Animals maybe? But there would've been significantly more DNA left behind if that were the case.

A sudden voice at the door makes me leap to my feet.

"Miss Nikki?"

It's Arrick.

I put a hand on my pounding chest in relief, breathless from the scare. "Oh. It's you."

A deep V form between his brows. He knows I never come in here. His towering figure takes up nearly the whole doorway. He wears suit as always, gray tweed today, paired with the brown Hermes pageboy hat I got him for Christmas last year, but the frown? That's new. It looks foreign and out of place on him.

He's worried.

"Are you alright?"

I lower back into the desk chair, rubbing my heavy eyes. "Oh yeah I'm fine, just couldn't sleep."

His mustache twitches over his deepening frown. "How long have you been in here?"

I wince. "A while."

He beckons to me, outstretching his hand but remaining

at the threshold of the door, as if uneasy to come in here himself. "Why don't you come have something to eat? Maybe with a full stomach you can get some rest."

I take his hand, palms calloused and rough from a lifetime of hard work, grateful for the warmth there that brings some comfort to the chilling night I've had.

"Okay. Yeah, maybe."

I bring the journal with me, sending one last glance over my shoulder, hoping maybe the room will reveal something to me in these last seconds. It doesn't.

If Arrick notices the journal, he doesn't mention it as he leads me down the hallway and past my room.

"I'm just going to plug my phone in really quick."

I step to my side-table, and the vibration of a text feels like an electric shock in my hand. I drop it, and it clatters across the wood of the table. Unknown? *Lizzy?*

I allow myself to exhale when the screen shows Hunter's name.

HUNTER

good morning, fiancée.

Seeing his name, remembering I get to see him today, it takes a few layers of the pressure from the night off my throat, loosening it a little bit and allowing me another exhale.

We can talk through it together. He can help me figure all of this out.

I'm not alone in this.

I text back.

I needed a smile this morning.

AFTER BEA FUSSES over me for a little while in the kitchen, insisting I eat and drink water before I turn to dust—that traitorous Arrick must have told her I was up all night in Lizzy's room—I manage to escape and slink away to Aunt Wren's room. I've been desperate to talk to her about every-thing, like it's this huge monster of a secret that feels bigger every second I keep it all from her. She'll know what to do.

But I'm stopped at the door by Nurse Kayla.

Her lips are pressed together in a line that knocks the breath out of me.

"Is she okay?" I barely manage to get the words.

She nods quickly, hands out to reassure me. "Yes. I'm sorry. She just, well—" She stops herself, pressing her lips back together.

I look behind her—Aunt Wren lying there, eyes closed restfully, monitors beeping like usual. "What is it?"

She gently shuts the door. "I'll have to consult with my supervisor. He'll come and give a second opinion. But" —she pauses to squeeze my hand, looking at me with sympathy— "it's not looking good, Nikki. Without treatment, I'm not sure how much time she has left."

She may as well have taken a steak knife and stabbed it right through my back.

"I'm so sorry," she whispers.

"Wait, no." I rip my hand away, as if that will retract the words she's said. "I have a plan to pay for everything. I can access my inheritance if I get married."

I continue quickly as the alarm flashes across her expression, "Don't worry. He's my best friend. It's going to be okay."

She replies slowly, like I'm too fragile to engage in a regular-paced conversation. "Sweetie, in Oregon you can't get married before eighteen without a parent's permission. Isn't your birthday in June...?"

I nod emphatically. "Yeah, that's only a few months away."

Her eyes flick downward.

And she doesn't have to say anything. It's written in every pore of her face.

Aunt Wren doesn't have a few months left.

@blurrymoon7: is it not weird to anyone else that nikki's guardian let the police give up so easily? wonder what she's hiding

    @little21jazz REPLYING TO @blurrymoon I was thinking this as well. Huge house, Nikki's big inheritance to oversee. Seems like she has the most to gain from their deaths.

@pixel_raven: my vote is the butler. it's always the butler.

@33mossypines33: idk why I expected her to be ugly… lowkey kinda hot in a could kill you at any second way. I love a redhead. someone like this when she turns 18.

@lemonontop56768: kieran marry me and have my babies PLEASE

    @mysticmuffin REPLYING TO @lemonontop56768: srry he's already married to me

@susan_jones: Elizabeth was so young, it's so sad!

    @user889921 REPLYING TO @susan_jones: spoiled brat had it coming

    @susan_jones REPLYING TO @user889921: She was a child, how can you even say that?

    @user889921 REPLYING TO @susan_jones: she wasn't as innocent as she seemed

9

KIERAN

PART OF THE JOB, BUT I WISH IT WASN'T

I awake to the buzzing of an incoming phone call, the noise of the vibration intensified by my keys rattling in unison right next to it.

I ignore the call at first, pulling my covers around me tighter with a groan, but then I sit up sharply when I remember it could be Jason calling with an update about Albert's case, if they'll dismiss it or not.

It's far earlier than I wanted to be vertical, especially considering the late and restless night, but no hope of going back to sleep now.

The buzzing starts again, and I confirm it's not Jason from PD calling, before pressing ignore again. I don't typically answer unknown callers. Anyone who manages to find my direct phone number can leave a voicemail if it's important enough.

A huge part of my job is skimming through the mass of calls, texts, comments, and DMs, filtering past the trolls and fans, to find anything helpful. And then having to decide whether the information is actually worth looking into more, or if it's only local gossip or speculation. At any given time, there are thousands of leads and different directions I'm being pulled in, and I have to make constant decisions about which path is the most promising and which is just a distraction.

It's exhausting. I need to hire an assistant at some point to help with that, but I'm too much of a control freak. I'd probably have to fix everything they did anyway.

The caller buzzing in a third time makes me stop. Well, they sure are persistent. Vinnie stretches in his nook and hops up next to me, resting his head on my thigh.

"This is Kieran." I answer the phone in an overly formal way, lowering my voice to match my podcast persona.

"Hey kid," someone says breathlessly on the other line. "It's me, George."

I freeze in place, stunned to hear from him. "George, hey, everything alright? Missed ya the other day."

"I'm so sorry about that," he apologizes, still in an out of breath way like he's walking somewhere quickly and talking at the same time. Always the busybody. "I left my phone on the airplane by accident and then the airline lost my luggage. It's been a mess. Anyway, I missed my flight back home trying to get a new phone and whatnot, so I'm still stuck in Portland. Are you still around? Want to meet for an early lunch in about an hour?"

I breathe a sigh of relief. "I've been so worried about you. I thought someone—*never mind*. Yes, I'm around still, lunch sounds great."

"Okay, I'll text you an address." He mumbles to someone off the phone nearby, forgetting for a moment he's still on a phone call with me. I'm about to clear my throat to remind him I'm still here when he quickly says, "Okay kid, see you then."

The call disconnects. Wow, I am so glad I answered the phone call. Who knows when else I would have gotten the reassurance that he didn't get taken off in a mysterious van like I almost did or that he decided I wasn't worth speaking to anymore.

A text comes through with an address. I click the link, and it takes me to my GPS app. I groan. It's a restaurant up in the Hills. I hate prissy places like this. Leave it to George to be needlessly fancy. He always did love an expensive steak when we worked together. For a retired PI, he sure loves to splurge on big-ticket food. The time estimate says it'll take about twenty minutes to get up the mountain in current traffic.

"Vinnie, get your fancy pants on, we have a date at the country club."

He's not amused. He's waiting by the van door, back to me like he's shunning me.

"Oh!" I leap to my feet, realizing I haven't let him out yet. "Sorry, bud."

I grab his leash and give him full range of the parking lot to choose from. I adjust my insulin pump at my hip as the leash edge catches on it and pulls my skin uncomfortably.

We walk into the gym after Vinnie finishes his business, and I let the girl at the desk scan my membership barcode. She's about to tell me to enjoy my workout in the routine way they always do, but then our eyes meet, and she gasps.

My stomach clenches. It's too early for this.

"Kieran Bergstrom!" she breathes. "I saw on your sub-Reddit someone said they spotted you downtown, but I thought they were making it up!"

I huff a polite chuckle. "Guess my disguise wasn't very effective." I wave to the light stubble I've been growing out on my jaw.

"No disguise can hide this handsome boy," she coos, kneeling to give Vinnie some love, which he participates in with *enthusiasm,* licking her face, tail wagging like a turbine.

"I am obsessed with your podcast," she gushes, still kneeling with Vinnie, flinging full chunks of his hair everywhere. Sorry cleaning crew. "I just listened to the season two finale yesterday. I literally had chills. What case are you working on next? Wait, is it *here*?"

"Guess you'll have to listen and find out." I give her a roguish smile.

"Ughhh." She stands with a laughing wail, dusting Vinnie's hair off her black leggings. "Well, if you ever need a local gossip, I'm happy to lend my services. I know basically every ragey meathead in town." She gestures around to demonstrate her point.

I chuckle. "I'll definitely keep you in mind if I have any gym-rat suspects come up."

I wave goodbye and tug Vinnie away, my body needing rather urgently to take care of business... I admit, the reliance on public restrooms does certainly get old.

WE'RE DRIVING up the winding freeway of the Hills around thirty minutes later, passing under an archway as we enter the premises, and I instantly feel out of place. I pass the valet roundabout and park my van myself, knowing it sticks out like a sore thumb around here.

It's not a dumpy vehicle by any means, but people who

frequent places like these don't live in their van. They live in those estates you can see from here, up in the hills that surround this place.

I shove my unruly hair out of my eyes, feeling the sudden need to shave it off into a gentlemanly fade. Wow, and I haven't even stepped out of my van yet. What's next, I'm going to have the urge to start golfing? Wearing loafers? This place may morph me into one of them by proximity alone. George better not stand me up again.

"We have to be on our best behavior here," I tell Vinnie sternly as I slide on his vest and leash. He perks up in understanding.

I lock up the van and smooth down my hair in the reflection of the windows. I threw on a plain black long sleeve shirt with a nice, quilted vest I found stuffed in the very back of my coat closet, brown chino pants, and some lace-up leather boots that cost a surprising fortune at the last town I stopped in, but the saleswoman had assured me they were "cool and trendy." Which I don't really care about, but she had a pretty smile I couldn't say no to.

I step inside the warm foyer of the restaurant. It smells like freshly baked bread and garlic, and I'm instantly hungry. George isn't in the lobby yet, only a few rich snobs waiting to be seated by the pinched-face elderly hostess.

The door has barely even shut behind us before she turns her nose up at her podium and says, "We don't allow pets at our establishment."

She all but shoos us out the door.

I clench Vinnie's leash in my hand, trying to stay calm even though the heat crackles under my skin like static. "He's a service dog, ma'am," I reply quietly so as not to cause a scene, waving to his bright yellow vest.

She looks at Vinnie in a disgusted way that makes my blood boil. "Unless you can provide some documentation or a certificate, I can't just take your word for it. It's a health code concern. Are you members here?"

I take a hard swallow, trying with maximum effort to keep all the words I want to say safely inside my throat. "I'm pretty sure, legally, you can't ask me for that," I say thickly, a little louder. "I'm meeting someone here, ma'am. He made the reservation. George Marshall?"

And right when I thought I couldn't be more mortified, there is a tiny gasp from someone behind me, exactly the same kind as that girl's from the gym. The kind that, in moments like this, makes me want to slink into a quiet corner and evaporate into oblivion.

"It's you!"

10

NIKKI

THE DOG, THE MYTH, THE LEGEND

Arrick's eyes bore into me from the rearview mirror as we drive up the hill to the clubhouse.

He's worried about me. That frown under his mustache hasn't gone away since this morning.

But I'm trapped too deep under the pressure of every-thing to reassure him right now. My aunt is dying right before my eyes, and life is holding both of my arms behind my back and forcing me to watch from afar. I'm unable to help no matter how hard I try.

Marrying Hunter in June fixes nothing if Aunt Wren doesn't have that long. And there's absolutely no way my proud aunt would sign off on an underage marriage, even if it could save her life.

I'm watching the blur of the snow-powdered golf course out my window, the snowflakes delicately falling and melting on the glass, trying not to cry, when a glimmer of an idea settles in my mind like the gentle snowfall outside.

I do the math five times in a row, mumbling to myself and using my fingers to make sure I'm not counting wrong.

"Arrick?" I have to clear my throat and repeat myself when his name comes out as a strained squeak.

"Yes, Miss Nikki?" He glances at me in the rearview.

"Do you remember what year Lizzy was born?"

I need someone else to say it, someone else to confirm it, so I know I'm not making things up, not clinging on to some new fantasy I've constructed.

He thinks for a moment, and I can tell he wants to ask why, but he doesn't. "2003, I believe."

"Her birthday was in December," I say it slowly, worried if I say it too fast maybe the truth of it will pop like a bubble. "So wouldn't that make her twenty-one?"

He eyes me again while doing the mental math. "Yes, I believe that's right."

That delicate, fragile snowfall of an idea morphs into a raging blizzard in my head as he confirms what I wanted so desperately to be true:

That Lizzy would be twenty-one if she were alive.

If somehow—some way—these texts from Unknown *are* her... if she's really alive, and more importantly, if I can find her...

She could access our inheritance.

She could save Aunt Wren.

Lizzy is the answer to everything.

MY BODY BUZZES like I've guzzled twelve coffees as I wait to be seated in the lobby of the clubhouse. I fiddle with the buttons that go entirely down the front of my ditsy floral dress, the corset waist feeling tighter as the pressure rises under my ribcage.

I'm too fidgety to reply, and I wish it wasn't socially unacceptable to pace because maybe the movement would help the room not feel so claustrophobic. Is it getting hot in here? No?

What started as a seed of hope has now transformed into the realization that I have to do what experienced, adult investigators were not able to do: find out what happened to my family and hope it leads to an alive Lizzy.

I'm close to falling into panic entirely when I take notice of the adorable fluffy furbaby at the host stand, yellow vest signifying he or she is doing important work right now, which sends a glow to my heart. Sweet baby probably feels so proud to take care of its owner. I only see the back of the owner's blonde head, but he looks young, maybe around my age. It's nice to see a fellow young person around here. I'm usually the only one amongst all the grouchy grandpas.

I'm about to plunge back into my own flaming thoughts, when I overhear the host tell the young man that there are no pets allowed. Something about the condescending way she says "pet" perks my immediate attention. I must have misheard her because this dog is clearly a service dog, and there's no way she is being blatantly discriminatory? I'm in fight mode as fast as if someone has flipped a light switch in me.

Stop eavesdropping, you stalker, the more rational side of my inner monologue reminds me.

Except, hold on.

Did she just say they had to be members here? That is not true at all, anyone can eat at the club restaurant.

I look around, sure that one of the adults in the lobby will speak up, stand up for this young man, but everyone stares at their phones, pretending not to notice.

I'm already standing to intervene when the young man's voice roots me to my spot. "I'm pretty sure, legally, you can't ask me for that," he says, and I gasp.

I would recognize that voice anywhere in any dimension or galaxy.

"It's you!" It blurts out against my will, and I hate myself for it.

He turns and I'm face-to-face with the one, the only, THE Kieran Bergstrom. The PNW legend, the host behind one of my favorite podcasts. I've sent him so many DMs about my family's case over the past couple years, *begging* him to investigate. I don't think the messages were ever opened, and honestly, I'm kind of glad about that in this moment. I'd probably want to melt into the floor with embarrassment if I knew he'd seen them.

I'm struck almost speechless with how unexpectedly good-looking he is. I knew in theory he was handsome, and he has a beautiful voice, but his social media doesn't do him justice. Like, he's not on Hunter's level, of course, but I can appreciate him as one would appreciate art—the strong nose, brown eyes you can get lost in, crisp jawline, swishy blonde hair some girls go crazy for.

Now I'm blubbering, and I can't stop, "Oh my gosh, I can't believe it's you. I love you. I mean not like *love* love, but I love your work. And your voice. But not in a weird way. Wow, you're younger than I thought you were, how old are you anyway?"

He looks less than amused.

My cheeks burn hotly. Did I actually just word vomit all over him right now? Maybe melting into the floor wouldn't be so bad after all.

There's so much I want to ask him about his cases, about his work, but I force myself to shut up (although it physically pains me, like I'm twisting my own tongue).

I look past him and straight to the hostess, giving her the sternest eyebrow I can muster despite my obvious blush. "Is there a problem? This man is clearly within his rights to have his service animal here, or should we give the ADA a call?"

The hostess's eyes look like they may bulge out of her eye sockets to be spoken to this way by a young person. I don't believe old people should automatically get a free pass, simply because they're old.

"If he were a member, I'd be happy to verify his membership," she splutters, nostrils flaring.

"Anyone, member or not can dine here," I interrupt. "But take it up with my membership if there's something you need to 'verify.' Sinclair."

Her face reddens with anger. My family has had a membership here for generations. This isn't the hill to die on today, and she knows it, especially with the eyes of the rest of lobby on us now.

I take her lack of response as an answer and step away from the hostess stand.

"I didn't need your help," he grumbles, crossing his arms. "I had things under control."

I'm shocked. He almost seems angry with me? Sure enough, his melty brown eyes are glimmering with anger.

"I think you meant to say, 'thank you, kind stranger." The sheer disbelief comes out nearly a squawk.

"Thank you, kind stranger," he deadpans, voice dripping with sarcasm. "How have I ever been able to live day-to-day for my whole life so far without your help?"

My ears sizzle with embarrassment, but I lift my chin. "Well, I can't just stand by when I see someone being treated unfairly."

He sighs. "I'm sorry." His tone is still tight, but a single slice of anger melts off the top. "I just hate places like this."

"I do too." Finding common ground with THE Kieran Bergstrom? *Be cool, be cool.* "People here are the worst."

I'm desperate to greet his fluffy helper, whose tongue is lolling adorably, tail wagging happily, but he's working right now, so I resist the urge. I'm trying to remember the dog's name from the podcast. Male, I'm pretty sure. Vincent? Steven?

"Stop," Kieran hisses to the dog under his breath, pulling the leash tighter as he attempts to come over to me.

"Wait." I gasp. The idea zaps me like a bolt of electricity from Mount Olympus itself. Kieran looks concerned, my wide eyes probably making it look like I'm experiencing a seizure or something.

"You ok…?" he says slowly, allowing the dog a little extra leash to come over and assess me medically. He licks my fingertips.

I am instantly more at ease. "Oh, you're good at your job," I tell him, scratching behind his ears.

I've already put my foot in my mouth, but I'd never forgive myself if I didn't at least ask. If he could help me with the investigation, maybe I'd actually have a real shot. This is my only chance. I have to. For my family.

"You probably get strangers asking this all the time... I'm sorry. Um, long story short, my whole family was murdered ten years ago and—" He exhales, and I quickly finish before he tunes me out completely, "No wait, please just look it up. It would be great for your next season. It's right up your alley. Sinclair family, Sapphire Pines. I've already messaged you about it. Several times actually... so you can search my name in your DMs. Nikki Sinclair."

He looks as if he's about to decline in a way he probably does often, but he's interrupted.

"Hey, kid."

A stout, bearded man shuffles past me to clap Kieran on the back.

The hostess glowers as she begrudgingly instructs the men to follow her back to their table.

Kieran moves to follow, looking at me over his shoulder with a polite wave. "Have a good rest of your day."

"I can pay you a lot of money," I call after him, the desperation rising as he walks away. "Please, I'm desperate to solve—"

But he's gone.

And he takes away every shred of hope with him.

11

KIERAN

BLACK EYES AND EXPENSIVE STEAK…
ANOTHER DAY IN THE LIFE

I tug Vinnie away from the girl, trying to be as polite as possible, but it's nothing I'm not used to—people asking me to look into cases for them. Ever since the podcast took off, I get a handful of people in public every so often who approach me like this. It used to get me down, that I had to say no. That I couldn't help everyone. But unfortunately, there's only one of me. I can't say yes to them all.

Although the name Sinclair does sound vaguely familiar, I already have my eye on a couple potential cases for next season, and I'm hoping George can look over them and give me his professional opinion. Since this is my livelihood, sadly there are more factors I have to consider than simply picking any random case.

Especially since I've managed to aid in solving my last two cases somehow by sheer luck. Having to do that a third time? It's a lot of pressure.

We take a seat at our table, other guests around side-eyeing us. Vinnie tucks in close to my feet like he's hiding, somehow feeling in the atmosphere that he's not welcome here. It makes my cheeks burn with a simmering anger. It's fine for me to feel that way. But making my dog feel unworthy? I want to burn this place down for making him feel like that.

George lowers into his chair a little clumsily, nearly knocking over the glasses at his place setting.

"Long time no see," he says with a breathy laugh as he straightens his place setting hastily. "How ya been?"

"Just been relaxing since the finale." I take a sip from the glass of ice water that was already waiting at the table for us. "What about you? How's retirement? Wait—" I get a good look at him for the first time. "Do you have a black eye?"

He waves me off. "Oh, it's nothing. Took a fall getting off the plane. Retirement? Yeah, good, great."

I stare at him. His fingers drum an erratic rhythm on the stem of his water glass. He's fidgeting more than me today, and that's saying something. I'm usually the antsy one.

I arch an eyebrow. "Are you okay?"

"I'm fine," George chuckles, sitting up straighter as if trying to convince me of his fine-ness. "Just a bit out of sorts today. Any ideas for next season?"

"Out of sorts?" I repeat skeptically, ignoring his question entirely. A retired PI like George doesn't get 'out of sorts.'

I narrow my eyes at him like a parent who knows their child is lying, the silence spanning between us for a moment. He doesn't say anything, or even look at me. He fidgets with his napkin, folding and refolding it over and over on his plate. Something's off.

He realizes I'm not letting it go. Heaving a sigh in defeat, George reaches inside his coat. His hand trembles as he slides a folded piece of paper across the table to me.

He meets my eyes at last and the sorrow laced through

every wrinkle, every fiber of his face, makes my mouth run dry. I struggle to swallow.

"George, tell me what's up," I repeat again, slower, as I take the paper from him. Vinnie senses the change in my heart rate and puts his head on my lap under the table. He knows how adrenaline can spike my glucose levels.

"I'm so sorry, kid," he whispers. "I had no choice."

He hangs his head as I slowly unfold the piece of paper, terrified of what it must say for him to react this way. What's going on?

A stark chill covers me from head to toe as I read the typed note:

"We could have done this the easy way, but the stakes have raised now. You will cooperate, or I will kill George and his wife the same way I killed Roger Mackenzie."

"What is this?" I breathe.

"I'm so sorry." George shakes his head miserably. "I showed up the other day to meet you for lunch, and these men in a van grabbed me. They took my phone and my wallet. Said they would kill Tina if I didn't do as they say."

"What do they want?" I can barely formulate the words, but I already know. *Ciphered Voyager.* So, it *was* him who shot Roger Mackenzie. He wanted me to take down my podcast, but I blasted him on it instead.

My phone vibrates on the table next to my place-setting. The preview shows a text from an unknown number.

George winces. "That's probably him. I think that's why they stole my phone, so they could get your number."

I open the text with shaking fingers. A series of text bubbles come in one by one.

CIPHERED VOYAGER

> Hello Kieran.

> All you had to do was take down the podcast.

> Now in addition to that, I'd like five million bitcoin in exchange for George's life.

My eyebrows fly to my hairline, jaw dropping to the ground. Three dots dance in front of me as the sender types another message. I stop breathing as I wait.

CIPHERED VOYAGER

> And as for his wife Tina's life? We'll let you know.

> I'm sure you know how ransoms go in your line of work, so no use getting into all the specifics of what will happen if you involve the police or put this on your podcast.

My phone nearly falls right out of my shaking hands as I attempt to send a text back.

KIERAN

> I don't have that kind of money.

CIPHERED VOYAGER

> I'll give you a month.

> Talk soon.

I clear my throat, attempting to form a coherent sentence. "Have—have you heard from Tina? Is she okay?"

"I called her as soon as I could get a new phone. She— she's fine, she's on vacation with her sister, but..." He pauses. "They have some kind of surveillance on her. They showed me images of her. Videos." He shakes his head. "In all my years of work, I've never encountered anything like this. The threats were always empty, amateur. Easy to ignore."

He shows me his phone and swipes through different blurry photos and videos of his wife Tina, a beautiful and joyous Black woman, completely unaware, shopping or sunbathing in a warmer climate somewhere.

I pat Vinnie reassuringly and try to get my pulse down, so I can think this out. I really don't need my liver overreacting right now and giving me insulin resistance on top of everything else.

Calm, calm... I'm calm, liver, see?

"Why does he care so much about my podcast?" I finally ask, the mental fog of the shock finally wearing off enough that I have a sliver of access to my brain.

"I don't know, kid." George is making an effort to calm himself down too, speaking slower and taking deeper breaths. He, more than anyone, knows you have to keep your head in a crisis. "When they had me in the van, they said if I didn't get you to cooperate, they'd kill me. Then they threw me out onto the street with nothing. I—" He averts his eyes with a guilty wince. "I had to steal this phone. I don't know if TSA is going to let me get back on a plane without my ID."

"I don't know how he expects me to pay that kind of money. I'm barely in the red from the podcast. My van, all my equipment." I shake my head. "I don't *have*—What's the bitcoin exchange rate today anyway?"

I pale as the impossibility of the number in bold at the top of the search engine screams at me.

"George, he's asking for half a million dollars."

～

An hour later and we've barely touched our food. The server looks at us with no shortage of judgment when George orders another refill of his cocktail. He doesn't seem worried that he's blown nearly a hundred dollars in alcohol so far, even with money being the forefront of our dilemma.

We've had our heads together the last hour, trying to pool together all our resources. If he cashes out his IRA and sells his condo, and if I sell all my crypto and my van, we've calculated that we can probably pull together close to 300k.

Even after making ourselves homeless and destitute, we'd still be two hundred thousand dollars short.

It feels futile, the gravity of it all sinking in and nearly smothering me.

He slides his whiskey glass across the table to me, an offering I wave away with a flat-lined smile. "Underage, remember?"

"Oh, right. Sometimes I forget you were just a little runaway when we met." He chuckles, shaking his head.

"Emancipated adult," I correct with sniff, hating that term. "But I've crossed into official adulthood now. Eighteen, finally, as of September."

"Well, I'll drink to that. Happy birthday." He holds the glass up in a cheers motion and downs it.

The positive moment is fleeting. Within seconds I've remembered the absolute black hole we're in. An impossible hole to climb out of that's all my fault. Maybe if I hadn't blasted Ciphered Voyager on my livestream, or maybe if I'd cooperated with the men in the van better, George wouldn't have to be involved in this at all. Or Tina.

Luckily George and I have solved a tricky case together before. If we can track down Ciphered Voyager, it won't matter if we don't have all the money. We can find this guy together.

I'm about to suggest we outline our strategy when he looks at the time on his stolen phone with a sigh.

"I hate to leave you like this, kid. If I have any chance of the airline letting me on board, I have to get there early."

All I can do is stare at him wordlessly. Leave?

His face twists in apology. "I need to be where Tina is. If this psycho is serious, I can't be away from her. Once I know she's safe, we can make a plan."

I clench my teeth together to keep myself calm. I nod. "Of course."

"Forward me that email you got. I have a few contacts that are very," he whispers, "discreet. They might be able to help us find this guy. In the meantime, let's keep thinking of ways we can get the money together. Don't sell your van just yet. Don't take down the podcast. We'll figure something out. I'll be alright."

How is he the one reassuring *me* when he's the one being held for ransom?

He claps me on the shoulder, gives Vinnie a pat on the head, and then he's gone.

I sit at the table alone and pull out the notes I had prepared for season three, the ones I wanted to go over with George, staring at them, feeling like they're so insignificant now. Contributors to the problem, even. All Ciphered wanted me to do was quit the podcast, yet here I still am, not even considering that as an option.

Even if I could manage to solve a third case in a month, it wouldn't make anywhere close to the extra two hundred grand we need. I crumple up the paper and toss it across the table. It lands in the wine sauce of George's uneaten steak. That I have to pay for.

Then a thought comes to my mind. A desperate voice saying, "I can pay you a lot of money..."

I spin around in my chair.

The girl. She's gone.

I rack my brain, the name of the family right on the tip of my tongue.

Sebastian?

No.

I pull out my phone to my search engine.

Sinclair Family. Sapphire Pines.

Secrets in Ice Season 3, Episode 2: The Crash, the Car, the Crime

[Secrets in Ice opening theme music plays]

KIERAN BERGSTROM:

A family with money, power, and seemingly no enemies, beloved to the community and staff members. Or so everyone thought. Suddenly gone and never seen again.

In the last episode, I introduced you to the Sinclair family—Sapphire Pines royalty, known for their wealth, but also their warmth. Murdered. With no justice, even ten years later.

In this episode, we'll retrace what we know of their final hours and take a hard look at what was—and what *wasn't*—found at the crash site.

Looking for answers among the shadows of the iciest cold cases, I'm your host Kieran Bergstrom, and you're listening to *Secrets in Ice.* This is episode two, "The Crash, the Car, the Crime."

[Secrets in Ice opening theme finishes playing over static police radio chatter]

DISPATCH *[over radio]* *[archival recording]*:

Unit 7, we've got a report of a black sedan off Forest Road 22. Caller found vehicle crashed into a tree off the road. No signs of life.

OFFICER *[over radio] [archival recording]*:

10-4, en-route to the crash site with K-9 unit.

[a beat as suspenseful music plays]

KIERAN BERGSTROM:

Saturday, October 17th, 2015.

It was a regular morning in Sapphire Pines, a crisp 46 degrees. Clear skies, slightly breezy. The trees in the hills were exploding with vibrant oranges and yellows. Fallen leaves decorating the earth like confetti.

The Sinclair family prepared for their busy Saturday like normal. Had breakfast, got dressed, packed their bags for a day out. They were heading to the next town over, Lake Oswego, for Elizabeth's statewide figure skating tournament.

Sources say they left home around 9:33 a.m.

No one knows why they left seven-year-old Nikki at home with a babysitter.

And no one knows why they never arrived at the tournament.

EMILY WRIGHT *[recorded voicemail]* :

I'm Emily Wright. I was Lizzy's coach. It was very unlike her to not show up. Skating was her whole life. We assumed she got sick or something. I had no idea until the next day what had happened to her. It's just really sad.

KIERAN BERGSTROM:

They were expected at the tournament by 10:00 a.m., and Elizabeth was on the schedule to perform midway through the roster. When Elizabeth's name was called, she was nowhere to be seen. No calls, no texts. They were just gone.

EMILY WRIGHT *[recorded voicemail]:*

I called their driver, Arrick, when they didn't show up for warmup, because he would sometimes be the one to bring her. Like I said, it was very unusual. He said they'd left on time and didn't know why they hadn't shown up.

9-1-1 CALLER *[archival recording]:*

Hello, I'm calling to report an accident I just passed off the I-5. Car's in bad shape. Doesn't look good.

KIERAN BERGSTROM:

Although the exact location of the crash site hasn't been revealed publicly, I was able to deduce that their car was found in Thurston County, Washington, on a smaller county road off the Interstate, over one hundred miles away from their intended destination.

OFFICER *[over radio] [archival recording]:*

Dispatch, this is a code 10-13. Immediate backup needed. Suspected foul play, no bodies on scene. Deploying K-9 to search area. Suspect at large, likely armed and dangerous.

[suspenseful music plays]

12

NIKKI

THOUGH THE WEATHER BE FOUL

Back at the house, Hunter and I look around in Lizzy's room for anything helpful, and I'm trying really hard to forget about a horrifically embarrassing encounter at the country club.

What's the saying? Never meet your heroes and spill your verbal guts all over them, or they'll think you're weird and won't help you solve your family's murders? Should have remembered it *before* the gut spilling.

Well, screw him. I'll do it myself. Maybe I'll even make my own podcast. Everyone has one these days, anyway, why not me? And he'll sure regret it when mine is better than his. Take that, Kieran Bergstrom.

Hunter clears his throat from Lizzy's closet, pulling me from my spiraling thoughts of declaring audio warfare. He keeps glancing at me through glittery leotards, making sure I'm not going to seep into despair the longer we're in this room, actively confronting hard truths. He knows I prefer cozy denial, and we're way past that.

He was worried about me at lunch. He could tell I was

keeping something from him. It took some persistent convincing on his part (okay, all it took was a flash of a dazzling smile and a flutter of lashes over eyes that are the color of seaglass), but I finally told him everything. The additional texts from Unknown/maybe Lizzy, the journal, the conversation with Nurse Kayla that expedited the timeline. The reality that I need solve my family's case to save Aunt Wren. No pressure or anything.

He listened politely and didn't make me feel insane when I spoke the crazy thoughts about Lizzy into existence aloud for the first time. He helped me plan out the next steps, held my hand while I called and requested the full case file from the police department.

I don't know why I waited so long to tell him everything. I feel lighter now that I have someone to share the load with, someone to help me carry the weight.

Until the case file comes in, the plan is to look around the house for clues. I'm sure there will be nothing that police wouldn't have already found when they did their own inspection, but I have to try.

I'm lying flat on my stomach, looking under Lizzy's bed. I call to Hunter over my shoulder, "I'm sorry to waste your last day here like this."

It physically hurts thinking about the fact that he has to leave today. Yes, we'll still be able to talk like we always have, but now that I've gotten a taste of what his presence is like, it's irreplaceable. The squeeze of hands, the brush of shoulders, the smell of his cologne.

Now that I know what his cologne smells like, how will I survive without it when he's gone? It's unfair to have to go back to everyday smells.

He puts a shoe box he's just inspected back up on a shelf

in the closet I never would have been able to reach on my own. "Don't be. It's not every day you get to help your fiancée solve a murder." He smiles. "This is way better than snowboarding, which is all I would have been doing otherwise."

"Do you really think she could be alive, or are you afraid to tell me what you actually think?" I blurt the words out before I can convince myself I don't want to hear the truth.

He removes the lid from the next shoebox, pulling out a handful of hair accessories from it and looking through them. He glances at me cautiously over the box. "I just don't get why she'd stay away all these years if she's alive? And where could she have been hiding out this long?"

It's nothing I haven't already asked myself a million times, but hearing him say it injects doubt directly into my bloodstream.

I stretch to reach a plastic box pushed far under her bed.

"It's worth looking more into though," he hurriedly adds, sensing my disappointment. "If anything, to find the answers no one else could find. Closure is good regardless."

Closure. Closure is accepting an end. It's a goodbye.

He doesn't think she's alive.

I get it. It's impossible and impractical and hopeless and makes me feel so ridiculous.

But I feel in a way like I let Lizzy down by simply accepting her death all this time. For ten years I've been okay with not knowing what happened to her? What kind of sister am I? I owe it to her to find answers, whether she's alive or not.

I believed the investigation was complete because that's what the adults told me. I accepted there was nothing else they could do because that's what they told me.

Well, I'm not a child anymore. I'm old enough now, and

sufficiently hardened by the realities of life, to not simply believe what an adult tells me at face value anymore.

Adults lie.

Sometimes it's out of love. *Yes, sweetie, there is a little fairy that takes the tooth from under your pillow and leaves a dollar in its place.*

Sometimes it's to protect you. *Your family is in a better place now.*

But sometimes it's to hide things. *We did the best investigation we could do, and there is nothing further that can be done.*

Adults *lie*. How else can three human beings get murdered, and everyone who could do something about it simply gives up?

Aunt Wren did her best. I will never blame her.

She thought she was giving me peace by allowing the police to give up without a fight. And for years, honestly, it did. The grief has always been there, but at least it was never fear. The loss was always smoldering, but at least I could sleep at night. As a child, it was better that there were never bodies I had to see every time I closed my eyes or had to imagine a figure lurking in every shadow to come for me next.

She gave me the best semblance of a childhood she could. She uprooted her own life to care for a child that wasn't hers and pick up all the pieces when that little girl's family never came back, putting them back together the best she could. Distracted that little girl with messy art projects, picnics on the property in the summer, princess tea parties with tiaras and tutus.

That's why I can't just let her die.

I clear my throat, deciding to keep things light with

Hunter. "Well, on the bright side, if we find Lizzy you don't have to marry me."

"I don't know, I've gotten kind of attached to the idea." And he does one of those grins that makes my heart soar.

I rifle through the plastic box I pulled out from under the bed. It's full of paper. Pages and pages of old school assignments, tests, essays. I didn't realize Lizzy was such a paper hoarder.

My breath catches when a familiar spread of colors peeks out of the stack. I pull it out from the pile carefully. It's a page taken out of a children's book. The artwork style is unmistakably Dr. Seuss. There's no text on either side of the page, artwork only. On one side, there's a lone character in a boat, passing by groaning monsters in the dark blue water around him. On the other side, the same character stands right in front of a different monster, seemingly braver. No cats with hats to be seen. *Oh, The Places You'll Go*, maybe?

But with a corner missing.

I jolt up, forcing away the dizziness in my head from standing too quickly. Hunter looks at me from the closet with curious eyes. I don't pause to fill him in, scurrying to my room without a word.

I kneel in front of the sock drawer where I hid Lizzy's journal, feeling Hunter's eyes on me from the doorway as I shake the journal from the spine. The scrap of paper falls out into my hand.

I set the journal down to confirm what I already know.

The scrap from the journal. It fits perfectly in the missing corner of the paper. Blue water on one side, reddish orange on the other side.

I breathe a shaky breath, holding it up so Hunter can see.

I analyze the numbers on the scrap again. *3-7-0-5.* It's

obviously important because she took the time to hide it in this journal. A combination maybe? Password to something? I'm struggling to remember if she had a phone or a computer—having to rely on the fading memories of an oblivious child is so frustrating—but I'm sure any of that would have been taken into evidence by police if it were left at the scene or in the house somewhere. Hopefully the case file will provide that kind of information.

"What do you think it is?" Hunter asks after giving me a moment to think.

I stand up methodically, even as my brain whirs at Nascar-level speeds.

I slide past Hunter through the doorway. He lets me past without a word, only there to lend support if I need it, bless him.

I skip down the stairs three at a time, hearing the clattering bustle of Bea preparing dinner in the kitchen. The aroma of whatever she's cooking is drool-worthy—some variation of a buttery, savory potato and something citrus. Fish maybe? I take a left to the sunroom, which is on the opposite side of the downstairs foyer from Aunt Wren's suite.

I instantly feel more at ease stepping into the sunroom.

This is my favorite room in the house. I love curling up with a book or podcast in my reading nook in the corner. Or I'll sometimes take a nap or work on homework when I need a change of scenery from my desk. The whitewashed brick fireplace is the only wood-burning one in the whole house (the others are gas or electric), and in the cold months, Arrick keeps a fire going to keep the room cozy for me. In the summer I come in here to absorb the warm sun into my soul. Floor to ceiling windows on two entire walls of the room provide an unimpeded view of the expansive acreage around the house and the neighboring forest drenched in a warm golden hour-glowing snow.

Light oak bookshelves line every inch of space surrounding the fireplace, packed full of books and memorabilia and plants I've collected over the years. Without Mom to put her foot down, and an aunt with no opinion on the matter, I've pretty much gotten to fill these shelves up however I want. Mom wasn't here to disapprove as I got rid of her decorative books that weren't meant to be read, aesthetic figurines or vases, and oddly shaped bookends. Things she only used as fillers on these shelves, never touched or used or *felt*. My plants give it life in here. In a house that sometimes feels like a living tomb, this is where I can go to feel somewhat alive.

I go straight to the bookshelf on the far left, the only one I've left completely the same all these years. The bottom two rows I've ignored for so long, I sometimes forget they're even there.

Our books. From when we were kids.

Colorful, non-aesthetic books Mom probably hated having in here where everything else was so strategically curated and placed to fit a certain style, made to look like it was pulled from a magazine.

Our two shelves of books I've never been able to bring myself to get rid of. Books Lizzy had loved. Books she had read to me before I knew how to read myself. Books I'd flip through and pretend to read just like her.

I kneel in front of the rows, setting the page beside me. Hunter sits on the huge loveseat in the corner, my reading nook, taking in the room but not interrupting my train of thought. I adore him for that.

I hesitate, my outstretched hand pausing before touching

the books in front of me, terrified to disturb this little shred of childhood I can simply shove down into oblivion whenever it hurts too much to think about. Touching them makes them real. Brings them back to life.

I sniff away the tears as I finger the spines one by one. I pass a dozen books, *The Cat in the Hat, Go, Dog, Go, Pete the Cat,* feeling the grief clawing inside me at the memories these familiar titles bring up.

There.

I exhale before taking it off the shelf. I can do this.

I pull the book out, leaving a small gap in its place, like I'm pulling a slice of a memory out of a tangible block of consciousness.

I look at Hunter over my shoulder.

"I'm scared to open it," I admit sheepishly.

"Do you want me to do it?" He reaches his hand out from the loveseat.

I squeeze my eyes shut and puff out a breath. "No. I can do it."

I *have* to do it. Too many people are counting on me; dead and maybe not dead and almost dead.

I open *Oh, the Places You'll Go* and flip through the pages one by one, the colorful illustrations matching the style of the torn page exactly, just like I suspected. I flip halfway through it before finding where the page was torn from, fingering the frayed edge in the spine.

I murmur the passages from both sides aloud. "*Though the weather be foul... though your enemies prowl...*" I raise an eyebrow at Hunter. "Are these supposed to be clues or something? '*On and on you will hike... you'll hike far and face up to your problems whatever they are.*'"

He kneels by me, stretching his neck to take a look at the

pages himself. "Maybe?" He repeats it thoughtfully, *"'Onward up many a frightening creek'*?"

I flip through the rest of the book, looking for any more writing, or missing pages with missing corners.

"I don't know what any of it means, but I sure don't like the sound of *'enemies prowling'*," I mumble. "Or hikes for that matter."

I'm about to return to the clue pages to read them again when I notice something on the back cover.

I freeze.

Lizzy's handwriting. In the same glitter gel pen as the scrap of paper, written so small I never would have noticed it under regular circumstances, the green ink blending in with the illustrated grass on the artwork: *"pair left beck burn."*

After repeating it in my own head countless times, I read it aloud to Hunter.

He reads it for himself over my shoulder before meeting my eyes, mirroring my own confusion. I hand him the book and pace around the room. Maybe I can spark some sense into my head, a kinetic reaction to hopefully zap new ideas into my brain the more I move.

At first, I think it's working, that static electricity must be flooding into my body and heading for my brain, but it's my phone vibrating in my back pocket.

I take it out quickly in case it's Unknown again.

It's not.

I scream.

"What? What is it?" Hunter is at my side immediately.

The message is from @kieran_bergstrom CHECKMARK. The verified, the kind-of-rude-but-still-legendary, *THE* Kieran Bergstrom.

KIERAN BERGSTROM

Hello Annika, I wanted to apologize for my rudeness in the restaurant today. I took a look at your family's case. I'm still in town. When can you meet to talk more?

I scream again and throw my phone at the loveseat. No freaking way.

13

NIKKI

THOUGH YOUR ENEMIES PROWL

Arrick peeks his head in from the doorway, trying to act casual and not like he just heard me screaming bloody murder.

He and Hunter meet eyes, sharing a look like they don't know what to do with me, but I don't care. My pacing increases in both speed and vigor.

Kieran Bergstrom looked up my case.

And he wants to meet.

The stubborn part of me wants to leave him on 'read,' to make him pay for blowing me off at the restaurant. But I guess it wasn't really his fault... I'm the one who threw my family's case at him the second he breathed at me. He's probably used to that. My cheeks warm at the thought of being another fangirl throwing herself at him, especially now that he has probably seen my prior messages. *Alllll of them.*

Arrick clears his throat. "Beatrice wanted me to inform you both that dinner is ready."

Hunter thanks him and says we'll be right there, but I'm barely listening. He stops my pacing mid-step by putting his hands on my shoulders gently. "Breathe and explain. Did you get another text from Unknown?"

I shake my head, stepping over to the loveseat to show him the message from Kieran.

Hunter looks at me with a quirked eyebrow. "Who is this?"

"You never listened to that podcast I sent you."

"Sorry," he says with a sheepish grin. "You know blood and gore isn't really my thing."

I shake my phone. "It's his podcast. He does investigative work on *local* cold cases! I ran into him at the restaurant yesterday." I'm nearly shrieking at him at this point. "He looked into my family's case, and he wants to meet to discuss more!"

"And being on a public forum with someone you don't know will help how?" He keeps his features neutral, but the doubt cords across them like tiny rivulets.

I deflate a little that he doesn't see how promising this is. "Hunter, he has *solved* his last two cases. Cold cases are what he does."

He takes my hand. "You don't know this person, Nik. It's weird to me that he would reach out to you like this. It could be some kind of scam." He continues his thought quickly before I can interrupt like he knows I want to, "Even if he is who he says he is, all being on a podcast will do is invite more strangers to speculate on every detail of your life. Your parents. Lizzy. You. Are you sure you want that?"

I look away, trying to shake away the frustrated tears burning in the corners of my eyes. I wanted him to be excited with me. If I wanted a voice of reason, I would have told Arrick. "If it means finding answers, I don't care about that," I sniff. "I don't really have any other option. My *aunt* has no other option."

He presses his lips together. I can tell there's more he wants to say, but he doesn't. He tugs my hand toward the doorway. "Let's go eat."

DINNER IS TENSE, and I hate it. These are my last moments with Hunter before he has to go, and it's ruined. I pretend to eat, pushing my food around the plate aimlessly until Bea comes out from the kitchen and asks me what's wrong with her salmon. I take a big bite quickly and assure her with a full mouth that nothing is wrong, and it's delicious as always, shoveling in more until she's satisfied.

"I'm sorry to be a buzzkill," Hunter says when she leaves. He feels so far away across this ridiculously huge dining room table we hardly ever use, but we don't have guests often, so Bea wanted to go all out. "I should've let you be excited about the podcast thing."

I forgive him instantly. How could I not with a face like that? "If he does my family's case, will you listen to it then?" I tease.

He takes a long-drawn-out bite off his fork as he pretends to think about it. "I'll consider it."

I toss my napkin across the table at him with a snort. "Some fiancé you are."

"Some what?" A sudden booming voice in the dining room makes me leap to my feet.

The blood drains from my whole body because *it's Hunter's dad.*

He's leaning against the entryway. He's gotten grayer in

his hair and beard, but I recognize him from my childhood right away.

My dad's best friend.

"Mr. Vanderwaal," I blurt, suddenly unsure of what to do with my hands. "It's great to see you, um, I didn't realize you were coming in. Bea can make a plate for you."

Hunter's countenance sours immediately, and all the warmth is sucked out of the room. He sinks deeper into his chair, his cheerful appearance slipping into an emotionless mask.

"No need, Nikki, I wanted to come in to check out the place for old time's sake. My, how you've grown." His smile goes all the way to his eyes, but it doesn't make him any less intimidating.

I've always had a hard time reconciling the Hunter's dad I remember as a child—goofing around with my dad on family vacations, swinging me upside-down until I was laughing so hard I was breathless—with the Hunter's dad *Hunter* tells me about. Cold. Strict. Ruthless.

"You've become a lovely young woman," he says, appraising me like family friends always do when they see you again after a long time. "What's this I hear about fiancé?"

He looks at Hunter pointedly, but not angrily. More like... assertively curious.

I expect Hunter to shrink down under his father's gaze, but he straightens in his seat, lifting his chin defiantly. "We're getting married."

I, for one, would love to turn into an ooze so I can seep into the cracks of the hardwood and disappear forever. I look back and forth between the two. Being in the middle of two men each trying to take up more space than the other creates a deep twinge in my stomach that I fear may eat itself.

Mr. Vanderwaal quirks a surprised eyebrow at his son, but he remains otherwise indifferent, almost like he was expecting him to back down too. "Is that so?"

I lower back down into my seat slowly and take a deliberately long drink of my Coke, dreaming again of becoming ooze. Or even a nice slime would do. "I'm sure Bea really wouldn't mind preparing another plate," I say to no one.

"In three months," Hunter adds simply, casually, as if merely discussing a golf match. I can tell he's just trying to get a reaction out of him. A small sliver of me wonders if that's all our engagement is to him, a way to piss off his dad. I shove that possibility deep, deep down before I can dwell on it.

The cool edges of Mr. Vanderwaal's composure heat ever so slightly, and I can't tell if it's because he doesn't approve of our engagement, or if it's the way Hunter is leveling his gaze and not backing down. "Well, in that case, I suppose congratulations are in order." He thinks we're bluffing. "Arrick, did you hear the happy news?"

I wince, as Mr. Vanderwaal pulls a passing Arrick into the room. It's not that I didn't want him to know, I just didn't want him to know *yet*.

Arrick's reaction as Mr. Vanderwaal tells him the news is impossible to discern. All he says is, "I hadn't heard. Congratulations. Miss Nikki speaks very highly of your son."

My ears burn at Mr. Vanderwaal's attention returning to me at the mention of my name. "Indeed," he says, appraising me again but with new eyes, like this time he's trying to figure out what I'm up to—what I'm trying to get out of him.

He snaps out of it quickly, pasting a smile back on. "Well,

we have a flight to catch, but it was lovely to see you again, Nikki. Next time I see you, I guess will be the wedding." He laughs sharply, emphasizing 'wedding' as if it's the most ridiculous thing he's ever had to say. It's clear he doesn't take us seriously at all.

"I'll let you two say your goodbyes." He claps Arrick on the shoulder and leaves the room. Arrick gives me a nod and follows him out.

The silence stretches between us like molding clay, tightening and drying the longer neither of us speaks.

"I hate him," Hunter growls, his fist visibly tightening on the table by his plate.

"I'm sorry." I look down at the mashed potatoes on my plate. "It's my fault. I shouldn't have said—"

"I'm not sorry," he interrupts me firmly, his eyes warming in a way that makes me melt. "I'm glad he heard you." He stands and takes my hand. I can barely look at him as we walk out of the dining room and across the foyer to the front door.

Don't cry, don't cry.

But the second I look at him, the dam breaks, and *I* break.

"I don't want you to go," I sob.

Going back to being alone after getting used to him *here* seems cruel.

He pulls me in tightly, stroking my hair as I cry into his chest. "I wish I could stay. I'm sure he's going to try to keep me from coming out here again, but I'll be back as soon as I can, I swear."

I sniff into his sweater and take one last big inhale of his cologne, woodsy and musky, before pulling back to take a final look at him. He strokes my cheek, a conflicted flicker in his eyes as he looks at my lips.

I want to scream at him to do it, to kiss me, but I hesitate too, also unsure of where exactly we're at, when only yesterday we were *just* best friends and now we're engaged. That doesn't exactly come with clear instructions or defined milestones.

He must see my doubt, so he presses a gentle kiss to my forehead instead, a gesture so sweet that it makes me cry again.

"Are you trying to make me miss you, Canada?" I laugh through tears.

"Of course I am." He shoots me a deadly perfect smile. "How else will I make sure you don't go off and get a better-looking fiancé to save your aunt with?"

Arrick returns to the front door after helping Mr. Vanderwaal and his driver get to their car. A light layer of snow dusts his hair and jacket as he opens the front door. "Ready, Mr. Hunter?" Arrick offers a hand to help him down the steps, but Hunter shakes his hand with a thank you instead.

He waves before sliding into the back seat. Arrick shuts his door and may as well have shut my entire soul in there with it.

I watch as the car crawls away, taking pieces of me with it as it goes. Leaving me here alone.

I crumple into the chair by Aunt Wren's bedside and let myself cry silently while she sleeps. I take her hand carefully in mine, wishing more than anything I could talk to her about this. I've always told her everything. It feels too big on my shoulders, too heavy.

For a while there, I actually felt like a normal seventeen-year-old. A normal teenager who could fall in love and make stupid decisions and take risks with her life like normal teenagers do.

But it was all a very brightly colored fantasy.

Annika Sinclair is not a normal seventeen-year-old.

She doesn't get to cry in her aunt's arms over a boy.

So, I blow my nose on a tissue as quietly as I can, take out my phone, click to my DMs, and type a reply.

NIKKI SINCLAIR

I'm available to meet tomorrow.

14

———

NIKKI

PRO-TIP: BRING A SHOVEL WHEN YOU'RE DIGGING FOR SECRETS

I pace back and forth outside my father's office door, deliberating. Mourning what I have to do.

The ugly truth has been tickling at the back of my head ever since I found Lizzy's journal, uncurling ever so slightly until I acknowledged it, and now that the distraction of Hunter is gone, I can no longer ignore it:

For some reason, Lizzy didn't trust my parents with whatever her secret was, or she wouldn't have gone to these lengths to conceal it. She would have just told them, and they would have dealt with it, and that would've been the end of it.

A sad ache blossoms in my chest. I fear digging around will taint my memories of my parents. The parents I loved, who loved me, who I trusted wholeheartedly as a naive child. But I need to confront the reality that I might not like what I learn about them.

Because why didn't Lizzy trust them?

The last time I went inside my father's office was an accident. This time will not only be intentional, but an intentional invasion. Because this time I don't intend to sit in here and breathe in the smells of a life I used to have. This time, I plan to cut through them and find answers to secrets that were hidden right before rose-colored eyes. I hesitate at the doorknob, giving my parents one last moment.

One last moment where I allow them to hide in their secrets and remain the parents I knew and loved.

One last moment before I dig.

And dig I do.

After an hour, all I've gotten through are the drawers of his desk, and I don't find anything useful. I've found financial papers and spreadsheets neatly stacked in piles, certificates and licenses that are long expired, tax documents full of figures I don't understand. No titles to useless metal piles of money in the garage. No clues.

I move half-heartedly to the closest bookshelf, losing steam quickly after finding nothing in his desk. The bookshelf has a storage cupboard on the bottom half of it, which I open hesitantly, afraid a nest of spiders could be lurking inside or something. Luckily there are no spiders, only more stacks of books and documents. I attempt to take the stack out carefully, but it topples over into my lap.

In the stack are a few old yearbooks from my father's high school and collegiate days that I peruse quickly, finding nothing of substance in the messages from classmates written in the margins. I'm setting them back in the cupboard when something catches my eye. It's the same color as the backing of the cupboard, so I would have never noticed it if I weren't sitting so close to it.

It's a handle to some kind of interior compartment. *Purposefully out of sight.*

Maybe he kept the titles to the cars in here? I hold my

breath as I reach for it, finding it to be cracked open slightly, as if it were shut in a hurry.

I open the small door, lying on my belly and using my phone flashlight to illuminate the inside. The inner compartment smells musty and stale. It's lined with a rough, gray fabric.

At first glance, it looks like a random assortment of trash, but when I analyze it more, it's not trash at all. It's the remnants of an emergency. The scraps left behind in duress.

The items closest to me are several hastily torn scraps of paper of different colors that each have a different dollar amount printed on them. Paper bands that go around stacks of cash. Quick math shows nearly twenty-thousand dollars here, grabbed quickly.

Why would my father need twenty-thousand dollars cash in a hurry?

I move those aside, and my heart stops.

Stacked boxes.

Of gun ammunition. One torn open and halfway empty.

Which means not only did my father have a *gun* in this house, but when he took it in a hurry, he needed it *loaded.*

I nearly miss the last item completely because it's tucked further into the shadowed corner. I squint.

My hands break out into a cold sweat as I pick it up carefully.

It's a black, older model smart phone, thick and heavy. I press and hold the power button cautiously, as if it will sound some kind of alarm at my touch.

The screen remains black.

I blow out a frustrated breath at myself. *Did you really expect it would be charged after ten years in storage, idiot?*

My father didn't want this found, or it wouldn't be

hidden in some weird hole in the wall, but it wasn't important enough to take with him when he took the gun and the cash. I have to know what's on this phone. What *secrets* are on this phone.

I try to find a charger for the phone, looking in the storage cupboard, and then the next one, and then the next one, moving stacks and books around in a near frenzy of adrenaline.

The energy fizzles quickly when I can't find a compatible cord anywhere.

Curse you tech companies for always changing the chargers!

I tuck the phone into my pocket and dart down the stairs, determined to check every drawer we have.

After a frustrating hour of rifling through every drawer and cabinet I can find, searching through my dad's bedstand and closet, even venturing into the garage and digging into the various drawers and toolboxes there, I plop onto my bed in defeat.

After an internet search, I find a compatible charger online which I buy immediately, but it isn't expected to be delivered for a few days. I groan, bashing my forehead into my pillow.

As if pulled there in a hypnotic trance, I'm back in Lizzy's room, needing to feel close to her. I can't believe I spent so long avoiding this, trying to pretend I don't need her close in whatever capacity available. I think I've always needed her closeness, I just never acknowledged it. Not consciously anyway. What I thought was simply a deep cavern of loneliness was always her. The absence of her. And now that I've cracked that awareness, I don't think I'll ever be able to go back to pretending I don't need her.

I plop down onto her bed, the exhaustion from the day

quickly settling in. I lie my head back on her pillow, and take the burner phone out of my pocket, allowing myself to reflect on it, knowing a heavy weight will follow whenever I confront the fact that my dad had secrets he didn't want found.

Why did he hide this phone? And most importantly, why did he need a gun and twenty thousand dollars?

Who were you really, Dad?

There is a *buzz*, and I'm struck into a frozen shock, psychotically thinking his phone has come alive in my hand. But it's my own phone in my pocket. I have to do a complete 180 to wrench it out.

It almost feels like a relief at this point to receive another text from Unknown, since I'm operating under the assumption it's Lizzy, that she's alive, that she needs me to find her. But then I read it:

UNKNOWN

don't trust anyone

PODCAST TRANSCRIPT

Secrets in Ice Season 3, Episode 2: The Crash, the Car, the Crime, Cont.

[suspenseful music plays]

KIERAN BERGSTROM:

There wasn't much public information about the team that investigated this case. It seemed like the more I dug, the less I found. Even what were supposed to be public records were heavily redacted or missing completely. I found that really strange. And even suspicious. I asked a friend if he could help me make sense of the crime scene, at least what I could find of it.

[sound of phone dialing]

KIERAN BERGSTROM:

Adam, we're recording now, can you introduce yourself?

ADAM KIRBY:

My name is Adam Kirby, I'm a forensic scientist in the state of Idaho. My specialty is examining crime scene evidence and giving investigators an expert opinion on what could have happened.

KIERAN BERGSTROM:

Can you help explain to listeners what we were able to find out about the crime scene? Icers, please be advised that the following details may be hard to hear.

ADAM KIRBY:

Sure, Kieran, although I do agree it's strange how little we were able to find. Hopefully your client will get better information from the case file. Anyways, okay, here's what I understand of the crime scene. The car was found collided with a tree off a county road near Interstate 5 in Washington. There were no bodies in the car or on the scene, and a search of the area was done as well with no luck.

Three distinctive blood pools were found inside the car, on the windshield, ground, and seats, and when those three samples were tested and compared to DNA of Gunnar, Ingrid, and Elizabeth, they were matches.

The direction of the blood spatter and bullet fragments they recovered in the windshield and backseat indicated a firearm was discharged multiple times.

They also found tear marks in the seats, scuff marks, and broken glass and deduced there was a struggle of sorts, although it's unclear if the struggle was before or after the firearm was used.

KIERAN BERGSTROM:

If you had been on this investigation team, what would have been your next steps?

ADAM KIRBY:

I would try to begin working backwards. First, I would want to figure out if the gun was fired before or after the crash. That would at least give me some insight on the timing and nature of their deaths.

KIERAN BERGSTROM:

From what you can see of the scene, what's your theory?

ADAM KIRBY:

It's hard to say without more evidence available to look at, but I'd guess the perpetrator probably caused the crash and shot them afterwards to finish the job.

KIERAN BERGSTROM:

For no bodies to ever be found, even ten years later, I mean, what kind of perpetrator are we dealing with here?

ADAM KIRBY:

For there to be no DNA around the scene, no slip-ups, no trail, this is someone experienced, organized, and intelligent. This was planned meticulously and carried out impeccably. You're looking for the perfect murderer.

[suspenseful music plays]

15

KIERAN

I'M GETTING A LITTLE TIRED OF ANONYMOUS MESSENGERS

The second I begin researching the Sinclair case, I regret everything immediately. Why couldn't a rich heiress of an *easy* case need her family's murders solved?

The lack of information, theories, coverage, anything, is both surprising and discouraging. It feels like a mile-long cliffside I have to scale without any safety equipment, with the very real possibility I'll fall to my death. Or George's death... Or Tina's.

I've been scouring the internet for any concrete information about this case, but I'm coming up frustratingly short. No wonder no other podcast has touched this with a ten-foot pole. Apart from about a hundred news sources reporting the initial shocking deaths of the Sinclairs next to headlines about Hurricane Joaquin and President Obama's involvement in Syria, there's not much on the internet about this case at all. It seems to have been forgotten quickly.

How could the deaths of a high-profile couple and their child not have received more media coverage?

I have to remember that the internet ten years ago didn't

have as much of a viral nature as it does now, but the amount of social media buzz regarding this case is suspiciously low. I found a few Tweets and a couple Reddit posts that discussed theories when the news originally broke, but otherwise, it's like no one cared at all. Coverup maybe? If that's true, this case will be even trickier than I thought.

The further I dig and the less I find, the more the dread stretches and elongates. How am I going to do this? The last two cases had significantly more public information than this, so many theories available I could pull from, cooperative communities willing to help. And even then, I still barely pulled it off.

The secret I could never admit on my podcast? *I don't know what I'm doing.* I never have. I put on a confident front, make promises to families that I might not be able to keep, rely heavily on luck, and fake it until it works out.

And now I'm a fraud *and* a con artist.

Never before would I have considered charging money to solve a case, and not two hundred thousand dollars, no less. Will this case even be worth that much to Annika Sinclair? Does she even have that kind of money to work with? Because unfortunately those are the terms I have to present to her. Hand over 200k or I won't help you solve your family's murder. It feels so wrong.

But I don't have a choice. I can't think of any other way to get the rest of the money together for George. He's depending on me. His wife is depending on me.

And it's a case so impossible that even professional investigators and the internet gave up on it?

It's so much pressure that it makes me want to vomit.

I push off my bed and begin pacing back and forth across the floor of my van. Vinnie assesses me from his nook but luckily gives me space. My kettle hisses at me from the counter, signifying my hot water is ready.

It's almost three o'clock in the morning, so coffee at this hour is a decision. A commitment that I'm not sleeping tonight.

There's no way my brain could turn off right now anyway. Ciphered Voyager, George, the Sinclair case. Everything is too cluttered and tangled in my head. I'd never be able to sleep even if I tried.

So might as well drink the coffee and get to work.

I wipe down the whiteboard mounted by my bed and write notes on the Sinclair case, trying to organize what little I know about the case before meeting with Annika in a few hours. If I'm asking her for two hundred thousand dollars, I have a lot of work to do. I'll need to put my best foot forward. I have to look confident, make her feel like I can really solve this. I have to be the best fraud I can be.

George and Tina's lives depend on it.

A FEW HOURS LATER, I'm sitting at a table in the coffee shop she sent me the address of. It's a more alternative place than I expected from the perky country club princess. It's a pleasant surprise. The walls and ceiling are black, with trendy huge bare bulbs hanging down to cast a cozy ambience and actual guitars and vinyl records mounted decoratively on the walls. A mix of both tables and clusters of cushioned furniture pepper the room, all filled with people working on laptops or groups of friends munching on pastries and chatting.

I'm sipping on my second coffee today, fidgeting with my

napkin as I wait for her to arrive. I'm glad she didn't make us go back to that awful country club, and I'm equally glad she suggested we meet for breakfast and not any other mealtime. I don't think I could have survived any extra hours of pacing around my van hyped up on caffeine and anxiety.

Vinnie tugs on his leash the second he sees her, perking up immediately when she walks through the cafe door, which is held open for her by what looks like a literal retired member of the presidential secret service. Dude was probably huge and terrifying in his prime. He's dressed to the nines, cool mustache, and despite his intimidating aura, he opens the door for her affectionately. Speaks to her gently.

Dang, this girl has a bodyguard on staff to drive her to downtown cafes?

I hiss at Vinnie to relax. He wags his tail, aggressively impatient, as he waits for her to see us and get closer. How quickly I'm shoved to the side when a girl is involved.

"Vinnie, don't you know it's bros before—" I cut myself off because she has found our table. She looks different today, but maybe the change in environment is affecting that. Less stuck-up princess... more normal. Pretty, even.

Her hair is down, the long red waves tumbling down to her waist. She holds a black puffy coat in the crook of her elbow. I'm surprised she's not dressed in something flashier or more expensive looking, considering how much her net worth is. She's wearing a simple black cropped sweater, light blue jeans with huge cargo pockets on the sides, and low-rise tennis shoes. Very casual. Again, *normal.* She crouches to Vinnie on the ground enthusiastically with a sing-songy voice. He nearly tackles her.

"Hi," she says to me as a second thought, once Vinnie is properly greeted. "I'm Nikki. I—I think we got off on the wrong foot yesterday. I'm so sorry for coming at you like a psycho."

I paste on the Kieran Bergstrom I have to be for my podcast and set aside any doubt or guilt, plastering on all the confidence I can muster.

"It's okay, I'm used to psychos in my line of work." I smile so she knows I'm joking.

"I'm sure you are. Luckily, I'm not one of *those*—" She gasps in happy surprise, plopping down in her seat across the table. "Coffee! Thank you!"

I watch in horror as she dumps an obscene number of sugar packets and cream into her cup and then sips it blissfully, completely oblivious.

With effort, I allow the crimes against coffee to slide so we can get right to business. "No problem." I clear my throat. "Before we start, I have to make sure... Are you positive you want to do this? People can get pretty cutthroat on social media and stuff. You'll probably receive some nasty comments and messages once this goes live."

She grimaces but nods. "Yeah. I'm prepared for that. I'll try not to read the comments."

"And when we dig into this case... There's always a chance you might not like what we find."

She considers that for a moment as she pets Vinnie dazedly, whose head has somehow ended up on her lap. Suck-up. "I was thinking about that last night actually. When I was looking through my parents' things." She gives a decisive exhale. "At this point, I just want the truth."

Well, I gave her an out. Now I have to rip the band-aid off like the bold and confident Kieran Bergstrom would.

For George and Tina. For George and Tina.

"Okay. Well, if you're sure, I have to let you know my

terms for taking on your case. I've looked into it, and" —her eyes widen when I pause for effect— "let's just say, it's going to be a challenge."

She sets the coffee cup down slowly and delicately, like she's bracing herself for the worst. And maybe she's right to do so. I have no idea what two hundred grand means to someone like her.

"Do you think—" The sentence is strained, like she's exerting a lot of effort to get this question out. She clears her throat and tries again with forced determination. "Do you think it's even possible?"

"Like I said, it'll be a challenge," I hedge. Luckily, she can't see my knee bouncing anxiously underneath the table. "It's going to require a lot of additional resources and tools that I'm not currently equipped with."

She nods emphatically as I talk, like she knows what I'm saying before I even say it.

"I'll of course pay for whatever you need," she assures. "How much are you thinking?"

My eyes flicker downward against my will, unable to keep contact with her hopeful blue eyes. The guilt tugs at my gut, my confident facade wavering.

She mistakes my guilt for reluctance, and her voice raises an urgent octave as she tries to convince me. "I will pay any price. I have to solve this case. I have no other option."

I meet her eyes, which fill at the edges with desperate tears the longer I don't answer. Great. Make me feel worse.

"Two hundred thousand dollars," I say quickly, having to nearly blurt it out before I lose the nerve entirely. "That's my price." I fold my arms, leaning back into my chair now that all my cards are on the table.

She blinks at me in surprise.

Your move, Heiress. (Say no, so I don't have to do this to you…)

She doesn't say anything for a long while, taking an extra-long sip of her sugar-with-a-side-of-coffee as she thinks, and for a moment I wonder if she'll say no, after all. Part of me hopes she does.

She sets her mug down with determination, drips of it flinging out from the force. Vinnie licks them up happily. "I have one condition."

My eyebrow quirks.

"My aunt is off limits," she says. "No interviews, no questions. I don't even want her to know I'm working on the case. You have to promise."

"Why?"

I don't like that at all. In cases like these, more often than not, it's someone the family knows well. How can I promise I won't question someone that close to the case?

Her lips harden stubbornly, so she must sense my reluctance. "She's very sick, and it would probably kill her knowing I'm doing this, and do you really want to be responsible for the death of a sweet old lady? You want to speak at her funeral?"

I narrow my eyes, about to object, but she interrupts me to add, "Plus, she's unquestionably innocent, and I know that with 100% certainty."

I mull it over. I'll definitely be looking more into the aunt on my own, whether Nikki likes it or not, but I suppose I can agree not to interview her.

I reach out my hand to seal the deal. "Fine."

"Great!" She shakes my hand, and I'm struck by how soft her hands are. My goodness, has she never been outside? These are hands that have never thrown a baseball, made a sandcastle, used a shovel. "You have a deal. I'll get the money together ASAP."

At the mention of the money, an oily guilt settles in my stomach. I hate using people, and she seems like a nice girl. I wish I wasn't so desperate.

"Great," I return with feigned enthusiasm. I pull out my notebook. "Let's get started. Tell me what you—"

"I think my sister could still be alive," she blurts. Her eyes widen like even she is surprised that came out of her mouth.

"Your sister Elizabeth," I repeat slowly.

According to all the sources I could find, investigators found too much blood to attribute it to normal car accident wounds. That doesn't look good. The odds of her being alive after all this time with no contact are impossibly small. The logical side of me discounts this possibility immediately.

But I will say... the part of me that loves a good story, a shocking plot twist... that side of me can't resist the seductive pull of what a good ending that would make to this season. Elizabeth Sinclair, alive? Think of what that could do for my podcast. Well, and for Nikki. Happy reunion and whatever.

"I know it sounds crazy," she says with a sheepish chuckle, pulling me from my thoughts.

My logical side wants to agree, to tell her how low the likelihood of that would be, but she keeps going before I can.

"I've listened to all the podcasts; I've watched all the documentaries." Her flaming blue eyes are determined, immovable. "I know how this usually goes. I *know* the odds, but—"

Nikki's phone vibrates on the table, plucking her train of thought out of the air entirely as she reads the text that has popped up on her brightened lockscreen. I can't make it out from here.

Her face pales, eyes flicking back and forth between the message and me as if trying to decide something.

She finally hands it to me to read.

"I told you not to trust anyone," the text says. From an unknown number.

She flicks her finger upwards to give me permission to scroll up in the text thread.

I start at the top to read them chronologically.

"And these texts are why you think she's alive?" I ask carefully, the good-story-loving side of me fizzling out entirely as I'm presented with the reality.

Someone has clearly taken an interest in her family's case and is determined to be involved in some capacity, but it's not her sister. It can't be. After ten years? No. It could be someone obsessed with the case, a stalker, a witness, even the killers themselves like to re-insert themselves back into their own cases eventually. But whether it's the killer or not, the person sending these texts could still be dangerous.

I know from experience how dangerous anonymous people can be... Ciphered Voyager seemed harmless enough at first, too.

"This text here" —she points out the one about the window seat, leaning closer— "led me to a series of strange... 'clues' I guess you could call them? Clues I don't think anyone else could have known about other than her."

Which piques my interest, that pull of curiosity tugging again.

She sets her phone down and meets my eye with a lift in her chin. "I know it's sounds crazy," she repeats with a new boldness, a sturdy confidence she has pulled from somewhere. "But I have to believe she's alive, and you're going to help me find her."

16

KIERAN

I'VE NEVER FELT SUCH INSTANT REGRET

I raise an eyebrow at her, intrigued by this absurd confidence she has in such an impossible outcome. "And what if this doesn't turn out the way you hope?"

She averts her eyes, the mood shifting as she clacks her icy blue painted nails on her coffee cup. "It has to."

I analyze her like I'm profiling her, seeing all over her body language that she has her own reasons for needing to solve this case all these years later, some urgent ulterior motive for why she needs her sister to be alive. I suspect it has something to do with the off-limits aunt, but I don't grill her on it. I mean, I can't share my own motivations, so how can I expect her to? I soften a little bit, understanding how desperation can fuel delusion.

"Okay," is all I say.

She blinks at me, looking at me through long eyelashes. "Okay?"

"It's worth exploring every possibility. I usually start with the more likely ones, but you're the boss. We can do it your way."

I pull out my phone and click to the camera. "If I make a public post on my page of us together and announce that I'm starting your case, we can begin to collect leads, get tips, and gather testimony from your community. Are you cool with that?"

"Oh, yikes." She untucks her wavy hair from behind her ears and pulls it in front of her shoulders. "I really should have done my hair better. Okay, let's do it."

She stands to drag her chair next to mine. She smells strongly of laundry detergent and coffee, with a citrus undertone, which is an interesting combination, I note, but not unpleasant. Vinnie wedges himself between us happily, his tongue flopping out.

I'm about to apologize for his lack of boundaries, but she laughs and nuzzles his head. She doesn't seem to be bothered by him at all, even as clumps of his hair coat her clothing which was probably expensive.

I get the feeling he would push me in front of a bus to get to her at this point.

I hold the phone up and take a picture of the three of us and within seconds have it posted to my accounts. Caption: *"Season three teaser. Meet Nikki Sinclair, the sole survivor of her family of four. If anyone has information about the Sinclair Murders of Sapphire Pines, please email me at kieran@secretsinice.com."*

I set my phone on the table and flip to a new page in my notebook. With a click of my pen, I say, "Okay. Tell me what you know."

∽

AN HOUR LATER, there's a spread of pastries and notes between us. My heart swells with the thrill I've come to love from starting a new case, and for just a moment I've been able to forget about George and Ciphered Voyager and remember why I love doing this. Gathering theories, outlining a timeline, listing suspects and motives. It's my favorite part.

And the thing is?

Nikki seems to love it too.

She enthusiastically participates in putting our baseline together, offering surprisingly informed, albeit annoying sometimes, suggestions. I guess she did say she was a fan.

I tap the papers between us that we've arranged into a makeshift CSI chalkboard. When I get back to my van, I'll organize them on my whiteboard.

"Let's review what we have so far. When the department gets back to you with the case file, we can confirm the times, but your parents and sister" —I touch the paper furthest on my left— "left the house in the morning to go to a tournament in Lake Oswego. Instead, their car was found in the opposite direction in Washington."

She stares at the paper thoughtfully. "Which is so weird. Lizzy's skating tournaments were her whole life. I don't know why they'd miss it. And to go to Washington of all places? Why?"

"Unless they were—" I quickly cut myself off, forgetting for a second to have some tact. This is her family we're talking about here, after all.

"Unless they were what?"

She only needs a second to think before she answers her own question at the same time I do:

"Running away."

"Fleeing the country."

She nods cynically, almost hysterically. "Yep, just go ahead and leave the country and leave me behind too, no worries!"

I gulp, not sure what to say.

She shakes her head, visibly pulling herself back together with a deep inhale. She taps our next paper to continue the review. "Police arrived on scene and found their car totaled on a forestry road, but no remains were in the car or anywhere on scene."

"We can take a break you know," I offer, a little concerned about how quickly she compartmentalized and then got straight back to business. That can't be healthy.

She meets my eyes with a determined set of her jaw. "I've been taking a break for the last ten years. I owe it to my family to give them the closure they deserve."

"Okay." I clear my throat awkwardly at the details I have to say next, still very aware this is her family we're discussing. "Police analyzed the, uh... They examined all the—"

"Don't euphemize."

"Euph—what?"

She stabs the part of our notes I'm struggling to verbalize with a sharp finger. *Blood spatter. DNA. Remains.* "Everyone has been sugar-coating these details in front of me this whole time. I never understood the gravity of this case back then because it was so downplayed to me. You know I always thought they were going to come back one day? Imagine my surprise when, plot twist, they never did." She laughs bitterly. "It was to protect me, okay, yes. But I'm not a child anymore. I need cold, hard facts now, so I need you to always give it to me straight. Can you promise me that?"

"I mean, I get it, but you can still ease in a little bit. You don't have to dive right into the deep end." I push my hair out of my eyes. "All I'm saying is cases like these can get heavy. You have to do it in a way that takes care of—"

"I'll take care of myself when my family's killer is brought to justice."

We look at each other for a moment, and I remind myself that even though she's younger than the clients I'm used to, I'm not her guardian. So therefore: I'm not responsible for her mental well-being. She's simply a client who is paying me—a lot of money—to do a job. I don't have to run diagnostics on her wellbeing every time I speak.

"Okay," I relent with a shrug. "I promise to give it to you straight."

She straightens her shoulders, satisfied. "Great."

"Great." I continue on, as requested, "This is where the public details get fuzzy, but we know the forensic team examined the interior and concluded there was a struggle. I have a friend in Idaho I'll call later to help me get some clarity on this."

"What's weird to me is the lack of blood outside the vehicle," she muses.

"I agree." I add a scribbled note to the paper as I say it, "That suggests to me that there was probably more than one perpetrator. How else could the bodies have been moved without a significant blood trail left behind? It's not like they could just bleach the forest ground to clean up afterward."

"I hope they get back to me soon with the case file. I really want to know if there was a cadaver dog used in the search."

She reaches for my notebook at the same time I do, and

my hand brushes up against hers for a moment. She rips her hand away like I've burned her.

"Sorry, go ahead." Her cheeks turn a soft pink that brings a pretty vibrance to her face. Like, objectively. "It is your notebook after all."

"Oh, by all means, take it," I joke. "You've already turned my own dog against me—I mean *look* at him—might as well take this from me too."

Vinnie side-eyes me from where he's resting his head on her crossed knee. Traitor.

Nikki laughs. "Forgive me for being so loveable."

With a smirk, I rip a paper out of the notebook and slide it over to her. "Contacts." I hand her my pen. "Make a list of any notable people in your life you can think of. I'll reach out to them and see if they'll do an interview. See what information they can give us, anything they remember about the case."

"No aunt," she reminds me sternly before jotting down a name. "But here, I'm sure my fiancé would do one."

My jaw drops. I peek over her shoulder at the paper, confident I must have misheard her. Sure enough: *Hunter Vanderwaal, fiancé.*

She does a double take when she sees my disbelief. Her soft pink blush turns blood red. She tucks her copper hair behind her ears. "What?"

She knows.

"Aren't you—?"

"Seventeen," she finishes for me, her tone attempting to feign obliviousness, but the blush that has now reached the tips of her ears says otherwise. "So? You can't be much older? You're what, eighteen?"

I'm trying to keep the judgment out of my voice, I really

am, but it slips through against my will. "Has no one ever told you that seventeen is too young to get married? And that it's also illegal?"

She takes a long bite of a cream cheese Danish and avoids my question. "Mm, this one's good."

"This guy" –I check the name again on the paper— "Hunter, is it? Yeah, he's the very first on my suspect list. What weirdo marries a seventeen-year-old?"

That gets a reaction out of her. She waves the pastry at me with vigor, wielding it like a weapon. "Hunter is *not* a weirdo. He's my best friend. And not that it's any of your business, but our wedding will be in June, and I'll be acceptably eighteen by then. Happy?"

"Just because you *can* do something, doesn't mean you *should*." I snatch the Danish out of her hand and take a bite with the full intention of finishing the rest of it to make her mad. "I'm suddenly doubting the reliability of any of your witness accounts. Are you even really Annika Sinclair? Maybe you're just some imposter who likes to impede on murder cases and get married to weirdos."

She huffs in outrage, ripping the Danish out of my literal teeth and shoving it into her own mouth. "How dare you sit and judge me when all you have going for you is—" She gestures to me erratically with crazy hands, trying to come up with something. "Blonde hair."

"Good one." I lean back in my chair. "I'm just holding up my promise and giving it you straight: You are insane to get married this young. If he was really your best friend, he'd tell you that himself instead of *marrying you*."

She catapults to her feet, her chair nearly toppling over. "I don't need your opinion on my personal life." She points at me sharply across the table. "All I need you to do is solve this case. Keep your judgment to yourself, or the deal is off. I'll text you the rest of my contacts."

She swipes her phone off the table, yanks her little purse and coat off the back of her chair, and storms off. She gets nearly all the way to the door before she whips around and stomps back. She kneels to say goodbye to Vinnie, cooing to him something unintelligible but overly sweet. Then she snatches the last pastry off the table *and the rest of my coffee* and marches out the door.

Oh boy. It's going to be a very long season.

YOUTUBE COMMENTS SECTION
Season 3 Episode 2: The Crash, the Car, the Crime

@ghosttrain94: bro... THREE separate blood pools in the car but no bodies? that's nightmare fuel.

@7765chairenthusiast: imagine being the K-9 on that scene. can dogs get traumatized?

@kpop_or_die: um why is no one talking about the fact that the aunt is literally a voting member on the board of the Sinclair business??? her name is listed ON their website right now. motive??

    @toastbagel83241 REPLYING TO @kpop_or_die: wait omg ur right I just looked up the website. wren delaney BUT ALSO ANNIKA SINCLAIR! I wonder if anyone told her that she's a voting member of a billion dollar business?

@ramen_addict: okay but how did nobody see a car get run off the road in broad daylight

@cometcrashcourse: 100 miles off course??? no way that's accidental.

@caffeinatedsloth: so we all agree the family driver was in on it? he's the last person confirmed to have seen them right?

    @bubblewrapbandit REPLYING TO @caffeinatedsloth: he def knows something

@th3otherguy: lack of paper trail is super suspicious, can you say COVERUP

17

———

NIKKI

HIM.

It's been over twenty-four hours since I've seen or spoken to *him*. I'm dying for an update, but I'm giving him the silent treatment he deserves.

I'm trying to focus on schoolwork—because with the chaos of everything, I've been neglecting that recently—but it's taking everything in me to resist pulling out my phone and stalking his social media for updates.

I won't, though, not after what he said. Call it pride, call it sheer genetic stubbornness, but I'd rather die than have my name listed together with all the other fangirls watching his Stories right now.

I can't believe or forgive the audacity! The gall, the gumption, all of the above! The way he felt entitled to have any kind of opinion on my life choices after knowing me for a whole hour is wild. The unsolicited advice on my personal matters when he knows nothing about me? It enrages me! And that rage far outweighs my curiosity about the case. Or his whereabouts when he's in my town. Or what he's up to.

Or... who he's with... I care about none of it. Not even in the slightest.

No. I don't need to engage with him unless necessary for the case. He will contact me when something dire comes up.

I've also been avoiding going into my social media because the last time I popped unawares into my favorite app, I was met by an angry red pop-up on my notifications bar that said I had more than two *thousand* people requesting to follow me and over three-hundred message requests. I turned off notifications, and I'm simply ignoring the problem until it goes away. (It's worked for me this far in life, so why stop now?)

I knew in theory this would be the result of going public about working with *him*, but the reality of it is still overwhelming.

Not to mention I'm still not exactly sure how I'm going to pay him for doing this case...

I have to keep telling myself that when we find Lizzy, she can access our trust, and everything will work out. I'll get him the money then.

He doesn't need to know that I don't currently have access to *two hundred thousand freaking dollars.*

I'm getting really close to mental-spiral territory, so I take in a long inhale through my nose and try to focus on my geography notes. The problem with doing online school is there's no one to hold you accountable when you get distracted. Sometimes I wish I had a nagging teacher to take my phone away and tell me to get back to work.

When I was younger, before she got sick, Aunt Wren would work through the courses with me. She was absolutely zero help with the math, and we'd always laugh together that she was so helpless in that department, but she'd always help me draft my essays or conduct experiments with me for science projects. School work never felt lonely, even though I was doing it at home.

But now it's one more thing I have to do alone, and I can't even escape my reality with my favorite podcast anymore. For... reasons.

This morning, Aunt Wren was awake and alert, and I was so excited to fill her in on everything, but Nurse Kayla needed my help taking her on a walk around the house, to get her up and moving. We had to cut it short because she couldn't get the coughing under control to catch her breath. Nurse Kayla had to get her back on oxygen after only a few minutes of laps around the foyer.

So, I set up a canvas with her by her bed, and we painted like we used to and made idle chit chat about positive things until she fell back asleep, while I tried not to cry.

It's getting painfully clear that she's running out of time. The moments she's conscious are getting more and more precious. I don't want to waste that time with such dark topics when I should be raising her spirits.

My phone pings.

HUNTER

miss you already, fiancée

I set my phone down without replying. I miss him so much it hurts, and I can't take any more things that hurt right now.

There's a gentle knock on my door, followed by Arrick's voice. "There is someone here to see you, Miss Nikki."

I scramble to my feet and crack my door open, knowing it can't be Hunter, but a flutter of hope swells anyway. "Who is it?"

"A young man. A one Kieran Bergstrom." Arrick eyes me with no shortage of protective suspicion. It's rare for me to have visitors of any kind, let alone a boy he's never met.

"Excuse me for one moment."

I shut the door and scream internally. He's just going to show up?! Completely uninvited? How does he even know where I live?

I throw off my sweats and pull on the closest pair of jeans I can find, which fortunately only have one small visible stain, and try unsuccessfully to smooth my hair down. I give up and throw it into a messy ponytail instead. I pat down my bed like I'm giving it CPR to locate my phone under the covers.

After several minutes of Stress Tornado, I'm striding past Arrick and down the staircase—the epitome of Casual and Unbothered, ready to demand an apology from *him* with my chin held high.

He's waiting by the front door, annoyingly unbothered himself. Not even a shred of regret in his countenance.

I don't say hello, only cross my arms when I reach the bottom of the stairs, keeping the span of the foyer between us. "You came to my house."

He apparently takes that as an invitation and sheds off his shoes. "Ready to get to work?"

His unchanging expression says he clearly doesn't see anything wrong with that. Just showing up completely uninvited to a stranger's house? I have minimal contact with the real world, and even I know that's weird.

"I need to start interviewing the staff here."

"You showed up to my house," I repeat. "How did you even know where I live?"

He gives me a look. "I solve murders for a living.

Googling 'The Sinclair Estate' didn't take much detective work. Ready?"

I can't believe the unabashed continued lack of apology. "Don't you have something to say to me?"

"I'm gathering you're upset..." His eyes flick up and down as he takes exaggerated note of my crossed arms, my expression, my posture.

For a 'detective' he sure is dense.

"You completely overstepped the other day!" I cry, giving up on him ever figuring it out himself. "When you commented on my engagement. That was totally unprofessional."

He blinks at me. "Are you expecting me to apologize for being the only one in your life willing to tell you the truth?"

I gape at him in disbelief. He's really doubling down? "Oh I'm sorry, I didn't realize I actually hired a therapist. Do you want to talk about my feelings next? Dissect my childhood trauma? Decode what my dreams mean?"

He shrugs. "It might help. You obviously have a lot of unresolved issues."

My blood turns to lava, the prior annoyance morphing fiercely into full-fledged anger. "How dare you?" I seethe. "You don't know a single thing about me."

Arrick has sensed the elevating tension and joins us at the foot of the stairs. "Is everything alright, Miss Nikki?"

His presence grounds me. I take a long regulating breath. "Yes, everything is fine. My friend here was just apologizing for being a lizard-faced ass."

Kieran visibly chokes down a shocked laugh to nod solemnly instead. "I was. Right after she begged me to forgive her for acting like a spoiled pampered princess."

Interesting, the *act* of murder might not be off the table for me after all. I'm beginning to see the appeal.

I try to stay calm for Arrick's sake mostly. He looks completely lost, eyes ping-ponging back and forth between us.

"Where is Vinnie?" I say through gritted teeth. "He's the best part about you."

"I told him to hang out in the van. I didn't know if you'd want him running rampant in your" –Kieran waves his hand at the foyer— "*palace.*"

"He'll need to be present at all times if we're going to continue doing business."

"I accept your terms." He steps past me to shake Arrick's hand. "Sorry for the rough start here. I'm Kieran Bergstrom. Has Nikki explained why I'm here?"

A FEW MINUTES LATER, the four of us are seated at the dining room table (which has seen more action in the past few days than it has in years). Vinnie is sniffing around, tail wagging happily, grateful to be included instead of stuck in the van.

Kieran has an assortment of equipment scattered around the table. Computer, microphones, headphones. He's getting his podcasting program fired up on his laptop while we wait tensely.

Arrick's back is as straight as a board, lips pursed under his stiff mustache. He agreed to do the interview, but he was justifiably wary when I told him about the investigation. I'm not surprised he's worried about me. The engagement news, finding me in Lizzy's room the other day, and now this. He's probably wondering what's gotten into me, if this is the downward spiral right before I crash and burn.

He knows how careful I am with my hope. My heart. He knows it'll kill me if this doesn't all pan out. If I can't find Lizzy. If I have to accept that she's dead all over again.

I'm aware of that too.

That's why solving this is my only option.

Kieran sets a microphone in front of Arrick, who is still as a statue.

"You don't have to do this," I whisper to him. "You can answer his questions privately."

Arrick's eyes flick to me. "I trust your judgement, Miss Nikki. If you feel this will bring you the answers you're looking for, I'm happy to help."

I reach for his hand, my throat feeling tight as he squeezes it back.

"I think they finally deserve the truth at any cost."

He nods.

Kieran takes the lapse in in our conversation to begin, pointing at the microphones to signify they are recording.

[The Secrets in Ice opening theme music plays]

KIERAN BERGSTROM:

In our last episode, we looked over what we could find about the crime scene. The blood pools matching all three victims. The evidence of a firearm used. The lack of bodies. Everything pointed to a very methodical perpetrator and ruled out the theory that this was a spontaneous killing. That the Sinclairs were just in the wrong place at the wrong time. It took planning. Experience. Careful clean-up.

I've read through your comments and messages. I appreciate all of your theories. Many of you have the same questions that I do. If the Sinclairs were so loved, why would someone do this to them? What were they hiding?

Looking for answers among the shadows of the iciest cold cases, I'm your host Kieran Bergstrom, and you're listening to *Secrets in Ice.* This is episode three, "The Butler."

[Secrets in Ice theme finishes playing]

KIERAN BERGSTROM:

Joining me today I have Arrick Kensington, the longtime household manager for the Sinclair family. I'm hoping he can give us some further insight. Thank you for being here.

[muffled response]

If you could speak into the mic, Arrick, thank you.

ARRICK KENSINGTON:

I apologize. I'm happy to help however I can.

KIERAN BERGSTROM:

I assume you were heavily interviewed by investigators ten years ago when the case was ongoing, but I'd like to create my own picture of what happened.

ARRICK KENSINGTON:

Yes, I understand.

KIERAN BERGSTROM:

How long have you managed the Sinclair's household?

ARRICK KENSINGTON:

Seventeen years. I was brought on shortly after Miss Nikki was born. They found two children to be... hard to manage.

KIERAN BERGSTROM:

What are your primary duties here?

ARRICK KENSINGTON:

When Mr. and Mrs. Sinclair were here, I was much busier. Greeting guests, driving services, maintaining the property and vehicles, managing the staff. But nowadays... I mostly arrange landscaping services and care to Miss Nikki's needs.

KIERAN BERGSTROM:

What can you remember about the day the Sinclairs left and never returned?

ARRICK KENSINGTON:

The details are blurry now, as you can imagine, but from what I remember it was a very ordinary Saturday morning. It was planned that Mr. and Mrs. Sinclair would be taking Miss Lizzy to a competition in the neighboring town. They had hired a babysitter for Miss Nikki as they would be gone most of the day and evening.

KIERAN BERGSTROM:

Did Mr. and Mrs. Sinclair travel a lot for Lizzy's sports?

ARRICK KENSINGTON:

Saturdays were often a busy day, yes. Sometimes one or both of them would take her to her practices, sometimes I would myself. It varied day to day. On this particular Saturday, it was the state championships, which they both wanted to attend.

KIERAN BERGSTROM:

Did they usually hire a babysitter for Nikki when Lizzy had sports?

ARRICK KENSINGTON:

No. She typically went with them or had her own soccer practice. But it is my recollection that she wasn't feeling well that day.

KIERAN BERGSTROM:

In the days leading up to their disappearance, was there anything unusual or out of the ordinary that you can remember?

ARRICK KENSINGTON:

[unintelligible, off mic]

KIERAN BERGSTROM:

Icers, I should mention that sitting here with us also, off-mic, is Nikki Sinclair herself. She has generously invited me to come to her home today.

[unintelligible, off-mic]

KIERAN BERGSTROM:

She is a very gracious host. Anyway –

ARRICK KENSINGTON:

Right, my apologies. Miss Nikki usually doesn't like hearing about her family, so I was just making sure she was okay. What was the question again? No, the days beforehand were mostly normal. I already told this to police then, so it's nothing new, but there was only one thing I could think of that was a bit out of the ordinary.

KIERAN BERGSTROM:

What's that?

ARRICK KENSINGTON:

Miss Lizzy was usually very even keeled. Very calm demeanor, very collected. However, that week she had multiple unusual outbursts.

KIERAN BERGSTROM:

What were the outbursts about?

ARRICK KENSINGTON:

It was a culmination of a lot of small things that set her off, not one particular instance, which is why it was so odd. Forgetting her skates at the rink, a project for school that she didn't want to do, not being able to find her iPad, a friend who stopped by that she didn't want to see, I believe. Just a combination of things that didn't seem related.

KIERAN BERGSTROM:

What do you think caused her to be so upset?

ARRICK KENSINGTON:

I don't know. Maybe stress from school or trouble with friends. There were a few instances where I discovered her crying. Something was certainly off, but I don't know what.

KIERAN BERGSTROM:

So to clarify, the week before she was killed, Elizabeth Sinclair was acting unexplainably strange?

ARRICK KENSINGTON:

Yes. She wasn't acting quite herself, and then she disappeared.

[suspenseful music plays]

18

NIKKI
BECK, BECK, GOOSE

"Everybody okay?" Kieran asks as I make a noticeable effort to swallow the giant lump in my throat. "The first one's always the toughest."

It was harder than I expected to hear Arrick talk about them, to hear the grief in his voice. Sometimes I forget I'm not the only one who misses them.

But once I got past the initial pain, it was almost nice to hear about my family again. For someone to talk about them in front of me and not pretend as if they never existed, like a huge elephant in the room we always have to tiptoe around.

It made them feel a little bit alive again for a glimmer of a second. Like speaking their names brought a little bit of their souls back in the room for just a flicker.

"Yep." I inhale, pulling myself together. I will not cry in front of *him*.

Arrick reaches across the table and squeezes my hand. "Are you alright, Miss Nikki?"

"I am. Are you?"

He nods, the deep lines in his face crinkling. "Is there anything else you need me for?" He stands and smooths down his trousers. "If not, I'll finish up my duties here and head home for the evening."

"We're all good on my end," Kieran answers, eyeing me for the final word.

"Thank you, Arrick. You're amazing as always," I add.

Arrick gives me a quick upward jut of his head to gesture he wants me to follow him out of the room. He lowers his voice when we're out of Kieran's earshot.

"We're getting into new territory here, Miss Nikki," he says, a quirk of an uncomfortable smile at his lips. "I understand you are reaching adulthood, but I'm not sure how your parents would have felt about you being here alone with a boy we don't know, and I do—"

I spare him the rest of this talk. "New territory for sure. Two boys in one week? Who am I?" I laugh. "But it's okay, it's not like that. I extremely, incredibly, very much dislike him. But I do believe he's a good person. He's just helping me out with the case. We'll brainstorm a bit, and then he'll head home."

"Would you like me to stay?"

"No! Enjoy your weekend. Please. I'm all good. Reaching adulthood over here and whatnot." I give him a look to reassure him. "Really, it's okay."

A flash of emotion crosses his face. "You are growing up into a wonderful young woman. Your parents would be very proud of you."

I bear-hug him. "Thank you."

He chuckles, patting my head. "Send a note if you need anything."

"It's text, Arrick, we've gone over this. *Text*."

"Right." He smiles, and then he's gone.

I return to the dining room with a glow in my soul that only Arrick can provide.

Well, and Vinnie, who greets me happily as I lower down into the closest chair.

Kieran is adjusting sound levels from the interview on his program, bars and waves of multiple colors sprawling across the screen. "Good?"

"Yeah. Good," I say. My phone vibrates.

HUNTER

> you know what I was thinking?

I don't reply, waiting patiently as the typing icon blinks.

HUNTER

> there is only one word she repeated multiple times

> creek... could that be important?

NIKKI

> creek? it only said creek once, I think. right??

HUNTER

> oh you sweet little american. beck is another word for creek, nik.

"Pair left *beck* burn." I repeat it multiple times aloud, standing to pace next to the table. "Is that what it said? Or was it 'pair left *back* burn?'"

Kieran looks at me blankly.

"Be right back."

I run upstairs to my room and grab everything of Lizzy's.

The clues, the journal, the book. In seconds I've darted back out the door and down the stairs, my abdomen heaving as I try to catch my breath.

I drop everything down in front of Kieran, giving him a breathless rundown of everything, while I confirm if Hunter is correct, flipping through the pages like my life depends on this.

I flip to the back cover to read it again. "'Pair left *beck* burn.' I can't be the only one who didn't know beck was a body of water."

"I've never heard that either." Kieran looks it up on his phone to confirm. "Guess it's true."

"We have a creek on our property," I think aloud, gaining enthusiasm as the theory forms while I'm saying it. "In the winters, Lizzy and I would ice skate on it. I fell through the ice once. It was actually quite traumatic," I laugh to take the edge off. "Could she have left something there?"

As if anything could have made Hunter *hotter,* he's been thinking about clues we found for my dead family's murder case and actually giving me a lead?

NIKKI

you might be on to something

HUNTER

you're welcome

Kieran is nonchalant, but I can see in his eyes that he's curious. "It's worth looking into. When was the last time you went there?"

"I used to go out there all the time when I was younger, and the weather was nice, but never in the winter. It made me too sad to see the creek iced over. It would remind me of her too much. So, it's been a few years, at least, maybe more."

"Care for a field trip?" He quirks an eyebrow at me, almost like he's daring me.

I'm already halfway to the garage, and it gives me a strange sense of satisfaction that he and Vinnie have to scramble after me.

The hexagon-shaped lights overhead in the garage gradually increase as they detect our motion and power on, illuminating the rows of covered, priceless, and *useless* vehicles that at this point are just here to mock me, perched here like gargoyles on a mausoleum, keeping watch in that haunting, unmoving way they do. Kieran's low whistle just irks me further on the subject. Unless I find those titles somewhere, these will continue to be useless to me. Useless to my aunt.

He peeks under the cover of the closest one and gives me a look like I'm guilty of a heinous crime. "A McLaren? Really? You have a McLaren just sitting here collecting dust, and you didn't think that was worth mentioning?"

"Sure, next time I'll include that in my introduction. 'Hi, I'm Nikki, I like true-crime podcasts, and I also inherited my dead dad's McLaren, but I don't have the legal right to sell it or drive it, so it collects dust in my garage, nice to meet you.' Would you have answered my DMs then?"

"Might have helped. No license? The little Heiress is too good to go to the DMV with all the common peasants?"

I give him a death glare. "Stop calling me that." I grab a coat, hat, and gloves for each of us off the rack by the door and throw him one of each like I'm pitching him a baseball, loving the way they bounce off him with a *thud*. "And no. I've just never needed a *license* when I have an *Arrick*."

I pull two rings of keys off the hook and make a point of ignoring his smug look like I've proven him right somehow, as I stride past him toward the other side of the garage where Vinnie is sniffing around curiously.

I click the button on the opposite wall, the carriage door of the garage opening outward with a groan into the recently shoveled driveway. Vinnie immediately darts out and dives into the closest snow pile. I pull the cover off the vehicle next to me, revealing the pair of ATVs underneath.

"Want to drive your own or ride passenger?" I ask, zipping up my coat to my neck.

"You just admitted you don't know how to drive. Why would I risk my life on the back of your vehicle?"

I throw the key at him. "I *know* how to drive," I insist. He doesn't have to know I've only ever driven these, not an actual car. "I said I'm not legally *allowed* to drive."

"Sure, Heiress." He hops onto one of the quads and turns the key. It powers on with a growl. "You take these out often?"

"Not in the winter because I'm not insane."

I check the cargo box attached to his rear rack, making sure there's a shovel and first aid kit in there just in case. I slam it shut and return to my vehicle, loving the way it rumbles to life under me. Vinnie hops around the driveway excitedly, impatient to get going. I give Kieran a thumbs up as I pull on the beanie on over my ears, which smells like Arrick. It smushes down my ponytail, probably making me look bald, but I don't care.

Kieran revs his engine, looking frustratingly good on his quad, curls of blonde hair poking out from under his own beanie.

"Don't go off the trail," I yell over the engines. With fresh snowfall like this, there's no telling how deep it could be.

"I'll follow your lead," he yells back, giving me an exaggerated salute. Then he makes some kind of hand command to Vinnie, who backs up out of the way.

I speed out of the garage, and Vinnie whizzes past like a furry rocket, darting ahead, not even sure where we're going just happy to run uninhibited. I take a right on the circular drive, past the pool house, off the pavers, and onto the unpaved trail that leads to the back acreage of the property. The snow isn't plowed out here, and the branches overhead are packed with undisturbed snow, creating a thick canopy of white over our heads as we barrel down the trail. Vinnie runs and explores but doesn't wander too far off. I've never seen him happier, and it's adorable.

My jeans are soaked, the snow flying up and around me as I plow through it. I forgot how cold snow is when you're not just looking at it through a window.

The trail itself is hard to see but muscle memory takes over, guiding me down the path and into the thicket of trees that surround our property. Arrick and I have blazed this trail many times over the years, racing each other through the trees and around the land so many times I could probably do it with my eyes shut.

I'm remembering now how beautiful it is out here during the winter. The expansive white of the snow is almost heavenly. Tranquil.

My heart squeezes as we pull up to the creek. Vinnie approaches it cautiously, his tongue out and panting. The creek is iced over and glassy, reflecting the warm hues of the late afternoon sunlight. It brings a flood of memories that hurt so bad it makes me breathless. I cut the engine of my quad, remaining seated and taking a painful moment to look around as Kieran pulls up next to me. His cheeks and nose are reddened from the chill, smile huge from the thrill of the ride, until he sees me.

"You okay?"

I expect to see impatience or agitation, or even mockery, on his face, but the question is genuine. Concerned, almost.

I press my lips together and nod. "Just a lot of memories." I appraise the frozen creek, remembering the knife sharp freeze of the water as I fell in. The paralyzing terror as I tried to come up for air and found only ice above me, trapping me in. The pure relief of seeing Lizzy's hand, almost like it was a shining beacon. Reaching for her hand knowing with full certainty she'd save me. *She always saved me.*

I remember the laughs here, the giggles, *the fun.* Echoes of them are still here, soaked into the very roots of the trees and immortalized in the evergreen branches.

The trail was always plowed regularly when we had a full staff, so we could come and go as often as we wanted. Days of skating on this creek until our legs felt like jelly, completely immune to the cold as children are somehow. And then tromping across the trail when daylight began to melt into sunset, kicking piles of snow at each other as we'd walk back home to Bea's homemade hot chocolate. And then we'd do it all again the next day.

The joy enshrined here is what hurts the most. Memories of two sisters who laughed and played and fought and cried and tattled on each other. Two regular sisters who never knew their time together would be cut cruelly short.

Would we have skated a little longer if we'd known? Walked back home a little slower?

I blink tears away, remembering Kieran is here, embarrassed at how long I must have been trapped in my thoughts.

I shake the memories off and plop down into the snow. It comes halfway up my shins.

I'm much less confident now that I'm standing here. What did I possibly think I'd find out here? Especially under a foot of snow? I'm beginning to think this was a really dumb idea.

19

NIKKI

THANKS, WHIPLASH, NOW I'M COLD

Kieran joins me off the quad, and Vinnie hops around us happily, ready to get to work. We get the shovel from the cargo hatch.

"Is there a certain place in particular you guys would sit or hang out?" he asks, throwing the shovel over his shoulder like some kind of lumberjack, and I'm ashamed of the double take I may have just done.

I refocus to appraise the clearing thoughtfully, repeating the clue in my head. *Pair left beck burn.*

"We'd sit over there in the shade." I point to the bundle of trees on the other side of the creek. "Oh my gosh," I gasp, my eyes widening at him. "Kieran, those are *pear trees*. We would eat the pears every summer and throw the cores into the creek. Do you think she could have meant 'pear' instead of 'pair'?"

He tightens his grip on the shovel. "Only one way to find out."

We trudge through the snow around the edge of the frozen creek, not daring to step foot on the frozen surface.

What is it about reaching near-adulthood that makes you so much more aware of potential danger? How did Lizzy and I skate across this deathtrap daily so fearlessly? Even after falling in and nearly dying, I came right back the very next winter.

A nervous buzz prickles in my gut as we approach the thicket of pear trees, now beginning to fear what we might find, what she might have wanted to lead me to.

"The next word in the clue is 'left', which would be" —I point— "either that one from this angle, or that one from the other way."

"Vinnie, you have an opinion on the matter?" Kieran makes a spanning gesture across the snow. Vinnie sniffs around the trees, and I wait with bated breath, sure I'm witnessing some canine magic happening right before my eyes. But after a while of sniffing around, he just plops down in the snow and lolls his tongue at us.

I share a look with Kieran. He shrugs. "Might as well start there." He begins digging by the tree nearest where Vinnie has sat, shucking snow out of the way like he's burying a bone. I stand over him, absolutely no help at all, watching as he clears the snow around the tree. He stabs the shovel into the ground, but it only goes a few inches.

"The ground is pretty frozen, but I've had worse." He jumps his full bodyweight onto the edge of the shovel, and it goes all the way in. I watch in wonder as the hole widens little by little. He pants with exertion as he works.

Nearly an hour goes by, and my toes are growing numb from the cold. We've found nothing by the first tree and have begun clearing the snow around the second tree. I'm very little help with the actual digging, but I'm holding my own on the snow removal, at least.

Vinnie brings me a branch he's found, and I play fetch with him for a bit while Kieran works on the next hole. I'm feeling sillier by the minute, the longer we're out here. What if all of this is for nothing?

"I can take a turn," I offer.

Kieran smirks a little but steps over and drops the shovel breathlessly into my outstretched hand with no objection.

He plops down onto the ground to catch his breath. "Have at it, Heiress."

He pulls out a small package of freeze-dried strawberries from his pocket and munches on them while he watches me with amusement. I ignore him, though I do catch a glimpse in my peripherals of a surprising set of abs when he wipes sweat off his forehead with the edge of his shirt. An entirely objective glimpse. Impartial. Detached, if you will. As one would simply notice the blue of the sky.

With every measure of confidence I have, I thrust the shovel into the ground and kick my heel onto it, feeling certain it'll go in deep like it did for Kieran. It hardly makes a dent at all. A sharp pain shoots up my leg from my heel.

Next, I attempt to jump on it like he did, but I miss it entirely and fall onto my butt. Multiple times. I mumble every curse word I can think of at the shovel, convinced it must have a personal agenda against me.

In a last-ditch effort to restore any shreds of dignity I have left, I grab the shovel like a knife and stab it repeatedly into the earth with all the repressed rage I have in me, shouting at the top of my lungs for good measure.

"You're going to hurt yourself." He makes no effort to intervene, though. He's lying in a pile of snow with his arms behind his head, seemingly entertained by my futile efforts.

I throw the shovel into the snow after it lands me on my butt again.

"Giving up so soon? But you were finally getting somewhere," Kieran deadpans.

I lie back into the snow like a fallen snow angel, gasping for air. "I hate you," I pant.

Vinnie prances over and rests his snout in my armpit, licking my ear encouragingly like he's telling me, "At least you tried."

Kieran clambers up with a satisfied chuckle while I lie here unable to move, staring into the clouds like I used to when I was kid.

But then a *clunk* reverberates off the surrounding trees. Vinnie and I perk up immediately.

Kieran looks at me over his shoulder. "A box maybe?"

I scramble to my feet, waiting next to him in anticipation as he digs more eagerly, throwing huge mounds of dirt and snow behind him at an even quicker pace.

With effort, he manages to wrench free a medium sized weather-proof box from the hole. I've never seen it before. It's green, like some kind of military box. Something they'd store heavy duty computers in or ammunition they didn't want to get wet.

He gives it to me, panting, and I take it in my hands, surprised at how heavy and thick it is. Even as I hold it, I doubt its existence. I can't picture Lizzy owning something like this, much less taking the time to bury it in the earth. Yet here it is.

I drop to my knees to examine it closer, and Vinnie takes a good long sniff. I turn it all around to figure out how it opens.

I fling the box into the snow in frustration when I find a small lock on the front latch.

"Of course she would lock it," I groan. "Lizzy, why did you have to be *so freaking thorough?*"

Kieran takes a turn inspecting it and Vinnie sniffs it some more. "I assume you don't have a key for this somewhere."

"That would be too easy, I guess." And something inside me deteriorates. Without a key, we're no closer than we were before.

He fingers the brand name embossed on the top of the box, eyebrows scrunching together. "*Impenetra,*" he murmurs to himself thoughtfully. "Where have I heard that before?"

My teeth chatter as the cold and disappointment really set in. "I don't know, but if we stay out here much longer, my brain will be of no use whatsoever. We can think more next to something warm."

Kieran has to hold the shovel across his handlebars, but we're able to squeeze Lizzy's box in the cargo storage.

I take the drive back slower, feeling both physically and emotionally numb. Even Vinnie trots along slower, maybe sensing the shift in mood.

I hate that I'm frustrated with Lizzy. You're not supposed to be mad at the sister you've thought to be dead for ten years and now could miraculously be alive, but I can't shake it.

She must have had a reason to go to these lengths to keep all this hidden, trying to keep someone away from whatever she knew, but why didn't she tell *me*? Why did she have to leave me in the dark then, only to reveal tiny infuriating puzzle pieces of truth that don't fit together all these years later? Why now? Why this way?

If Unknown is Lizzy, why can't she tell me the whole truth instead of leading me on this ridiculous scavenger hunt?

My thoughts are busy and cluttered as we park the ATVs and shuck off our wet coats and gloves in the mudroom, hanging them up on the hooks that line the shiplap walls, leaving wet shoes behind in melted puddles. Kieran brushes the snow off Vinnie and dries his paws off with his beanie before leaving that behind with the rest of the wet clothes.

We head back to the dining room, and Kieran sets the box on the table with a *thud*. Vinnie is alerted to a noise on the other side of the house and leaves us to investigate.

That's when the ear-splitting screams of my aunt rattle the windows.

20

———

KIERAN

DECEIT WASN'T IN THE JOB DESCRIPTION…
OKAY, MAYBE IT WAS

I race after Nikki, following her out of the dining room and toward the sound of screams, my soul leaving my body and staying behind.

I skid to a stop behind Nikki, seeing a frail old woman with a nurse holding her up by the arm. The woman is pointing in fear at Vinnie, coughing so badly she can barely get out more than a couple words at a time.

"Wolf!" she screams in terror. "Nikki! Run! Get—shoo!"

"He's not a wolf, he's very friendly!" Nikki rushes to comfort the woman, working with the nurse to calm the coughing fit. I call Vinnie to me, hanging back and holding him by the collar. The nurse shoots eye daggers at me.

"It's okay, bud," I reassure Vinnie in a whisper, who droops at my feet sadly. "You didn't do anything wrong."

"I'm so sorry," Nikki apologizes to the old woman, rubbing her back gently and helping her take sips of water. "I didn't know you were awake—I should have told you they were here."

The old woman—who I'm assuming is the off-limits aunt

—finally gets the coughing under control. She eyes me with glassy, beady eyes. "I always knew you'd try sneaking a boy in at some point. I just didn't expect he'd be so big and furry."

I step closer to her to introduce myself. "Sorry for the scare, ma'am. This is Vinnie, and I'm Kieran Bergstrom, I'm a true—"

"Boyfriend!" Nikki shrieks, cutting me off, scurrying over to me. "He's my boyfriend."

I knew I couldn't reference the case specifically, but I didn't realize I couldn't tell the aunt who I am at all. But she gives me a glare so sharp it could cut through metal, so naturally, I shut up immediately and play along for the sake of my life. She loops her arm through mine, putting her head stiffly on my shoulder.

Her voice is higher when she's lying through her teeth. Noted. "This is my *boyfriend* Kieran, and his dog Vinnie. We met... online. Yeah, online."

She's terrible at this.

I clear my throat to salvage the situation. "It's wonderful to finally meet you" —I quickly replay the interviews with neighbors I did yesterday, trying to remember this woman's name— "Ms. Delaney. I've heard so many great things about you."

I step forward to shake her hand and she takes it hesitantly, but not out of mistrust, just surprise. "Great things, huh?" she rasps with a dry laugh, shaking my hand in return, hers bony and wrinkled. "I didn't realize my niece was such a liar."

I give that charming radio-style laugh I'm known for and take a risk: "She does have incredibly poor judgment, so don't worry, I didn't believe any of it."

For a moment the aunt doesn't say anything, so I worry I've misjudged her humor. Nikki's nails dig into my arm with an unspoken message of, 'I'm going to kill you.'

But then the aunt laughs, sending relief through my bones.

"Alright you can keep him," she tells Nikki. "And the furry one too."

Nikki laughs in a forced way. "Isn't he. Just. So. Funny? I knew you'd like him."

The nurse nudges the aunt back toward her room, which appears to be nearly the entire west wing of the house. "Sorry to ruin the moment, but Wren needs to eat something while she's awake."

"Come fill me in when he's gone," Wren says pointedly to Nikki, with a wrinkled quirk of her eyebrow, like it's less of a suggestion and more of an indisputable order.

"I will, as long as you promise to take your meds," Nikki calls after her.

When she's gone, Nikki nearly leaps away from me as if I'm contagious. She lowers down to pet Vinnie apologetically, tutting to him in that way she does that he adores. "I'm so sorry. You'd never hurt a fly, would you?"

"Fake boyfriend wasn't in the original job description, you know," I say ribbingly, tucking my hands into my pockets. "That'll add an extra ten thousand onto your tab for the extra deceit."

She ignores me, striding past me to the dining room.

I decide to mess with her a bit more. It's the least I can do after playing the part so well with such little prior notice, and maybe the more I joke about the money aspect of it, the less sick about it I'll eventually feel. "We'll say an extra 10k to add the fake boyfriend clause, and any handholding or kissing will be one thousand each."

Her eyes flash. "There will be no such thing! I'm *engaged*, thank you."

"And she knows that? Maybe I should go ask her how she feels about your little underage engagement?" I challenge.

I startle a bit as Nikki gasps out of nowhere, but she has only received a notification on her phone. "Wait here!" She flies out of the room, stomping across the wood of the foyer to the front door.

When she leaves, I quickly swipe away an incoming notification of my own: *"This is your last warning."*

Let's just say Ciphered Voyager hasn't been happy since I announced I was doing the Sinclair case. But I try to put it completely out of my mind, no matter how insistent the threats are becoming. I have to stay focused here.

How else am I supposed to get the money together for George?

When I spoke to him yesterday, George said his contact is trying to pull whatever he can on Ciphered, but it'll take a few days. He sighed with deep regret when I told him what I'm charging Nikki to take on her family's case. But he agreed there aren't many alternatives. He's been speaking with a realtor to see what they can get from his and Tina's condo. He made me promise not to sell my van. *"And don't you dare quit your podcast on my behalf, kid,"* he had ordered. *"You've done too much good with it."*

So onward we go.

Nikki returns with a small poly-bag package that is slightly wet from the snow outside. She rips it apart and yanks a black cord out of it. Then she rifles through the pile of things she dropped in front of me earlier—the journal of her sister's, the book, the papers.

Seeing that journal, the desperate clues left behind, my mind hasn't stopped spinning since. There's always a turning point in the cases I've done so far, when it becomes less of a job and more of a deeply intimate mission. The point when I get personally invested in a case. When it's no longer just a name written on a case file. It's a person. An innocent person that I feel I know.

Reading the hasty handwriting of a scared eleven-year-old was it for me.

Elizabeth Sinclair is no longer a name on a file. She was an innocent little girl. And I believe finding out what she knew is the key to everything.

Nikki spins around with an object in hand, plopping on the ground in front of a wall outlet on the other side of the dining room table. Vinnie and I are nosy—it is our job—so we join her on the ground.

She has plugged in an old blocky smart phone and taps it impatiently, waiting for it to come back to life.

"I found this in my dad's office," she explains as we wait. "In a hidden safe. There were also torn bands for stacks of money and boxes of gun ammunition."

"What's your theory?" I don't try to inject any theories of my own yet, considering she knows her family better than I do. I don't tell her that a burner phone is never a good sign. I'm sure she knows.

The screen brightens, accepting the charge and powering on. Her impatient tapping gains enthusiasm.

"Yeah, I know it doesn't look good." She read my mind. "Hidden phone. Hidden safe. To me, it looks like he left in a hurry. Prepared for anything. Whether that was the day they died or a different day, though, I don't know."

"Do you remember your dad acting weird that week?" I ask, remembering a comment one of the neighbors made in an interview: "*Erratic, strict.*"

I never take neighbor testimony too seriously because the gossip mill is very unreliable, especially when the case happened so long ago. Things tend to compound and exaggerate in people's minds. But they still make for compelling soundbites, nonetheless. It adds bits of mystery and intrigue when everyone is adding their outlandish theories and recollections of events, true or not.

"No. My dad was so normal it was almost boring," she says with a dry laugh. "Racing was the only exciting thing he ever did, and it wasn't even that often. Other than that, our life, even in this place, was so incredibly *normal.* But clearly, there was a lot I didn't know."

The main screen of the phone finally loads, and she looks at me with widened eyes. "No password," she breathes. "He must have thought the safe was good enough. I think he probably meant to lock that."

Her fingers twitch as she clicks the calls icon on the screen. The operating system of the phone is clunky and old, even for 2015 standards. Among a long list of incoming and outgoing calls to the same number, are five missed calls in red.

She holds the phone closer to inspect it. She murmurs something to herself before repeating it to me louder, "This call right here was over an hour long, and it was the day before they died. All these missed ones? That was the day they died."

21

KIERAN
BURN BABY BURN

Everything in me wants to snatch the phone out of her hand and comb through it myself, with the burning curiosity that guides me through these cases, with my own investigative eye. It's killing me to have to wait here as she does it *so excruciatingly slow*.

But I restrain myself, obviously, trying to respect the position she's in here, and giving her the time to do it herself. As much as it may kill me.

She presses the home button, which takes her back to the main screen. Nikki clicks the messages. There's only one conversation thread. It's with the same number as the call history. She clicks into the text thread.

Suddenly she lets out a scream that makes me jump out of my skin, tossing the phone away like it's on fire. It clatters on the ground next to her, bouncing off the baseboard. "I think I just saw something of my dad's no daughter should ever have to see!" She makes a retching sound, covering her face with her hands. "No, no, no. Why me, God? Why?"

I try not to laugh. "That's... unfortunate."

"Unfortunate?" she repeats in disbelief. "I'm going to be traumatized for life because of this! This was worse than burying him!"

"You didn't bury him. His body was never found."

"Exactly," she hisses, pressing her palms into her eyelids. "I never had to *see anything*. Stop laughing, it's not funny."

"It's a little funny," I snort. "I'm sorry. But we're going to need to figure out who he was talking to. It could be substantial to the case. Just pretend it's not him."

"Oh, *I'm* never opening that phone again." She uses the very tip of her toe to slide it over to me. "Luckily I'm paying this really great amateur detective a lot of money."

"I mean, I wouldn't say amateur. But touché," I concede, picking up the phone and turning it around in my hand to inspect it, the cord stretched its full length across her. "You know we're lucky he didn't password protect this?"

"He was notoriously bad with technology. I'm honestly surprised he even figured out how to send pictures like that."

"It's a very deep-rooted male instinct. I'm sure even a Neanderthal could figure that out. They were probably sending them via petroglyph back then."

"Ugh why are men so disgusting?" she groans into her hands. Vinnie thinks she's crying and is quick to lend comfort. He lies his head on her lap. "Except you," she corrects, nuzzling his face. "Never you."

I scroll through the text thread, and sure enough, there it is. So. Many. Images. The messages themselves are... very hard to read. I'm cringing so hard reading old people's flirting that I've nearly separated from my skin. It's very clear that Mr. Sinclair and this woman were romantically involved.

"How bad is it?" Nikki asks cagily.

I wince. "Pretty bad. It looks like they met up in person on several occasions. There are texts of 'I can't wait to see you again' and mentions of 'Last night was amazing.'"

"I can't believe he would do that to my mom," she sniffles. "Who is she?"

"They were very careful. I'm trying to find anything identifiable about this woman, but they never say names or show their faces. Only... everything else."

I show her a picture of a fair-skinned woman in red lingerie, cropped at the neck. She's posing in front of a bathroom mirror, though it's pretty zoomed in.

Nikki stares at the photo in horrified awe for a moment. Then her eyebrows pull together.

"What?"

Her eyes flick to me above the phone. "Nothing. I thought there was something familiar about it, but I can't place it. I don't know who this woman is. We're going to call the number, right?"

I give her a look. "Of course we're going to call the number."

I pull out my own phone and enter *67 to block my number, carefully inputting the digits from the other phone. I click the 'record' button as it dials. Nikki scoots closer to me as it rings. I put it to speakerphone so she can hear it better.

It rings and rings. No answer. No voicemail.

I try again.

Ring. Ring. Ring.

I'm about to end the call when the line connects. "Hello?"

Our eyes widen at each other. Nikki's hand claps to her mouth.

Because it's a man's voice.

"Who is this?" he says angrily. "How did you get this number?"

I clear my throat, scrambling to think of something to say. "Hello, thank you for answering. I'm wondering if you can answer some questions for me. How did you know Gunnar Sinclair?"

There's a pause on the other line and then, "Never call me again."

"Wait!" I say hurriedly before he hangs up. "I have photos that were sent to and from an old cell phone, dated before his death, to this number. Do you know anything about that?"

"Is that a threat?" The voice lowers to nearly a growl.

"No, I only want to know how you know Gunnar Sinclair." I take a chance: "I'm solving his murder."

Another pause, and a shuffling around. Maybe the slightest muffled sound of someone else there too?

"Never call this number again."

The call disconnects with a *beep*.

Nikki exhales in a short puff like she's been holding her breath. "A man?!"

I shrug. "I don't know. The pictures were pretty *graphically* female, but it has been ten years. A lot can change."

"I need a break," she declares, standing up in a huff. "You hungry?"

Twenty minutes later, we're sitting at the granite countertop island in her massive kitchen, eating a delicious meal left behind by her personal chef.

"Personal chef is a bit of an overstatement," she had

protested as she reheated the tray. "Bea is more like a family member at this point... who we happen to pay."

Vinnie sits next to me, begging with puppy-dog eyes, as if Nikki didn't just give him his own plateful of filet mignon that he devoured in seconds.

I throw him a carrot to get him off my back, which rolls across the gleaming white tile. He stomps clumsily after it.

I savor my bite of butter and herb roasted potatoes, which are heavenly, trying not to make it obvious how long it's been since I've had a meal this good, much less a home-made one.

Nikki's phone vibrates with an incoming call. *Montgomery Law Group* says the caller ID.

Nikki sets her fork down to answer it. "Hey, Michael. I hope you have good news."

I munch on my food and try not to eavesdrop. I'm sure she'll fill me in if it's important to the case. I do notice how her face falls, though.

"Oh," she says, lips pulling into a frown that looks unnatural on her normally bright face. "Okay, well thanks for trying. I'll keep looking for the car titles, then. If I don't find them, what other options do I have?"

She fidgets with her fork as the call speaks on the other line.

"Oh." She nods as if the caller can see her. "Thanks, Michael. Well, let me know if you have any luck pulling the vehicle records. Okay, you too, bye."

Vinnie startles at the sudden slam of her phone on the counter, and is quick to the scene, sniffing us out for danger. "I feel like insurance is the biggest scam on the planet. Literally what's the point of paying for it, if they don't cover *anything?*"

I snort in agreement. I've asked myself that question so many times over the course of my diagnosis. "Don't I know it. Everything okay?"

She waves it off. "Yeah. Just my lawyer giving me an update on an insurance thing. Okay, here's my theory," her eyes turn busy as she changes the subject. "Since the number my dad was contacting is still in use all these years later, it was probably her everyday phone she was using, not a burner. The man who answered didn't sound surprised when you said my dad's name, so he must have known about their affair."

I nod. "Yeah, maybe. If that's true, that means this man could have a motive to want your dad gone."

She looks at me, eyes wide. "Is it possible you just spoke to his murderer?"

A sudden chill shoots down my back that I try to play off by straightening my shoulders. "It's worth looking into more. I mean it's more of a motive than the police ever found."

She stabs her fork into a potato on her plate. A shadow of sadness crosses over her face. "You know, I've heard so many rumors and speculations over the years. Everyone assumed it must have been that. Because it's always that." She waves her arms wildly as she talks, near hysteria. "'Husband of rich businessman's mistress seeks revenge.' What a cliché. I never even considered it."

I let her words hang in the air for a moment, the silence, not uncomfortable, but heavy with the pain she usually tries to hide. I don't want to disrupt whatever healing vocalizing these feelings could bring her.

"'My dad would never,' I always thought."

"I'm sorry," I add genuinely, hoping to convey I actually

mean it. "It sucks finding out the worst part about someone you always believed the best in."

"I was naïve to so much," she laughs bitterly. "No wonder Lizzy didn't trust me with whatever she found out. I never would have believed her."

"Don't blame yourself. You were literally a kid." And I repeat it again until she's really hearing me. Her blue eyes glisten with the tears she's trying to hold back. "Kids *should be* naïve to stuff like this. You did nothing wrong."

She presses her lips into a small grateful smile. "Thanks for saying that. Maybe you're not the grouchy swamp gargoyle I thought you were."

"No, I definitely am," I chuckle. "Honestly, you're still the same spoiled princess I thought you were" —I gesture around the glamorous kitchen for emphasis— "but maybe you're a little less intolerable."

She laughs, crossing her arms to hug herself as she shivers. "Oh great, a little less intolerable is all I aspire to be in life."

She pushes her barstool back and steps over to the black, wall-mounted electric fireplace that takes up nearly the entire back wall. She flips the switch and purple flames power on, emitting immediate warmth into the room.

Nikki gasps, and I drop my fork at the startle. Vinnie darts over to her side immediately. "You have got to stop doing that!" I shout.

"*Burn,*" she says, with emphasis, pointing to the fireplace. "On the clue. *Pair left beck burn.* There are like six other fireplaces on this property. Or more. What if the key to the box is in one of them?"

She's already running out of the room. "Let's split up!" she yells over her shoulder.

I scramble to my feet. "Wait!" I shovel the last few bites I can into my already full mouth. "I don't know where to go!"

"Back patio!" Her voice is already far away.

I circle back to steal a few bites off her abandoned plate before I go, tossing Vinnie another carrot.

Then a text with a photo comes in on my phone that makes me skid to a stop.

It's a photo of Nikki and I sitting at her dining room table. Today. The only possible angle this could have been taken from is through the window.

CIPHERED VOYAGER

I've given you every opportunity to obey. For the final time, take the podcast down and cease further investigation. Next time I won't just take a picture.

PODCAST TRANSCRIPT

Secrets in Ice Season 3, Episode 3: The Butler, Cont.

[a beat, as suspenseful music plays]

KIERAN BERGSTROM:

Mr. Kensington, in your time here managing the household, how involved were you in Mr. and Mrs. Sinclair's personal lives?

ARRICK KENSINGTON:

I wasn't directly involved, but Mr. Sinclair became a good friend. He confided in me from time to time.

KIERAN BERGSTROM:

Did he ever mention any problems between himself and Mrs. Sinclair? What was their marriage like from what you could observe?

ARRICK KENSINGTON:

They had many early years of stress as Mr. Sinclair's business got off the ground, and when the children were very young, but from what I could tell, at that time they were in a good place. They went out on dates and attended social gatherings together, laughed often. They seemed happy.

KIERAN BERGSTROM:

What is the nature of Mr. Sinclair's business?

ARRICK KENSINGTON:

Oil transportation, primarily between the United States and Canada.

KIERAN BERGSTROM:

The oil industry can be pretty cutthroat, especially on the billion-dollar scale. Do you think he had any enemies? Or anyone who could have profited from his death?

ARRICK KENSINGTON:

Not to my knowledge. Mr. and Mrs. Sinclair were both very well liked in the community. Everyone loved them, me included. I never would have ever guessed someone would do them harm.

KIERAN BERGSTROM:

If they were so well-liked in the community, why do you think everyone accepted their deaths without justice?

ARRICK KENSINGTON:

That is a mystery to me as well. The staff and I begged for help from the community—friends, coworkers, anyone— and at first, they were involved and willing to help, but then everyone became more reluctant to talk to investigators until eventually no one would even answer the calls at all.

KIERAN BERGSTROM:

It must have been very hard for you to find out what had happened to them.

ARRICK KENSINGTON:

Yes. Losing them was the second worst day of my entire life. When Miss Nikki woke up in the morning, and we had to tell her, that was— *[voice breaks]* that was the first.

KIERAN BERGSTROM:

What were the days after like?

ARRICK KENSINGTON:

The police were here for probably four days straight. Searching the property, taking some of their belongings into evidence, interviewing us, looking for leads. It was unclear at first who would be caring for Miss Nikki, but we were all happy to help. We were all so heartbroken for her.

KIERAN BERGSTROM:

Why do you think even the police gave up on the investigation?

ARRICK KENSINGTON:

Lack of bodies and lack of motive they could find is my assumption.

KIERAN BERGSTROM:

Please don't take offense to this, Arrick, I'm only asking because I have to do my job, and many of my listeners are wondering this as well. But can anyone confirm where you were on October 17th, 2015?

ARRICK KENSINGTON:

I understand. It was a Saturday, so the staff was off for the weekend. I normally am as well if my driving services aren't needed, but I came in that morning to wish Lizzy good luck and help get Nikki's babysitter situated. I ended up staying around most of the day to catch up on a landscaping project. It was so long ago, I doubt the babysitter would even remember me, but you're welcome to reach out to her.

[pause]

We did have a guest later that day, however, now that I think of it. He can confirm I was here.

KIERAN BERGSTROM:

Who?

ARRICK KENSINGTON:

Peter Vanderwaal. He was one of Mr. Sinclair's good friends and business associates, but he lives in Vancouver, so he didn't visit a lot. He came by around noon. One o'clock perhaps? He didn't stay long. Just came by to drop off some paperwork. He didn't linger when I told him they weren't home.

KIERAN BERGSTROM:

Can you think of any reason Mr. Vanderwaal would have wanted to do the Sinclairs harm?

ARRICK KENSINGTON:

Not that I know of. However, I suppose is quite strange that he happened to be in the country on the day of their disappearance.

[suspenseful music plays]

22

NIKKI

IS THIS LIZZY'S REVENGE FOR ME BEING A PEST OF A LITTLE SISTER?

I start looking in the fireplace in my room first, even though it's doubtful Lizzy could've hidden something here that Bea or I wouldn't have already found. I just want to rule it out. I comb through the ceramic logs and artificial embers but find nothing.

Next is Lizzy's room. Her fireplace is also lacking anything extraordinary, except dust. It hasn't been powered on since she died.

I'm most hesitant to check my parents' room, feeling like an intruder every time I step through their door. Their huge primary suite takes up the entire north wing. The white walls and gold finishes may have once felt luxurious and warm. The plush carpet, high vaulted ceiling, and glittering chandelier may have once felt airy and inviting. But after all these years it has all grown stale and stiff. Cold. Dead, just like them.

I find myself tiptoeing across their soft carpet, as if I'm sneaking back into a sleeping house after curfew, even though I've never done that. Sneaking just feels like something mandatory you have to do in your dead parents' bedroom.

A slit in their beige velvet curtains lets in some of the warm sunset from outside as it slips slowly into dusk. I forget sometimes that they had the best view in the house. Our property itself is meticulously maintained. Perfectly placed pavers and stones outline the huge circular drive with a carefully trimmed hedge border. Our expansive lawn is white half of the year, and brilliant green the other half and meets the surrounding forest of snow-dusted maples and firs, which spans for miles around us. The entire city is visible in the valley below with the sprawling Cascade mountains melting into the pastel sunset beyond that.

With how alive and vibrant it looks outside, you'd never know how dead it feels in here.

It's a beautiful view, but the stark contrast is yet another painful reminder of what this place used to be. The *life* that used to be here, no matter how rose-colored it may have been to me.

But we were happy. I know we were.

I admire it a second longer, wondering when Arrick last saw his hard work from this angle. I'll have to remember to bring him up here on Monday when he gets back in.

I shut the curtain with a *snap* and search through my parents' fireplace, finding nothing here too.

The guest bedrooms and sitting rooms are also lacking.

I'm losing steam quickly. The constant up and down is exhausting and discouraging. I don't know how Kieran can do this full-time. The emotional roller-coaster alone is enough to make me want to hibernate, let alone the mental exhaustion of my brain always being in hyperdrive, afraid to rest in case I miss something or fail to remember something vital.

I return downstairs, and I'm about to sneak into Aunt Wren's suite when Kieran and Vinnie come barreling in from the back patio.

"I found something!" he whisper-yells.

I meet him halfway in the dining room. "On the patio?" I ask, no louder than a hopeful breath.

"The. Gym. In. The. pool house," he pants, handing me the key. He must have sprinted all the way back. Even Vinnie looks winded.

"There's not a fireplace in the gym." I tilt my head.

"Wow, I didn't realize how of shape I was." He takes another gulp of air. "Sauna."

My jaw drops nearly to the floor. I stare at the key in awe. "Of course. Sauna. *Burn.* How did you even think of that?"

He gives me an arrogant smirk. "Told you I'm no amateur, Heiress."

"Where was it?" I roll it around in my palm. It's tiny. There's no keychain or loop attached to it. Just a single metal key. You would have never found it if you weren't looking for it.

"There are gaps in the wood on the bench. It was under one of those."

I'm impressed, but I neutralize my expression. Can't have him being *too* proud of himself. "Good work," I say formally instead.

"Thanks, boss." He returns the formality and gives me a mocking salute that I ignore.

I chew on my lip as I stare at the box on the table warily.

I'm almost afraid to try the key. Lizzy went through all this trouble to hide whatever is in here. But I don't know what I'll do if all of this leads to nothing. Could I have mistaken this entire thing? What if this was all some game? A fun, mysterious little excursion around the property she designed for her annoying and curious little sister. Maybe when she was alive, she knew I'd go snooping around her room one day and this was her elaborate planned payback.

I hold my breath as the key goes into the lock. It's a perfect fit.

Kieran's presence over my shoulder is surprisingly comforting, considering how much I further dislike him every time he speaks. I'm glad I don't have to do this alone. Weekends are so painfully lonely on a normal basis, let alone when I'm uncovering hidden clues left behind by a murdered sister.

An *alive* murdered sister. She's alive, *she's alive,* she has to be.

And that reminder gives me the courage boost to turn the key and open the box.

Every inch of the inside, lid included, is padded with a firm gray foam, apart from the empty square with a white iPad in a glittery pink rubber case nestled inside it.

"No way," I breathe, feeling doused by a splash of nostalgia. "I remember this."

I pull out the iPad carefully. The tablet is heavy and thick, and I'm struck by how quickly technology updates. This feels like a dinosaur, yet not that long ago, it was the newest tech available. I nearly cry out in relief when I see the charging cord coiled up under it.

"She certainly thought of everything, that's for sure," Kieran says, impressed.

I press the power button stupidly, even though there's no way it'll still be charged after ten years in storage inside the literal earth. Who knows if it'll even turn on at all.

I return to the same outlet my dad's stupid, nasty phone is plugged in at, and I resist the urge to kick it into oblivion, only because it could be potential evidence.

I will never get that image out of my brain. It's seared there forever, and I'll never forgive him for that.

I lean down to plug in the charger, but Kieran gives a little cough behind me. "Uh, is there anywhere else we could set up?"

"Oh, I'm sorry this didn't meet your expectations." I look up at him in exaggerated shock from own sore knees, too stubborn to admit he's right, that it's silly to sit on the floor of my dining room when we have this entire house. "Who's the spoiled princess now?"

His eyes flick to the window. "Second floor maybe?

I bundle all the items in my arms. "O-ho," I mock. "Is the big, brave detective scared of the dark?"

He gets the rest of the items from the table and follows me out of the room. "Oh yeah, deathly," he says flatly, but doesn't elaborate further.

"I didn't account for you requiring such lavish accommodations when we made this arrangement." I lead him up the staircase. "We may have to revisit our terms and conditions. At the very least, I feel like this neutralizes the fake boyfriend clause."

He's distracted by my house, and I try not to feel embarrassed by its excess. I know it's overkill. I'd sell this beast to live in a cottage in the woods in a heartbeat if I could.

My stomach somersaults into my throat as I trip on the last step of the stairs and fly forward to my knees. Everything

I'm holding scatters to the hardwood around me. Kieran gathers everything up and adds it to his own pile, still managing to find a free hand to help me up.

"Thank you," I mutter as I continue down the hallway toward the south wing, feeling a blush spread across my cheeks.

"What was that?" he calls after me.

He heard me.

"I said I hate you," I reply over my shoulder unnecessarily loud.

I push open the door to the theater and cringe a little at Kieran's whistle behind me, cheeks still hot with embarrassment at being a clumsy idiot.

"Now *this* is what I'm talking about," he says, lowering the pile of evidence into the closest armchair.

The windowless room is dim, lit only by the red LED recessed lighting overhead and on the edges of the stairs that lead up to two rows of huge leather recliners. I had a lot of homework I was catching up on, so I haven't been in here all week, but apart from my sunroom, this is my favorite place to be. I've watched so many hours of true crime documentaries with a bowl full of popcorn in here.

I rifle through a few drawers of the black built-in shelving under the huge projector screen and cheer in victory when I find an extension cord in the bottom drawer.

Kieran and Vinnie have both already made themselves comfortable in two separate armchairs. Kieran's is reclined, legs out, arms behind his head.

"Making ourselves comfortable I see."

"Yeah, finally, now that you're not keeping all the—what was it?—'*lavish accommodations*' to yourself."

"I'm used to having this whole house to myself. I'm remembering why I struggled to share as a child."

"I'm so shocked to hear that. I never would have guessed that about you."

I ignore him and find the closest outlet, plugging in the extension cord and pulling it over to the open armchair next to him. I plop down and plug the iPad into it.

A red battery blinks in the middle of the black screen. I sigh loudly. I'm much too impatient for this. The anxiety creeps back in, oozing through my stomach and up my chest. Now that the distractions are over, I have to confront whatever is on this iPad.

"What do you think is on there?" Kieran asks in a forced casual manner, even though he's every bit as anxious as I am. Fingers tapping, knees bouncing when he thinks I'm not looking. He never sits still. He and Vinnie are basically the same, just different species.

"Hopefully something that gives us actual information, instead of more vague hints."

I gasp as the screen brightens.

"I thought we talked about the gasping!" he says exasperatedly. "Let's save it for when someone's dying, yeah?"

The lockscreen finally loads, and it feels like a sledgehammer to the gut. It's a photo of Lizzy and me. Our smiles are so bright it nearly blinds me. It's unfair that those two smiling little girls don't exist anymore, for one reason or another.

It was taken after one of her figure skating competitions. She's holding a bouquet of roses we brought for her, wearing a bright blue leotard, bright pink blush across her fair cheeks, blonde hair pulled back tightly in a slicked bun. I was always so jealous she got to wear makeup for her competitions, and all I got for my soccer tournaments were ugly cleats. I'm next to her, nearly a half-foot shorter, my hair pulled into two braids.

Looking at my unaware smile, so oblivious to what was apparently going on around me, hurts. How could I have not seen any signs of something off with my dad? With Lizzy? How could so many secrets have been right in front of me the whole time?

Kieran's knee bounces more vigorously, and I can sense the restrained impatience bubbling up inside him. He may combust at any moment. Part of me wants to take longer on purpose to torture him, but I guess he did find the key and help me up when I fell, so maybe I'll go easy on him.

I press the button on the bottom of the iPad again, and it pulls up a numeric keypad for her password.

I stare at it blankly for only a moment before the idea comes to me.

I shoot up and over to the pile of evidence Kieran dropped in the armchair nearest the door. That scrap of paper from the book that was in her journal; where is it, where is it? It has to be her password.

"Aha!" I find the scrap and pump it in the air like it's a winning lottery ticket.

3-7-0-5

I kneel on the armchair, not even bothering to sit fully, plugging the digits in carefully. One by one.

It's slow and lagging. I drop my butt down onto my heels and set the iPad on my lap. I twirl and untwirl my hair around my index finger impatiently.

Kieran is also frozen in anticipation. Vinnie too, but it's because he's napping tranquilly, resting on his own armchair like it's his second home. I envy him a bit. I don't know if *I've* even felt that at peace in this house.

I squeal when the iPad unlocks, kicking my feet under me like a toddler.

Kieran lets out a celebratory *whoop*. "Let's goooo."

I did it. I'm in.

23

NIKKI

EYEBALLS? MEET SCUM

Her home screen photo is the same as her lockscreen, and our blurred smiles peek through the small, squared app icons, all categorized by color.

"Of course her apps are color-coded," I laugh. That is so Lizzy.

I go first to her messages, scrolling through inconsequential messages with friends. Making plans, sharing homework answers. Texts with Mom letting her know practice was over or asking for permission for hangouts.

Her FaceTime log is similar, nothing out of the ordinary for a preteen girl. A few red missed calls from friends but all of them returned within minutes.

Nothing in her notes app.

No other apps that look unusual, mostly games I doubt she ever even played. Did my parents know she had Snapchat? Although a quick scan doesn't show anything suspicious there.

Her photos app is my last hope. I hold my breath as I click the icon.

The grid view of her camera roll is full of a random assortment of photos and videos, most so blurry that I can't even make out what they are from the grid-view. None appear related, and none of them are even of her. I scroll upwards quite a bit before I find any photos or videos of Lizzy at all, and they're just silly selfies with her friends.

I return back to the end of her camera roll grid to enlarge the most recent video. Might as well work backwards.

The video begins with movement, hastily, the camera taking a second to focus. It appears to be recorded in some kind of bar or lounge that has a goal of privacy. The lighting is very dim, ornate chandeliers hanging low above tucked in booths with curtains, some pulled shut, and some not, revealing pockets of couples and groups enjoying their evenings respectively.

I finally take a full sit, leaning back in the armchair and closer to Kieran, setting the iPad on the arm between us so he can see better. Our heads are close together as we watch.

In the video, the camera zooms in on a pair at a table. The man is a great deal older than the woman. Girl? Hmm. She seems *very* young, like maybe even younger than me. Long black hair, low-back dress. They appear to be having a great time. Their food is untouched, but they are... not. They are all over each other. Their faces are hard to see in the dim lighting and with the camera pixelation, but I don't think I recognize either person.

What was Lizzy doing at a bar? Who are these people? Is the girl one of her *friends?* Oh, I hope not.

My skin crawls by the time the video finally ends. I share a confused look with Kieran.

"Okay..." I say.

I swipe over to the next video.

This one is rowdier, and the sudden spike in volume startles me. I nearly drop the iPad. Kieran holds the other edge to steady it. This cameraman is in a group of boisterous people, cheering on two men fighting each other in the middle of what appears to be the billiards hall of someone's estate. There's a window on the right that takes up most of the wall that looks out into a moonlit night sky.

The fight is an equal match, until one of the men becomes gradually more angry. He starts hitting harder, cursing louder, even spitting at the opponent. The other man stumbles for a fraction of a second, and the angry man takes advantage, pushing him back into the pool table with a *crash.*

I gasp as the man's head cracks on the edge of the table. The onlookers shift into commotion and frenzy as the blood pools out of the man's head.

And he doesn't move.

The video ends in a blur of motion.

My hand covers my mouth. I don't think I'm even breathing. Did we just watch someone die?

Kieran looks at me with eyebrows pulled together, eyes busy "Wait a minute. Are you able to zoom in on the video at all?"

I fumble with the iPad for a second, realizing it will let me zoom when it's on pause. I zoom into a still frame of the two men.

"Pause it where we can see his face better," he instructs, pointing to the angrier man.

I do so.

"Nikki," he breathes. "Isn't that Nathaniel Mooresbury?"

"Why does that name sound familiar?"

"Nathaniel Moorsebury is the attorney general."

"No," I exhale in disbelief. I fumble with my phone and plunk the name into my search engine.

Sure enough, the first photo that pulls up looks exactly like the man in the video, sans the bloody lip and rage. I show it to Kieran, who is far too proud of himself.

"I knew it. But why haven't we heard about this?" He takes the iPad to inspect the still-frame closer, the extension cord stretching across me. "Quite possibly killing a man in a fistfight? Search 'Nathaniel Moorsebury fight video' and see if anything comes up."

I type that into my phone. There are no exact matches. Nothing on Reddit, no news articles, no social media posts.

"Go back to the last video we watched," I tell him. "Is it the same guy in that one?"

We watch it back a few times, pausing and zooming to inspect their interlocked faces. We conclude the hairlines are too different, and it's not Nathaniel Moorsebury.

Kieran hands me back the iPad, allowing me to be the one to continue the search.

"I'm scared to watch any more of them," I admit.

"I can finish up if you want," he offers.

But I steel myself with an exhale. "Thanks. I can do it."

I slide to the next video, cringing in anticipation, as if a Jack in the Box is about to spring out at me.

It's a video of a man, a different man than the other two, snorting a white powder off the black granite countertops of a luxury bathroom. He's wearing a business suit like he's at work, not the suit you'd wear to a party or dinner. It almost looks like the camera is recording through the crack in the bathroom stall. Either way, he doesn't seem to know he's being recorded. It ends.

Painfully, we watch sixteen more videos like this.

More drugs, paid escorts, strip clubs—overall way more naked people than I've ever needed to see tonight—violence, public outbursts. Scandals of every flavor, all completely different people.

As the videos go on and on, a churning anxiety settles into my stomach like tar. Because each and every one of these men could have wanted Lizzy dead if they knew she had these videos.

And one of them likely did.

This adds so many suspects. How will we ever know which one of them was responsible?

The camera roll grid indicates we have three left, and I don't know how much more of this I can take. My eyelid twitches, somehow knowing I'm seeing things I was never supposed to see. Things that a lot of people probably went to great lengths to hide, yet here they are.

Kieran holds the iPad now. I handed it to him six videos ago, so I can cover my eyes when it's too much. He smirked at me and called me 'Little Innocent Heiress', causing any headway we had made toward an amicable professional relationship to dissolve into thin air. He's clearly completely determined to make me dislike him.

He pushes play on the video, and I force myself to watch, telling myself I can do this—I have to do this—if it can help lead to the person who hurt Lizzy.

I gasp when this video's subject comes into view, feeling my entire stomach fall through my knees.

Kieran looks at me to scold me about the gasp, but I point with a shaking finger.

"That's—that's Mr. and Mrs. Vanderwaal."

He raises an eyebrow at me. "As in…"

"Yes. Hunter's parents."

YOUTUBE COMMENTS SECTION
Season 3 Episode 3: The Butler

@**truecrimetina:** not Arrick casually namedropping Vanderwaal ten years later. convenient he only remembered this now. guilty much??

    @**hamsterprophet REPLYING to @truecrimetina:** if it's true he actually stopped by that's so sus, who hand delivers paperwork across a border even in 2015??

    @**icepick42 REPLYING TO @truecrimetina:** 100%. Vanderwaal is shady af. nobody just happens to be there.

    @**GaryBrown REPLYING TO @icepick42:** Peter Vanderwaal is a decent guy, I've known his family for years. I believe he's innocent.

    @**hamsterprophet REPLYING TO @GaryBrown:** found Peter's alt account guys

@**loulou:** Kieran, your interview style is so respectful but still gets to the point. I appreciate how you asked about Arrick's alibi without being accusatory.

@**cozy_crime_watcher:** ARRICK IS INNOCENT. the way his voice broke when talking about Nikki... man, that hit hard. you can hear the grief even after all these years.

@**whispersofthemoon:** I'm from a town like Sapphire Pines. Trust me, in a small town like that, everyone knows everything about everyone. If they're not talking, it's intentional.

24

KIERAN

THREATS ARE BASICALLY MY ALARM CLOCK
AT THIS POINT

I've dealt with some creepy stuff over the last few years investigating for the podcast. Some threats that have hit pretty close to home, and it was whatever. But I won't lie, I'm a little freaked out right now.

Maybe it's the unique combination of watching all these blackmail videos that belong in digital dumpsters getting to me. The threat from Ciphered. The photo of Nikki and me.

I'm trying my best to act natural, but I'm jumping at every shadow, expecting to look over my shoulder and see a lurking figure watching me or a group of masked men. And it doesn't help that Nikki gasps like someone has stabbed her every other second. I'm just glad there are no windows in this room.

No more texts have come through from Ciphered, so who knows, maybe he clocked out for the night. I sent a screenshot over to George, who then sent it over to his "guy," and they're looking into it, but they haven't found anything on Ciphered so far.

"There is a reason this person wants you to stop. It's

because you're probably on to something. Keep yourself safe, but it sounds like you must be on the right track," George had texted back.

Nikki has taken the iPad back to get a closer view, to really confirm what she thought she saw. The video is paused on Mr. and Mrs. Vanderwaal. Nikki's "in-laws-to-be." This video is security footage from an elevator, bird's eye view, looking down on them from the top corner. It's grainy, but their faces are pretty unmistakable. I don't know them personally, and even I would have eventually recognized them on my own from the research I've done on the case alone. They are dressed formally, likely going to or coming from some kind of dinner party or gala. He's wearing a black-on-black tuxedo, and she's wearing an emerald-green evening gown that drapes off her shoulders elegantly.

"You want me to push play?" I offer, trying not to sound impatient, though it's always bubbling there right under the surface. "Or we can give up. Tell your sister good luck."

She chews on her lip. "Judging by the state of the other videos, I'm scared to watch it. These are Hunter's *parents.* Mr. Vanderwaal was my dad's best friend."

Vinnie sighs deeply in his sleep from the armchair next to mine, and kicks his hind leg out like a rabbit, which softens the tension a bit.

She gives me the iPad back. "Okay. You do it." She covers her eyes. "I can't watch."

I press play on the video and see her peeking through her fingers. The video has no sound, but Mr. and Mrs. Vanderwaal are clearly tense. They appear to be arguing. Or rather, Mr. Vanderwaal is arguing, and Mrs. Vanderwaal is trying to placate him. He is stiff, angry. She has a hand on his arm in comfort, speaking to him gently, brows furrowed in concern.

Nikki takes her hands off her face finger by finger, the video much milder than the others we've seen tonight. Everyone argues.

But then there's a shuffle of motion as Mr. Vanderwaal rips his arm out of her reach. His muted volume escalates as he yells at her—face reddened, arms outstretching and flailing, fingers pointing like daggers. The silence of the video is so loud, like they're trapped inside a snow globe or a bottle out at sea. Mrs. Vanderwaal steps closer, arms out to lend comfort, but he grabs her by the throat and pushes her up against the wall of the elevator. He throws his wife to the ground, and even though there isn't sound, the *crack* of her head still ricochets off the epoxy flooring.

The video ends.

Nikki gives me a bewildered look. "Is *everyone* in my life a secretly terrible person? What is happening?"

I attempt to lighten the mood. "Yeah, you really should have better friends and family. This isn't a good look."

She buries her head. "It's too much."

"Maybe we should be done for the night."

I give her a minute. As much as I'd hate to admit it, for a spoiled princess, she has actually been handling all of this like a champ. That revelation about her dad alone would have been earth-shattering for most people. That's the dark side of this line of work. You uncover people's darkest shadows; the ones they'd do anything to keep safely tucked away in the dark. But the truth comes out eventually. It always does.

Doesn't make it easier to face, though.

However, I can't tell her any of this. That would be too

nice, and I can't be too nice. I have to remain carefully balanced between kind-of-a-jerk and still professional. If we dislike each other, it'll be a lot easier to continue using her for her money. For George and Tina...

I try to focus on the videos, and push everything else out of my mind before the guilt eats me alive. Better to just compartmentalize entirely.

So far, we are up to twenty-six potential suspects.

We haven't watched them all yet, but there are twenty-two total of these career-ending, reputation-exploding, and prison-inducing videos. Any one of them could have committed murder to keep these secrets hidden, including Mr. Vanderwaal. So that's twenty-two.

Then add Mr. Sinclair's affair partner (23), add her husband (24), who I assume I spoke with on the phone.

Mrs. Sinclair if she had found out about the affair (25).

And Hunter Vanderwaal (26).

Just because I don't like the guy (he would have been eight-ish at the time, so probably not, but psychopaths can be any age, you know).

Nikki sits back up, but her shoulders are slumped, and her voice is flat and defeated. I don't blame her. "Hunter hates his dad," she says. "But he's never said anything about this. Could it have been an isolated incident?"

I play the video again and analyze their body language more closely. It's subtle, but there are signs, which I point out to Nikki as they happen. A flinch here, a look of fear there. Being overly apologetic to calm him. No. This wasn't the first time. And it likely hasn't been the last. Men like him never change.

Nikki puffs out a breath that turns into a groan. "We still have two more videos."

"You're right." I swipe over to the next one, bracing for impact. It's another drug one, someone neither of us recognize.

Okay. Last video.

It appears to be filmed in some kind of spacious warehouse. There are huge shelves with pallets and boxes stacked high. The camera zooms in past a forklift to a group of men congregated around a few open boxes of merchandise on a table.

Two of the men have their backs to the camera, but the other three faces are visible from the side. One of them reaches into a box and pulls out a huge gun to inspect. A gun no regular civilian would have access to.

Something catches my eye. "Wait." I pause the video and zoom in on the shelf nearest the group. These boxes are labelled.

Nikki looks at me with ocean-wide eyes, seeing it too. "*Impenetra*," she breathes. "The box Lizzy hid all of this in. That's where it was from. Coincidence?"

I pull out my phone to do a Google search, still unable to place why that name sounds so familiar.

Their website comes up. I read their description. "At *Impenetra,* we design and manufacture high-performance storage solutions built to withstand the harshest conditions." I gesture to the iPad. "Doesn't say anything about firearms. How convenient."

She looks over my shoulder as I swipe through their website, and I get a nose-full of her laundry detergent and citrus scent, a splash of vanilla in there today too. "Click the 'About Us.' Maybe we can match some of the faces in the video with names."

When the page loads, I know immediately why this name sounded so familiar.

I read the names of the executives aloud. "Derrick Shaw, Logan Pierce, Grant Holloway, and Marcus *Mackenzie*."

Nikki gives me a look when I emphasize the final name, knowledge flashing in her eyes. "Mackenzie? Isn't that—?"

I nod, feeling an eerie feeling grow inside me like an ooze. "I know why this name sounded familiar now. Marcus Mackenzie is Roger Mackenzie's father. Roger was a key witness in my last case."

"Small world." She shivers, and I resist the urge to do the same. "Do you think they're connected?"

I don't answer right away, my brain going into sonic speed.

There are notable similarities between the cases that I can't ignore. Albert Jimenez from season two was connected with Roger Mackenzie, and he's dead now. Lizzy had this video of the Mackenzie family business, and she's dead now (well, hopefully not actually). Then add Ciphered Voyager, and now Roger Mackenzie is dead too. Are the Mackenzies the common denominator? Does Albert's killer, Frank Holt, have something to do with this case too?

Does Ciphered?

I had guessed Ciphered Voyager just didn't want Roger to testify in Albert's trial, that maybe he has some relation or friendship with Frank Holt, and that's why he wants me to stop investigating so bad. Until now, I had never even considered that Ciphered could be connected to the Sinclairs too. Because why does he want me to stop the podcast so badly? What doesn't he want me to find?

The Mackenzie coincidence is too big to ignore. What's the connection here?

"There's a reason Ciphered wants you to stop. It's probably because you're on to something," George had said.

I can't tell Nikki any of this. I can't tell her about Ciphered because then I'd have to tell her I'm using her for George's ransom money.

The realization comes to me slowly like a sunrise over the horizon:

If Ciphered Voyager is somehow connected to the Sinclair case too, that means solving this is the answer to more than I thought. Solve this case, out Ciphered Voyager, save George and Tina, help Nikki, help Lizzy if she's out there somewhere, too. It could be the answer to *everything.*

No shadows for an anon to hide in, no ransom to pay. No deceit or using good people for their family's money necessary.

I stand up, and Vinnie lifts his head curiously, half asleep. "I should—"

I'm interrupted by shouts from downstairs.

Nikki jumps to her feet, letting the iPad fall onto the armchair. She's already in the hallway, and Vinnie and I race after her.

It's her aunt's night nurse, wearing a frown of unmistakable concern.

Nikki flies down the stairs two-by-two. "What happened?"

"Her levels are dropping critically low. We need to call it in."

Nikki pats her pockets wildly, but her phone is back in the theater. I toss her mine.

"Thank you." She dials 9-1-1.

I return to the theater to retrieve the iPad. With the

threats from Ciphered, I don't trust any evidence like this to be left lying around

When I come back downstairs—iPad, Lizzy's journal, Mr. Sinclair's burner, and Nikki's phone in hand—she is holding her aunt hand in her suite.

All due respect to her aunt, but I'm a bit relieved Nikki has somewhere to go tonight, somewhere public and monitored, where Ciphered probably won't venture into.

Nikki sees me peeking in from the doorway and comes out, shutting the door gently behind her. "The ambulance is on its way." Her voice quivers.

"Is she okay?"

She presses her lips together. "I don't know. We had an episode like this a few months ago. I thought I was going to lose her then, but she pulled through."

"And she will again. She's a fighter, I can tell." I give her the most reassuring smile I can muster. I hand her phone to her, and she gives me mine, though I struggle to take it with everything in my hands.

Nikki looks at the bundle I'm holding, confused. "Oh. You didn't have to do that. I could've cleaned it up later."

How do I burst her naïve little bubble in the most minimally jerkish way possible?

"You need to be more careful with this stuff," I tell her, handing it all over. "I'm happy to keep it secured myself if you want, but you can't leave it lying around. This is our only evidence so far."

"In the safety of my own house?" she challenges, eyebrow quirked.

I blow out an exasperated breath, pushing my hair up and out of my eyes in frustration. "Do you have to argue everything? Now that your family's killer likely knows we're doing the case, you think they're going to happily stand aside and let you? You're in more danger now than ever. Just be careful, okay?"

A frown pulls at her lips as that sinks in, and I'm satisfied. Good. She needs to realize this is the reality of the other side of investigative work. The dangerous side. This is real-time real life, not something she can chime into and listen when she feels like it or pause when it gets too scary. This is real.

"Fine," she says stubbornly. "But only because of my own will to live, not because you asked me to."

"Will to live? You have the survival instincts of a baby bird."

"What I'm hearing is I'm tiny and adorable." She lifts her chin in that infuriatingly prissy way she does.

My jaw ticks with growing annoyance. *For George. For Tina.* "Do you know you're very stubborn?"

"Thank you, I inherited it with the house."

I feel a renewed sense of urgency to get this case done as soon as possible so I can be done with this maddening princess.

I swallow down anything that could potentially be ransom-money-ruining before saying, "I think we should keep the videos to ourselves for now." I nod to the iPad.

She tucks it under her arm and nods. "What should I be doing?"

I give her a look. "You should probably ask your fiancé a few questions."

"I was afraid you were going to say that." She grimaces. "How does someone casually ask, 'Hey so by the way did you know your dad beats your mom?'"

I mimic her tone to add, "And also, just wondering, did your dad happen to murder my family?'"

She shakes her head with confidence. "No. There's no way. I'm not excusing the abuse, but he's not a murderer. I can't see a motive there that makes sense to me."

I shrug, keeping a lot of thoughts to myself with a practiced amount of restraint. "We can't rule anyone out. Do you know how to record a phone call? Record every incoming and outgoing call from here on out. All of them. And tell me if Lizzy texts you again."

"Okay—"

An approaching siren blares outside, and the glow of blue and red grows as it makes its way down the drive. Nikki sparks into action, hurrying to secure the evidence items in a backpack she pulls from the nearest coat closet, while the nurse prepares her aunt for transport.

I whistle to Vinnie and grab my coat and equipment from the dining room.

"Stay close," I tell Vinnie as we make a quiet exit. "Don't get in anyone's way."

I toss my stuff in the back, load in Vinnie, and as I'm about to pull away, my phone vibrates with an incoming call.

It's George. I check the clock. It's almost ten o'clock here, so even later for his time-zone. I hope this means he found something on Ciphered.

"Tell me you got this guy," I say, skipping the 'hello.'

The reply is a surprise. Female.

"Kieran." There is a tremble in her voice that makes the hair on my arms stick straight up.

"Tina?"

She breaks down into a muffled sob. "He's gone, Kieran. George is dead."

25

NIKKI

SAY THE WORD, I HAVE THE MATCHES

I know ambulances are lifesaving emergency vehicles and aesthetics aren't their top priority, but can't they make them at least a little homier? A little less cold and coffin-like?

They just aren't much for encouraging hope. Maybe it would feel less like sure death if they offered you a cozy blanket or even a smile. Lit a candle or something? These are the thoughts I have as I sit in the back with my aunt, teeth chattering, feeling like I've already lost her, begging her to hold on a little longer.

I only had time to grab the closest bag and coat before the ambulance arrived, and per Kieran's—annoying but probably wise—advice, I've stuffed everything that could be potentially evidence-related in it, and I'm keeping it on my body at all times.

So, I feel... heavy.

Not only because of the extra very important items I'm lugging around (no pressure), but mentally and emotionally too.

After discovering my dad's affair, watching all those

terrible videos, Hunter's parents, and now this... I don't know how much more I can take. There has to be a limit at some point, right? Like when you've reached a certain threshold, the universe says, 'Okay we can give her a break now.' Right?

We finally get admitted into a room, and I'm numb as they hook Aunt Wren up to more machines and monitors. I hoped we'd never have to be back here after her last episode. It was scary, but it ended so hopeful, with around-the-clock homecare and the promise of treatment soon.

But now here we are again.

Will they even let me make any decisions about her care since I'm still a minor? Will they deem her a lost cause, and let her die here?

She has more fight in her. I know she does.

I will try to get them to schedule the surgery. They can send me a bill, they can take my house, I don't care. They can do that in emergency situations like this, right?

When I find Lizzy, we can pay it all back.

I refuse to let her die.

Since it's the middle of the night, and the specialists don't get in until morning, we've been mostly left alone. Nurses come in occasionally to check on her and make sure she's still alive. They offer a polite greeting, occasional pity. I've been in and out of sleep, curled up in the stiff chair I dragged over to her bed, so I can still hear her breathing. It's cold in here, and the scratchy blanket a nurse handed me is basically useless.

I wish Aunt Wren didn't have to be back here, but at least she's safe.

If what Kieran said is true—that my family's killer could know we're reviving the case—I'm glad she's out of that house. I would never forgive myself if something happened to her because I opened this investigation back up.

Soft warm hues of morning peek in through the curtains, dragging me officially from my troubled, patchy sleep. With a sigh, I get up to check my phone.

6:43 AM.

Same time in Vancouver. Hunter is probably wrapping up his morning run about now.

I hesitate before pressing the call icon. He will be alarmed to hear from me this early, considering it's usually my preference to stay up way too late and wake up way too late.

I'm nervous to bring up his dad. That's already a topic he hates under normal circumstances.

But I have to. If he doesn't already know about this incident in the elevator, he should. If he does know... well, at least I can have a friend with a common experience—dads who do crappy things to their moms.

I also desperately miss him.

The past few days have been so busy with the case that we've barely talked, apart from scattered texts here and there that I answer when I can. It's like we've been playing tag and barely missing each other.

I exhale and steady myself as the phone dials. He picks up on the second ring.

"Nik?" He's breathless. Maybe he hasn't finished his run yet, after all.

His voice brings instant warmth to my cold insides. Instant sunshine to the darkness I've been feeling being back in this place. Life to a place with so much death. Warm comfort to the chilling fear.

"Hi." And I'm in tears before I can even help it, like a dam has cracked. But they are tears of relief, almost, tears that I've held in so tightly, but now I'm safe to let them go because he's here, he's listening.

I grab the evidence bag, step out of the room, and find a quiet secluded corner in an empty hallway. I press my back against the wall and sink down onto the floor, pulling my knees and the backpack close to my chest.

There is a shuffling on the other side as he switches his phone off Bluetooth, the muffled sound of city noises and wind blaring into my ears. "What's wrong?"

I try to get a handle on the tremble in my voice. "My aunt is back in the hospital. They've been stabilizing her and trying to figure out next steps."

"I'm so sorry, Nikki. What can I do to help?"

"A hug would be nice," I say with a small laugh.

"I'll book a flight."

It's a joke, but my spirits raise a little at the thought, like pure concentrated hope being injected straight to my veins.

I sigh, unable to keep any form of a secret from him. "Do you want to call me back when you can? Somewhere... private. We found out something you should know."

"What is it? I can talk. I'm just on my run route, there's no one around."

"Are you sure? I don't want to disturb your run."

"You're freaking me out, Nikki. What's up?"

"It's a long story, but that clue you figured out?" I fidget with the straps of the backpack nervously. "The one about the creek? Well, it led us to Lizzy's iPad. There are tons of videos on there. Like bad videos. They're freaky, Hunter. So many awful videos of people doing terrible things. I have no idea how she got them."

"Are you serious?" He blows out a muffled breath that

mixes with the blare of the wind. "Damn. Are they people you know?

I grimace. "That's the thing... one of them is actually of your dad."

There's a tense silence on the other end that makes my stomach clench. "Doing what?" he finally asks dully, as if he already knows.

I rip the Band-Aid off the rest of the way. There's no sugarcoating this, anyway. "It's a video of him hurting your mom in an elevator. I'm so sorry. Did you know?"

Another pause. "Did he see the video?"

"Your dad?"

Hunter's reply is thick, and it catches me off guard. "Your little detective."

"Kieran? I mean, yeah, it's all relevant to the case since Lizzy had them. Why...?" I'm confused by his reaction. Shouldn't this anger be directed toward his dad? Kieran has done nothing wrong.

"If you want to bring him into your family's private business, that's your choice, but he needs to stay out of mine."

"So, you did know about this?" My voice is smaller than I want it to be.

I have no right to feel betrayed. He's right, it's *his* family's business. I just really thought we told each other everything. How could he know something like this and not tell me?

There is another long silence. "It's why I haven't moved out." He sighs. "I won't leave her alone with him."

"Why won't she leave him? Or call the cops?"

He laughs mirthlessly. "Your guess is as good as mine. I've been begging her to leave him for years. She refuses."

"I'm so sorry, Hunter." I wish I could reach through the

phone and hug him. "But you can trust Kieran, I promise. We aren't telling anyone about the videos for now."

"What do you mean *for now*?" There's an edge to his tone.

I reply quickly to reassure him, trying not to take it personally. He's just being protective of his mom. "Well, we have to figure out how they're even connected to the case. But I'll ask Kieran to let you decide how you want to handle your parents' video."

"Nik, I really don't think you should be working with this guy." Reluctance wraps around the words, almost like it's something he's been wanting to say for a while but has held back. "I just have a bad feeling about it."

"What? Why?"

A breeze picks up on his side of the line, and it blows in my ear. "Listen, I wasn't going to bring it up, because you were so sure about him, but I saw some things about him on Reddit..."

"What things?"

I scour my brain, trying to think of what he could have seen. I'm very active on true crime forums. I remember some people during season one accusing him of invading the family's privacy for 'clout,' but now that he's solved two consecutive cases, a lot of the negative comments have stopped. As far as I could tell, he has a good online reputation. Should I have done more digging?

"Some people are saying he has a ton of unpaid gambling debts." And then he rushes to add, "Which doesn't really affect you necessarily because, I mean, I assume he does the cases for free since his podcast is monetized, so I'm sure he won't ask you for money, but be careful. I don't trust him."

It's like my very voice has been plucked straight from my throat. Like Ursula herself has snatched it away for herself.

My silence must be telling because Hunter's tone shifts. "He hasn't asked you for money... right?"

I don't answer. I don't know how to.

"Nikki." I know if I could see him, he'd be face-palming right now. His disappointment in me nearly kills me. "Tell me you didn't give him money."

"No!" I protest. I'm so glad he can't see the hot blush spreading across my cheeks. "I haven't given him a penny."

Which is true... I haven't given him a penny *yet.*

I feel so dumb I could cry. Why didn't I even question why Kieran would need me to pay *him* to do the case? Let alone two hundred thousand dollars?

He doesn't care about this case. He just needed me to settle his debts.

Humiliated tears burn in my eyes.

"I should probably—" My sentence is interrupted by three consecutive *dings* from my phone. I peel it away from my cheek to look at the screen.

My breath hitches.

Three new texts from Unknown. Two videos.

"Hunter," I breathe.

"What, what is it?" Hunter voice is distant. I switch the call to speakerphone so I can open my messages.

"I got two videos from that Unknown number claiming to be Lizzy," I whisper, instinctively looking around to make sure the hallway I'm sitting in is still empty.

I read the accompanying text aloud quietly, "'I am trapped. I need help.'"

I press play on the first video, fearing the worst after all the awful videos I've already had to watch in the last few hours that are seared into my eyelids forever.

I hold my breath as booted feet in dim lighting come to life, crunching on deep snow. The video pans upwards, showing that the area is completely surrounded by thick forest, a faint sunset almost entirely dipping below a distant snow-covered mountain range.

The video ends. "That's it?" I huff frustratedly. Why does everything have to be a puzzle?

"What was it?" Hunter asks, and I jump a little at the sound. I forgot he was still on the line.

"A video of someone walking in snow. Trees around. Maybe I'm supposed to recognize the place?"

"Send it to me," he suggests.

I press play on the second video, which is almost the same, but instead of panning upwards, this one turns to the left side, showing a brief and blurred glimpse of a corner of a building before it ends.

I groan. "Is it so hard to send a location pin, Lizzy?"

But she's right to be suspicious. To be careful. She was so careful with the iPad and all those videos, and yet she still ended up dead. *Dead but alive. She has to be alive...*

I want to crawl into a hole myself after watching all those videos, and no one even knows I have them. I pat the bag close to my chest instinctively, assuring myself that the iPad is still safely inside.

I send the videos to Hunter, the message delivering with a *swoosh*. "Do you recognize this place?"

He shuffles with his phone. It's quiet as he watches the videos.

"No," he says slowly, almost like there's a question mark after it.

"No?"

"Hold on, let me watch it again. I could be wrong..."

I wait in fidgety anticipation.

"The mountain... Googling it now to double check..." he finally says. And then more confidently, "Yeah, okay, that's Mount Rainier, isn't it?"

My jaw drops to the floor. "You're some kind of expert on American mountain ranges now? How could you possibly know that?"

"Nikki, Mount Rainier is literally an active volcano, and it's right by you, how do *you* not know that?"

Can there be one single solitary moment today where I don't feel like a complete idiot?

"I know what Mount Rainier is... but it looks like literally every other mountain," I grumble as I peck that location into my maps app. "That's only two hours from here."

"And? You're just going to march through a National Park in the snow until you find a corner of a building that looks like the one in the video?"

"If you found out your dead sister could be alive, she's saying she needs help, *and* sends you her location, wouldn't you?"

"I don't have a sister."

I push myself off the ground with an exasperated huff. He's joking, but I'm not in the mood right now. It's been too long of a day.

"I need to go check on my aunt. I'll talk to you later."

"Don't do anything dumb," he warns. "Seriously Nikki, don't try to go there all alone. It's a suicide mission in this season. If you really want to go check it out, wait for me. I'll see if I can book a flight."

He doesn't give me a chance to reply before doubling down. "Promise me?"

I chuckle. "If you insist."

"And at least consider cutting ties with the shady detective?"

"If you actually book a flight to come help me, I'll consider it."

But do I mean it? Shady or not, can I do this without Kieran?

I disconnect the call and step back into my aunt's hospital room, which is silent except for the beeps of the monitors and her haggard oxygen-infused breaths.

I drop down onto the armchair with a heavy sigh, feeling stupid and hurt and exhausted and embarrassed *and furious.* I put my elbows on my knees and hang my head for a minute, trying to comb through all the muddled-up thoughts, so I can make a plan. Figure out what to believe and what to do about it.

If I find out Kieran did just use my family's case for money, his podcast will go up in flames.

I have the match ready and waiting.

PODCAST TRANSCRIPT
Secrets in Ice Season 3, Episode 4: The Cover-Up

[Secrets in Ice opening theme music plays]

KIERAN BERGSTROM:

In a case like the Sinclairs', the most obvious question was: Who would want them gone? But as I dug deeper into the original investigation, another question began to loom even larger. Not just, "Who killed them?"

But also: "Who has the most to lose the more we dig?"

Looking for answers among the shadows of the iciest cold cases, I'm your host Kieran Bergstrom, and you're listening to *Secrets in Ice.* This is episode four, "The Cover-Up."

[Secrets in Ice opening theme finishes playing over crowd chatter, press camera shutters clicking]

SHERIFF DEPARTMENT SPOKESPERSON *[archival recording]*:

At this time, we believe the tragic vehicle accident of the Sinclair family is unrelated to any larger criminal activity. We're following up on all leads, but there is no cause for alarm in the community.

CHANNEL 12 NEWS ANCHOR *[archival recording]*:

The Thurston County Police Department is urging residents not to spread unverified information about the Sinclair case. Officials say they will not be releasing photographs of the crash site at this time, citing, 'respect for the family and integrity of the investigation.'

[a beat, as suspenseful music plays]

KIERAN BERGSTROM:

When I first requested the police incident reports from the Thurston County Police Department in Washington, since that was where the crime happened and they would have the jurisdiction, they told me the case had been transferred. It's not completely unusual for there to be a change of venue, especially if the next of kin in the case is a minor and resides in a different state.

But what I found strange was that when I contacted Portland City Police Department to access the file that was now in their care, I was denied. In fact, the entire department and original investigating team refused to speak to me at all.

[sound of phone dialing]

KIERAN BERGSTROM:

Hi Denise, thank you for speaking with me today. Icers, this is Denise Marlowe, a reporter for the Sapphire Pines Chronicle who originally reported on the Sinclair story. Tell the listeners what you told me about the crime scene photos.

DENISE MARLOWE:

Ugh it still makes me so mad. My article was one of the first to report on the Sinclair murders because I have a contact in Thurston County where it happened. I obtained my own crime scene photos and everything. But they made me take it down.

KIERAN BERGSTROM:

Who did?

DENISE MARLOWE:

The investigative team. The department called my editor and told him I needed to turn over the photos I had, that the crime scene was 'confidential.' He said that I was 'stirring up fear,' and the family wanted privacy. My access completely dried up after that. Nobody at the station would talk to me, and my editor wouldn't run any more of my stories on the case.

[suspenseful music plays]

26

KIERAN
MESSAGE RECEIVED

Vinnie nudges me with his snout. I ignore him. I ignore the beeps on my CGM. I've been frozen here in the driver's seat for who knows how long. An hour? Three? I can't move.

I don't want to move.

I want to decompose with the van. Let the earth swallow me whole. Even buried alive would be fine.

Anything would be better than this.

It's a hollowness, a chasm. One that's evolving, growing where there's no room to grow, like an invasive species, a chemical spill leaking out into an ecosystem, destroying everything in its path.

Impossible to tiptoe around. Impossible to breathe. Move. Even cry.

It's a paralyzing abyss. One I wish I could give myself over to.

George is gone.

And it's my fault.

Roger wasn't innocent. He made his choices and made

his own enemies. So, with him, I used that anger as fuel to work harder. It was motivation to seek justice, to push on.

George, however, was completely innocent.

He wasn't even directly on this case. Not even a threat.

Only a means to send a message.

Well, message received.

You want me to quit so bad, Ciphered? Fine. You win.

Nothing matters anymore.

I WAKE to the persistent sound of my phone buzzing, clattering against spare change in the cupholder. My cheek is pressed against the steering wheel, and Vinnie snoozes with his snout in my lap. Early hues of morning brighten the sky around me. I guess I slept longer than I thought. My neck is stiff enough to account for that.

I don't move, ignoring the incoming call until it stops, not wanting to deal with anything right now. But then it starts up again.

I groan. Vinnie stirs at my movement as I reach to pick it up, rubbing at my eyes as the caller ID comes into focus.

The name on the screen makes my throat tighten. George Marshall.

It's not him. It can never be him again.

So seeing his name pop up on my screen is a stark reminder of the loss. The guilt.

My fault.

It must be Tina. She ended the call last night in a hurry to speak to the police.

I hesitate before answering.

I don't know if I can face her, knowing what I've taken from her. Knowing I'm the reason George is dead.

If I would have taken down my stupid podcast, Tina would still have the love of her life.

The call ends.

But then it lights up again, a third time.

I slide the icon over to accept the call, swallowing hard. "Hello?"

"Hey, hun, it's Tina."

The undeniable sorrow in her voice kills me. I hate myself for doing this to her.

"How are you?" I rasp. What a stupid thing to ask. *She's having the worst day of her life, idiot.*

She sniffs. "Oh, you don't mind me, sweetheart. I just had a feeling I needed to give you another call. Check on you."

I choke down a sob that threatens to escape. "I'm so sorry, Tina. This is all my fault."

"Don't you even think that. I told George to go to the police right away, but that old mule insisted he wanted to do it his way." She chuckles sadly. "Always so stubborn."

"All the anon wanted me to do was take my podcast down. If I would have listened, he could still be alive," I insist.

Her being so understanding hurts worse somehow. Yell at me, Tina. Tell me I'm an awful person. Hurt me like I deserve.

"Do you know how many near misses he's had over the years doing this job?" She laughs. How can she laugh? "How many dangerous people he's gone toe-to-toe with and somehow come out unscathed? You can only evade destiny for so long, and he's been slipping out of the Reaper's reach for years. He chose this life. He *loved* this life. If he could pick how to go out, he'd pick it this way every time."

Hot tears streak down my cheeks. Vinnie lies his head back in my lap with a soft whine. He hates to see me cry.

My throat is too tight to reply. I don't know what to say anyway.

"I need you to promise me something, Kieran," Tina says firmly. "You can't quit this."

I open my mouth to protest, but she cuts me off.

"I need you to find out who did this. For George. For me. But also, for the Sinclair girl. From what George told me, that girl needs someone who won't give up on her."

That hits me hard, as someone who was given up on, left behind by everyone who claimed to care about me.

"That's why we need people like you and George, Kieran," Tina continues. "The justice system fails more victims than it helps sometimes. I've seen it so often from the people George worked with over the years. You have a talent for this, and people need you. They deserve justice. They deserve peace."

All the insecurities I've felt about this case, the imposter syndrome, the doubts that I can even solve this, all come bubbling to the surface and settle like a vise clamping down on my neck.

I can barely choke out the words. "What if I can't, Tina?"

"Then you get up and keep trying until you can, hun," she replies gently. "Don't give up on George. Find us answers."

I mean, how can I argue with that? I blow out a breath, wiping the moisture from my eyes and cheeks. "You have to promise *me* you'll stay safe, though. Do you have somewhere you can go?"

"Yes, honey, I'm safe. Don't you worry about me."

"Okay. Good. Please be careful until I can find out who this psycho is."

"One more thing." Tina pauses, hesitating. "A text came in from George's contact that may or may not help."

I perk up. "Really?"

"From what I understand of the text exchange, they found security camera footage and picked up a license plate number of that van of men that beat him up. No videos of the attack, unfortunately, but they found an angle of the van waiting around the corner."

My breath stills in anticipation.

"How do I screenshot this?" Her voice gets muffled as she pulls away from the phone. "I'll send this over to you if I can figure out how to do that. I'm sure you'll understand it better than me. It looks like they traced the plate, and it led back to a fleet belonging to an organization located in Washington state." She stumbles over the name, "Ae—? *Aetherline?*"

My phone dings as the screenshot comes through.

"I'll also send you the number of George's contact in case you have any other questions."

"Thank you, Tina," I say with awe. "I don't deserve your kindness. I'm so sorry again for George. He was a great man."

"He was," she agrees affectionately, that sorrow coming through again, and I'm amazed she can even keep it together right now, let alone lend comfort to someone else. "And so are you. You deserve it all and more. Keep up the good work, sweetheart."

The call disconnects, and I cry a little bit more. Tears of guilt but also tears of gratitude. That Tina thought to reach out to me at all. I don't know if I've ever been shown that kind of kindness before. A tenderness that even my own mother never showed. It makes that growing, hollowed-out chasm in my chest a little bit smaller. That someone cared.

I swivel my seat around to grab a tissue from my kitchen counter and blow my nose. I spend a second reassuring Vinnie that I'm okay, and he perks up with relief. Then he leaves to get an apple juice carton and drops it gently in my lap. He must have known I wouldn't have accepted it before.

I feel a little numb as I sip the juice. Exhausted from the crying. A headache brewing from my forehead's quality time with the steering wheel.

I'm furious that this happened to George.

But now there is a miniscule glimmer of determination flickering inside me. A tiny spark of resolve to solve this for Tina, to get justice for George.

A promise made to a kind old woman to not give up.

So that's what I'll do.

I stand up as if that decision alone will be what fuels the spark into a flame, what gets the momentum going, but I just kind of look around for a second, not sure where to go from here. Mentally, emotionally, with the case, with my life, physically with my van... I never even pulled out of Nikki's driveway.

Fresh snow surrounds me, covering her entire property like a white blanket, and I dread that I'll have to shovel myself out to drive anywhere, but that's a problem I'll deal with later. I'm sure she wouldn't mind if I camped in the driveway for now.

I get my hot water heating in the kettle, take a few human and Husky moments by a nearby tree, stabilize my blood sugar, shove the sadness deep, deep down, and get to work.

27

KIERAN

SPEED LIMITS ARE JUST SUGGESTIONS

A text from Nikki a couple hours later pulls me from my work, which all feels very pointless and unimportant, but I'm trying to make do on my promise to Tina. I've been editing the latest podcast episode, getting it ready for upload. It's something that always takes at least ten times longer than I expect. You never realize how many times you say the word 'um' until you record yourself speaking.

I get to a stopping point and open Nikki's text.

NIKKI

where are you? I need to talk to you

Nothing like the good ol' "we need to talk" text. An irritability settles in my gut, latching onto the hollowed-out space for George that is much a piece of me now as my organs. I don't know if I can take a run in with an annoying spoiled princess today.

"Out and about," I lie, sending it off with a *swish*.

NIKKI

[location pin]

KIERAN

I'll see if I can fit you into my calendar.

No answer, so I assume she's laughing too hard to reply.

I click the pin, and the address to the hospital she's at with her aunt loads. It's twenty-eight minutes away. I groan.

Part of me considers not showing up at all. Maybe I can ghost her and pull all the episodes down quietly. George is already dead. Without that desperation for the ransom money hanging over my head, not having to deal with Nikki's frustrating stubbornness is sounding more and more appealing.

I SLIDE OPEN the van door as she approaches. She hesitates before stepping up, eyeing the inside warily. Vinnie's butt wiggles so hard at the sight of her he nearly knocks me out of the van.

"I feel like you should be asking me to help you find your dog or offering me candy or something," she says, at least thoughtful enough to dust the snow off her boots before stepping in and greeting a wiggling Vinnie.

"What does it say about you that I didn't have to offer

anything?" I reply flatly, unable to even fake a smile or cheery attitude right now. *Fire me, go ahead, please.*

I slide the door shut, shivering at the freezing breeze that followed her in. I gesture to the passenger seat that is already flipped around in social mode. She doesn't sit, only clutches her bag tighter as if I'm going to rob her.

She looks around with a frown I can't quite decipher, and I suddenly feel like I want to shrivel into myself. I rarely have guests in my van.

It feels... intimate. Like I'm stripping off a layer of my soul and baring it for her to see. I'm way too exposed.

I give an awkward cough as I kick a stray dirty sock into Vinnie's coop, hoping she didn't notice it.

"What?" I finally ask her after a tense silent moment, uncomfortable with the analysis she's conducting on my home.

She meets my eyes, and I still can't quite make out what she's thinking. She's almost... disappointed?

"It's different in here than I expected. When someone tells you they live in their van, you expect sleeping bags and top ramen. This is" –she clears her throat— "um, it's... cleaner than I thought it would be."

"Right. How surprising a mere peasant would take pride in his humble belongings."

She crosses her arms, a frown forming. "It just looks like it cost a lot of money to get it like this."

Why does that seem like an accusation?

Vinnie is oblivious to the increasing tension and is over-joyed to have her in his home. He's brought over about four of his chew toys and has piled them at her feet while we've been talking.

"I did most of the work myself," I reply a little defensively because why is it any of her business how much I spent on my van? Hypocritical, if you ask me, considering she lives in a sickeningly excessive castle and the boots she's currently wearing likely cost several hundred dollars, maybe more, I have no idea.

There is a brief silence as she stares me down. Now I'm getting impatient.

"Why don't you just say what you came here to say, Heiress? You clearly have something on your mind."

She takes the permission and runs with it, the anger crossing over her countenance like lava. "Fine. Is it true you only took my case to settle a debt?"

I rear back like she's slapped me, like she's taken her lava and chucked it at me.

"What?" is all I can muster, a sharp, clawing sensation piercing my chest. How did she find out about the ransom? Did Ciphered Voyager contact her too? Is he going to target her next?

"I can't believe he was right." She shakes her head with an outraged laugh. My body language must be the only confirmation she needs. "You used me for money."

I can't meet her eyes. The slimy guilt I've felt all along about doing this to her bubbles over now that it's exposed, coating it in a mixture of relief and dread. "I had no choice."

"You had no choice," she repeats incredulously, her eyes full of blue blazing fire. She points at me sharply like she's wielding a dagger. "You took advantage of my desperation and used me. *You* made that choice. Did you do this to the other families you 'helped' too?"

"What, no, of course—"

"So I was just the perfect target to get you out of the hole you got yourself in."

My brows furrow. I pause. What is she even talking about? "Okay now I don't know—"

My words are cut off by a *crack* that reverberates off my cabinets.

I whip my head around as another one comes from behind. I stare in shock at the hole in my back windshield.

Bullet hole.

"Is someone shooting at us?!" Nikki shrieks, crouching down with her bag and pulling Vinnie into her. "We're at a *hospital!*"

"Stay low!" I order as another one cracks. I squat and swing the driver's seat around. My chest seizes and turns to stone when I look out the front windshield.

A group of masked men are closing in on all sides, popping off shots with handguns as they get closer.

Ciphered's men have found me again. And it looks like they're more prepared this time.

"Hold on!" I yell.

The rear windshield explodes, shards of glass flying everywhere.

Nikki screams.

I fumble with the ignition as the men get closer. I slam it in drive and peel away, tires screeching on the pavement of the parking lot, which is slippery with dirty slush.

I slide on an icy spot and nearly hit a couple of the men, who have to dive out of the way as I speed past. Bummer I don't have better aim.

More shots *clank* off my exterior, and I roar in fury. "Leave my van alone!"

"Wait! My aunt! I can't just leave her here!"

"She's in the safest place she can be right now."

I've nearly made it to the exit, keeping my eye on the

men in the rearview mirror as I swerve around pedestrians and giant piles of snow that have been plowed into corners, dodging obstacles like I'm in one of those racing arcade games.

The men hop into their own van (the same windowless white one as before, the one that tried to abduct me when I was meeting George the other day). They're hurrying to follow us.

I have to lose them before they get in motion.

I take a curb at full speed, and we're nearly airborne for a moment before crashing back down onto the other side, the tires struggling to catch on the pavement. I drift for a heart-stopping second before I gain traction back.

I'm on the main road now, and I take the closest right, weaving in and out of cars.

"Take a left at Belmont!" Nikki yells, plopping into the backwards passenger seat and fumbling with the seatbelt.

I obey, flying through a nearly red light, horns from the cars around me blaring furiously. "Why?"

"They won't follow us into a police station!" She holds out her phone to show me that she has navigation in progress.

I eye the rearview mirror, wincing as the van flies right through the now fully red light and nearly collides with three other cars.

Vinnie materializes over my shoulder, and I reach behind me to pat his head. "Vinnie, nook," I tell him as I jerk the steering wheel sharply to avoid a turning car.

He lolls his tongue out to drool on my shirt before obeying. Guess I deserve that.

"Who are they? Are they after us because of the case?"

Nikki eyes are wide as she watches them out the shattered back window.

I increase my speed as the van gets closer, having to cut off several honking cars. "Sorry!" I wave at them uselessly.

I give Nikki a sidelong glance. "Not entirely."

She gasps, reaching over to punch my shoulder. "Is this your bookie?!"

"First of all, ow," I say, rubbing my shoulder and glaring at her. "Secondly... bookie?"

I'm more confused than ever.

"First you manipulate me into giving you money to pay off your gambling debts and then you put me in direct danger with your debt collectors?!" Her shrieking has risen to octaves that nearly reach dog whistle frequencies. Even Vinnie tucks himself deeper into his nook at the sound.

"Okay now I *really* don't know what you're talking about!" I throw out my hands in exasperation. "What gambling debt?"

I finally get to a clear stretch of road, so I press the pedal down as far as it goes, the other van getting stuck behind the cars I cut off. My engine groans as my speed increases over ninety miles per hour. Then one hundred.

Nikki gawps at me over her shoulder, because her seat is still backwards, and it's almost comical that we have to argue back-to-back. I should tell her how to swivel it around. Sometime.

"Your debt!" she insists, but less confidently. "Take a left!"

I lurch the steering wheel to obey, but then she screams, "MY LEFT!" and I almost hit a pedestrian in the crosswalk correcting course who justifiably flips me off.

I snatch the phone out of her hand to navigate myself.

"The debt is the reason you made me pay you to do the

case." She sounds like she's trying to convince herself, mostly. "To pay off your gambling debt!"

I scoff a disbelieving laugh. "What? I've never gambled a day in my life. All the money I have, I've worked for. Plus, most places around here, you can't gamble until you're twenty-one anyway."

Nikki's mouth snaps shut, and she gets quiet for a moment, which is actually a very welcome change.

No van behind us. I hope this means we lost them.

"So, who are those people then?" she asks with that frustratingly stubborn tone, not looking at me.

"I'll explain later." I obey the GPS and take the next right to fly into the police department's parking lot. I screech to a stop, earning several glares from officers walking into the building. Fortunately, they must be on lunch or something because they don't make a fuss about it.

I roll my window down to poke my head out. Nikki clambers over to kneel on my seat next to me and look around, too. Her closeness catches me off guard. Her citrus scent has a hint of hospital antiseptic today. A tingling sensation torrents over my skin at her proximity and fuses with my frustration at her to create this strange, buzzing electricity.

I jerk her down as the van comes into view. We duck beneath the dash, as if hiding our heads will make my very conspicuous van invisible, sharing the seat as we hold our breaths.

Her face is right in front of mine on the other side of the steering wheel, so close I swear I can hear her heart pounding. We stay frozen, waiting to find out what the van will do. She licks her lips nervously, which makes me suddenly realize how close her lips are, which is an irrelevant and ill-timed observation I shove away quickly for the sake of focusing.

I peek over the steering wheel. The van slows right in front of the entrance to the parking lot. Then it speeds off down the road and out of sight.

I whoop, and Nikki pops up, looking for herself.

"Are they gone?!"

"They're gone!"

We cheer together, bumping shoulders. Vinnie joins the celebration, spinning in circles and knocking things over in the back.

Nikki snaps out of it quickly, remembering that she's still mad at me. She goes back to her own seat and points at me cuttingly. "*You* have some explaining to do."

28

NIKKI
SERVING, PROTECTING, GASLIGHTING

An hour has passed, and we're still parked in the police station parking lot. We swept up most of the broken glass and taped up some parchment paper he had in his cabinet to the shattered back window. Every now and then I'll get a gust of chilly air, but the heater is cranked, and it's surprisingly comfortable in here.

Kieran made me coffee—which I drank only to be polite because it was very bitter and tasted like something miserable people drink to punish themselves—and then he told me what happened to his PI friend, George.

I've been trying to hide the tears welling up in my eyes as he has told me everything. I came here guns blazing, with Hunter's voice in my head telling me Kieran is a liar and a con-artist. And I hardly know Kieran, I know that. I don't have a lot of experience with people, I know that. People lie, *I know that.*

But as I've pushed Hunter out and truly listened, I believe every word Kieran has told me. The quiver in his words, the guilt engraved into his pores, the pain in the brown of his eyes. You can't fake that.

I stare down at my mug, feeling terrible for flying off the handle at him after he had barely learned about his friend's murder. How quickly I believed the worst about him. A slow but mighty anger is growing inside me about this Ciphered guy. It's terrifying the anonymity technology can give psychopaths. How they can hurt innocent people, both physically and mentally, and then simply retreat back to their shadowed keyboards without any consequences.

"I wish you had told me from the beginning," I whisper to the mug. "Maybe there was something I could've done."

He sets his own empty mug in his little sink and lowers himself back down onto the floor in front of his bed.

"I hardly knew you," he says, bringing his knees up to his elbows. "I didn't know how you'd react, and I didn't want to risk making it worse with Ciphered."

I nod, knowing exactly what he means. I, myself, haven't even gone into all the details about why I'm marrying Hunter, my aunt's treatment, my lack of access to my inheritance... And I thought *he* was the liar? I've used Kieran every bit as much as I accused him of using me.

It's hard not to blurt out everything and come clean, after he's been so vulnerable and honest. But this isn't the right time. It's not about me right now.

"So, your theory is this Ciphered person is somehow connected to my case?" I pull myself in tighter as I get a chilly draft from the broken window.

He shrugs, less sure than I hoped. "That's the only explanation I can think of for why he'd go to these lengths to get me to stop. There must some connection through Roger Mackenzie."

"Well," I say, smacking my knees in finality.

"Well, what?"

"Well, we have work to do. Let's get justice for George. I want this Ciphered guy to rot behind bars."

The corner of his mouth quirks into an almost-smile, and it makes a little warmth flicker in my belly seeing him cheer up again. Well, *his version* of cheer, I suppose.

"Me too," he agrees, and Vinnie comes over and licks my face, so I take that to mean he agrees as well. I chuckle and pat him on the head.

"While we're here we might as well go inside and ask if the case file is ready," I say, while trying to discreetly dump the rest of the awful coffee down the drain behind my back. "They haven't called me, but maybe they forgot."

He smirks, and I guess I'm not as sneaky as I thought. "Too pure of a roast for you?"

"Oh, no it was delicious." I nod my head emphatically. "So good. I love... *earth*... flavor."

"You can ask for sugar next time, you know." He laughs. "I know you have the taste buds of a four-year-old."

"If that's because four-year-olds' palates are very dignified and classy, thank you."

"I think you would melt candy and marshmallows and add that to your coffee if that were an option."

"*Now* someone pulls out his best ideas?" I sniff. "Let's put this energy into detective work now, shall we?"

He does an exaggerated salute. "Roger that. Let's go annoy some civil servants. It's my favorite pastime."

∿

We're waiting in the lobby of the police station. I fiddle with the fabric of the evidence backpack looped around my shoulder. It's chilly, fluorescent, and sterile in here, and it feels a bit like the hospital room my aunt is lying all alone in. The guilt makes me colder, peppering goosebumps all across my arms.

Being in here also makes me feel like I'm in trouble, even though I haven't done anything wrong. I think. I run a diagnostic on my entire life every few minutes to be sure.

The desk officer looked up my request in her system when we came in, and didn't have a very helpful idea of when the file would be available. She said we were welcome to wait, that she'd ask around, though she didn't seem enthusiastic about doing so.

So that's what we've been doing. For thirty minutes now.

She hasn't even been back at her desk for the last twenty. Pretty sure she's avoiding me. I may have visited her desk to check up a few more times than she would have liked, but I have no shame. I'd rather be annoying than give up on my family. And now George and his wife Tina? It feels good to have an extra motivation that doesn't feel as selfish. This justice I'm searching for can do good for someone else too.

Kieran has his headphones on and is editing interviews on his computer, including a phone call he apparently had with Hunter that he won't let me hear. It's driving me crazy. What questions did he ask him? What did Hunter say about me? And why didn't Hunter mention it this morning?

NIKKI

you did an interview with kieran?

HUNTER

I wouldn't exactly call it an interview…

NIKKI

what was it then?

HUNTER

he didn't tell you?

NIKKI

no he won't let me listen to it

HUNTER

did you know he tried to contact my mom?
I told him to leave my family alone

"Sinclair?" The officer's sudden voice startles me out of my phone.

I leap from my seat, the heavy iPad in the bag bouncing off my hip, probably leaving a bruise. Vinnie follows, but he keeps a respectful distance. It's so incredible how well-trained he is. That's a credit to Kieran, I suppose, though I'd never tell him and give ammo to that arrogant smirk of his.

The officer hands me an envelope. "The case file."

I pull out the stack of papers greedily. But then my jaw drops.

I flip through the pages, gaining urgency the more I rifle through them.

"There must be some mistake," I tell her, and she raises an eyebrow.

Kieran joins me at my side and looks over my shoulder. "What?"

I show him the pages. They are almost entirely blacked out. "Almost every word is redacted."

He takes the stack of paper to look for himself.

"That's quite common in an active investigation," the officer says with tone of no-longer-disguised annoyance.

"Active investigation?" I repeat incredulously. "This case has been cold for over ten years."

"There has to be a mistake here," Kieran echoes. "This is Annika Sinclair. This is her immediate family's case. She should have access to way more than" –he gestures to the stack of paper— "whatever this is. Is there a superior in that we can speak to?"

Her annoyance melts quickly into molten anger. "This isn't a Kohl's, sir, you can't just ask to speak to the manager. You're welcome to make an—"

An older white man enters the room from behind the desk, crisp uniform and confident stature, intimidating mustache covering a frown. There's a gold badge sewn on his navy-blue hat that says 'Chief.'

"Is there a problem here?" His stare is so piercing it makes me want to crawl into myself and disappear.

"Yes, there is," Kieran replies, and his eyes flick over to me to make exaggerated eye contact, like he's trying to relay something to me, but I don't know what it is. He's looking back at the police chief again before I've figured anything out.

"This case file is ridiculously redacted," Kieran tells him. "My client is an immediate family member, the next of kin."

The man simply crosses his arms and doubles down. "As Officer Stapley has already explained to your *client*, we can't release any information during an active investigation."

"I was told the case was administratively closed in 2018," I correct in a moment of boldness, momentarily forgetting that I'm terrified of him. I remember again quickly after and shrink back down.

"I think it's a good idea for you to leave." Although the Chief didn't say anything threatening, his timbre carries the threat to us anyway. "We can't help you here, but you're welcome to submit any questions or complaints you have about the case to the IPR for review."

"Would you like their phone number?" Officer Stapley adds smugly, her arms crossed.

Kieran snatches the envelope off the desk, leveling the Chief's stare with one of his own. "I'm sure I don't have to tell you what the penalties are for sabotaging a murder investigation to keep your own secrets hidden, Chief" —he makes a show of reading the name on his nametag— "Hemlock?"

I gape at Kieran.

Is it the lighting or does the Chief pale a little bit? A miniscule twitch in the mustache?

"Excuse me?" he growls.

Kieran looks satisfied. "C'mon Nikki. It's clear they don't want this case solved. It's okay. We'll do it ourselves."

He tosses me the case file, which I fumble with ungracefully for a second before turning on my heel with a *hmmph* to follow him and Vinnie out the door.

The icy outside is even colder than the chilly inside, and we head toward the parking lot. I catch a whiff of delicious fumes from a barbecue smokehouse restaurant a block over, and I get a hungry pang in my stomach. I nearly slip on the ice as I shuffle like a penguin late to work to try to catch up to Kieran.

"Um?!" I call after him. My teeth chatter as I bark a laugh in disbelief. "Talk back to police chiefs often?"

I can't deny that I'm pretty impressed. I was shaking in my boots, but Kieran didn't back down.

"Didn't you recognize him?" he replies over his shoulder, opening up the van to let Vinnie in and the warmth from inside as the generator whirs to life is welcoming. He taps his snowy boots on the side of the van, and I do the same before stepping in.

"No. I don't think so? Why? Do you know him?"

He takes my coat for me, and I shiver, rubbing my palms along my arms as the heater powers up.

"iPad," he instructs.

I pull it from the backpack that is basically a second skin now. Is he implying that the police chief is on one of those videos?

"Fourth video," he adds from the other side of the van, kicking some broken glass we missed out of his way as he hangs up our coats. "I'm ninety-three and a half percent positive."

I swipe over to the video, and sure enough, watch Chief Hemlock fondle two very scantily clad women on his lap, in a room full of other scantily clad women, a gold wedding ring visible on his finger.

29

NIKKI

KNITTING A SCARF WON'T KILL YA

Kieran watches the video over my shoulder haughtily. "I'm so good at this."

I roll my eyes at him. He's right, though.

"He was still wearing the same ring in there," he points out. "So, I'm guessing his spouse doesn't know about his extra-curricular activities."

He pulls out a marker from one of his drawers. He writes 'Timothy Hemlock' on a very organized and tidy whiteboard, in the column titled 'Videos' that so far only has four names on it:

- Nathaniel Mooresbury, attorney general (video 2)
- Marcus Mackenzie, Impenetra (video 21)
- Peter Vanderwaal (video 22)
- Timothy Hemlock, police chief (video 4)

But the other column?

"Wait." I squint at the whiteboard, at his column for 'Other Suspects.' "Why is my aunt's name on that list?"

An uncomfortable grimace pulls on his lips. "You sure you want to know?"

"Know what?" My gut clenches.

He rubs the back of his neck. "I wasn't sure how to tell you this... but did you know you're a voting board member and shareholder of your father's company?"

I shake my head. "Huh? No, I'm not."

"And so is your aunt... It was a pretty big topic of discussion in the comments of the last episode. I got lots of DM's and emails about it too."

My mind whirs. *What?*

"I was hoping you knew," he says, pity darkening the warm brown of his eyes. "I've kept my promise, I haven't questioned her about it, but being appointed a part owner of a billion-dollar business when its CEO suddenly disappears would be a motive worth looking into if it were anyone else... don't you think?"

"If it were anyone else," I agree, shutting down this insinuation right away. "I trust my aunt *whole-heartedly*. I'm sure she had a good reason not to tell me."

But I swallow down the small lump of hurt so before he sees it. I don't know why Aunt Wren would keep something like this from me, and though I trust she must've had her reasons, it still stings. When she's feeling better, that'll definitely be a point of conversation. Until then, I can't dwell on it. I won't.

Luckily Kieran drops the topic, so I take the stack of papers out of the envelope to look through the file again. Maybe it's not as useless as it appeared at first glance. I don't realize I'm sitting on his bed until I notice him staring at me.

"Making yourself at home so soon?" he jokes.

I flush and fidget with the ends of my hair, twirling

them around my finger. I'm trying to think of a witty response to play off the embarrassment, but he lets it go and sits next to me to look at the case file too. I can barely focus on the file now that I've become aware of him next to me. On his bed. Where he sleeps. That I'm sitting on. With him.

I shiver.

He points to a line halfway down the page, and I shake my head to refocus. "They left us the time they arrived on the scene. Generous of them. We can add that to our time-line." He does so on the whiteboard. 2:17pm.

They also left most of the initial 9-1-1 report. A wave of sadness washes over me reading it, having to imagine the scene.

"Car's in bad shape. Doesn't look good," the caller had said.

A sentence further down catches my eye. I read it aloud. "'When asked why they were in a different state than their supposed tournament, a source close to the Sinclair family suggested they may have decided to visit their family cabin instead.'"

That brings a flood of memories I had long forgotten of trips to *a cabin,* but I didn't realize it was *ours.* We only went there a couple times that I can remember, and the images are hazy and vague.

"Family cabin," I whisper in wonder. "I completely forgot about that place. But we only went there a few times that I can remember."

How strange of a place, the mind. Memories, experiences, things the subconscious deems unimportant and then simply cleanses from storage.

"Do you remember where it was?" Kieran asks. "If this

was where they were heading, maybe it would have some answers."

I consider it for a moment. "Yeah, Washington, I think. So that checks out. Maybe my family's lawyer would have the address in our asset file somewhere."

I pull up Michael's number in my contacts and hold my breath as the phone rings. I switch it to speakerphone so Kieran can hear too.

"Offices of Montgomery Law Group, this is Michael."

"Hi, Michael, it's Nikki Sinclair again."

He sounds surprised to hear from me, slightly breathless. "Oh, hello, Miss Sinclair. What can I do for you?"

"Do you know anything about a property in Washington my family would've had around the time of their deaths?"

"Hm. Let me look."

"Thanks."

I wait with bated breath as he clacks on his keyboard, watching Kieran who fidgets with the edge of his bed sheet, plucking out stray threads one by one.

"Just a minute," Michael says, and then the line plays very distorted jazz music. Hold music, really?

I tap my fingers on my knee impatiently.

Michael comes back on the line, and it startles me a bit, like knowing the toaster is going to pop, but it still scares you anyway. Or is that just me? "Miss Sinclair?"

"Yes, I'm still here."

"Okay, so I looked back in the records, and I'm seeing a property your family had the deed for in Rainier, Washington."

"*Mount Rainier?*" I nearly shriek back at him, thinking of the videos Lizzy sent. Kieran looks at me in alarm.

Could this be the connection I needed? Could this be

where Lizzy is? I can feel the hope coming up my throat, bubbling and nearly choking me.

"No, no," Michael corrects, and I deflate. There goes that theory. "That's a common mix-up though. *Mount* Rainier is over an hour away from *Rainier*, Washington."

"Do you have an address?"

"I do," he answers slowly. "But you should know the property was sold years ago."

"Sold? How? Why?"

"Your guardian is able to make certain decision on your behalf like this until you become of age," he explains. "She may have thought it would be better to sell the property. Could have brought up painful memories."

"Does it say who the property was sold to?"

Another clack of keys. "The property was sold on January 3rd, 2017, to a one Peter Vanderwaal."

Kieran and I gape at each other.

Why would my aunt sell the family cabin to Hunter's *dad?*

I forget for a second that Michael is on the line until he speaks again. "Was there anything else you needed, Miss Sinclair?"

"Oh." I shake my head before I remember he can't see me. "No, that's it, I think. Thank you, Michael."

"You're welcome." He speaks hesitantly, as if worried he may offend me, "Um, so I heard on social media that you've hired a podcaster to reopen the case."

"Yes," I reply simply, exhausted to have to justify it to every adult I speak to.

"That's great," he says, surprisingly eager. Huh, I'm used to the people in my life telling me it's a dumb idea. "Have there been any big leads? I love true crime."

"Why don't you give tomorrow's episode a listen, and you can see for yourself," Kieran pipes in. I whack his leg.

Michael sounds embarrassed. "Ah, yes, of course, will do. You two take care now, and good luck."

"Thank you, Michael," I say extra sweetly, giving Kieran a pointed glare to shut up. "Can you text me the address to the property? The Vanderwaals are our good friends. I'm sure they wouldn't mind."

"No problem."

The call ends.

Kieran gets up and walks around the bed to the whiteboard.

"What?" I ask as I follow, glass crunching under my boots.

He pops off a square of paper that was held in place by a magnet in his 'suspects' column. He moves it from the middle of the column to the top and shuffles down the other squares, including one with Hunter's name, which I roll my eyes at. The square at the top now says 'Peter Vanderwaal.' Then he takes Aunt Wren's square and moves it right under that to second place.

I sigh. "Seriously? Sure, it's weird that he bought the property, but I still don't see a motive."

He gives me a look over his shoulder as if it's obvious. "Money?"

"The Vanderwaals are one of the richest families in Vancouver. They don't need our money. The whole Washington coincidence is weird though," I muse, and when Kieran gives me a confused look, I remember I haven't told him about the videos from Lizzy yet.

I quickly catch him up, and he's in the driver's seat before the second video even finishes playing.

"Wait!" I tell him as he turns the key in the ignition. "My aunt! I can't just go to Washington and leave her behind. I have to go back to the hospital. I've already been gone long enough. She needs me."

"Again. There's no safer place she could be right now. I'm sure she has a great team taking care of her. There's really nothing you could be doing there." His face softens. "But I can take you back there if you want."

I look at the whiteboard, the list of suspects ever-growing. Questions that beg to be answered, daring someone to come looking. How long have I been waiting for answers that could be only a state away?

I believe that Lizzy is alive, that she's counting on me. She needs me. Any number of those terrible men from the videos could be after her.

And now George and Tina are counting on us finding answers too? What if the answer to everything is in Washington?

I can't stand by and do nothing, but I can't just leave either. It feels impossible to choose, when I'm equally needed both ways, being stretched both directions limb from limb.

Kieran waits patiently at the wheel for me to decide, nearly glowing like some angelic figure with the promise of the answers I've been searching for.

When I accepted Hunter's proposal, I decided to do things my way, that I would take charge of *my* life. I can't forget that promise to myself. To put on my oxygen mask first, so I can save others.

I told myself I'd do whatever it took to save my aunt. That I would do the hard choice if it meant she could live. But can I save her by leaving her behind, or am I fooling myself?

And would I ever forgive myself if I missed her last moments chasing answers I could possibly never find?

A vivid imagining, almost a vision, comes to my mind of what my aunt would say to me, and for a second, it's like she's here. I imagine her saying, "You can stay here and knit me a scarf, or you can go. Knitting a scarf won't kill 'ya. But wondering what could've been... that might. It'll eat you alive. Ask me how I know."

So, I join Kieran up front, buckling into the passenger seat with the decision. I will find answers for Aunt Wren. For Lizzy. For George and Tina. And for me, too.

Kieran lights up like a boy discovering fire for the first time. I'm sure it's just the prospect of adventure, but it makes me smile too, nonetheless.

"I have to make one call first," I tell him and press the name on my contact.

He answers on the second ring. "Hello?"

"Arrick?" My throat tightens at the sound of his voice, which makes the distance between us feel so far. He's always been one of three people who hold my hand when things get hard, to wipe away my tears. "I need to ask you a favor. I'm so sorry, I know it's your day off."

"You are more important, Miss Nikki," he says in that way he does, and it makes the tears come to the surface and burn there. "Anything you need."

Vinnie puts his head on my lap in comfort, and I rest my hand on his head, feeling a little lighter the closer he is.

"Aunt Wren was admitted again," I sniffle. "Adventist off 96th. Kieran and I... we found something. It could be big. But it's in Washington. I don't want her to be alone."

There's a pause, and I hate myself for imposing on a Saturday. I hate to ruin his weekend yet again, like I've done so many times. It's not even noon, yet here comes Nikki needing something again. I wish I would have saved all the past times. I wish I could have known everything then was insignificant to this.

He's probably trying to think of a good way to let me down easy, to tell me he already has plans, to say this is finally the last straw, that I've already asked enough of him...

"Miss Nikki, are you sure that's a good idea? The roads on that route can get icy so easily, and I don't like the way the clouds look. If you perhaps waited until—"

Kieran flashes me his phone. It's his weather app.

"The forecast says it's all clear today," I assure him. "No storms the whole weekend. So, we'll be fine."

Another pause. Longer this time.

"Of course, Miss Nikki," Arrick finally says. "I'll go to Adventist. Just..."

"Yeah?"

"Please be careful. I—well, I can't lose you too."

My throat tightens again. There aren't many people in my life who care enough about me to worry. In fact, I can count all of them on one hand. But the sincerity in Arrick's voice easily counts for a hundred.

I may not have an army of friends and family behind me.

But I have an Arrick.

And right now, that feels like enough.

"I will," I tell him, and I hope I convey that. "I promise."

I hang up, and we head out.

PODCAST TRANSCRIPT
Secrets in Ice **Season 3, Episode 4: The Cover-Up, Cont.**

[crowd chatter, press camera shutters clicking]

SAPPHIRE PINES MAYOR, ALFRED HAHN *[archival recording]:*

It is tragic what happened to the Sinclair family, but we urge the community to let law enforcement do their jobs. I trust Portland PD completely to find answers and seek justice where it's due.

[suspenseful music plays]

KIERAN BERGSTROM:

As soon as I started this case, I tried pretty persistently to reach the community of Sapphire Pines. The ones that were there at the time of the murders. I wanted to hear their experiences. At first, a lot of them were willing to speak to me, to share rumors and theories, but almost every time I asked this question, they'd shut down. End the interview. That question was, "Why didn't you keep looking for them?" No one ever wanted to answer that. Or maybe they couldn't.

Then I received this message from a verified source. They have asked to remain anonymous. This is what the message said.

VOICE ACTOR READING MESSAGE:

Hi Kieran. Just wanted to say great job on the first episodes of the podcast. I'm sorry for ending our interview so abruptly. Honestly, I got a little scared. As you know I was the *[redacted]* at *[redacted]* at the time, and I led a community search party for the Sinclairs. Well... it was the day of the second search party. We were going to go search the woods around the accident site again. Um. Well, I had to cancel it because unfortunately my *[redacted]* caught fire. The fire department said it was an electrical fire but couldn't show me where it originated. Everyone was fine, and luckily it was contained quickly, but I got caught up in repairs and couldn't be involved in the Sinclair case for a few days.

KIERAN BERGSTROM:

Icers, you may be thinking, Kieran, this has to be a coincidence. An electrical fire is hardly proof that there was ill-intent. Well, listen to the next part of this person's message:

VOICE ACTOR READING MESSAGE:

I asked a friend in the community to take over the search while I figured everything out. He reorganized a new search party, and this time even more of the community was planning to come. It was looking like it would be a great turnout. But on his way to work that morning, his brakes failed, and he crashed into a tree. He survived, but he was hospitalized for weeks. This wasn't the only incident. There were other random attacks around town. Conveniently against anyone who took a lead in spreading awareness for the case. Safe to say the community got a little spooked after that. People wanting to help fizzled out pretty quickly.

KIERAN BERGSTROM:

Hmm. Strange that anyone trying to speak out for the Sinclairs was silenced. Sounds to me like someone was trying really hard to make sure this case was forgotten. And for a long time, it was.

It makes me wonder what they'll do this time to make sure it stays hidden.

[suspenseful music plays]

30

KIERAN

I HEAR CALIFORNIA'S NICE THIS TIME
OF YEAR

Washington here we come. The parchment paper rear windshield flaps and whistles noisily as my speed increases, but I manage to tune it out eventually. I finally showed Nikki how to swivel the passenger seat around, though I did strongly consider making her ride backwards the entire way there to mess with her, but I decided to play nice. She *was* surprisingly understanding about the George news and offering to help me take down Ciphered was cool of her. Really cool of her, actually. Though I hate to admit I'm wrong, it makes me think maybe I misjudged her.

Driving to Washington is a mixed bag of emotion. I'm hopeful about what we can find. There are so many leads there. We can visit the crash site, see if anything about the scene jogs up any ideas. We can pay a visit to Nikki's family cabin, maybe do a little breaking and entering (her in-laws won't mind, I'm sure).

All of that feels like progress. Momentum. It feels good.

But did it *have to be* Washington? Why not Idaho, Montana, or even good ol' California?

Luckily the state is big. I mean, it's never *felt* big enough, but I remind myself that the state is *objectively* large. So we'll be far enough away from any big cities, any big traffic-inducing events, and any big things I've been running away from for the past few years...

I don't have anything to worry about. At all. No worrying here.

I shake the thoughts away. I tuck them deeply back into their special corner of my mind where they belong and turn off the lights, before I panic and turn around.

Apart from the anxiety about the state itself, in some ways I feel... *lighter,* as my van trudges down Interstate-5, and not only because we're leaving the crowded city behind. I didn't realize how heavy the lie was, the act. The part I had to play to get Nikki's money for George. The pressure to keep everything together because the stakes were so impossibly high. I didn't realize how much it was affecting me.

Part of me wonders if Nikki and I might have skipped the whole disliking-each-other-profusely stage entirely if I had been honest from the beginning. I should've given her the benefit of the doubt. I was doing what I felt I had to do in a desperate situation. I can't fault myself for that. But all the same, I'm grateful she forgave me.

I can't deny how freeing it is to be doing what I love for the right reason again—for justice only. And, I admit, having a partner to do it with is surprisingly nice. We're getting close to answers, too (I can just *feel* it), so that's encouraging.

As long as I keep this van going North. Even though I've been trying to escape that very direction for years. But I'm not thinking about that. Not at all.

I click into cruise control as I reach a long, open stretch of interstate and explain to Nikki how to download an AI program I found onto the iPad that I thought we could try running the videos through. The program attempts to match faces from videos or photos with public social media, news sources, TV, or available public records like mugshots. A lot of these guys—if not all of them—appear to be high-profile, so I'm hopeful we can find matches for most of them. It's a tedious process, but Nikki picks it up quickly, adding more names to our whiteboard list.

"Another CEO of a billion-dollar company," she breathes, her legs crisscrossed on the passenger seat, the iPad balanced in her lap. "This list scares me. It's like a hornets' nest we keep getting closer and closer to."

"Buzz buzz," I joke, and I feel a twinge of pride that she laughs, terrible excuse for a joke and all. Her laugh is nice. It reminds me of wind chimes in a breeze, or the bell of a bicycle riding through town on a warm summer day.

Wait, what? I'm getting poetic now? I have no idea what deep, dark bricked-off crevice of me *that* crawled out of.

The steering wheel jolts and yanks me out of my self-analysis spiral, causing the van to swerve off-center ever so slightly. Nikki quirks an eyebrow at me as she stumbles back to her seat from the whiteboard.

"Wind." I stretch to look further out the windshield, eyeing the tops of trees around us and the sky above. The wind is picking up, but the sky is still blue and clear.

Nikki checks her phone for any possible weather updates. "It's still saying we're good."

Just keep going North. No turning back.

I turn the volume up on my music so it's loud enough to drown my thoughts of North and any other possible metaphors about laughs or smiles or long, wavy penny-red hair.

Nikki side-eyes me with judgment.

"What now?" I huff. Can she read thoughts now too?

"Oh nothing," she says with feigned obliviousness, a slight smirk on her lips. "I just knew you'd be a classic rock guy."

I bark an incredulous laugh. "What's that supposed to mean? If your music taste is anything like your taste in coffee, your critique of my music means nothing. You probably like Taylor Swift or something."

"Excuse me, Taylor Swift is an *artist!*" she defends, clutching her chest as if I've shot a hole through it.

"I knew it. You just scream *Swiftie* to me."

"That's a great compliment, thank you." She lifts her chin and pretends to busy herself with the iPad. "But for your information, I have very diverse musical interests."

"Oh yeah, like what, Sabrina Carpenter too?" I deadpan. "No wait, probably Olivia Rodrigo, so you think you're quirky and different."

She glares at me. "Who are both fantastic and talented women, you misogynist."

The next song comes up on my shuffle, and it just so happens to be a Sabrina Carpenter song. That I know every word to.

I snap my mouth shut, any comeback I would have said dissolving into thin air. A thick silence spans between us for a moment because there's absolutely nothing I can say.

I peek over at her, and she cracks, bursting into hysterical laughter.

And I can't help but laugh too. We laugh until there are tears in our eyes.

I SHIVER as we plop back in the van after a bathroom break for Vinnie and gas fill-up, clutching convenience store snacks in hand as we impatiently wait for the temperature to warm up inside. The shattered back window has been making that much harder.

"*Brrr*," Nikki says, pulling her coat tighter, her chip bag crunching. "It wasn't this cold this morning."

I take a right out of the gas station as the GPS instructs, away from the Interstate and onto an old highway road.

Nikki offers me some of her chips, and I grab a handful, the bright red powder immediately staining my fingertips. I offer her some of my protein bar in exchange, but she wrinkles her nose.

"You *would* choose something good for you as your road-trip snack," she says in a way like she has me all figured out now.

"Yeah, I got really into nutrition when I had to learn how to keep myself alive." I wave to Vinnie for effect.

She freezes, a flaming chip stopping midair on route toward her open mouth. "I'm so sorry. That was insensitive. I knew he was a service dog, but I didn't know for what."

I snort. "It's all good." And I almost don't elaborate, but she's looking at me with such genuine eyes, I feel compelled to. "Type I Diabetes."

"How long has it been since you found out you had it? Your parents didn't help?" Now the genuine eyes are making me squirm. I'm not used to people looking at me and trying to see *under* the layers I paste on. Most people are perfectly content accepting me at face-value, or voice-value, and I like it that way.

"I left home a long time ago." I keep a forced casual tone to play it off, but honestly it still stings. "I haven't spoken to them in years."

"That must've been so hard," she says softly.

I don't think about my family much. I don't wallow—I *work* instead. I have to. But her acknowledgement is surprisingly nice to hear. Because yeah, it's been hard as hell. And it's a battle I'll have to fight for the rest of my life.

"Yeah," is all I say, giving her a tight-lipped smile. "Parents. Who needs 'em, am I right?"

She chuckles humorlessly, finally crunching on the chip. "I mean, I'd say we're doing alright."

She returns her attention back to the iPad, and my eyes linger on her longer than they should, considering I'm operating a moving vehicle. The sun lowering into late afternoon is hitting her profile just right that it makes her glow angelically, and I'm distracted by it for a moment.

I blink out of it before I get poetic again.

"Weird," Nikki says, tapping the iPad screen to get the program to load. "Your satellite thing isn't working. It's worked perfectly this whole time."

"Huh. It usually only glitches when there's—" a flurry of snowflakes interrupts me and falls delicately onto the windshield.

"...bad weather," I finish slowly.

She points to the navigation display on my dash. "We have less than thirty more minutes. We're way too close to give up now."

The sky is still mostly blue, but the clouds are moving quickly with increasing wind.

I don't want to let her down, and we don't have anywhere else we can go anyway, so I keep heading straight ahead, down the old two-lane highway. It's mostly farmland around. Herds of cattle huddle closely together in their snow-covered pastures that span for miles. We pass huge trees that must have been here forever, shading modest farmhouses and ancient, crumbling businesses.

I catch a glimpse of a vehicle approaching in my side mirrors, since the rear mirror is useless now with a parchment paper window, and I pull as close to the edge of the road as I can so the vehicle knows it can pass me.

I blow out a frustrated breath when it doesn't, but I'm relieved it's a regular black pickup truck and not a windowless white van with bad intentions.

Aggravating all the same, though. Why are all pickup truck drivers so maddeningly impatient? Like where do you all need to be so bad that's more important than where anyone else needs to be?

"What?" Nikki swings her head around when she sees me eyeing it in the side-view. Vinnie senses the shift in mood too and comes to investigate.

"I just hate truck drivers," I complain, giving Vinnie a pat on the head.

Nikki looks at me with widened eyes after analyzing her own side mirror. "It's not..."

"It's not," I repeat, quickly discounting the ridiculous possibility that it's someone following us. We're in the middle of nowhere, there's no way.

Even as the truck tails me closer, refusing to pass, even with clear openings on the other side of traffic, I still assure myself it couldn't be that.

I increase my speed. Maybe they just want me to go faster and then they'll back off.

They don't.

31

KIERAN

DID I MENTION I HATE TRUCK DRIVERS?

The truck increases its speed too. It's following so closely on my tail that if I were to tap the brakes, it would rear-end me.

There is a *crash* from behind that lurches us forward, our heads nearly cracking into the dashboard. My laptop that was on the back counter flies forward and almost goes straight through the windshield, but Nikki catches it clumsily before throwing it in her bag with the iPad.

"He just rammed into me!" I yell in horror.

"Could it be Ciphered?!" Nikki yells back as she tucks Vinnie down by her feet. He rests his head on her shoe with a whine, his ears pulled back in fear.

I roll my window down and stick my head out. "What's your problem, man?"

"Kieran!" Nikki grabs the sleeve of my shirt and yanks me back in just as the passenger rolls his window down to aim a gun right at us.

I duck as the man peppers the van with bullets. Glass shatters all around us. His face isn't masked like Ciphered's men have all been so far. Could this be someone different? Is the Sinclair's killer finally onto us?

Nikki covers her head and curls low into Vinnie's fur.

I jerk the steering wheel left and right, trying to snake across the road and avoid direct fire.

There is nowhere to go.

There isn't even a real shoulder to pull over onto, only a narrow gap between the road and a thick line of trees, deep snow between them.

The wind howls through the cracks and holes of my windows like wolves as I speed up, my parchment paper windshield completely ripped apart.

The truck rams into me again, and there is a *pop* from one of my tires. The steering wheel spins out of my hands, and we fishtail. I fumble with the wheel, pulling with an exerted groan as I try to gain control.

We're sliding sideways on the road now, halfway into the other lane.

"Look out!" Nikki screams.

A car is coming directly toward us.

I jerk the wheel, slamming the brakes again, and the three in-tact tires finally catch, jolting us back over to the right side of the road. Our passenger side collides with a protruding branch of a tree, and it rips off the side-view mirror.

I straighten out and accelerate before the truck can hit me again.

Snow is falling in swirling masses of white now, blanketing the world around us, as if it weren't hard enough to see already. Burly hulking trees line both sides of the road tightly like a tunnel. We're trapped.

"Kieran..." Nikki points like she's seen a ghost.

A bridge ahead. Narrow, only one lane on each side.

A rushing river below it.

"Kieran, if we go on that bridge, we're dead." Her face is paler than the snow outside.

I squint. Right before the bridge on the right, the lining of trees opens into a field. Do I take my chances with the bridge, knowing they'll try to push us off either side, or take my chances with the deep snow? It's an impossible choice.

A bullet whizzes past my ear and lodges into the front windshield, creating torrents of cracks all around it. I can hardly see anything.

I slam my brakes to a full stop, and the truck has to swerve into the opposite lane to avoid crashing into me from behind. It drifts by, veering to a clumsy stop into the narrow gutter up ahead.

"No, stay down." Nikki pulls Vinnie back down by the collar as he misreads the stop. He whines. "It's okay."

I don't know how much good it will do with only three tires, but I have to try. I throw my van in neutral and activate the four-wheel-drive button before slamming it back into drive. *Gas. Go.*

The tires spin uselessly on the snow. Stuck.

I can't breathe, waiting as they spin and spin.

Catch.

We lurch forward, limping as fast as it will go. I pass the truck and flip them off.

I had hoped it would get stuck behind traffic, but there are hardly any other cars on this rural road. The truck peels off into the road, nearly colliding with a semi-truck going the other direction, but then it's right behind us again. They must be out of ammo because the shots have stopped. I fear what they'll resort to without that option.

I accelerate *faster, faster,* busted tire thumping and screaming with the speed. As soon as the trees end, I swerve off the road into the field.

We nose-dive into the snow, and the engine groans as I push forward. My ears freeze into numb icicles as the wind roars past me from my open window. Visibility is low with a busted windshield and increasing snowfall. I narrowly dodge a powerline, nearly hit a group of cattle, swerve around a tree.

"Where are you going to go? There's still a river!" Nikki shrieks unhelpfully.

"Would you rather they push us into the river from on top of the bridge?" I yell back, pushing the pedal down harder as the truck follows me into the snow.

The trees thicken as we get closer to the river. The skies overheard have darkened into a ghost-like gray.

My biceps scream in exertion with how tightly I have to pull the steering wheel to stay in control as we trudge through the snow.

The truck speeds up on the passenger side and slams into us from the right.

I groan through gritted teeth and pull the steering wheel tighter, the tires sliding underneath.

They slam again.

"They're trying to push us toward the water!" Nikki screams, head low into Vinnie, her door crunched inward from the blows.

"Keep your seatbelt tight!"

I tighten mine too as we curve in and out of thickening trees, hardly able to see anything as branches snap around us.

Nikki reaches over to yank the steering wheel as I nearly crash into a tree I couldn't see.

On my left is a berm that curves down into the river fifty feet below. We are running out of flat ground. It's getting narrower and narrower. Fear sluices through my veins, cold and fierce, paralyzing.

I don't know what to do.

Nikki must notice my fear because it darkens on her face too, as the reality of the situation dawns on her like a shadow. She opens her mouth to say something, but the truck slams into us one final time.

My tires slip off the edge, and the world turns upside down.

"Vinnie, jump!" He leaps as the air explodes all around us.

I'm transported to a different dimension where gravity subsides entirely. The sound of Nikki's fear shreds me apart from the inside out. She's too far away. Her screams are muffled and distant, like we're trapped on opposite sides of thick glass I can't break through. I can hear her, but I can't reach her.

I grab Vinnie's collar as he flies backward, and my elbow crunches into the seat, sending a shooting pain all the way up to my shoulder. The fiery pain makes my vision go blurry but with every ounce of strength I can muster, I yank Vinnie back toward me and pull him in tightly to my chest. We tuck into each other as the van rolls. My seatbelt wrenches on my insulin pump at my stomach, threatening to rip it out with every bounce and jolt.

The roof is folding in above us, or is that the undercarriage below us? It's impossible to know which way is up and which way is down.

Half-speed shatters and cracks blast all around me, but I hardly register them. Sound is now pulled completely out of this reality somehow. A terrible, paralyzing, silent dream.

My hurt arm is going numb, the momentum threatening to pull Vinnie out of near useless fingers, but I don't let go. I'll never let him go.

I turn and with horror see Nikki's head drooping and lolling, knocking against the headrest. There's a gash on her forehead, the blood coming out of it defying gravity like we're suspended in space. I scream her name at the sight, terrified that she's gone. *She can't be gone.*

For a moment I think we're trapped in this never-ending loop of roll after roll, crash after crash, until eventually the van will crumble down to dust and eat us whole.

But then everything stops with a final *clank*. My forehead slams against the steering wheel, my seatbelt knocking the air out of me. I gasp for air, inhaling a huge clump of Vinnie's fur. My pump hangs down by the tubing, swinging and pulling at the adhesive on my skin that is hanging on by a thread.

We're upside down, the nose of the van in the water.

We would have been completely submerged if we had fallen ten more feet.

My vision darkens, the blackness trying to lull me into its embrace. It seems so quiet there. So calm...

But a soft whine in my arms, a panting ball of fur who licks my face, pulls me out. I claw my way out of the dark back to him.

I groan as I come to.

With my full consciousness, I first register a pain in my head, a throbbing ache that snakes down my neck, then the sharp fire in my elbow. Then to Vinnie squirming in my arms, his movement alone transporting a physical relief that nearly washes the pain away. He's okay.

"Nikki?" I call out, fear slithering back into me when she doesn't answer. *Please be okay.*

With effort, I manage to turn my head to look at her. Her hair hangs, drips of blood from the gash on her forehead streaking into it and reddening it further, as her seatbelt holds her in place upside down. The backpack hangs down off her shoulders.

I breathe again when her chest moves up and down with a labored breath of her own. My chest relaxes an inch.

I can't believe we're alive.

"I'm gonna drop you down," I tell Vinnie.

I lower him down slowly, trying not to scream out in pain as my elbow extends. I drop him gently onto the wrinkled-up roof.

Motion flashes beyond Nikki's unmoving head.

"Play dead," I whisper. He obeys.

The truck has pulled to a stop from the top of the berm, and the men stretch out of their windows, watching us. *Confirming life.*

I stay as still as I can, keeping my arms dangling for effect, holding my breath. I squeeze my eyes shut. It feels like an eternity that I hang here.

"Stay," I hiss to Vinnie without moving my lips like a ventriloquist.

We're dead. Drive away.

We're dead.

I nearly cry in relief when the tires kick up snow. The truck peels away.

I peek through squinted eyes to confirm.

It's gone.

"Good boy," I tell Vinnie. "First aid kit."

He digs around the debris that is my van. He won't find it. But I need him out the way so I can—

Clunk.

It's a short fall, thanks to my van being crumpled up like a soda can, but I still land on shards of broken glass and branches.

"Ow," I tell the glass and branches.

I push myself up into a crouch because there isn't enough room to stand up anymore, which I try not to dwell on. The adhesive on my infusion site is barely sticking to my stomach anymore, but I readjust the needle and press the adhesive down as best as it will, tucking the pump and tubing back into my pocket. It doesn't appear to be broken, though it is a little wet. Leaked insulin, maybe. Hopefully not because those are disgustingly expensive. Thanks, American healthcare.

I don't pause to look around. I can't. I don't have time to sit and cry about how everything I own is destroyed and everything I've worked for is pounded up into dust right now. As always, I don't wallow, I *work.*

I rush hunched over to the passenger seat, stumbling a bit as the throbbing in my head intensifies now that I'm upright.

"Nikki!" I tap her shoulder gently. She's still and frozen like a doll. "I'm gonna get you down."

The upside-down drawer behind her seat is intact. I reach for it and rip it out of the tracks. Everything in it falls out. I rifle around in the debris for the pocketknife I keep in there.

I cut the straps of her backpack and toss it behind me onto all the pillows and bedding strewn around everywhere, thankful Nikki thought to keep my laptop protected in it with the iPad.

I kneel, glass digging into my jeans. I brace myself for her weight and then cut her seatbelt, crying out at the impact on my hurt arm. Stars explode behind my eyes. I'm lightheaded, nearly toppling over entirely. I let myself fall back onto my butt, so I can brace her up against me. The snow intensifies just out the windows, surrounding us in a flurry of white.

"Nikki?" I brush blood-caked hair off her face, tapping her cheek gently to get her to come-to, and I suddenly weirdly understand the appeal of coming across a beautiful girl in a castle, who is trapped in an eternal slumber, and pressing a kiss onto her lips. I don't, though, because I'm far from a prince. She has one of those already.

Vinnie comes up behind us and pokes his snout into my shoulder, whining. "I think she's gonna be okay," I reassure him.

But he whines again, pressing his snout into my shoulder more insistently, and when my monitor beeps a second later, I get it. I reach around me to look at my pump.

Great.

Of course it would be here, of course it would be now, in the middle of a snowstorm, next to a river where no one will find us, with a useless vehicle that resembles a mangled-up toaster...

Yes, of course, my pump would choose right now to be empty of insulin and my blood sugar would decide to be critically high.

This just went from bad to extremely bad.

February 15, 2025 | Elise Moreno

Popular Podcaster Presumed Dead After River Crash

THURSTON COUNTY, WA – Authorities responded to a call around 4:30 p.m. from a local hiker who spotted a partially submerged vehicle in the Deschutes River. Search and rescue crews located the white conversion van upside down in a shallow bend of the river.

Details are still emerging, but initial reports suggested a fatal accident for the three deceased individuals discovered in the vehicle. Investigators noted shattered windows, bullet damage, and what the sheriff's office is now calling "strong indicators of foul play."

Though the identities of the individuals have not been officially confirmed, sources have indicated that one of the victims found potentially matches the description of 18-year-old Kieran Bergstrom, host of the PNW true crime podcast *Secrets in Ice*. The other victims remain unidentified.

Law enforcement is urging anyone with information or anyone who may have seen the van near Deschutes River Bridge this weekend to contact the Columbia County Sheriff's Office tip line.

More updates to follow as the story develops.

32

NIKKI

NICE TO MEET YOU, PLEASE DON'T KILL ME

I wake from the blackness with a jolt, like a bad dream where you feel like you are falling into bottomless depths that swallow you whole. My heart drums faster as I try to register where I am.

I remember the truck pushing us off the berm. Rolling, crashing. Hitting my head.

So why am I comfortable? Is this what the bottom of a river feels like? Is this where I'll find my family?

I pat around as my vision adjusts to the dimness, feeling blankets and pillows and... fur. Fur that moves right away.

Fur that is now licking my face, an excited tail whacking my legs.

Thankful for something familiar, I giggle.

"Who's the best boy?" I croak, my throat dry and gravelly. "Is Kieran okay?"

Vinnie seems happy enough, so I take that as a sign that his person is safe. I rely on that. I'd never forgive myself if something happened to Kieran, leaving Vinnie without him. Unimaginable.

I finally decide that I'm in an apartment—hotel room maybe? It's minimally decorated and furnished simply, lacking photos or other unique touches. There is a kitchenette on the other side of the room with a small, round table next to it. It's impersonal, but comfortable. Warm.

My phone is plugged into a charger on the side table. It's shockingly not even cracked. Wow, I'll definitely be writing a glowing review for that phone case. *"10/10, can withstand rolling into a river, also cute."*

I can't tell what time it is, not even if it's morning or night, but I'll need to call and check on Aunt Wren as soon as I get the umph to move my stiff body. I hope she's okay. I just have to trust that Arrick is looking out for her, which is what I should be doing, instead of rolling into rivers. But I hope she'll forgive me when I find Lizzy, get our inheritance, and save her life.

The only door in the room is shut, but a halo of light surrounds it, leaking in from the other side through the cracks. There are faint, muffled sounds on the other side. I strain to listen, but I can't figure out what they're saying.

It's either another language that they're speaking, or I have some kind of head trauma that must be causing words to not make normal sense.

I'm really hoping for the first option.

I take stock of the rest of my body, testing fingers and toes. I find a thick bandage on my forehead and a bruise on my cheek that is tender to the touch.

I can't believe it wasn't worse. We *rolled* into a *river*. I send a silent prayer of gratitude to my parents, who I'm convinced are my own personal guardian angels. They had to have aided in this miracle, because there's no other way I should be alive.

Vinnie snuggles into me, putting his snout on my shoulder.

"Where are we?" I whisper, petting his head. "Where's Kieran?"

Vinnie barks once, and I wince, the sound ringing in my throbbing head.

The door cracks open and, to my relief, Kieran steps through, but not before pushing a figure behind him back into the hallway, hissing something to them in... Russian?

He smiles when he sees me. And that makes me smile. The relief of seeing him okay is tangible. It's warm in my chest, like the glow of a gentle fire on a cold night you want to draw in close to. By looking at him, you'd think he simply got into a fistfight behind the bleachers somewhere. There is a bandage on his forehead similar to mine. Purple bruise flowering under his eye and down his cheek.

It could have been so much worse. Such a miracle. Thanks Mom and Dad for looking out for him too.

"So do you remember who you are, or do we have to invent a new identity for you?" Kieran asks, sitting on the edge of the bed. Vinnie greets him by nearly tackling him. They wrestle a bit, and it's cute.

"Hmmm," I take a dramatic moment to think about it. "I think I'll be a beautiful heiress with a tragic backstory and a cool sidekick."

"Cool, *handsome* sidekick," he adds, puffing out his chest in an overly theatric way, his chocolate eyes sparkling. I don't even notice the little flip my traitorous stomach does. Not at all. Didn't even happen.

I ruffle Vinnie's fur and joke back, "Yes, he is."

Kieran laughs in surrender. "Yeah, I really can't compete. How are you feeling?"

"Well, I've never been in a boxing match before, but I imagine it feels something like this. I'm surprisingly okay, though. How are you? And where are we?"

"I'm fine." He flaps his elbow. "Nothing a ton of Tylenol and ice packs can't fix. And don't worry, we'll head out in the morning. I just got off the phone with Arrick, your aunt is doing fine. He's going to stay the night there."

I blink at him. "You called Arrick? To check on my aunt?"

His eyes flick over me, trying to figure out if he's done something wrong. "I just figured you'd be worried about her when you woke up."

I struggle to find an adequate response, the thoughtfulness of the gesture locks up my tongue. "I am—I... thank you. That was nice of you to do."

"No problem. Are you hungry? I can bring you something to eat?"

"Who was that?" I nod to the door, pulling myself up to a sitting position, which makes my head whirl a little bit.

"No one." He scowls and pats a pile on the end of the bed by my feet. "Here's a change of clothes. They won't fit perfectly, but at least they won't be covered in blood."

I raise my eyebrow at the very deliberate change in subject. "Thanks. And you suddenly know how to speak Russian?"

He stands and smacks his thighs. "Sounds like you're hungry. I'll go get you some food and you can change. I'll be right back."

The door clicks behind him as he shuts it.

I eye Vinnie to explain why his person is so frustratingly unwilling to talk about himself, why he's more guarded than freaking Area 51, but he lolls his tongue at me adorably like he's smiling at me, and all is forgotten.

I pull the covers back and find my tattered clothes, indeed covered in streaks of blood. Did I really hit my head that hard? I swing my legs off the bed and test my footing, finding that my feet are covered in someone else's socks. Pink and fuzzy.

The clothes he left for me consist of a black classic rock band tee that's a little oversized, but kind of in a cute way, an unopened package of ladies' underwear—where did he get these?? How humiliating!—and a pair of gray sweats that are a bit big, but I roll the waistband down and tie the drawstring tight. The shoes are black lace-up boots, surprisingly trendy. With the thick fuzzy socks, they fit fine.

I don't even consider sitting on this bed and waiting for him to come back. With my curse of innate curiosity, it's simply not an option. After a slight dizzy spell passes, my steps become surer, and I crack the door open, immediately hearing faint music, laughter, and noise. I follow it.

"Stay close," I whisper to Vinnie. He tucks his ears in and creeps slowly next to me.

The din increases in volume with every step, leading me down a narrow, carpeted hallway, passing a few doors identical to the one I came out of. I find a staircase at the end of the hallway, and I peek around the corner.

Down the stairs is a bar, not packed tightly with people, but still busy. The music is loud but not overpowering. A fast-paced rock song I don't recognize. The atmosphere is energetic but not rowdy. I'm a little embarrassed of my sweats and t-shirt as I slink down the stairs, holding Vinnie by the collar as we come down, so I don't lose him.

I scan the patrons and find Kieran quickly. Well, I find the back of his head, at least. He's speaking closely with a gorgeous young woman who looks to be in her early twenties. Pale blonde hair, enviable curves that many women pay for, homicidal eyeliner, cool skirt, cool boots.

She's stunning and cool and for some reason I immediately dislike her.

Is it the way she's leaning in closely to hear what he's saying when she could probably hear him just fine at a reasonable distance? Is it the way she laughs loudly at whatever he just said even though I know he's not *that* funny? Or the way she insists on flashing every one of her perfectly white teeth at him as if she's never sipped coffee or missed a floss a single day of her life?

I've never felt so hideous. I'm furious at Kieran for not finding me something more flattering to wear. Sweats, really?

Part of me wants to turn around and hide before he can see me, but another very inquisitive part of me wants to hear what they're talking about. To understand what could possibly be so funny.

Vinnie sees Kieran too and pulls a bit, wanting to run to him, but I tug his collar back. I don't want Vinnie giving me away yet.

Two older women join them, and their group talks easily to one another.

I'm nearly close enough to hear their conversation when one of the older women spots me, grabs the arm of the woman next to her, and immediately shrieks, "Kai brought a girl home?!"

The entire bar goes silent. *Kai? Home?*

Kieran's head snaps to the younger woman angrily. "You told them?"

She simply folds her arms and nods in my direction,

meeting my eye with a smile I can't quite decode as friendly or unfriendly.

Kieran turns and does a full-body exhale in exasperation when he sees me, throwing his hands out as if I'm a toddler getting into mischief again. I'm sure not *everyone* in the bar is looking at me. But it sure feels like it.

I let Vinnie go, and he pounces on Kieran, which defuses an ounce of the awkwardness. The group around Kieran has grown, a few more older people, and a couple other young adults.

"I said I'd be right back," Kieran hisses through gritted teeth as he steps to me. "Do you have any idea what you've done?"

I jerk my head to the younger woman, an angry prickle popping up at the back of my neck. "Right, how rude of me to interrupt your *peacocking*. I'm sure you were really in your game."

His brows knit together. "Huh?"

The two older women interrupt us, approaching me with delighted expressions. They coo at me in Russian (I think?), touching my cheeks and smoothing my hair as if I'm a newborn baby.

Kieran simply crosses his arms when I implore him with my eyes. "You brought this on yourself," he says helpfully.

"Well, aren't you going to introduce us to your girl-friend?" one of them says, pulling Kieran close and squeezing his cheek against hers.

Kieran sighs. "Not girlfriend. Client." He gestures between us with an exhausted wave. "This is Nikki. Nikki this is Babulya Nina, and Babulya Tamara, my *very nosy, very meddlesome* aunts."

Aunts.

Like *my* aunt. Who gave up her whole life to take care of me, and at the first opportunity, I've left on her deathbed in a whole different state. The guilt about that is relentless, just slowly gnawing me apart from the inside out.

One of the aunts pats my head affectionately. "A good girl to bring a boy home to his family. Our Kai hasn't been home in years. He's gotten too big." She pouts at him.

Kai. Home.

The beautiful blonde young woman comes over and, to my surprise, pulls me in for a hug. "Hi, I'm a hugger, sorry," she says, voice angelic and melodic. Of course it is.

Kieran glares at her. "Give it back."

She flashes those blinding teeth at him innocently. "What?"

He reaches over and yanks *my favorite gold ring* off her finger. "She's off limits, Ofeliya."

I look at my hand in disbelief as if it were the one who handed the ring over without my permission, jaw fully on the ground. *How?*

"I wasn't going to keep it," she lilts, handing it back to me with a sparkle in her eye. "It's just a fun party trick."

I slide the ring back on my finger, huffing in an impressed way. "Wow. I've never been to a party, and the only 'trick' I have is I can eat an entire pizza. Sometimes. With advance notice."

Ofeliya laughs. Loudly. She must not know any actual funny people.

"I like her," she says to Kieran, then pulls the Babulyas away, who are about to begin fussing over me again, chiding them in Russian and distracting them with someone else across the room.

"She's cool," I say simply, trying to be chill and casual. "Sorry again to interrupt."

Something dawns on him, like he's been zapped with understanding, and he guffaws a single laugh. "Right. My *peacocking.*" He nods to Ofeliya. "Cousin."

Cousin.

Why am I relieved? I don't care who he talks to. He can talk to anyone he wants, cousin or not. Because I am very happily engaged to my best friend. My very hot and very rich best friend, I might add.

"Her dad owns a tow company. He's the one I had to call when we... you know." He whistles as he makes a spiral motion with his finger of the van rolling down the hill. Then his finger splats on his palm and he does a crash sound effect.

Another sharp pang of guilt adds itself to the layer already there for Aunt Wren. I was the reason he had to contact his family again. On the drive earlier, I could tell how hard it was for him to even talk about them. And now we're here.

A man at the bar shouts that name. *Kai.*

I give him a quizzical look as we make our way over there, and he blows a resigned sigh, like all his cards are already out on the table anyway.

"Like I told you," he explains. "I left home a long time ago. When I emancipated myself, they asked me if I wanted to pick a new name. Thought it would be a good fresh start." He flashes a big showy smile that he's probably used to girls swooning over. Unengaged girls who are into that kind of thing, big smiles and nice teeth. "Plus 'Kieran Bergstrom' just has better podcast pizzazz, you know?"

We reach the bar, and the man slides him two takeaway

boxes. The man leans closer to Kieran and whispers something to him that I can't make out. Kieran tenses right away, his shoulders going taut.

"Let's go eat these up in the room," Kieran tells me hurriedly, nudging me back toward the staircase. "We should probably go before—"

The front door opens with a *bang,* and the bar goes silent. A huge man with a gray beard stomps in and tosses his coat on the nearest table. Tattoos cover all his visible skin except his face, even his hands and neck. A chill rolls down my back as he steps toward *us* slowly. Whispers hiss around the room like a nest of snakes.

Vinnie steps in front of us, growling at the man he perceives as a threat, and I don't blame him; I myself want to shrink into the peeling wallpaper of the nearest wall as he advances. Kieran tugs Vinnie's collar back to keep him close, but the man sneers at him unbothered, waving him off like he's a little yapping puppy.

His timbre is so low and deep it probably just caused an earthquake somewhere. His Russian accent is throaty and rough. "Thought you could show your face around here, and I wouldn't find out? In my bar, no less?"

Kieran squares his shoulders, meeting the man's eyes with admirable nerve. "Hello, Dad."

33

NIKKI

PAKHAN'S STORY

My eyeballs nearly pop out of my skull. *Dad?*

"I knew you'd be back eventually." His laugh is cold. "Ran out of money, yes?"

Kieran's hand balls into a fist, and a wave of heat radiates off of him.

I clear my throat, stepping forward to extend my hand, the guilt of forcing him back to this place driving me to action. I can be brave when it's literally my fault.

I paste on a toothy smile that mimics Kieran's earlier, the irresistible one (for unengaged girls who are into that kind of thing) and make my voice sugary sweet. "Hi, I'm Nikki. You can blame me that we didn't call ahead. Sorry for the surprise. I'm a client of his, and I had urgent business up in this area."

His father shakes my hand tightly, probably crushing several of my metacarpals, his hard face shifting into slight surprise. Impressed surprise, maybe? "Hello, Nikki," he rumbles. "Lovely to meet you."

"You, too. You have a lovely... bar." *Please don't kill me.*

He lets go of my hand and side-steps me to Kieran. There's a brief moment of silence so tense you could slice it as they stare at each other. Are they going to fight or something? But then his dad's lips curl into a smile so big that it disappears into his beard. He tugs Kieran into what is surely meant to be a hug but looks more like how an anaconda suffocates its prey, patting his back with such force it has to hurt.

Kieran pats back half-heartedly, looking exhausted.

His dad bellows to the room, arm around Kieran, "My son is back!"

The room cheers, lifting their drinks to the air.

"Drinks all around!" Kieran's dad announces, and the cheering intensifies.

He leaves to mingle with the room, taking the bubble of intensity he exudes with him and allowing me to breathe normally again.

"Well, he seems nice," I squeak.

Kieran laughs, and I'm glad to see his face unclench for a moment. He takes our takeout containers over to the bar and sits on one of the barstools. "Cat's out of the bag now, so I guess we can just eat here."

He opens the containers to reveal unfamiliar but drool-worthy appetizers.

"Ooh, what's this?" I grab a crispy golden roll, splitting it apart in the middle to find a mixture of rice and meat inside. I didn't realize how starving I was until I smelled all of this.

"Pirozhki," he grunts, tossing one to Vinnie, who inhales it in a second and immediately begs for more with big eyes I'd never be able to say no to. I slip him some of mine when Kieran is distracted plugging numbers into his phone, which I realize must be for his diabetes.

The second takeout box is filled with stacks similar to crepes or thin pancakes, drizzled with honey and jam. "And I absolutely need whatever this is."

"Blinchiki." Kieran's mouth is stuffed full with his own hefty serving.

They are both divine. One savory, one sweet. I'm no better than Vinnie as I devour every scrap.

Various people from the room come and greet us while we stuff ourselves happily, and I've lost track of everyone's names, but nearly everyone here seems to be related to him in some way. Kieran loosens gradually as time goes on, like the layers of pressure keeping him so tightly bound are slowly letting up the longer we're here. An actual smile returns to his lips for the first time since his dad showed up.

"Why did you leave home, anyway?" I venture, taking a chance on the looser energy I'm feeling from him. Everyone here adores him. But I know from experience you never know what goes on behind closed doors. Sometimes even in your own house.

He picks at the leftover crumbs in his Styrofoam tray. "I didn't want any part of this." He gestures around the room. I follow with my eyes, as if what he's implying will reveal itself to me if I look hard enough.

He sees my confused expression and luckily elaborates. "It looks fine on the surface. Everyone's here having a great time. My dad's acting normal. He's good at that." A shadow crosses his demeanor as he looks around, seeing it completely differently than me, like through an X-ray lens that reveals the hidden bones of a place. "It's all a lie."

"How?"

Kieran murmurs, "It's a front, Nikki."

I clamp my mouth shut in surprise.

"You have no idea the darkness that comes when the lights go out and everyone leaves." He shakes his head. "After my mom died when I was eight, my dad started showing me the ropes in his... industry. The 'family business.' He wanted me to take over one day."

"That sounds really dangerous for a child," I whisper, wanting to cry for that little boy without his mom.

"I ran away when I was almost sixteen. I wanted to do something *good* with my life."

I smile at him. "And you have."

"Right," he snorts. "Albert's case may not even be able to go to trial without Roger Mackenzie's testimony, and George is dead. So much good."

I force him to look at me, which puts our faces closer than I expected. "That wasn't your fault," I tell him with emphasis. "You've done so much good. For all those people, and for me too. I can't thank you enough for helping me."

He holds my gaze, something shifting in his eyes that makes my insides turn to jelly. "You can thank me when we find your sister."

"I'll thank you then too."

A voice behind us startles me like I've been caught red-handed doing something wrong, but I haven't done anything. Nor would I have!

"You are going to freak out!" Ofeliya squeals.

She puts her face in between us and throws her arms around our shoulders, bringing us in for a squished hug.

Kieran brightens, but only a fraction, like he's trying not to get his hopes up. "Did you...?"

Ofeliya straightens up and shoves her phone in his face. "I did."

Kieran looks at the screen in awe. She whips the phone away as he reaches for it. "I have one condition."

"What." Kieran doesn't even ask the word like a question. He groans it like a flat statement he's dreading the response to.

Ofeliya smiles brightly. "I want to cohost your podcast next seas—"

"Absolutely not."

"Aw," she pouts. "Well, guess you'll never know the coordinates I found from the metadata of those videos her so-called dead sister sent which would tell you almost the exact location of the sender."

My jaw hangs. "Wait, what? Are you serious?"

"Mhm," she says proudly, giving a pointed look to Kieran.

"Kieran!" I screech, eyes bulged. "You have to!"

"Your podcast needs a female touch anyway, and I'm extremely likable." She nudges his shoulder. "Plus, you *know* my talents could come in handy for the investigations."

"What good is a hacker and pickpocket when I'm trying to get *legitimate* by-the-book justice for people? You'll get me arrested!" Kieran protests.

She crosses her heart. "I'll be good, then. Still very likeable. I'd be doing you a favor."

"She is very likeable," I add helpfully.

She raises her eyebrow at him like, "*See?*"

He glares at me like I've betrayed him, but I show my teeth innocently.

"*Guest* cohost. One episode only."

"Permanent cohost. Full season. Or no coordinates." She waggles her phone for emphasis.

I implore Kieran with wide eyes, as if I'm Vinnie begging for human food insatiably. If what she's saying is true, we could have Lizzy's *location* and we could just *show up?* I could finally know for sure if someone has been messing with me, or if it's actually her. If she needs help or not. If she's really *alive!*

Kieran evaluates me and must see all these thoughts written all over my face. He sighs. "Fine."

Ofeliya and I simultaneously squeal, squeezing each other's arms and bouncing up and down like we've won a contest.

She hands me her phone and chatters off all her ideas for the podcast to Kieran, but I'm not listening.

There's a pin in her navigation app in a town called Grayford. I zoom in, seeing if it has a street view. It doesn't. From the bird's eye satellite view, it shows only trees. No buildings, no homes, not even roads. I study it for a minute, hoping the blocky shapes on the terrain will speak to me somehow, lead me to her.

They don't.

I interrupt her ramblings, which Kieran seems thankful for. "This pin is in the middle of nowhere. This is where she is?"

She takes the phone and zooms out to demonstrate. "When I ran it through my program, the metadata would only show me a radius." She points a very long acrylic nail, which has a bright orange French tip at the end of it, and outlines the shape of a circle. "The coordinates are in this area. Worst case scenario, you ask around. It's a super small town."

I sag into the barstool. "I was hoping you meant a little more precise."

She pats my back in comfort. "But it's closer than you've

had so far, right? Here, put your number in my phone, I'll text this to you."

I do.

It must have crossed into after-hours now because a DJ has set up in the corner, flashing lights around as some kind of signal, the atmosphere shifting.

Kieran's dad takes a microphone, and a crowd gathers in front of him.

Ofeliya claps excitedly. "Time for *Pakhan's* Story!"

"He's still doing this?" Kieran groans.

"Come on!" Ofeliya takes our arms and pulls us toward the group. Vinnie follows behind, receiving the admirations of a long line of adoring fans along the way, which he loves. He struts through like he owns the place.

The thought crosses my mind like a zap of static that Hunter is probably worried about me. I left my phone back in the room, and I haven't spoken to him all day, which might be the longest we've ever gone without talking, and I have so much to tell him about—nothing eventful like this ever happens to me! I doubt Kieran called him to let him know I was okay, like he did with Arrick. Which is fine. The thought of the two of them speaking makes me squirm for some reason. I'll just finish up here and give him a call in a little bit.

Kieran's dad at the front of the room sees us join the crowd and raises his glass to us, saying something in Russian into the microphone. Everyone turns to look at us. A muscle in Kieran's jaw ticks. Funny how much he hates to be the center of attention considering what he does for a job.

Then Kieran's dad's tone shifts into some kind of speech, entirely in Russian, and the crowd listens eagerly (are this many people in *Washington* really fluent in Russian?), the spaces between people getting closer as more people enter the room. There are way more people here now than there were even thirty minutes ago. I notice only a younger crowd remains. All the Babulyas must have officially turned in for the night.

He's like a pastor giving a hellfire sermon at a mega-church. People hang on his every word, offering up Russian forms of *hallelujahs* as he speaks.

He eventually concludes his speech by raising his glass again. This time everyone does the same, cheering. The DJ turns the volume on the music up right at a bass drop, and movement erupts all around us as everyone dances. The room darkens, only strobes and lasers flashing all around.

"What did he say?" I have to yell over the music.

"He's got this weird thing about mirrors," Kieran grumbles, not elaborating further. He kneels down to rub down Vinnie and gives him a command to go back upstairs and to bed, which he obeys like such a good boy.

Ofeliya is more helpful. "He has this long-standing story about a mirror in the sky. Every Saturday night he tells another piece of the story," she explains eagerly in my ear. "It's like a metaphor or something. So, everyone spends all day looking in this mirror in the sky, admiring themselves and making sure their reflection is more beautiful than the other reflections. They rely on the mirror to decide what's beautiful, rather than looking around themselves. Well, tonight, the mirror shattered, shards of it falling down and horrifically mutilating the vainest of the onlookers."

I grimace. "Yikes. Then what?"

She shrugs happily. "We'll find out next week. Let's dance!"

I brighten, excitedly joining her as she jumps up and

down to the fast-paced music. I'll just dance for a little bit and then I'll call Hunter. The crowd has tightened. There are people close to me in nearly all directions, but I surprisingly don't mind. I've never experienced anything like this, and I love it. The music, the feeling of it in my bones. The collective breaths and sweat. Dancing in a room much too full of people is a formative experience any regular young person would have.

So, it's nice. To feel like a regular young person for once.

I tug Kieran over to us, and with a sigh—a sigh that's mostly for show because he doesn't take much convincing at all—he relents and dances with us.

And we dance.

For an hour? Two? I lose track of time to the music.

Ofeliya leaves to get us waters to drink, after I insisted multiple times that I'm really not interested in her vodka flask but thank you for the very kind offer.

As soon as she leaves, the crowd sucks in closer like a sponge, absorbing the space that was once hers. Kieran and I are left alone in the crowd, and I'm aware of his proximity for the first time now that our triangle has become... this.

His body is so close I can feel how heavy his breaths are from the movement. We move together in sync, swaying with the rhythm and with each other, the song shifting into something deeper, a heavy bass rumbling between us.

Someone behind pushes into me and makes me stumble into him. I collide with his chest, which is surprisingly hard. He laughs and helps straighten me out, and I look up at him to apologize but his face makes me pause. The lights from the DJ booth are bouncing off the ceiling and dousing him in blue. It makes his laugh look frozen in time, the light making him seem... carefree. It's a look I've never seen there before, and it catches me by surprise. It makes me think about all the worries he must stack so heavily on his shoulders all the time. The people he helps. The people he can't help. It's like I'm seeing him in a new light entirely, and I can't look away.

The music fades to the background entirely, slowing to half speed, as his eyes flick down to my lips. Our noses are nearly touching. I can feel his warm breath on my lips, his heartbeat. It's fast. Unsure.

He moves slowly to close the rest of the distance between our lips, and some internal force of nature wants me to pull closer to him too, but I turn my head away. That inner force screams as I step away, a very real, very confusing part of me that *wanted* him to kiss me. That wanted to kiss *him!* A part of me so palpable that it still lingers. I can't deny it even if I tried, can't pretend it was never there.

"I'm engaged, Kieran," I whisper. "I'm sorry if I led you on in some way."

"No, I'm sorry. You're right." He stumbles back. "This place makes me not think straight." His face is unreadable. Is he hurt? Angry? Relieved?

And what am I?

Ofeliya returns, holding three water bottles, sensing the tension immediately. "What's up?"

"Just answer me one thing." Kieran shoves his hair off his forehead, unrepressed frustration taking over his demeanor. "Why are you *marrying* him? You have your whole life ahead of you, and you're throwing it all away for him?"

Ofeliya's eyes play tennis between us.

I swallow hard. "I'm not throwing my life away. I love Hunter."

And as I say it aloud for the first time, the truth of it glimmers in my chest, confirmation that I *do* love Hunter. He is a constant in my life I need like oxygen. He has been for years.

So, I leave it at that. I don't need to explain everything about my aunt. The inheritance clause. It wouldn't make a difference anyway.

Kieran just nods, the words he clearly wants to say, but is holding back, so visible on his mouth. *His lips.*

"It's late," is all he says. "We should get some sleep."

And we do.

And when I'm alone, back in that little apartment, a stranger's pillow under my head, I cry a little. And I don't know why.

34

KIERAN

HUSKIES ARE BETTER THAN HUMANS

In the morning, I feel stiff and sore. Dense. Like I've been packed full of tar and tossed around a washing machine. And it's not just because I slept crammed up on Ofeliya's tiny couch, clutter from her messy apartment surrounding me, suffocating me.

It's also, because, well, we don't need to talk about it. About *her*.

I wait as my cousin's Keurig spits out some hazelnut monstrosity into a bright pink mug. It's a different color than coffee should be, but it's caffeinated and warm, and right now that's all I care about. Out the window, through the horizontal slats of Ofeliya's blinds where bright morning sunlight streaks in, I have a great view of the alleyway where my uncle dropped off my crunched-up soda can of a home. I haven't had the heart to inventory what's still usable inside, only quickly picked out what necessities I could grab. Because what's the point?

I wanted to come back to this place at a future point in my life when I had more things figured out. When I could flaunt my success and confidently say, "See? I didn't need this kind of life after all." Not when everything I've worked for can so easily be nothing at all, gone in an instant like sand from an incoming tide.

Ofeliya still snoozes loudly on her bed on the other side of the studio, so I shush Vinnie and gesture for him to follow, carefully stepping out into the empty hallway. Most of my father's tenants live here because they like having frequent access to the nightly festivities downstairs.

"Coffee" in hand, I step down the stairs and out the door, keeping to the front of the building so I don't have to see my van, and allow Vinnie a few moments to himself while I make a phone call. A phone call I probably should have made sooner, but maybe I was holding out a selfish bit of delusional hope.

Back inside the apartment, I scoop dog food into a salad bowl I found in the cabinet for Vinnie. He devours it, and I'm slightly jealous he has something to eat that he loves so much and all I have is "coffee." I cringe a little when my CGM beeps, feeling extra loud in this quiet apartment. It's been having a hard time regulating my levels. The algorithm has been wonky ever since the accident.

But as much as I hate this place, I'm grateful my uncle was able to get to Nikki and me after the accident so quickly. By the time he arrived to pull us out of the riverbed, though it was less than an hour, I was so hyperglycemic that my headache threatened to explode out of my head, and my toes were going numb from the cold.

My mind flashes back to huddling close to an unconscious Nikki to keep us warm as we waited, the way I was able to stay calm just because she was there in my arms... Nope, we don't need to talk about it. About *her*.

Fortunately, at least Ciphered has finally been quiet thanks to the favor I called in with a friend at the *Herald*. I'll let him think I'm dead for a while longer, get my ducks in a row, hopefully track him down, though I do feel bad for any listeners who may be upset at my 'death.' I hope they'll forgive me.

I set my laptop and the case file from Nikki's backpack on the tiny kitchen table tucked into the corner of the studio. I don't know when Nikki usually wakes up in the morning, or if she's already up, but just in case she's still resting—head injury and all—I'll wait for her to initiate contact. I'm not avoiding her, of course not. It's for her recovery.

I evaluate everything set out in front of me, not even knowing where to begin. Everything feels so cluttered and chaotic without my van. Without my whiteboard, my equipment, my coffee. My brain no longer knows how to operate outside my normal environment. Plus adding Ciphered, George, and now being back here in this place that holds so many memories I've tried really hard to forget, I can't even think straight. Something I'm normally good at feels impossible to tackle, like the person who solved the last two cases wasn't even me. Maybe the "stage persona" I've taken on for the podcast has been more all-consuming than I thought. Maybe I've been pretending all along, wearing some kind of mask in real life too, and this fumbling boy with nothing to his name is who I truly am. Who I'm meant to be.

I take the next couple hours to flip through the case file and try to organize, but I'm too distracted by all the inadequacies surrounding me, like they're simply part of the oxygen here, impossible not to inhale.

A text from Nikki pops up on my phone, and I'm grateful for the interruption.

NIKKI

you alive?

KIERAN

Define alive.

NIKKI

same

KIERAN

Meet me downstairs.

Vinnie and I grab a spot downstairs at the bar, though there's not much competition with only a few other patrons here, and order from the very limited breakfast menu. There are only packaged pastries, muffins, and select fruits (subject to availability), but I order a few of everything.

After a few minutes, Vinnie's tail whacks my stool with such force it echoes across the whole room, so I know Nikki has arrived. She greets him with coos and tuts and slides into the barstool next to me, setting her backpack on the countertop next to her. Her hair is down and wavy, blue eyes bright, her face is makeup free except for a glittery lip gloss shining on her lips. She's so pretty it hurts a little.

I hate that it hurts a little.

"Morning," I say with a mouth full of muffin, sliding the options toward her. She chooses a banana and packaged Danish.

"Hi."

The awkwardness between us is thick and claustrophobic, so concrete I may be able to reach out and grab it. I guess I'll address the elephant in the room head-on before it crushes us. "I'm sorry about last night."

She shakes her head emphatically. "*I'm* s—"

"No," I interrupt, full stop. "It's completely my fault. I was out of line. I promise I will be nothing but professional from here on out."

Her icy eyes flick across my face like she's reading me. I wish I knew what she was seeing. "Right. Professional. Of course."

She returns to the banana quietly, looking like there's a lot more she wants to say but doesn't, and that infuriates me. Why does she have to be so infuriating?

She changes the subject and that infuriates me further. "So, when are we heading out for Grayford?"

"*We* aren't," I correct as the well-timed car pulls up outside. I quickly look at the carb totals on the plastic wrappers of my eaten pastries before throwing them away across the room.

She gives me a confused look, but I pretend not to notice and busy myself with bolusing my carbs, which is very urgent at this very second and necessary for my survival, certainly not just a way to keep myself busy so I don't have to look at her. I'm sure it'll all make sense when—

The front door *dings* as he enters, and he looks so out of place here it's kind of hilarious. This place would eat him alive. I might not mind seeing it.

"Hunter?!" Nikki squeals. She flies past me to fling herself into his arms.

I look away. I've spent a lot of time unlearning my upbringing, choosing a different way. Instincts and behaviors that were battered into me from infancy that I make the choice to suppress, not wanting to give into my roots, into this kind of life. But this is one of those times I might let genetics take over, give into the constant pull of who I could be—if I'm not careful. One look at him might pull me straight under, especially here, in the middle of the very life that is trying to consume me as we speak.

So, I return to my barstool, let Vinnie regulate me, and pretend to busy myself with the tubing of my pump, twisting it and untwisting it uselessly.

He approaches, and my jaw clenches. *He* holds out his hand to shake mine, and I allow myself to meet his eye, exercising probably the most restraint I've ever had to.

"Thanks for the call," he says, and his very voice makes the back of my neck heat up.

I shake his hand only for Nikki's benefit. *She loves him.*

"You called him?" She's looking back and forth between us with a look I can't quite figure out, different hues outlining the blue of her eyes.

I clear my throat. "I thought you might want your fiancé when you go look for Lizzy."

"Oh. Thank you. So thoughtful, yet again." She smiles, but in a way like the edges of her mouth are being pulled externally, like strings of a puppet.

He puts his arm around her shoulder, pulling her in tightly, and I have the urge to punch him again now that he's touching her. Which is totally unreasonable, considering they are engaged. To each other.

"Now we can figure the rest of this out together," he tells her brightly. I hate the stupid clean lines of his fade, and the stupid green of his eyes. At least I could probably beat him in a fight.

"Together," Nikki repeats, that same smile frozen on her lips.

Hunter brightens at the sight of Vinnie. "I love dogs! Can I pet him?"

I smirk into the collar of my jacket when Vinnie growls at

him, answering that question himself. Hunter leaps back. "Geez, okay, sorry."

"You're sure you don't want to come?" Nikki asks me, petting Vinnie between the ears absentmindedly as he tucks himself into her shins.

"We can cover more ground if we split up." Which is regrettably true. "I'll see what else I can get out of that case file. Maybe Ofeliya can drive me over to the crash site since my van is a little *under the weather* right now."

She winces. "I'll buy you a new one. I'm so sorry."

I wave it off and gesture to her backpack, to the iPad inside it. "Want me to hold onto that?"

Nikki clutches the bag. "No, I'll keep it. Especially if I do find Lizzy—*when* I find Lizzy—I want to be able to tell her I kept it safe myself. And maybe Hunter would recognize some of the men we haven't been able to name yet. We'll work on it on the drive over."

I don't like the sound of unnecessary eyes on our only evidence. But who am I to say what she can and can't do with her own sister's tablet?

"You have the GPS coordinates from Ofeliya?" I ask, but I already know she does. Maybe I'm prolonging the part when she leaves. With *him*.

"Yep. You have the case file?"

She knows I do.

"Yep. Good luck." And I mean it. "I hope you find what you're looking for."

And I mean that too.

"We will." She looks at Hunter. "She's there. I know she is."

She kneels to say goodbye to Vinnie, and he whines, sensing that she's leaving. "I'll be right back," she tells him, rubbing his face down affectionately. "And hopefully I'll be back with someone else you'll love just as much. She's the best."

And then they're gone, driving away in the shiny black car that brought him here. Off to see if her dead sister is alive. Together.

35

KIERAN

I DIDN'T ORDER THIS FAMILY THERAPY SESH, CAN I RETURN IT?

Vinnie and I slump up the stairs, the mood between us bleak. It's been only Vinnie and me for years, and *I like it that way.* I prefer it. So how come now it feels so off?

We step into Ofeliya's room, and I find her awake and sitting at the table, flipping through the case file I left there. Her laptop is sitting open next to her.

"This is bullshit," she says through a mouth full of cereal. But then she gets a good look at me and swallows quickly. "What's wrong?"

"What? Nothing. Just sent Nikki and her *fiancé* off to look for her sister, but it's fine. I'm fine."

She blinks. "Oh, you're down bad for her aren't you."

"Shut up, Ofeliya. For once in your life, shut up." I drop down at the table and tear the case file out of her hand.

"Because shoving something down deep inside and pretending it doesn't exist is totally the right move. What could go wrong?" she replies sarcastically, snatching the file back.

I throw out my hands. "What am I supposed to do about it?" My volume spikes. "For whatever reason beyond my understanding, she loves *him*. She chose *him*. She's *marrying him*."

"Did you forget I was also there last night?" She gives me a look. "The energy there was... well, it was a little sickening to be honest, but it was *mutually* there."

"She made her choice. I have to respect it."

"If you say so." She waves the file at me. "Well, at least when one of those idiot police officers opens my phishing email requesting that they change their login password, I can get us a non-B.S. version of this."

I gape at her. "Tell me you didn't actually do that."

She beams back. "You can thank me later. It works more often than you'd think. Most people are dumb. Truly so dumb."

"I don't do things that way, Ofeliya! I told you that! There are *laws*."

She takes another casual bite of her cereal. "You mean laws that say the next of kin is entitled to the details of their family's case? Laws that say civil servants shouldn't impede with investigations? Laws that prevent police chiefs from participating in coverups?"

I press my fingertips into my temples, feeling a headache coming on that I don't think is blood sugar related. "I cannot believe you."

"You don't have to look at it if you don't want to," she sniffs. "I think Nikki would want the information though."

"If you want to actually be helpful, tell me what you can find about this name."

I show her the text from Tina about the Washington-based organization connected to Ciphered Voyager that George and his contact found, that I've hit nothing but dead ends on.

"Aeth-er-line," she sounds out as she types it on her computer. "Hmm. Yeah there's not much other than that, what your friend found about the fleet of vehicles registered to it."

"Yeah," I tell her. "I couldn't find much either. Super unhelpful. I already knew he had vans. I know *quite well* he has vans."

"Well, this is cryptic." She turns her laptop screen so I can see.

It's a landing page in the App Store for an app that costs eight *thousand* dollars to download. The icon is completely black with tiny gold lettering that spells out *Aetherline.* Other than inside the app icon, the name isn't anywhere on the page. No reviews. The only thing it says in the description section is: *To the absence of light all things return in time.*

"This makes it seem like Aetherline is bigger than just one anon. Ciphered Voyager must just be a member of whatever this is, or maybe he's in charge of it, I don't know. I don't like the idea of there being more of him out there, though."

"Wouldn't it be convenient if you were well-connected with someone who knows a thing or two about organizations like this... in this region of the country...?" Ofeliya gives me a sidelong look.

"No," I reply simply.

"Even if it could mean being *the hero* that solves this case for Nikki, bringing her family's killer to justice, you still wouldn't ask him for help?" She folds her arms, raising an eyebrow. "Your pride is worth that much to you?"

"You heard him last night," I grumble. "All the 'my son,

the bird who lost his wings, has returned to fly again' crap he was saying? I built something worth being proud of on my own, but he won't even acknowledge it."

"Have you given him the chance to? Leaving home and changing your name and blocking every way to contact you is a pretty clear way of saying 'don't acknowledge me.'" Her face softens. "It doesn't mean you're moving back in and taking over the family business or anything. But he's your *dad,* Kai. Don't you think your mom would have wanted you two to at least make amends?"

"My name is Kieran now. And *no,*" I shake the thought away. "You don't get to use her against me. She was every bit a part of the life I left behind as he is."

Ofeliya puts a gentle hand on my arm. "Just think about it. He might be able to help."

There's no way that is happening.

I GUESS IT'S HAPPENING.

I'm at the stone front steps of my father's house, recently salted for the thick ice that ripples down them like a waterfall frozen in time. Ofeliya's arm is laced through mine to lend moral support, but also, she's wearing ridiculous heeled boots that make her nearly as tall as me, and she made me swear on my life I won't let her slip as we walk up the expansive stone driveway.

The area around my shins feels incomplete and cold without Vinnie right on them. I left him at Ofeliya's place, which is the right move—Dad never liked Vinnie much—but it still feels wrong without him. We do everything together. Now I don't have Vinnie or Nikki? My mood is worse than ever.

The house inside is just as stony and unwelcoming as I remember. High ceilings that echo. Hardwood floors that your shoes clack across as you walk. Décor and furniture that speaks to years and years without a woman's touch—purely functional. Detached. Lacking any sort of warmth or homeliness.

His latest housekeeper escorts us through the cold hallways, and

we find my father watching a boxing match in his living room with his head of security, Sergey, who is grayer than I remember. There are empty beer cans on the side-tables around them. They cheer as one of the boxers lands a finishing punch on his opponent, knocking him to his knees.

The sweet housekeeper coughs politely to get his attention, cautious to interrupt.

"*отец*," I address him formally, impatiently, when he doesn't notice us.

His head whips around with a look that could kill at first, but then he sees us.

"мой сын!" he cheers, coming over to clap me on the back. "My boy!"

He kisses Ofeliya on the cheek three times in greeting, left-right-left.

"*Dyadya*," she says fondly, kissing him back. "Sorry to show up without warning. This one was changing his mind the whole way here."

My father shuffles us toward the couches. "Come, come."

Sergey shakes my hand as he moves to free up a spot for us.

"To what do I owe the pleasure of a visit from my Little

Golovastik?" He's goading me. He knows I hate that nickname. *Tadpole.*

Ofeliya senses me tensing up and puts a hand on my arm to keep me from blowing up at him. She deliberately gets to the point before I can fly off the handle. "We wanted to pick your brain about our client's case. There is something we've found that you may be able to help us with."

"*We? Us? Our?*" he repeats, accent thick.

I sigh. He's never going to let this be easy. "*I* wanted your help," I correct. "My client, Nikki, that you met last night, her family's case."

The intrigue sparkles in his eye like a candle flickering, but he doesn't let up. "And why might this be worth my time, eh? I'm a very busy man. For a son to never call, never visit, just to come into my home and demand my help? Why should I?"

I knew this was a mistake.

I stand to leave, but Ofeliya shoves me back down. "Which he is very sorry for," she grinds out, emphasizing every word and raising an eyebrow at me.

"Which I am very sorry for," I repeat robotically, feeling thoroughly dead inside as the words cross my lips.

Infuriatingly, my father's face shifts immediately. "Ah, yes, my son, now what can I do for you?"

No apology from his end, I see, but what was I expecting?

I speak through my teeth, trying very hard to exert the self-control I've mastered these past few years. I decide to treat my dad like one of my interviews. If I detach myself from the relationship, I can conduct business as usual. Keep things professional. No need to get into feelings, or betrayals, or abandonments. No questions of, "Why didn't you love me as a child?" and only questions like, "What knowledge do you have that can be of use to me?"

With that strategy in mind, I pull out a small lavalier mic that survived the crash and plug it into my phone. Most of my equipment—microphones, condensers, stands, lights—didn't make it. But that's a problem I'll worry about after I solve this case. I can make do until then.

"As you may know, I run investigations for cold cases," I begin as I get the recording app to load on my phone.

"Yes, your little tripod," my dad adds helpfully.

Ofeliya snickers.

"Podcast, Dad. Podcast." I'm exhausted already.

He points to his head of security. "Sergey saw it on his Face app and listened to it in the car sometimes. A bit violent, my son. It made me *toshnit*... queasy in belly."

"Facebook? And I've literally watched you take a hammer to multiple men's fingers, Dad," I tell him flatly. "You made me watch you take out someone's *molars* once. I was like nine."

He waves it away and prattles off some proverb, the Russian equivalent of "no pain, no gain."

"Anyway, can I have your permission to—"

"Ah, yes, you'd like me to be star of your tripod." He nods knowingly, like he anticipated this one day.

I look at Ofeliya with dead eyes. *"I really don't like you,"* I tell her silently.

"Deep breaths," she sings sweetly through a stretched-out smile.

"Is it okay if I interview you?" I say with my teeth clenched. "I'm not sure when I'll air the interview because I'd like certain people to continue believing I'm dead. Normally I like to release them as it goes on, but I probably won't put out any more episodes until after this is all over. Is that okay?"

"You know I always wanted to be big actor. People always say I look like, what's his name Sergey? Bradley Pitt."

"You do not look like Brad Pitt, Dad."

And with a very deep breath, I pretend this is any other witness and press the red record button. I begin the interview I never thought I'd make in a million years.

PRE-RECORDED INTERVIEW
Secrets in Ice, **Season 3: Bonus Episode**

KIERAN BERGSTROM:

Sitting with me is Pavel Voronov, a local expert on criminal organizations here in Washington State. Thank you for joining me.

PAVEL VORONOV:

[muffled noises from speaking with lips directly against microphone]

KIERAN BERGSTROM:

Move back a little bit so we can hear you, please.

PAVEL VORONOV:

Yes, of course. Thank you for begging me be star on your podpad.

KIERAN BERGSTROM:

Podcast. Anyway, I have some questions about an organization we've uncovered. We think it could be a network of some kind involved in illegal activities. Some names we've found that could possibly be connected are Roger or *[redacted]* Mackenzie? Any of those names sound—?

PAVEL VORONOV:

[a crashing off-mic]

Roger *[censored]* Mackenzie! That son of a *[censored]* owes me four hundred and fifty thousand dollars. That weasel double crossed me. Got like eight of my men arrested! Whenever he comes out of the sewer like the little rat he is, I will *[censored]* *[censored]* his *[censored]* *[censored]* until he *[censored]* *[censored]*.

KIERAN BERGSTROM:

Roger Mackenzie is actually currently on life-support at a hospital in Southern Oregon from an anonymous attack. He may be connected to this organization, but we aren't sure how. The network call itself *[redacted]*. Heard of it?

PAVEL VORONOV:

Those *[censored]* *[censored]* stealing *[censored]*! Mackenzie is part of them, you say? May have to pay him little visit. Little snip-snip on the cord, eh?

[more crashing off mic]

KIERAN BERGSTROM:

Try to focus, I know this can be hard to hear. What do you know about this organization *[redacted]*?

PAVEL VORONOV:

I have tried to get in talk with those bastards many times, but no person would come to meet me flesh and bone. They wanted to negotiate on app they told me to get—like Sergey's Face app, you see—but I only do flesh and bone. But they scared to meet with me because they know they took my biggest client, those rats.

KIERAN BERGSTROM:

Which client?

PAVEL VORONOV:

This was long time ago. eight or nine years, maybe ten? Sergey, do you remember? Oil transportation I believe. Big client.

[muffled voice from off mic]

PAVEL VORONOV:

EverNorth Oil.

KIERAN BERGSTROM:

Wait, could you mean TrueNorth?

PAVEL VORONOV:

Yes, yes, that's it. Why?

KIERAN BERGSTROM:

Holy *[censored]*. That's the name of the Sinclair family's business. Nikki's father owned that company. He was killed ten years ago. Looks like they *really* wanted that business.

36

NIKKI

HER SISTER WAS A WITCH

Welcome to Grayford.

The sign is small and inconspicuous against a backdrop of white-tipped forest. We creep into the town slowly against the fresh snow coating the road. We pass a few businesses along the main road, all tourist attractions for Mount Rainier visitors, gift shops and winter sportsman gear. That must be what keeps this town alive.

It's beautiful and charming and I've never seen anything like it.

This is the furthest I've been from home since my family died, and my feet drum against the floor excitedly. I add this experience to my mental inventory. My collection. First a dance party and now a risky road-trip to a small town with my best friend? I'm basically a regular teen.

NIKKI

how is she?

ARRICK

No change to report. Are you okay?

NIKKI

yes, we have a lead. one step closer to lizzy.

Hunter's driver, Gary, slows the car and turns into the dinky gas station, parking in front of the gas pump. I admire the crumbling building in wonder, imagining all the many eras this gas station must have served over time. How many different kinds of people must come through here? I wish I could sit in a corner and watch everyone come in and out.

"Snacks?" I beam at Hunter in the seat next to me, partly desperate for snacks, but also partly wanting an excuse to go inside and explore, ask around about Lizzy. We've nearly identified all the videos, using our hotspots to run the program on the iPad, which is great, but this stop is a welcome break for my eyes. There's only so much 'bad men doing bad things' a girl can take.

Hunter looks at the building skeptically, as if it may gobble him up entirely if he gets too close.

I pull his arm, slinging my backpack with the iPad in it around my shoulder. "Come on, Snobby. It'll be good for you."

He laughs it off, adjusting the longer top section of his hair and pushing it back into place. He's trying to seem like a good sport, but I can tell he's uncomfortable. It's not his fault. He's used to a certain way of life. I mean, so am I, really.

Hunter pulls me close as I shiver in my marshmallow of a coat. My soul feels righted and at peace to have him close again, and not through a phone. I put my nose close to his neck as we walk together into the building, inhaling the scent of him I've missed so much.

Inside appears to be a multi-service establishment. There are souvenirs and gift items scattered about on shelves, keychains with names on them, magnets with a snow-capped mountain. There are lottery tickets and cigarettes. Stacks and stacks of beer tucked away in the back corner. And also—

I sniff it out immediately, and I'm pulled nearly in a trance over to the back counter. Hunter tucks in close behind me as we approach.

"Coffeeee," I sigh, already able to taste it on my tongue.

The café also serves as a deli, and the competing scents of espresso and salami is unique, but not in a bad way. The attendant is a very tall man with the longest beard I've ever seen. It's salt and pepper gray, pointed at the end. To my delight, he's wearing a multi-colored yarn beanie with an adorable pink pom-pom at the top of it.

"I love your hat," I gush.

The man brightens. "Isn't it great? My daughter is learning how to knit. She insisted it wasn't good enough to be worn in public. I can't wait to tell her she was wrong."

I gesture to my own hat, which is also pink, and grin. "You can tell her I know a good one when I see one."

He rumbles a laugh, the sound warm and cozy like a crackling fire after a day playing in the snow. "I will. What can I get you folks?"

Hunter is busy analyzing the fading menu like it's a different language he's translating in real time.

I order a latte and an Italian sub, and Hunter eventually decides on a BLT, ordering one for him and one for Gary.

"Where are you folks coming in from? I haven't seen you in before," the man converses as he prepares our order, sliding on a pair of food-handling gloves as the espresso machine gets to work.

"I'm from Sapphire Pines. This is a lovely little town. You must love it."

Hunter tucks his hands into his light wash Versace jeans, and for some reason it makes me wonder if Kieran would ever wear twelve-hundred-dollar jeans. "Vancouver," he answers the man simply. "We met up halfway."

"Ah yes, a lovely time of year for cozy rendezvous," the man replies with a knowing smile.

I look at Hunter for encouragement before broaching the topic, and he gives me a reassuring smile. "I'm... actually trying to reconnect with a family member who lives up here."

"Oh?" says the man, layering slices of lunch meat on the bread.

"Maybe you'd be able to help me?" I pull my phone out of my coat pocket and open the videos Unknown sent with the house in the background. That's when I realize I have absolutely no cell service out here. How comforting.

"We were separated a long time ago," I continue, "so I don't have any recent photos of her. And I don't know what name she goes by now... but I knew her as Lizzy. Well, Elizabeth. I assume she probably looks sort of like me? But a little older, with blonde hair. At least she had blonde hair when I knew her..." I trail off, realizing how insane I sound. I look at him hopefully anyway.

The man wraps up the sandwiches quietly in paper and sets them on the counter in front of us. He looks at me with a new expression that looks slightly pinched. Curious? Maybe suspicious?

"You know, hun," he finally says. "There are only two reasons why people live here." He turns to work on my coffee. The espresso machine hisses as he pulls two shots. The aroma fills my nostrils, and I have to keep from salivating. "They live here because they grew up here... or because they're running away from something." He adds pointedly, "Or some*one*."

Is it really that common to escape here? Or does he know something about Lizzy after all? I don't even know what to say. The man pours steaming milk in the cup with the espresso and dumps a colossal amount of caramel sauce in there just as I requested. It's perfect.

He sets it in front of me, and I take it in my hands reverently. He doesn't know how much I needed this. The cozy brown liquid swirling in the cup is comforting, grounding, reminding me of a certain pair of melty brown eyes, but I shake off *that* thought quickly.

The man gives me another long look. What's he seeing when he looks at me? "Since you didn't grow up here, I'm assuming your family member probably doesn't want to be found."

Hunter pulls cash out of his wallet to pay for the food and coffee, and includes an extra $50 bill, which he drops on the counter, deciding now to chime in. "Look, sir, are you willing to help us or not? Her sister could be in danger. We're trying to make sure she's okay."

The man sees the money and stands up straighter, somehow stretching even taller, and I squirm a bit. He sizes Hunter up from the top of his head to the tips of his boots, somehow gazing through his skin straight to his soul. There is a long silence, the tension so heavy it's almost crushing. Now I'm wondering what he sees when he looks at him too.

"We look after our own here," the man says, making some kind of decision about Hunter. Based on what? His clothes? The way his hair is styled? That says nothing about the kind and loving person he is.

"Please—" I begin, but Hunter snatches the subs off the counter, leaving the cash.

"Fine. We'll go somewhere else." Hunter pulls me with him out the door.

"Wait—"

The door *clangs* shut behind us before I can even blink.

I gape at Hunter, wanting to punch him. "What was *that?*"

Gary has pulled the car into a parking spot by the entrance, and he shuffles out to open the back door for us.

"I don't like him," Hunter says simply, ducking his head to slide into the backseat.

"Well, *I'm* going back in. Don't follow me." And I spin around on my heel before he can try to convince me otherwise. The bell on the door *dings* as I walk back inside.

I think about the way Kieran interviews people, the empathy he has for others that makes them feel comfortable opening up and answering his questions. It's part of why his podcast has always been so compelling to me. He's so good with people. I, on the other hand, have no idea what I'm doing. I wish he came along with us. It's weird to do this without him, and I miss Vinnie desperately.

The man sees me coming and has already opened his mouth to probably tell me to leave, but I don't give him the chance. I'm going to try this Kieran-style. "I'm so sorry about my fiancé. He... doesn't get out much. I respect the community you have here; it's similar where I grew up, too. But I promise I'm not here to cause harm. Is there any way you can believe that I have a really good reason to need to find her?"

I hold out my phone to him, the video already pulled up. "Can you just take a look? This is her last known location. Can you tell me if it looks familiar? If you know anything at all... it could save multiple lives."

He looks like he's going to protest, so I cut him off yet again. "*Please.*"

With a sigh, he takes my phone. He watches it a few times before giving it back with a look of apology that fizzles out any glimmer of pride I felt. "I'm sorry, hun. I don't know where that is. There are so many remote properties out here. It could be anywhere."

I blink, feeling a prickle of tears at my eyes. I had gotten my hopes up too high. Thinking I could waltz in here, and the first person I spoke to would lead me right to her? Stupid.

"It's okay! Thank you anyway for looking." I force a smile. "I appreciate your help."

I turn to leave, but he stops me, sounding hesitant but resigned.

"My friend Stuart owns the tow company down the road... He does a lot of the plowing around town this time of year. He may recognize the house better. You can tell him Otis sent ya."

His eyes are kind.

"Thank you, Otis."

He nods, and I leave. As I walk out of the door, the thought crosses my mind that Kieran would be proud of me, and that feels really good.

I find the two men eating their subs as casually as if this were a normal lunch break.

"Turns out a little *manners* go a long way," I tell Hunter with emphasis as I slide in next to him. "He said the tow company down the road might be able to help us. Finish your lunch first, though, Gary, please. No rush," I hurriedly add as he springs to action, feeling bad for cutting his meal short.

I unwrap my own sandwich, my stomach getting jealous when it realizes it's the only one not being fed.

"Sorry I messed it up," Hunter says through a mouth full of BLT. He swallows and gives me a sheepish smile, green eyes shifting apologetically to a velvety moss, and I forgive him immediately, of course. "I think my impatience may have been a little hunger motivated."

I squeeze his hand. "It's okay. We just need to be careful in a town this small. They have no reason to trust us."

Gary turns back onto the main street, the tires crunching on the salted road.

"This one?" he asks as he approaches a fading building with a crumbling sign that says "TOW."

"I think so."

He parks and comes to open my door. Hunter moves to come with me, but I gently stop him. "Maybe I should—"

"I'm not letting you go in there by yourself, but I'll shut up," he promises, giving me the equivalent of puppy dog eyes that I'd never be able to say no to even if I tried.

"Fine." But secretly I'm glad. Now that I've gotten used to his real-life presence, I'm more at ease, more myself, when he's close. Life just feels better, *enhanced,* when I can smell that cologne, feel his tall proximity hovering over me. It's like getting a luxurious upgrade to life I can't give up now.

We are met inside by a small office with a cluttered desk in the corner. It's warm inside and smells slightly of tuna. A man stands to greet us, hurriedly setting down the plastic fork he was holding in the plastic Tupperware bowl on the desk.

"Afternoon," he says, swallowing quickly and swiping at his mouth. "How can I help you?"

I move to shake his hand. "Hi, I'm Nikki, and this is my fiancé, Hunter. Are you Stuart? We just spoke with Otis down the road, and he sent us your way. By the way, the roads here are fantastic. Not the slightest bit of slip. You do great work."

He smiles in a surprised way, like he doesn't get compliments very often. "Why thank you. It's a busy time of year for the whole town. Just doing my part."

"Of course. Well, I was hoping you might be able to help us." I keep my story simple this time, trying to avoid all the unsure rambling that made Otis so suspicious. Kieran-style. "My sister lives in this area somewhere, and she could be in danger. I'm trying to find her. This is her last known location. All I have is this short clip. Otis thought you might recognize it with all the hard work you do around town. Can you possibly see if it looks familiar?"

Stuart blows out a humble breath. "I don't know if I'll be any help, but I can take a look."

I hand him my phone. "Thank you so much, Stuart."

He watches it a few times. And then a few times more. Then he rifles around his desk for something. A pen. He sets my phone down on his desk and watches it again as he scribbles something down on the paper. Then again. And again.

I lean back into Hunter, and he tucks his head into the crook of my neck. The impatience and anxiety instantly dissolve. I'm content waiting however long Stuart needs as long as Hunter keeps holding me like this. It's nice that the more time we spend with each other, those unsure boundaries between former best friends and new fiancés are slowly melting away, creating something new, something *right* in its place.

"Okay," Stuart says, smacking his pen down. He shows me his paper. It's a list with four bullet points and scribbled directions that are barely legible. "The angle of Tahoma in the back helped me narrow it down quite a bit. Then I looked at the trees. I always remember a tree. Then the curbing style of the sidewalks."

He's explaining this so animatedly, so proud to be sharing his expertise on something.

"I deal with a lot of curbs in my line of work, you see," he explains.

"Of course." I nod emphatically.

"That plus the style of house... my best guess is it's one of these four streets. I couldn't remember house numbers, sorry."

"Four? Wow, Stuart, that's great!" I exclaim. "That's so much better than we've had so far. Thank you so much for your help."

He beams at me, handing me the paper. "I have a few more that it *could* be, but I'm less confident on the tree patterns matching up. If those four don't get you what you're looking for, come back, and I'll give you a few more."

"Thank you!"

"You should know though... there's one on that list that you need to be very careful with. I almost didn't put it on the list at all, because, well... Folks around here say..." He trails off.

"Say what?" I fold the paper and put it in my pocket carefully.

"Ah, it's just local legend." He laughs it off, but the sound is hollow.

"What do they say, Stuart? We really need to be prepared out there, and you know this town best."

"That one off the 706? Just don't even go around it okay? I shouldn't have put it on there." Stuart rubs the back of his neck, as if hesitant to say anything more. "A lot of people around here keep to themselves, you know? But that one there... that's a recluse like we've never seen. Last time kids dared to trick-or-treat there, she ran them off with a shotgun."

I gawk at him. "Did anyone get hurt?"

"Nah, but they sure learned their lesson. The people say... well, it sounds silly to say it now, but the local rumor is she's a witch." He chuckles drily.

"A witch?" Hunter repeats.

I shoot him a look like a stern teacher, and he flashes me his palms apologetically, recommitting to his promise to shutting up.

"Silly, I know. But bad things happen when people go around. They say her property is cursed. Even the post-master drops her mail off in a PO box downtown, though she never comes to get it. Won't touch her mailbox with a ten-foot pole after he sliced his hand open on it once. No one even knows what she looks like."

"But you know she's a *she*?" I ask.

Stuart shrugs. "Could be a grouchy old man for all I know. That's just the town rumor mill."

"Okay." I give him a half-hearted smile. "I appreciate your help so much, Stuart. Thank you."

"Of course. Come back if you need anything else."

And we walk out of the stuffy office, my feet feeling like they're floating, moving entirely on their own.

Grumpy recluse who has made the locals believe she's a witch?

That's my *first* stop.

I'd bet my life that's my sister.

37

KIERAN

OH, BLOOD? COOL COOL COOL COOL

My hands are in my hair. I'm on my feet, but I'm not sure when I stood up.

"This is huge," I say, pulse racing from the news about the connection between this Aetherline network and the Sinclair business.

"There's your motive," Ofeliya whispers, eyes wide. "They wanted him gone so they could use the company."

"Did I solve case?" Dad asks with a proud grin. "I solved case, Sergey."

I ignore his comment, my mind on a single track right now. "Dad, do you have any way of confirming a more precise timeframe of when they took your client?"

"I'd have to check with Yeliza, my assistant. She keeps track of those kinds of things better than me."

I yank a napkin off the closest side table and scribble down my number on it. "Can you please have her call me when she finds that out?"

Ofeliya's phone *dings*. "Well would you look at that," she

says brightly. "Officer Dipshit Collins from Thurston County PD has just changed his password."

"We should go." I ignore Ofeliya completely. I can't go down that rabbit hole, or I might never come back up.

My dad stands and... hugs me? He pulls back, hands on my shoulders, and looks at me with an expression I've never seen him have before. Constipation, maybe?

"You know," he tells me, "it's good what you're doing for this girl. Nice girl. I guess I— well, I'm proud of you, *мой сын*, my boy. You do good work."

I blink at him. *What did he say?* Wow, he must be really constipated.

He grabs me by the shoulder, his fingernails nearly digging into bone, as he leads us out the door. My knees almost buckle under the weight of his grip. "And when you find these cockroaches, let me have piece of them too, yeah?"

"THEN YOU DON'T HAVE to look at it!" Ofeliya yells stubbornly over her shoulder as we enter her apartment. She goes straight to the laptop sitting on her kitchen table.

Vinnie greets us as if he's been alone in the wild for years, and I pause the anger at Ofeliya to smile at him properly. "Hey, bud, who's my good boy?"

She's already typing on her keyboard, her long, orange-tipped nails clacking away, emphasizing the sound of her completely disregarding any wishes of mine on the matter.

I sit on her couch with my head buried in my hands, trying to ignore her. Vinnie nudges my leg and drops a bruised banana he found on her counter in my lap. I sigh and munch on it grumpily.

"These county records systems are so archaic it's embarrassing. They're basically begging us to take it, Kai." *Clack, clack, clack.* "Done!"

I cover my ears like a child. "*Kieran*, and la, la, la. I'm not complicit in this."

"Don't you at least want to confirm your theory about the police chief trying to impede the investigation, *Kieran*?" She gives me a sly grin.

"What should I do?" I ask Vinnie, as if he can materialize into a wise Magi that will lead me to the right path.

Ofeliya makes an exaggeratedly low cartoonish voice from the table, as if speaking for him. "I think you should rescue the princess, you idiot!"

"He doesn't sound like that," I tell her flatly. And then to him, "Is she right?"

He raises his ears, sitting up on his haunches straighter at the question. He gives a little yip.

I sigh, standing with relent. "Guess I'm the only one with *values* around here. Good, bad, right, wrong, who cares?"

"You *know* legal doesn't always mean right and illegal doesn't always mean wrong," Ofeliya reproaches from her computer, focusing intently on the screen. "You have to embrace the gray area doing what you do, or you're no different than the system that failed them."

I don't have the energy for an ethics lesson right now, nor do I want to give much thought to how many laws we're breaking right now, but I resign to the decision. It's a means to an end. For Nikki.

Whatever this means for me, for my soul, my conscience, she deserves answers regardless.

I drop into the chair next to Ofeliya, and she tilts her screen so we can both see. She points to a line on the file and reads it aloud, "'Overseeing officer: Timothy Hemlock.' Though he was only Sergeant Hemlock at the time. I wonder if Aetherline pulled some strings to get him up to chief in exchange for his help covering this up."

"I knew it. Bastard." I skim the rest of the case summary page for anything else useful before she scrolls to the initial report page. "Maybe he's one of them. If he's *in* Aetherline, imagine how many cases like these he can 'oversee' and close quietly for their benefit. He was in one of those videos..." I think of the rest of the videos. Important people doing really bad things. "Maybe those are the rest of the members?"

If that's true, that would mean Vanderwaal and Mackenzie are in Aetherline too... Was Mr. Sinclair?

"Maybe," Ofeliya says. "Definitely another possible motive. Get the business, get rid of the girl who had the blackmail videos. Hopefully this will tell us more."

Our heads pull together to read the rest of Ofeliya's screen.

"Do you not have a printer?" I mumble.

"The location of the crash," she points again, ignoring me, a faster reader than me. "That was redacted in the other one. All it said before was off the I-5. Maytown Road? Does that mean anything to you? Seems random."

I pull out my phone and spread my fingers to zoom in on the map, analyzing it for a moment. I switch it to the street view. "Definitely a narrow highway. Thick forest on both sides. Not unreasonable that they would have simply lost control." I test a theory, plugging an address in. "Look."

I show Ofeliya, pointing to the two different pins. "That's her family's cabin. The crash site is directly on-route. That confirms they were going there after all."

I look at the map some more as I ask, "What does the report say about the search of the area? It was pretty much blacked out in the other one."

"'A search and rescue team, including K9's, were deployed to the area after the initial report. The team conducted a six-mile radius search on foot, and a thirty-mile radius search by aerial drone. The search was unsuccessful.'"

"Six miles, you said?" I ask, zooming into the map. Ofeliya watches over my shoulder. "There's a lake less than two miles away. Does it say anything about that in the report? Seems like an obvious dump site to me."

Ofeliya looks back to her computer to scan the report. "Here," she says. "'Forensic recovery dog search and side-scan sonar of nearby lake was inconclusive.'"

I gape at her. "They didn't deploy a dive team?"

I read over her shoulder to confirm, not that I don't trust her, but I can't comprehend it. Standard protocol would dictate a *thorough* search of any nearby bodies of water. And all they did was a cadaver dog and sonar?

"This goes way beyond reasonable oversight," Ofeliya murmurs, her eyes busy on the screen looking for the answers between lines. "This is blatant obstruction of justice. Someone made sure that lake wasn't inspected. Hemlock?"

"Makes the most sense."

I blow out a slow breath to steel myself for what I know is coming in the next section of the case file. The crime scene documentation. This is my least favorite part of investigations.

She looks over at me, sensing my unease. "Gotta thing with blood?"

I swallow hard. "Maybe a little."

"Odd choice of career path, murder. Perhaps surgery or phlebotomy instead?" she teases, flicking her thumb to scroll to the next section. These pages weren't even included at all in the file they gave us.

Embedded images load in the report. First are images of a crumpled black sedan, the front half nearly swallowed whole by a huge tree. Next are images of the interior. I cringe.

Ofeliya glances at me. "You okay?"

So. Much. Blood.

You'd think the interior took a bath in it with how much there is. I gulp and shake off the nausea. *Get it together.* I take off the eyes that see *people* behind these splashes of blood and put on analytical glasses instead. Look for patterns, look for inconsistencies. Look at the *data.*

So, I do that.

Like the public details I garnered from my own research said, there are in fact three distinct blood pools. One at the driver's seat, one at the passenger's seat, and one in the rear. The summary confirms that it came back a match for Gunnar, Ingrid, and Elizabeth Sinclair, which is why they were all concluded to be dead. I knew this already.

There has to be something I'm not seeing.

I ask Ofeliya to scroll back up to the photos of the rear.

I look at it for a long time. Ofeliya doesn't interrupt, but I can feel her curiosity radiating off her the longer I don't say anything.

"Doesn't it—?" I stop myself, looking at it again. No, probably not. It couldn't be.

Like she's about to blow from impatience, she blurts out, "Doesn't it what?"

I point to the pool in the backseat belonging to Lizzy.

"This may be a dumb observation and maybe there's a scientific reason for this, her being so young and all, but... doesn't hers look much smaller?"

"Well, we're operating under the hope that she's alive right? Could this confirm her injuries weren't lethal after all?"

"Maybe," I muse, taking another look. "'Ballistic evidence was found in windshields, dashboard, and rear seats, although no firearm was found on site.'"

I stand, my brain moving too fast to allow me to sit still anymore. Vinnie senses my quickening pulse and perks up, following me as I walk from side to side. I speak aloud as I do, trying to envision the scene that feels so tangled up in my head.

"It doesn't make sense," I think aloud. "If the car crashed first and *then* the gunman shot them to finish the job..." I raise my arm like a gun to visualize it, moving to one side of an imaginary car and 'opening the door' to shoot. "And assuming their heads wouldn't be upright because of the force of the crash, and assuming the gunshots would have probably come from outside the vehicle on either side..."

Ofeliya is hanging onto every word I'm saying, looking like she'd be eating popcorn right now if she had any.

"Wouldn't the blood spatter be—" I point around in my imaginary car. "On the sides? Or even on the seats? Or the ground?"

Ofeliya whips back around to zoom in on the photos. I lean over her shoulder. "They're on the front windshield and the lower back of the driver's seat." She looks back at me with wide eyes.

A chill covers me from head to toe as I point my imaginary gun to visualize it.

"The shots came from the backseat," Ofeliya breathes, verbalizing my inner thoughts that are still materializing in my head.

I try to stay calm as I work it out verbally. I'm sure there's an explanation I can come to that makes sense.

"It doesn't make sense that they'd be upright after *that*." I wave to the tree and smushed vehicle. "So, the killer would have shot them *before* they crashed, and that's likely what caused the driver to lose control. And with no fourth person's DNA uncovered in the backseat... No spatter on the rear windshield or back windows..."

We share a moment of heavy eye contact, the entire room filling with the tense fog of truth that slithers in through my nostrils and down my gut.

"Lizzy," I whisper, barely able to say it. "Lizzy killed them."

Nikki.

I jump to action, feeling like I've been struck by lightning. Ofeliya stands, reading my mind and grabbing her keys.

"Vinnie, stay. Sorry, bud, no car rides for you for a while."

Nikki is on her way there right now.

To unknowingly confront her parents' murderer. *Lizzy.*

We have to stop her.

Or she could be next.

38

NIKKI

DROP-INS DROP DEAD

Hunter's driver holds Stuart's handwritten directions as he turns onto the road he sent us to.

I squeeze Hunter's hand so tightly he may be losing circulation as we creep down the road, comparing the houses we pass with the video Lizzy sent. We're halfway down the road and we've only passed two houses. They're a little hard to see from the road—modest cabins tucked deep into spread out properties that back up to the most beautiful view I've ever seen.

The volcano itself is capped with snow, giant and towering, low-hanging wispy clouds draping around it like a misty halo. It's a majestic canvas of pure white that is both blinding and impossible to look away from. The afternoon sun reflects off the ice like millions of tiny mirrors, and I think of Kieran's dad. His mirror story. And then I think of Kieran...

I try to focus on the next house as we pass the third and don't find a match. My breath hitches as we approach the fourth property. The air shifts as we get closer. That has to mean something. You're supposed to be able to *feel* life-changing moments in your bones, right?

I squeeze Hunter's hand even tighter, and he squeezes back, holding up my phone to the window so we can both look.

An unnerving fog has materialized around us, casting a gray blur around everything, making it impossible to see more than a hundred feet ahead.

The property has a chain-link fence all around it, and where most of the other houses cleared away a lot of the trees on their properties to make better use of the land, this one has trees everywhere. There's barely a driveway. It's narrow and leads back to a house that's hard to see from the road in this fog.

I squint, nearly sitting on top of Hunter to press my nose against the glass of his window.

"That tree looks similar," I declare. But then less sure, "I think."

Hunter's breath is warm on my cheek, his face so close to mine that if I looked at him right now, our noses might touch. Our lips. *Focus, Nikki. This is a life-changing moment.*

"Want me to get out and look closer?" he offers.

I climb over him clumsily and nearly fall out as I push his door open and clamber out. I'm struck breathless by the contrast of the cold out here. My cheeks instantly go numb from the chill.

Poor Gary scurries out of his seat to help me, looking simply exhausted by me, and Hunter laughs, "There were easier ways you could've done that."

I dust myself off. "I'm good, Gary, you stay warm," I tell him.

"We're going to look around," Hunter adds. "Be ready. We might need a getaway vehicle from the town witch."

We share a laugh. I love laughing with him.

"It *has* to be Lizzy," I say with pride at the thought. "She once told me it was her lifelong dream to live in a retirement community because it seemed quiet. This" –I gesture all around to the spacious property, the views, the privacy— "is all so her."

Hunter holds up the video on my phone as we stand at the gate to squint at the house.

I gasp and point. "The corner! On that side of the house, look! Doesn't it look the same?"

He looks carefully, and I can tell he's trying not to get my hopes up. "It's hard to know for sure with how quickly it showed the house in the video, but it definitely looks—"

I've already opened the gate. It creaks and groans as I push it open.

"Wait!" he whispers loudly like we haven't been talking at a regular volume this whole time already. "What are you doing?"

My legs act on their own, as if I'm on a wire that my sister is pulling from her end. I couldn't stop if I tried. "I have to know if she's here," I whisper-yell back. "I can't wait a second longer."

I walk down the narrow driveway, hardly breathing as my boots sink into the un-shoveled snow. It's several inches deep. Hunter follows reluctantly behind, helping me keep my balance as I step through the snow.

Closer now, the house finally becomes visible through the mist, and I tell Hunter over my shoulder, "It's the same house. I know it."

I shriek at the sudden sound of a thunderous *bang!* I

duck right away, now all too familiar with the unmistakable sound of—

Bang!

Gunshots.

Warning shots. For now.

Hunter crouches in a low squat, fear distorting his entire face. "Let's go!" He pulls me backward by the arm, and I nearly fall onto my butt.

I rip my arm away and rebalance myself. "*No.* It's Lizzy. It has to be. She won't hurt me."

I stretch to my full height, waving my arms high above my head.

"Lizzy!" I yell as loud as I can, but it gets partially absorbed by the fog and the snow. "It's me!"

Another shot sounds, and I flinch but keep my arms waving high.

"Lizzy!" I yell again, hoping the wind will carry it to her, begging nature to be on my side here.

I make it down the driveway and tromp toward the front porch, fueled only by the buzz of pure confidence that it's *her.* She's *here.* She's *alive.*

"Nikki, wait," Hunter begs from somewhere behind, but I hardly hear him.

That string is pulling me again, forcing me toward her front door. I can't resist the gravity pull of my sister. *My alive sister.*

I knock on the door, and the sound echoes, cutting through the eerie quiet like ice. The quiet intensifies as no one answers. The window by the door has blinds pulled shut. No way to peek in. No doorbell.

I knock again, pounding a little more urgently. "Lizzy, it's me! Nikki!"

Pound, pound, pound. My knocking blends together with my beating heart.

"Liz—!"

I'm cut off by the sobering sound of a shotgun being cocked behind me.

Hunter and I whip around.

He puts his hands up right away, but I'm rooted to the spot. Stunned. Frozen.

I'm met by blue eyes behind a shotgun that are just as shocked.

Her eyes.

The gun falters, lowering slightly. "Kiki?"

She's wearing a flannel trapper hat with a brim that hangs low over her forehead and flaps that go nearly to her shoulders, blonde hair long and tumbling down underneath.

"Lizzy," I breathe, throat tightening. Hot tears prickle at my eyes. "You're really alive."

And then I nearly tackle her, sliding around the shotgun as if it's a silly play sword. It falls out of her hand and clatters to the ground. I squeeze Lizzy in my arms tightly and she's stunned and unmoving underneath my embrace.

"You're alive!" I sing, bouncing excitedly. I pull back to really look at her. Maybe seeing her up close will make this feel like less of a dream. "You're alive!"

Her eyes well up, tears clouding the bright blue. "Kiki?" she whispers again, eyes zigzagging across my face.

I take her hands in mine. "I'm here."

Lizzy shakes her head as if slowly coming back to consciousness, to reality. Her brows draw together. "How did you find me?" She pulls her hands away, her head still shaking. "I don't understand. How are you here? *Why* are you here?"

I step toward her, reaching for her hands again, but she takes a step back.

Her pupils dilate, the black almost swallowing her icy blue irises whole. She looks around wildly, noticing Hunter for the first time. "Who is this? Does anyone else know you're here?"

She bends down to pick the gun back up. I step toward her again to lend reassurance despite the warm hurt bubbling in my gut at her confusing reaction. "This is Hunter, remember him from when we were kids? It's okay. I'm here. You're safe now. I came as soon as I got your texts."

She holds a hand up to stop me in my tracks. The words she says are clipped and frozen. "What. Texts."

My jaw hangs. Did the temperature just drop further? "Your texts you sent. You asked me to find you... Didn't you?"

"I didn't send you any texts." Her words shake with a fear I don't understand. Her grip tightens around the shotgun, and she looks around again. "You need to leave. Hurry, go. Before anyone sees you."

I reach for her again. "Lizzy, you're alive, I'm not leav—"

To my surprise she points the shotgun at me. Hunter steps in next to me, his hand firm on my forearm.

"Leave. Now." Her features stack into a fierce glare, a warning as sharp as the gunshots. "You can't be here."

I feel dizzy as Hunter pulls me away from her. I stumble, my limbs and brain not communicating.

His voice feels far away. "Okay, easy, we're leaving," he tells her. "We don't want any trouble."

Hunter guides me back to the car. It's like I'm levitating, in some kind of daze. Disoriented. I barely even register we're sitting back in the car until Gary is driving away, slipping a little on the slick road.

"No, wait!" I protest, coming back to life. Doesn't he realize we left a piece of me behind? I bang on the window. "Lizzy! Lizzy!!"

I hit Hunter furiously, arms flailing. "What are you doing? We have to go back! Gary, turn around! We can't just leave her there! We can't—"

Hunter's eyes are so full of pity that it takes the words right from my mouth, snatching them away. I can't pretend or hide from the truth, because it's glaring on his face. It's impossible to deny it.

She's alive. But she didn't want me.

I crumble into him, a sob bursting from my throat like it was held for ransom.

He holds me and runs my hair through his fingers while I cry.

And I cry for a long, long time.

39

NIKKI

ANTIFREEZE TO THAW A FROZEN HEART

I rouse from a combination of numb shock and sleep—not the restful kind, the kind your body forces you into after you cry your guts out—as the car comes to a gentle stop.

Hunter's arms around me loosen as I move, and I look at him apologetically, noticing the uncomfortable angle I forced him to sit in for who knows how long while he held me.

He puts my hair behind my ear, a gesture so pure and gentle I have to swallow hard, so I don't burst into tears again. "Are you okay?" he asks, his lips pressed into a worried line.

My eyes flick downward to my lap.

"Stupid question," he scolds himself, raising my chin with his fingers, forcing me to meet his eyes. So green they nearly have a yellow glow in this light. "Let me rephrase that. You're *going* to be okay."

I smile weakly. "I don't know what I'd do without you. Honestly."

He puts his forehead on mine, and I force myself to breathe in the scent of him while he's close, even though there's a sharp ache under my rib when I take a full breath. I inhale and exhale, and here, when I'm his and he's mine, everything's okay for just a second. For this single second, I can block out the rest of the world when *my* whole world is right here. But it's fleeting. Over in a blink. My chest hurts too much to ignore.

Hunter takes my hand and kisses it. "You don't need her. Your aunt will be okay until the wedding. You'll save her yourself."

She's alive, but she has stayed away from me all this time... by choice. Made me believe she was dead, so she didn't have to be around me...

I smile weakly. I take stock of our location for the first time since the car stopped.

"Where—?" But then I gasp, a flash flood of memories hitting me over and over. "Wait! I *do* remember this place."

It's the family cabin.

With a chuckle, Hunter opens his car and holds my hand to help me out. "I figured we'd both rather stay here than some hotel with bedbugs and tiny cameras hidden in the showers."

"You watch too much American TV," I tell him with a light chuckle, looking around at cabin. It's a strange feeling to be back here again, but without my family. Without my sister who would rather be dead than be with me.

"You also said the crash site is nearby... I thought you might want to go check that out. Well, I don't know if you're doing the case still, after the whole Lizzy thing, but—oh no, I was wrong. You hate it. This made it worse. I'm so sorry." He's rambling. It's cute.

I take his hand and squeeze it reassuringly. "No, it's a great idea. Just a lot of memories is all."

Isn't it strange how smells can hold so many more memories than your mind sometimes? Like you don't even realize when a smell is holding a memory you've long forgotten until you smell it again, and it all floods back?

That's the smell of this cabin. It's pine and freshly chopped wood and cinnamon and that's *my family*. What my family used to be. It hurts. It hurts so bad I can't breathe.

Fortunately, it looks mostly the same, at least from what I can remember. Hunter's family hasn't changed it much since they bought it.

I set my backpack down on the sofa and keep exploring the main room, dusting off old memories and storing them in a place I won't forget them again.

Like sliding down these wood floors with Lizzy in our socks like they were a slip n' slide. Sprinting down the hallways to our room soaking wet from the hot tub, freezing and giggling. Sneaking Christmas cookies from loud traitorous cookie tins in the middle of the night and getting caught by our mom, thinking we were in big trouble, but she poured the milk and ate some too.

"Why did your dad buy this place anyway?" I run my hand across the back of the couch, remembering the texture under my palm.

Hunter leans back in one of the armchairs. "He said the bank was trying to liquidate everything. They wanted to put it on the open market, but he thought you may want to come back here one day."

I'm moved by the kind gesture. "And to have it upkept all this time, too? Really thoughtful."

My humanness catches up to me suddenly, and I realize

how long it's been since I've used the bathroom. "I'll be right back."

Muscle memory takes over, and I step down the hallway and open the first door on the left. I'm overcome by a strange nostalgia, but not a comfortable one, as I stand in the middle of the bathroom, looking around at the floral wallpaper behind the mirror, the textured tile, the dark green walls. My skin prickles for some reason.

I have my human moment, and then the sudden solitude becomes stifling. There's no place to hide from any troubling thoughts or repressed emotions when it's this quiet. I sit on the edge of the bathtub and put my elbows on my knees, trying to give myself a moment. I beg my brain to catch up, but nothing makes sense.

She's alive.

She pointed a gun at me.

And she didn't send the texts. Didn't even know about them.

So, who did? Has it been Kieran's Ciphered Voyager messing with me, too?

How did Unknown know she was alive? All those clues in my house? In her room? Did Lizzy even put those there for me to find? Or did Unknown...? The very thought of that makes my bones cold.

And most of all, why did they want me to find her, just so she'd turn me away? Shoo me off like a stray cat?

I pat myself down, feeling for my phone, but it's not in either of my pockets. I must have left it in the car. I need to call Kieran, talk this out with him and figure out our next steps. He can help make some sense of it all, and I need to look at those texts from Unknown again, see them with fresh eyes.

Texts.

Wait.

I shoot up from the bathtub like the porcelain electrocuted me to look around again, to really *see* this room. I stare in the mirror, seeing myself—eyes red from crying, braid messy and lopsided—and the reflection of the green walls, floral wallpaper.

This room. That vaguely familiar tingling feeling is here, but it's not quite right...

I throw open the door and dart further down the hallway, taking the next right to the primary bedroom. To the bathroom that is almost identical but a little bigger. Same wallpaper, same green walls, same tile. But one thing is different.

The mirror. A mirror I've seen *recently* but couldn't place then.

I stare at it in shock, and my knees begin to shake.

That feeling. My skin prickling. The familiarity my body picked up on before my cluttered brain did.

I put both my hands on the sink counter to steady myself for a moment, to pull back and see the whole picture I completely missed.

When Kieran and I were going through that burner phone, I had made assumptions before even opening the texts, figuring I knew what I would find, that I had it all figured out. So, I *saw* what I had pre-assumed I'd see: texts between my father and a secret mistress.

I had already fully resigned to that being the truth that I didn't even take into account other possibilities. Didn't even consider that the phone itself was from an entirely different decade. It was an old phone, even for 2015's standards. Why didn't I consider that the text bubbles could have been *reversed* back then? That the sender's texts could be on the left side?

Kieran had shown me a picture of the mistress. Everything about it had seemed so familiar then, but I couldn't place it.

But I know now.

That photo was taken here.

In this bathroom.

At a time when *my family* owned this cabin.

I was looking at the photo with such distorted lenses I didn't even register the zoomed-in and out-of-context, but *familiar* curve of a shoulder I've leaned on hundreds of times. A neck I've cried into. Arms that held me, rocked me to sleep. Fingers taking the photo *in this mirror,* fingers that held my hand to help me cross the street or during scary parts of a movie.

My mom.

I'll have to look at the photo again to make sure, but as the thought stitches together in my mind, I know it's right. The woman in lingerie was my mom. The woman sending the texts *was my mom.*

My world spins as the realization fully forms.

The affair wasn't my dad's after all.

The safe.

The cash, the burner phone, *the gun.*

Were my mom's.

I stumble out of the bathroom a little lightheaded, beelining to my backpack I left in the main room. I'm almost positive, but I want to confirm—

I stop in my tracks.

My backpack. It's not where I left it.

It's crooked, like it was thrown back on the sofa haphazardly. The zipper isn't all the way closed.

I rush to it, throwing it open.

"No, no, no," I cry, turning it upside down and shaking it out desperately, spare change and mechanical pencils and lint falling out onto the sofa.

But not the burner phone.

Not Lizzy's journal.

Not the iPad.

"Hunter, have you seen—"

His presence looms behind me, and I whip around, backpack in hand.

His expression freezes me in place, a cold chill slicing into me as if I've been impaled by ice.

Guilt.

It's unmistakable. So vivid, so clearly painted in every curve of his face. Has it been there all along, and I've blindly ignored it?

"Hunter?" I squeak. I drop the backpack, and it falls to the carpet with a *thud.*

His eyes well up, the rims of green filling and clouding. "I'm so sorry, Nikki." His voice cracks. He looks at his palms, severing the eye contact between us, *severing me.*

"What did you do?" I breathe, that eternal cold engulfing me, spreading from my skin to my tendons, to my soul.

"I had no choice."

He doesn't look at me. His eyes flick to the fireplace, a fire burning there that I didn't even notice before.

I stumble toward it as if he's pushed me, dropping to my knees. The flames devour them greedily, swallowing them whole. The iPad screen is broken and cracked like it was stomped on before being thrown in. The phone is snapped in half, the journal ripped apart. Melting and morphing in the fire.

Everything is gone. All our evidence for the case. *Gone.*

"Why?" I whisper.

My eyes widen as the only possible explanation forms before me in the flames. I stand slowly, steadying myself on the arm of the sofa. "Your dad was the man in the texts, wasn't he?" I nearly choke on the words as I say them. "He was having an affair with my mom. *Wasn't he?*"

Hunter's guilt-ridden silence is the only answer I need.

"Did—" I swallow the sob. I will never cry in front of him again. "Did he kill them?"

He drops onto the couch in a defeated way, exhaustion blending with the guilt, creating a morphed, agonized version of the face I've grown to love. "I don't know."

"Why are you doing this for him then?" The anger seeps through the cracks of the hurt and ticks up the volume, giving it wings.

"It's *not* for him." He finally looks at me, an anger of his own shimmering in his eyes.

"Then why?" I yell, throwing my arms out.

Hunter stands. "He made me, Nikki! He said he'd hurt my mom if I didn't get that phone!"

I point back to the fire. "You just destroyed the one thing that could help her! That video, it—"

"*That* was for her." He shakes his head in a resigned way, almost like he doesn't agree either. "My dad sent me for the phone, but my *mom* sent me for that video. He doesn't know you have it. He'd probably come here himself if he knew. When I told my mom that you had it, that she could use it against him, she made me swear to find it and delete it. You don't think I've been trying to get her to leave him my entire life?"

"You could have told me, Hunter. We could have figured something out together. Now I can never trust you again." I bite the inside of my cheek hard, forcing the tears that are threatening to fall back down. "Was it all a lie? The proposal? Everything?"

He steps closer, that beautiful and sad face contorted. "I still want to help your aunt—"

I step back, putting up a hand to stop him. "Stay away from me. Answer the question," I grind out the words. "Was it all a lie? Why marry me?"

He looks away. His Adam's apple bobs. "After your mom died, Dad said he'd have to get your dad's business another way. He told me to befriend you, that one day when I was older, we'd get married, and then I'd finally be useful."

That coldness devours me entirely, creating a heavy glacier in my chest. I can't breathe. I have to hold myself up on the couch arm to keep my knees from buckling.

His dad didn't just put him up to the marriage, but to our entire friendship.

He steps forward again, but I stagger back.

"The way I feel about you isn't a lie, Nikki." The words tremble as he says them. "You're my best friend. My *only friend.* You have to understand I had no choice. Please underst—"

"If you ever cared about me at all," I force out breath-lessly, "give me my phone and let me leave."

"I can't let you leave... My dad—"

"Let me rephrase that," I growl. I seize strength through my anger. I force the betrayal to fuel me instead of crush me, at least for right now. I swipe the cast iron stoker from the fireplace next to me and wield it like a sword, holding the sharp end out toward him. His eyes widen in shock. *"I'm leaving.* Give me my phone, Hunter. Hard way or easy way, you pick."

He moves slowly to his pocket, as if afraid I'll pounce like a lion if he makes any sudden movements. He holds my phone out to me carefully, and I snatch it out of his hand.

My stomach folds in on itself as at least ten missed calls from Kieran and even more texts cluster on my lockscreen. All over the last two hours. He must have sent these when I didn't have any service.

KIERAN

Answer the phone.

Analyzed blood spatter, will explain later, Lizzy killed them!!

SHE IS DANGEROUS NIKKI COME BACK

DO NOT GO LOOKING FOR HER

Nikki please respond so I know you have seen this.

SHE IS THE KILLER NIKKI DO NOT ENGAGE

If you don't respond I'll assume you are in trouble.

ASSUMING YOU ARE IN TROUBLE

I'm coming Nikki please don't do anything stupid.

Lizzy killed them?

I don't have time to unpack that. The only thing I can think of is how easily she held that shotgun. How easy it was for her to turn it on me, her own sister.

Let alone a stranger, or to an animal willing to do anything to protect his owner.

Whether she killed my parents or not, Kieran and Vinnie are in trouble.

I have to get there now.

Iron stoker in hand, I throw open the front door to the car in the driveway. Gary has the hood open, pouring a thick fluid out of a bottle labeled "ANTIFREEZE" into the radiator.

I stomp over to him and brandish my stoker, feeling terrible but desperate. "Keys, Gary. Now."

Poor Gary widens his eyes and closes the hood, keeping one hand raised in surrender. He fumbles in his pocket and holds out the keys with shaking hands.

I take them gently, lowering the stoker apologetically, with a little pathetic bow. "Thank you, Gary, I'm so sorry. I wouldn't do this unless I had to."

I drop into the driver's seat and turn the ignition, taking a second to take stock of the machine. I've never driven a real car before, but how different from a quad can it be?

Gary dives through the air as I lurch forward, nearly running him over. "Sorry!"

After a clumsy few seconds with the pedals, I peel off, sliding a bit on the slick road. My navigation app tells me to turn right. I cut the corner too tightly and knock over the mailbox with a *crunch*. Oops.

But I manage to make it to the main road which is fortunately more maintained, only sliding through one stop sign accidentally, feeling more capable with every turn. I increase my speed each time another call to Kieran goes to voicemail. I try again over and over. Voicemail each time.

I'm coming, Kieran. *Just hang on.*

I should have never left.

40

———

KIERAN

THIS WASN'T ON MY SEASON THREE BINGO CARD

When I open my eyes, I'm engulfed in a darkness I don't understand. I barely move, keeping still as I try to figure out where I am, trying to get my foggy brain to contribute anything at all.

What do I remember?

I register the ache radiating from the back of my head as it comes back slowly, hazily.

As I had sped down the interstate in Ofeliya's tiny car, feeling like we could swerve off the road into gulfs of snow at any moment, Ofeliya had worked to narrow in the coordinates she'd given Nikki to get us a more precise location, using a complicated system she tried to explain to me that involved cell towers, metadata, landmarks, and—in her words—good old trusty Google Earth.

Ofeliya shouted directions as I flew down the narrow county roads of Grayford toward the house that she said, without the confidence I was hoping for, was *"most likely"* the right house. We didn't see their slick black car parked out in front, which gave me a slight flutter of hope. No driver parked outside? Maybe Nikki never even found the house. Or at the very least already left and got away scot-free.

But why wasn't she answering my calls?

The longer we waited, pulled barely out of sight past the house, watching for any signs of them, the more anxious I became. If Nikki *didn't* find the house, wouldn't she want me to confirm if Lizzy was really in there? Isn't that what I agreed to do when I took on this case? And if she *did* find the house... well, that possibility left me a lot more anxious.

Either way, I only had one choice before me.

Confront a killer.

The motive was still unclear to me. What reason would an eleven-year-old girl have to shoot her parents dead? I consider the fear she wrote with in her journal. That "they knew." Was it her parents she was so afraid of? And how was Aetherline connected? Why the coverup?

I didn't know. But I didn't want to take any chances just because it didn't make sense to me yet. People did things for all kinds of reasons. I'd figure it all out after I made sure Nikki was safe.

I made Ofeliya promise to call for help if I didn't come back in fifteen minutes.

"Don't you dare come in after me," I told her. "You're smarter than that."

And she replied, "Oh, don't worry, at the first sign of trouble, I will leave you behind to save myself."

So, I had stepped through the chain link gate and tiptoed up to the closest windows to peek in, but the blinds were pulled too tightly to see anything useful.

I heard footsteps behind me right before everything went black.

And I guess that brings me to now.

Sitting in a dark room... tied to a chair? Yep, that's definitely duct tape around my wrists. Ankles, too, to the legs of the chair. She's thorough. Great.

As my vision adjusts to the dimness, I squint to identify shapes around me. I'm shoved in the corner of a small living room. There's a lamp on a side table nearest me. A sofa with a throw blanket draped over the arm. Bookshelf, I'm pretty sure. And I think that's my phone lighting up on the coffee table.

A shadowed figure moves across the room.

"Elizabeth Sinclair?" I call out. "Look, I think we got off on the wrong foot. I don't want any trouble. I'm looking for Nikki. Is—" The figure steps closer, and I can make out the very unmistakable shadowed shape of a shotgun. Pointed right at me. Two years of investigative work, and I have to say, this is a definite first. "Is Nikki here?"

"Who are you?" Her voice is low and gruff. Her eyes are a lot like Nikki's, but where Nikki's blue is warm and kind like gentle waves of a crystal ocean, Lizzy's blue is hard and cold, like an immovable glacier.

"I'm Kieran, I'm a friend of Nikki's."

"Liar," she growls. "I saw your phone."

I'm not sure what she saw, so I'm not sure what to say. Did she see social media notifications? Texts from Ofeliya or Nikki? *Ciphered?*

"Okay," I concede, deciding to ramble and maybe something lands. "Kieran is my legal name now, but some family call me by my birth name, which is Kai. I run a true-crime investigative podcast, and Nikki hired me to do your family's case. I specialize in cold—"

An edge of panic laces through her voice. "A *podcast*?"

"Yep, and I'm pretty good at what I do, Lizzy." I try to

soften my tone. Maybe I can negotiate myself out of this. "If you let me go, I can help you tell your side of things. I'm sure you had a good reason to do what you did."

She takes another feline-like step forward. "And what exactly is it you think I did?"

"I know you killed your parents, Lizzy," I say gently. "I just don't know *why*."

She rears back with widened eyes, gun faltering ever so slightly. "And you've put this on your *podcast*?"

"No," I assure her. "Not yet. Like I said, I still don't know why you did it. You can tell your own story. I can help you."

She shows her teeth, barking out a mirthless laugh. "No one can help me. It's something I deserve to live with for the rest of my life."

So, I'm right? Is this a confession?

"Help me understand why, then. What happened?"

There's a *clang* of a door closing from across the house that makes me jump. Is there someone else here? Nikki?

"Don't even think about trying to get away," she snarls, before turning and walking down the hallway toward the noise.

I strain my ears to listen, hearing only the muffled, indistinguishable sounds of a conversation in the other room.

"Nikki, is that you over there?" I shout at them, but the inaudible conversation carries on.

I wriggle in the chair I'm strapped to, trying to assess my duct-taped appendages. My wrists feel the tightest, taped together behind the back of the chair. The elbow I hurt in the accident is stretched painfully. Which ankle has the most give? If I can get even one ankle free, maybe I can kick and break the chair with my free leg.

"Tell me what I'm supposed to do with him then! This *is*

your fault!" Lizzy's volume increases from the other room, as if she's arguing with someone.

There's a window nearby, only ten or so feet to my left. It has a heavy curtain around it that blocks nearly all the light from outside, only a slice of light coming from the crack down the middle. Maybe I can send a signal to Ofeliya down the street, assuming she didn't already leave me behind to save herself.

My phone lights up on the coffee table again. I decide my first priority should be trying to get to it. Maybe there's better signal inside than there was outside. I squirm and scoot as quietly as I can in the chair toward the coffee table, only budging mere inches each time.

I think that was a squeal of tires outside, but I'm too far from the window to be sure. But then there is an unmistakable *clank!*, like a car has rammed through the chain link gate, followed by a screeching of brakes. Someone is definitely outside.

Ofeliya, that better not be you, I silently beg. I scoot with more urgency, sure Lizzy will be back any moment to check it out.

Suddenly the front door slams open, and all the walls in the house rattle.

"Kieran? Kieran!"

My pulse slams to a stop at the sound of her voice. *No, no, no.*

Nikki.

She rushes over to me, dropping to her knees front of me with eyes wide and fearful. "Where's Vinnie, is he here too?"

"Get out of here!" I hiss at her. "Hurry before she—"

Lizzy is back, gun aimed, eyes ablaze with a flaming

ferocity. "I told you to leave and never come back," she grinds out.

"Or what, you'll shoot me?" Nikki shouts over her shoulder as she fumbles uselessly with the tape at my ankles. "Kill me like you killed Mom and Dad? Let him go, Lizzy."

"I can't!" Lizzy's beginning to unravel. "Do you have any idea what you've done, sending him here? This podcast?"

"No, I don't actually! Care to fill me in?" Nikki whips around, facing her sister and pointing an angry finger at her like a dagger. "Because *I thought* you were dead all this time! So, I don't actually have any idea at all, because *you chose* to make it that way!"

The volume and tension is heightening, and I'm hoping Ofeliya is making progress in the "call for help" department because I really don't want to meet the end of that shotgun.

"Everything would have been fine if you never came looking, but now you've probably led them straight to me!" Fear flashes in Lizzy's eyes.

"*Who?*" Nikki cries exasperatedly. "Stop pushing me away and tell me what happened!"

Our heads whip around as that door down the hallway *clangs* again and two figures step out of the shadows, one staggering forward as if being pushed.

"Let me go," one figure protests, thrashing around in the other's grasp.

The air around me thickens. Her impossible-to-miss orange-tipped nails nearly glow in the dimness. *Ofeliya.*

"I found their lookout," the other figure says gruffly, letting her go so she stumbles to her knees right next to Lizzy. That voice... so familiar. So deep and smooth.

The lighting is still dim, so I can't make out who it is right away, until Nikki gasps, *"Arrick?"*

Sure enough, Arrick steps into view. "Hello, Miss Nikki."

I blow out a surprised breath, feeling a sharp crack inside me as Nikki crumbles to her knees. There has to be some kind of explanation here.

"What's going on?" Her voice breaks, and a piece of me does too at the sound of her pain. The hurt and confusion carves itself across Nikki's face, and I wish she was closer. I wish I could do anything at all, but I'm completely helpless, stuck to this chair.

Lizzy shares a look with Arrick, and he makes the tiniest flick of his head, conveying some kind of decision to her.

"Please," Nikki begs, a devastated sob breaking free. I wish so desperately I could reach out to her. "Just tell me the truth. For once."

Arrick is unreadable as he says, "I was the one who sent you the texts, Nikki."

"Why?"

Lizzy's hands tighten around the shotgun, eyes sharpening. And then she begins to speak.

YOUTUBE COMMENTS SECTION
Season 3 Episode 4: The Cover-Up

@**historynerddd**: he releases an episode, exposing a possible police coverup and then his van is found in a ditch??? I mean we know who's responsible right? no question there

@**cold_caseclara**: I refuse to believe vinnie is gone!!! I'm literally sobbing

    @**goldenyeti** REPLYING TO @**cold_caseclara**: same, idc if people die, but animals? nah. this ruined my day fr

@**monochromemoose**: guys I've been saying this for years and no one will listen to me. I was on the original investigative team. I reported another person's DNA that I found ON THE CRIME SCENE but they didn't test it, didn't even include it in the case notes! They just blew me off completely!

    @**_jellyshoes_** REPLYING TO @**monochromemoose**: wouldn't that probably be the DNA of the main suspect??? why wouldn't they want that tested?

    @**monochromemoose** REPLYING TO @**_jellyshoes_**: when I asked those same questions, they called me crazy, said I was no longer fit for fieldwork. my career was pretty much ruined.

@**jacobunderwood231**: rest in peace Kieran, we won't let them cover this one up too

41

LIZZY

WEDNESDAY, OCTOBER 14TH, 2015

3 Days Before the Murders

I sigh at the sound of my parents arguing down the hall. Again. My bedroom is closest to theirs, and even in this house, the walls still aren't thick enough to soak up the angry hissing whispers they try to hide after dark. I slip out of my room and tiptoe over to Nikki's.

She's resting peacefully, snoring without a single care in the world. But I'm not jealous. I'm relieved, actually. I hope it stays that way forever. Even if I have to take extra on myself to keep it away from her, I will.

I slide into her bed, snuggling up and pulling the covers over her exposed shoulders. I don't sleep, but at least I can breathe now that all I can hear are Nikki's deep, undisturbed snores. In another life I might even be able to pretend the arguing down the hall isn't happening at all.

Except it isn't, and I can't.

They've been trying to hide it—only arguing in that whispery way they do when bedtime has fallen, no staff or nosy little girls around in earshot—but something's been going on with them. I've been watching them carefully. I can't help it. I notice the way they tense up when the other enters the room, the frustrated sighs after sentences, the stiff hugs like they're putting on some kind of puppet show.

I can't ignore it. It's an obsession that keeps consuming more and more of me, like I have to figure out what's going on with them, or it might eat me alive. I can't accept they'll figure it out themselves, that this is a problem they'll work out. It's different this time. It feels like they're not even trying, that they've both just given up. And I'm supposed to accept it? My family is burning alive right in front of me, and I'm supposed to stand by and watch? Or worse, pretend it's not even happening at all?

So that's why I can't help sneaking out of Nikki's room when my dad's heavy footsteps stalk by as he retreats to his office. I tiptoe down the hallway and sit outside the cracked door, barely breathing as I try to listen.

My dad talks to someone on the phone in an exasperated way.

"Yes, I got your 'present,' but I've already told you a hundred times, Mack. I'm not interested. Find another trans-porter for your shady side deals."

There's a long pause before my dad's tone darkens. "Is that a threat, Mackenzie?"

Mackenzie? I have a friend from school, Ava Mackenzie. Could he be talking to her dad? Why would Ava's dad be threatening my dad?

Dad smacks his desk, and it makes me jump. "You leave my daughters out of this, you son of—"

He cuts off when I accidentally bump the door with my shoulder, and it opens a sliver with a *creak.*

I leap off the ground and sprint to Nikki's room as lightly on my feet as I can, closing the door behind me and nearly jumping back into Nikki's bed. I close my eyes and pretend to be asleep.

I hold my breath as her door cracks open, the light cutting in from the hallway sharp on my eyelids. *Don't move.*

After a moment that feels like ten years, Dad closes the door quietly, and I finally let out a heavy breath, almost lightheaded. My pulse races.

Well, I know who I'm sitting by at lunch tomorrow. Maybe Ava knows something that could be helpful.

IN THE MORNING, I oversleep by mistake and Bea gives me a slice of peanut butter toast to shove into my mouth on my way out the door. Nikki is already in the back of the car. Mom gives me a kiss on the cheek as I pass and shuts the front door behind me.

"One sec, Arrick!" He's waiting for me at the car's back-door, probably cold.

I scurry over to the garbage can that has been pulled out of the garage for trash day to throw away my napkin. When I open the lid, there's a bulky green box thrown in haphazardly, not inside a trash bag. I peek over the trash lid to see if Arrick is looking before opening the box. It's lined with gray foam and there are two tiny keys inside, along with a black note that says: *Our offer still stands. -Aetherline*

Strange. I quickly shove the box into my backpack and fortunately manage to zip it up, though it's a bit strained at the seams.

I rush to the car and apologize to Arrick breathlessly.

"Are you alright, Miss Lizzy?" he asks patiently.

"Yep, good to go."

And he closes the door after me, with a glint in his eye like he knows I'm up to something.

THE SCHOOL DAY IS A BLUR. I'm sleepy and distracted. I keep staring at the edge of box peeking out of my backpack, trying to figure out how it fits into the puzzle of what's going on with my dad.

Lunchtime isn't as helpful as I hoped. I carry my lunchbox Bea packed for me over to Ava's table. I keep things vague—you can't really say, "Hey I think your dad threatened my dad last night, any idea what's going on?" in casual conversation—but Ava doesn't seem to know much. I hint that we should hang out sometime, and to my delight, she invites me over to play at her house today after school.

I pull my tablet out of my backpack discreetly and shoot off a message to my mom, careful to keep it hidden so the lunch aides don't take it away. This—and everything— would be a lot easier if my parents would let me have a phone like everyone else in my grade. I'm almost twelve years old, but they insist on treating me like a little kid and having rules that don't make sense just because they can. It's embarrassing.

I keep the message ambiguous, only referring to Ava by her first name, hoping my mom has no idea of anything off between our dads. Luckily, I've played at her house before. If she were a stranger, it would take a lot more convincing.

I cheer in delight when the reply comes in. "My mom said it's okay if I come home with you after school." I swish away her second message with a roll of my eyes. It says, *stop texting during school. If you get your tablet confiscated, I'm not picking it up.*

We squeal together happily, and the bell rings, telling us to go back to class. She tells me where to meet her after school, and we part ways.

The rest of the day drags even slower than the first half.

AVA'S HOUSE is a lot different than mine. It's just as big, but my house is almost entirely white, on the inside and the outside. Hers is vibrant and colorful. Nearly every room is painted a different color, with oddly shaped furniture and decorations in bright patterns that don't seem to go together, but it works somehow. It's a little strange, but it's unique. It has personality.

Her cook serves us a snack at her kitchen island, and we giggle about a boy that Ava has a crush on and that he smiled at her at school today. When her older brother comes into the room to look through the fridge, we put our heads together and whisper and laugh in a way we know will annoy him.

Truthfully, her older brother has always made me feel strange. It's a weird prickle on my skin when he's around that I can't explain. He's always been nice to me, doesn't pick on us like some of my friends' brothers do. But even though he's almost eighteen, he always wants to hang out with us for some reason. If we're swimming in their pool house, he is too. If we're watching a movie in their game room, so is he. And even when he's not around, I can *feel* his eyes on me still somehow. It makes me shiver thinking about it.

He cracks open a soda can, leaning over to rest his elbows on the island.

Ava groans. "Ugh Roger, leave us alone! Lizzy is *my friend*."

He smiles at me as he sips on his soda. "Lizzy doesn't mind. Right, Lizzy?"

Luckily, I don't have to answer because Ava whispers in my ear that his head is shaped like a football, and I snicker into my hands.

"Come on!" She tugs my arm, and as I look at Roger over my shoulder, he winks at me.

I play a game with Ava in her room for a little while, where I make casual conversation and learn with disappointment that her dad is away for business for the next few days. Although I don't know what I thought I'd do if he were here. Confront him? Right.

I tell Ava I'm going to use the restroom. I step out of her room into a quiet hallway. Her housekeeper is vacuuming downstairs, so the faint hum of the vacuum is the only noise other than my own feet padding on the carpet. I walk slowly down the hallway, exploring as I go, peeking into rooms that are cracked open, not knowing what I'm looking for.

There is clacking of a keyboard from the last room on the left. I crane my neck to look in and see Roger sitting at a computer in a big study. The walls are lined with ornate bookshelves and a deep musk flows out of the room like cigars and pine trees, just like my dad's. This must be Mr. Mackenzie's office.

Roger's head jerks back when I ask him what he's doing.

"Geez, Lizzy, you scared the hell out of me." He puffs out a laugh.

"Sorry." I smile at him sweetly. "What's that?"

I stand behind him and point at the document he has pulled up. He minimizes it quickly, so only the desktop is showing. Mr. Mackenzie's wallpaper is a picture of him and his wife standing on a boat with a creamy sunset and ice-blue ocean behind them.

"Oh, I was just printing my homework for school," Roger says almost too casually. He turns to me. "Bored of my sister already? I don't blame you."

Something on the desktop catches my eye. In the very corner of the screen, tucked around other icons, is a blue folder named *Aetherline*. I recognize the strange name immediately. It's the same one from the note I found in the box this morning. It's in my backpack right now. Part of me wonders if I should show Roger and ask him straight-out what it means, but a deep twinge in my gut tells me to be careful.

"Yeah, super bored," I answer with a breathy laugh after a pause of silence, remembering a second too late that he had asked me a question. I turn my attention to him, an idea materializing. "Want to watch a movie or something?"

He blinks at me in surprise. "Sure." He moves to reach for the computer mouse. "Let me just—"

I stop him with a hand on his arm and another dazzling smile. "I have to go home soon, so we probably don't have much time."

To my relief, he hops to his feet, leaving the computer behind entirely. He tugs me by the hand, and my skin burns at his touch. "I have the perfect movie you'll love."

"Yay!" I force myself to sound girlish and enthusiastic, even though my whole body is recoiling at his proximity. I gently pull my hand away. "Can I meet you down there? I have to go to the bathroom really quick. Ooh you should make popcorn!"

When he leaves to take the stairs two by two, I know I only have minutes. My pulse races so fast I can feel it thudding in my throat. I race back to Ava's room.

"Hey!" She's waiting for me, scrolling on her phone on her bed. "Roger's making popcorn. He says he'll buy us a movie."

Ava perks up and darts out of the room. "It better be Jurassic World!"

"I'll be right there!" I call after her, but she's already halfway down the stairs.

I slide my iPad out of my backpack as I scurry back down to Mr. Mackenzie's office, switching it to the camera. I'm not sure what I'll find in that little blue folder, but I don't have a lot of time to make sense of whatever I do find. I'll snap pictures and look through them more thoroughly later.

To my relief, Mr. Mackenzie's computer hasn't locked itself yet, and the desktop still glows brightly. I close the door almost all the way but leave it cracked so I can hear if anyone is coming. My pulse has reached my ears now, and it beats so loudly they may be able to hear it all the way downstairs.

With shaking hands, I move the cursor to the blue folder and click it twice. *Aetherline.*

The folder is empty except for another blue folder called "untitled folder." I click it and find another one. And then another. I click the next one frustratedly, ready to give up all together when a group of icons appear. There are twenty or so. They look like... videos.

I click on one of them and nearly shriek when a man sitting with a topless woman on his lap appears on the screen, full volume. I fumble to close it hurriedly, barely breathing. My ears perk up. That might be someone coming up the stairs.

I unlock my iPad as fast as I can, and I could scream when it tells me to put in my password again after I did it wrong the first time. On the computer, I click to highlight all the video icons and drag them over to AirDrop.

"Come on, come on," I mutter as it loads, the icon spinning slowly. Footsteps have reached the top of the stairs, I'm sure of it. I have to go *now*. I don't wait to see if it's done, I just grab my backpack and sprint out of the room.

I collide face-first into Roger. I almost fly backwards from the impact, but he catches me by the elbow. "Woah, sorry, are you okay?" Then his eyes flick to the cracked door of the office. His red-brown brows pull together. "What are you doing?"

My iPad flashes in my hand with a notification. *AirDrop complete.* I click the lock button hurriedly, pulling it close to my chest. I send up a silent prayer to anyone listening that he didn't see it.

"Oh, sorry," I laugh in an airily way. "I, um... I was looking for your Wi-Fi password." I wave my iPad at him. "I needed to send my mom a message to ask her if I could stay longer for the movie. I was heading downstairs now."

His eyes flick to the computer behind me. "Okay," he drawls in a way like he doesn't quite believe me.

"Popcorn ready?" I say cheerily, pulling him away by the arm.

And the entire movie, I pretend to ignore the way he glances over at me from time to time, eyes tinged with a look that makes my skin prickle in a new way. A look that feels a lot like suspicion...

42

LIZZY

THURSDAY, OCTOBER 15TH, 2015

2 Days Before the Murders

"Are you okay?" Nikki nudges me at the breakfast nook when Mom steps away to refill her coffee mug. Dad is nowhere to be seen. He must have gone into work before anyone even woke up.

"Yeah, fine," I tell her, and I'm not, but I straighten my shoulders and paste on a smile. She doesn't need to be sucked into this.

After I got home from Ava's house last night, I watched all the videos I Airdropped myself from Mr. Mackenzie's computer, and hours later, I'm still nauseous. They're horrible. Every single one of them. And most of them are my dad's friends. Peter is his *best* friend, and he abuses his wife? What does that say about my dad that these are the people he surrounds himself with?

I couldn't sleep at all because of it. The awful videos replayed behind my eyelids every time I closed them, and wondering if Roger knows what I did made it worse. Even now, I still feel like my nerves are all being electrocuted at the same time.

I don't know why Mr. Mackenzie had these on his computer. I don't know what *"Aetherline"* is or why they want my dad to join, but they're obviously bad if these are the men that make it up. Dangerous, even. They clearly have a lot to lose. So, if Mr. Mackenzie or any of these other men knew *I* had these videos?

I'm not sure I'd live to see tomorrow.

But I don't know what to do with them. They're like a festering wound spreading all over me that I don't know how to get rid of. If I show them to my mom, that could make things worse for her and Dad. I don't want to add fuel to the fire when I'm trying to *help them.* Do I send them to the police? But then would they tell my parents? Ask questions about how I got them?

For a second, I don't realize my mom has asked me a question over the lip of her coffee mug.

"What?" I blink at her.

"I said are you feeling nervous for your tournament this weekend?" she repeats, and she may even look concerned if it weren't for her monthly injections that freeze her face.

I've always thought my mom was naturally so beautiful, with her dark hair and blue eyes, but she's been wearing so much makeup lately, it's hard to even remember what she usually looks like.

"Oh." In the commotion, I had forgotten about my figure skating competition on Saturday. I busy myself with stirring my oatmeal. It's gotten lumpy as it has sat here uneaten. "Yeah, a little. I'll probably go to the rink to practice my routine after school if that's okay."

I force myself to take a bite of the mushy oatmeal,

knowing Bea won't let me leave this table without eating anything.

"Sure, honey. Do you want Arrick to stay with you?"

"I want to come!" Nikki whines.

"No, Kiki," I grate, annoyed, and she slumps into a pout.

"Um, no that's okay, Mom. He can just drop me off. I'll only need like an hour."

After shoveling a satisfactory number of bites into my mouth, I jog upstairs to get my school stuff. I normally don't leave without my iPad, but I don't even want to look at it right now. The memory of the awful videos is enough. I pull the box I found in the trash from my bag and push my iPad into its inner foam. It hugs its blocky shape perfectly. I turn the lock and drop the key into the front pocket of my backpack. I don't want to risk it falling out of my shallow pockets. Then I shove the box deep under my bed just in case any of the housekeepers are cleaning in here today. I feel a little better as the videos get further away from my sight. Now to push them out of my memory next.

THE PARANOIA IS MAKING me jumpy today. Friends have snuck up on me multiple times without even trying, I've jumped at the most normal of sounds, and I even startle as Arrick opens my car door. I blow out a breath, trying to reassure my nervous system that it's not Roger lurking around in a shadowy corner to demand why I stole from them. It's just Arrick.

Except he notices.

"Are you alright, Miss Lizzy?" He helps me out of the car and loops the strap of my gym bag around my shoulder.

His eyes are glimmering with concern, and I almost tell him everything. The heartbreak of my family falling apart. The disappointment in my dad. The fear of having these videos. The pressure of keeping everything together, being the only glue this family has. He'll listen; he always does.

"Lizzy can I *please* come? I just want to watch," Nikki moans from her seat, giving me her best puppy dog eyes.

Any thought of telling Arrick flurries way in the wind with her listening in. I'd rather shove it down deep inside than have Nikki overhear anything that could dull her sparkling innocence. I'd hate myself if I was the reason she glowed even a little less. So, I'll keep pushing her away to protect that sunshine she deserves to keep as long as she can. And because honestly, I need her sunshine too.

"Not this time, Kiki," I tell her with an apologetic smile. "I'm just going to run my routine a few times. Maybe you can come with Arrick to pick me up and he could take us out for ice cream or something if we ask reeeallyy nicely."

"Yay!" She claps.

I shut the door and chuckle. "Sorry," I tell him.

He smiles in that ever-patient way he does. "Be back in an hour."

"Thank you, Arrick." I give him a hug, and he doesn't know it, but the fact alone that I felt like I *could* tell him everything if I chose to means the world to me. I don't think I have anyone else in my life who makes me feel like that.

I change quickly in the locker room and lace up my skates as fast as I can, letting out a full exhale for what feels like the first time in days when I'm finally on the ice, gliding and flying across it like I'm weightless. Being on this ice is the only time I feel truly free. I can shut out every stress, every pressure, and just *fly*.

I'm luckily the only one here, so I take full advantage of the open space and forget everything else—looping, spinning, leaping until I'm panting. I run through my routine for the tournament again and again until it's flawless. My legs feel like jelly by the time I'm done.

I drop down on the bleachers to unlace my skates, breathing heavily but feeling refreshed, hardly noticing when the door *clangs* open and someone else enters the arena. Open skate will probably be starting soon. The huge clock on the wall confirms I have ten minutes before Arrick will be here. Dripping wet skates in hand, I walk in my tights to the hallway that leads to the locker room.

I'm so distracted by my own thoughts, I run into a large figure in the hallway. I open my mouth to apologize, but my back is shoved up against the wall before I can speak. My skates fall out of my hand, clattering across the concrete floor, mirroring the sound of my thundering heart.

I can't move.

A man I don't recognize, face shadowed by a black hat, presses me up against the wall with a heavy arm. I writhe and squirm, but his hold is firm. I try to scream, but he covers my mouth with his free hand. His breath is horrible and hot on my face. I can't tell how old he is. Maybe my dad's age? Maybe a little younger?

I thrash my feet desperately, landing a kick in his calf. He sneers, flashing his teeth, and pulls my shoulders forward just to slam me back harder, making my head bounce off the concrete wall. Pain blazes down my neck.

"Where is it?" he snarls.

Where is what??

I manage to bite his hand *hard*. He rears back with a howl, cursing at me, letting me go for only a second, but that's all I need. I sprint toward the locker room. I'm nearly there, *almost to the door*, but then he grabs me by the hair, yanking me back. I cry out, hot tears welling in my eyes. He holds me from behind, crushing me, his hand over my mouth tighter this time.

His awful breath fills my nostrils. "The *iPad*," he grinds out through his teeth, squeezing me harder. "*Where is it?*"

Frigid dread replaces the blazing fear, confirming the nightmare that kept me up all night. *Roger saw. They know.*

There's another *clang* of the main entrance door. He loosens his hold at the sound of a group entering the arena, and I take advantage of the extra inch. I duck under his arm, sprinting to the locker room door and throwing it open. I race through the room and don't pause to get my gym bag from my locker. I run to the other exit that leads to the public lobby.

The teenager running the front desk watches me in confusion but doesn't question why I'm panting shoeless in the middle of the lobby in my sparkling performance leotard.

I nearly burst into tears at the sight of Arrick through the window, sitting in the driver's seat of the car at the curb waiting for me, but I swallow it down. I try not to draw attention as I fast-walk across the lobby and right to the car. I open the door myself and slam it shut behind me, feeling lightheaded as I try to make my breaths look more casual than they want to be.

He whips his head around, scanning me from head to toe. "What happened?"

And I really try, because Nikki is sitting right next to me, but I can't force down the sob this time. The cry erupts out of me.

"Lizzy?" Nikki's hand rests on my arm, and I know I have to say something, anything.

"I, um, I lost my skates," I blubber through sobs.

Arrick throws his seatbelt off and moves to get out, but the man in the black hat is walking across the parking lot.

"No, don't leave!" I yell at Arrick, shrinking down lower in my seat, and he looks at me in alarm.

"I mean—it's okay," I say calmer, pulling my seatbelt across my body. "I'll come back tomorrow and check the lost and found. I'm sure someone turned them in. We can't be late for *ice cream!*" I force a cheery tone for Nikki, counting on her to change the subject.

"Ice cream, ice cream!" she chants.

Across the parking lot, the man slides open the backdoor of a windowless white cargo van, and I allow myself to breathe as I watch it speed off.

It looks like there is a lot more that Arrick would like to say as he pulls out of the parking lot to meet Nikki's ice cream demands, but he doesn't. And for that, I'm grateful. I keep my face angled away, looking out the window like I'm watching the town pass by, because I can't stop the tears silently streaming down my cheeks.

43

LIZZY

FRIDAY, OCTOBER 16TH, 2015

1 Day Before the Murders

I tear apart my room with desperate wails. *No, no, no.* I throw aside blankets, books, stuffies, shoes. The iPad. It's not where I left it. It was here tucked in my blankets when I went down for breakfast, but now, only twenty minutes later, it's gone.

Last night when I got home from ice cream with Arrick and Nikki, I took it out of the lockbox and just held it for a while. I stared at it, feeling numb and hollow, wondering if I should just hand it over. If that's what they want so bad, maybe I end this and give it to them. What do I gain from keeping it? Encounters like that at the ice rink more often?

But now it's gone.

I get more urgent the longer I go without finding it. I've flipped apart this whole bedroom. I step out onto the balcony and shout over the edge, "Who took my iPad?!"

I run down the hallway, throwing open Nikki's door. She's not in her room.

"Kiki??" I shout. "Where are you? Do you have my iPad?!"

My mom and Arrick peer up from the foyer, shooting up looks of confused concern.

"What's wrong? Why are you shouting?" my mom calls up.

I yell back down, nearly reaching a shrieking octave. "Someone took my iPad! I need it back!"

I throw open doors and toss pillows around in sitting rooms and guest rooms.

"It's here, Miss Lizzy," Arrick calls.

When I glance over the balcony, he's holding it out like a peace offering. I take the stairs two by two.

"Where was it?" I breathe, almost about to cry again.

"Right next to these," he jokes with a glint in his eye, pulling my ice skates from behind his back like he's pulled a rabbit out a hat.

I gasp. "My skates! You... went back for them?"

He smiles with his eyes. They crinkle at the edges in that way they always do. "Couldn't have you competing without your lucky skates tomorrow now, could we?"

I hug him. "Thank you."

Maybe it's the close call with the iPad, or the thought of leaving this house—what if that man finds me at school?—but I feel queasy, a tingling sweat breaking out on my forehead. My tongue swells like I'm going to throw up. I run to the downstairs guest suite to retch into the toilet.

"You okay?" It's Mom.

I vomit again.

She holds my hair back, putting a gentle hand on my shoulder. "Oh no, sweetie. You should stay home from school today. Hopefully you can get some rest and tomorrow you'll feel better and ready to go for the competition."

I nod and carry my things up to my room, slouching miserably.

I drop into my bed and hug the iPad tightly, as if that will keep everything glued together a little longer.

I MUST HAVE FALLEN asleep because I rouse groggily at the sound of my iPad falling onto the rug with a light *thud*. I yawn and check the time, confirming I was asleep for a couple hours.

There are muffled voices coming from my parents' room next door. I perk up with excitement, hoping that means my dad got home early from his work trip. I was so disappointed when he told me he'd have to miss my competition. I slide the iPad back in its box and lock it, hurrying to go greet him. My mom laughs. Did her and dad make up? That makes a glimmer of hope glow in my chest.

I pause outside their closed door, hesitating before opening it because my mom laughingly says someone's name, but it's not my dad's name, Gunnar. She says *Peter*.

I stiffen. I only know one Peter. A pit grows in my stomach when I remember the video of him hurting his wife. Mom's entire charity organization is about advocacy for abused women. Why is she talking to *him*?

I knock on the door, and her laugh stops short. "I have to go," I hear her say.

"Mom?" I knock again.

Her door cracks open. She's tying a robe around her waist in a flustered way. "Hi honey, you feeling any better?"

"Who are you talking to?" I sound more pathetic than I

want to. My eyes flick to the room behind her, looking for signs of *Peter*.

She sees my peering eyes and opens the door fully to reveal an empty room. "No one, honey, why?"

"I... I heard voices."

"Oh, I was just watching TV." She stretches out her lips in an overly cheery way. "Why don't you head downstairs, and Bea will make you some lunch? I'll meet you there in a minute."

I nod, and she closes the door quickly. I step back in my room, wanting to cry, feeling that undeniable deep tug in my gut that something's off. It's why when her footsteps pass my door a few minutes later, I follow, tiptoeing after her as she sneaks into my dad's office down the hallway, feeling a bit of déjà vu from when I followed Dad like this just the other day.

The door is cracked only an inch, like she closed it in a hurry, but it's enough. She's kneeling in front of one of my dad's bookshelves, with piles of his yearbooks stacked around her. She presses buttons on a tiny safe tucked in the back of the bookshelf. *9-8-8-8.* She doesn't even try to cover the combination as she does it, not worried in the slightest that anyone, but especially not her obedient and docile daughter, would be spying on her.

She puts the books back in front of it, and that's my cue to leap down the stairs. I try to swallow down the huge lump in my throat as I sit at the kitchen island, wondering if Bea can see it if she looks closely enough. My world has flipped upside down, but I have to pretend I'm not dizzy. Finding out your mom isn't who you thought she was. That it's *her fault* your family is falling apart... but expected to simply carry on anyway? It's unfair.

I tense up as my mom sits next to me and thanks Bea for the lunch. There's a thick silence as she waits for her to hobble out of the room. She clears her throat and perks up her shoulders like she's preparing to say something ordinary but wants it to sound fun and exciting.

"I was thinking," she says in a chirpy way, taking a tiny sip from a green smoothie, "that all us girls should get away for a while after your tournament tomorrow. I think we could use some fresh air."

My head snaps in her direction. "What do you mean?"

She picks at the croissant on her plate, taking tiny crumbs off and placing them in her mouth. "It'll be good for us. We're going to go stay at the cabin for a little while."

"Like when Dad gets home?" That feeling in my gut expands, nearly crushing me from the inside out.

A strange expression clouds her face. "I think it should be a girls' trip for now. Won't that be fun?"

She's leaving him. And she's taking us with her.

"I don't want to." My lip quivers.

There's a flicker of hurt in her eyes. "It'll be good for us," she insists. "I promise."

"Does Dad know?"

She seems to understand there are layers to that question. She puts a gentle hand on my arm. "It'll be our little secret for right now, okay? Let's surprise Nikki. It's going to be so fun. It'll feel like we're on vacation every day."

She pats my arm and leaves the kitchen.

I toss my croissant in the trash numbly. I'm heading to the staircase to hide in my room and figure out a plan and probably cry, but Arrick's voice at the front door makes me stop. When I reach the foyer and see who's here, I stop in my tracks like I've been hit by a bus, stomach falling to the floor.

It's Roger Mackenzie. He's at my house.

"Oh hey, Lizzy," Roger says with a wave. Arrick looks over his shoulder at me. His posture straightens protectively when he sees my widened eyes like I'm a deer in the head-lights about to meet certain death. Is there any way I can tell him with my eyes to not let Roger in? *Please,* I beg with my eyes.

He came to my house.

There's no doubt he's here to get the iPad. Their black-hat-man last night was unsuccessful, so they sent Roger this time, hoping I'd let a familiar face waltz right in. Maybe they thought he could persuade me to hand it over.

"Ava sent me over to see if she could borrow your notes for the history test on Monday." Roger moves to *step into the house,* but Arrick stops him with a hand to his chest.

"Miss Lizzy isn't feeling well today," Arrick says firmly. He nudges him backwards ever so slightly, just enough for Roger to get the message.

Anger flashes in Roger's eyes, but he purses his lips as if trying to exert control. He must be able to sense that there's a quiet strength to Arrick under the suit and tie. It's unassuming, but it's there, waiting for someone like Roger to make it come out.

Roger takes a step back. "Okay. Well, maybe you can send her a text with the notes, then. Hope you feel better."

I don't waste a second. I'm up the stairs and in my room before Arrick has even shut the door in his face.

I have to hide this iPad. Now. Somewhere no one will ever find it unless I want them to. I have a feeling if I don't, people around me are going to get hurt.

~

BEDTIME WAS over two hours ago, and I've been lying in bed since then, waiting, skin buzzing with anticipation and anxiety. There haven't been any noises from my parents' room for over an hour, but I've been waiting a little while longer just to be sure.

I spent the rest of the day burying the iPad by the creek, and even though I'm exhausted and my eyelids are begging me for sleep, I can't sleep until I finish these final steps. I'd never forgive myself if I didn't at least try one last time to keep my family together.

I tiptoe out of bed and sneak down the stairs. It's completely dark, apart from some nightlights plugged into occasional outlets. A tremor spreads to my legs as I make my way through the dark. Every time I turn a corner, I expect Roger or the black-hat man to be there, waiting for me in the shadows.

I use a small pathetic keychain flashlight I won in a school contest last year to light my way as I dig through the cabinet by the fridge where Mom keeps all the medicine. I take a moment to decide on which bottle to grab, feeling a twinge of guilt at what I have planned. I hope Nikki forgives me one day.

I tuck it into my sweatpants pocket and pad back up the stairs. Carefully, I press my ear up to my parents' door, not breathing as I listen for a moment, waiting to hear the deep inhales and exhales of my mom sleeping before turning back around and sneaking into my dad's office.

I need to know. A secret safe hidden in plain sight in her husband's office doesn't look good, but if my mom really is hiding something big, something that could destroy our family, I have to know for sure.

I don't risk turning on the light. I use the feeble flashlight to illuminate the office instead, though it doesn't do much good. I move the books out of the bookshelf as soundlessly as I can, cringing a bit as the buttons of the safe beep when I press them. Can she hear them? 9-8-8-8. *Ding.*

I pat around in the safe, and my breath stills when something cool to the touch brushes under my fingers. Metal. I leap back when the flashlight lights it up.

A gun. Small and black.

With boxes of ammunition right next to it.

Why does my mom have a *gun*??

I stare at it in shock, feeling a panic rise in me. I've never seen a gun before, let alone *touched one.* What if I had made it go off somehow?

I force myself to shut everything out. *Don't feel.* Don't feel scared, don't feel betrayed, don't feel angry. Just push everything away and do what needs to be done.

I lie flat on my belly to look in the safe again, but it's hard to make out much in the darkness, the keychain not much help. I blow out a breath, pull bravery out of me from within somewhere, and I carefully nudge the gun to the side, as if it will detonate simply from touch alone. The only other thing I can make out in the safe are torn strips of paper. I hold one up to look at it closer. I think all these strips used to be around stacks of money.

I swallow down the lump in my throat. So, she really is leaving him... Why else would she need all this cash?

I look at the gun again. At least Mom didn't think she'd need it on our "girls' trip" if it's still in here. Something about it hypnotizes me like I'm a fly being lulled into a trap.

My memory slithers back to the man in the black hat, his reeking breath in my nostrils. The feeling of his hand around my mouth. His strong grip crushing me from behind. What if next time he brings a gun?

A noise from down the hall snaps me out of it. Before I can think myself out of it, I grab a handful of bullets and throw them in my pocket. I swipe the gun, and hurriedly close everything as fast as I can, throwing the books back into place. There's another noise. A door maybe?

I peek out into the hallway and sprint down to my room lightly on my feet. I shut my door behind me and gasp for air.

"Lizzy?" Nikki's voice in the darkness makes me leap out of my skin.

I drop the gun in my pocket, and squint in the darkness to see Nikki's little frame sitting on the edge of my bed.

"I'm scared," she whimpers. "I had a bad dream. A scary troll was trying to take me away."

I pull her in for a hug, smoothing down her hair. "Don't worry. I won't let any scary trolls take you away. Ever."

"Can I sleep with you tonight?"

"Sure, Kiki." The gun feels like it's burning a hole in my pocket. But I reach for the other pocket. "Take this medicine first, though. I threw up today, and I don't want to get you sick."

I swallow the guilt as my little sister, so trusting, chugs the laxatives straight from the bottle.

44

LIZZY

SATURDAY, OCTOBER 17TH, 2015

The Day of the Murders

I jolt awake to sound of my mom pounding on my door. "Lizzy! Are you not up yet? We have to go!"

Nikki isn't in bed. When did she sneak out without me noticing?

Mom is frazzled as she does my hair, pulling it tightly into its performance bun and slicking it down on the sides.

She answers a phone call as she sprays so much hairspray at me, it makes me cough. "Ahh thank you Maya, you're a lifesaver," she says into the phone. "Okay, see you soon, bye."

"Who was that?"

Mom sighs. "Babysitter. There's been a change of plans. Nikki caught whatever bug you had, and she's been stuck in the bathroom since early this morning."

"Change of plans?" I ask innocently. *Please tell me it worked.*

"Nikki will come join us at the cabin when she's feeling better."

My heart sinks. No. *We're still going to the cabin?*

She pulls my chin up to sprinkle glitter on my cheeks and spread lipstick on my lips. "Everything will be okay, sweetie, I promise. I have a bag all packed for you and ready to go."

My stomach sinks. Was she in my room?

"Where's my future gold medalist?" comes a booming voice from the foyer, front door slamming shut behind.

I gasp, leaping up from the table and sprinting across the room. "Dad?! Dad!"

I jump into his arms, and even though I'm almost twelve, he throws me up in the air like I weigh nothing. "You're here!"

"Gunnar?" Mom is trying not to let her anger show, but I see it. "What are you doing here?"

He squeezes me so tightly I almost can't breathe. He beams at me. "I came home early. I couldn't miss my Zizi girl's big day!"

"Nikki is sick." Mom folds her arms. "It makes the most sense if you stay back with her, so I can cancel the babysitter."

"No!" I say too quickly, nearly begging him. "Please come!"

He shrugs at Mom in a surrendering way like he has no choice on the matter. "See, Ingrid? She wants me to come. How can I say no?"

Mom storms past us and throws open the front door so hard it nearly flies off the hinges.

"What's her deal?" Dad asks me, and I shrug, hugging

him tighter, the tension in my shoulders unclenching little by little.

This doesn't solve everything, not even close. But at least it's a problem for another day. Today, I get to pretend a little longer that my family is fine.

I run upstairs to get my stuff. My gym bag is still in a locker at the ice rink, but I still have my skates and costume. Ice rink. The thought of that makes me stop. It makes me think of that man with the black hat... his snarling voice in my ear...

The competition is in a different town, but will he find me in a shadowed hallway there anyway? Will he be waiting for me in the locker room this time, where no one could hear me scream?

With shaking hands, quickly, before I change my mind, I take the gun from under my bed and stuff it in the bottom of my backpack, tossing the bullets on top of it. I don't know how to use it, but it can't be *that* hard to figure out. I've seen movies.

The concept of breaking a rule, doing something illegal and dangerous—it's chilling. But I'd rather break a million rules than ever feel that defenseless, that hopeless, again. I shove my skates and costume on top of the gun and zip it up.

I step down the hallway to say goodbye to Nikki who has luckily been granted momentary reprieve from the bathroom and is sleeping curled up in a ball in her room. She looks terrible, purple circles under her closed eyes, and I feel so guilty I could cry.

"I'm so sorry," I whisper, pressing a kiss to her sweaty forehead and pulling her covers up. "But everything's going to be okay. Our family is going to be okay. I promise."

I come down the staircase to my parents shouting at each

other outside by the car. My shoulders slump. So much for that.

To my surprise, since he doesn't usually work on the weekends, Arrick steps in from the garage.

"I came to wish you luck," he says with a smile, which falters when he sees what I'm seeing through the window. "Don't pay them any mind. Just do your best today."

I study the kind, wrinkled eyes I trust more than any other eyes in the world, and my own fill with tears.

"My mom was going to take Nikki and me to the cabin," I spill as if I'm confessing all my sins, the words catching in my throat. "She was leaving him. I didn't know what to do, so I made Nikki sick."

He takes my hand and squeezes it. "Anytime you don't know what to do, ask me. I'm here, Miss Lizzy. Day or night. Miss Nikki will be alright. I'll make sure of it."

My throat tightens, a tear streaking down my cheek. I nod.

He analyzes me for a moment before making some kind of decision. He pulls his phone out of his pocket and types something into it before pressing it into my hand.

"This is the work phone your parents gave me when I began working here. I saved my personal number in there for you just in case. Why don't you keep it safe for me this weekend?"

I take the phone like it's a baby bird. "Thank you, Arrick."

He uses his thumb to wipe the tear off my cheek. "You're going to do great today."

My dad cracks open the door and greets Arrick with a surprised hello. "C'mon Liz, we have to go, or we'll be late."

And with that, we're on our way.

The car ride is tense. Very tense. I watch the other cars pass by, wondering if their parents still love each other, or if they have guns stuffed at the bottom of their backpacks.

My mom's phone rings, and the bells of her ringtone pull me out of my trance. My dad gets one look at the screen, and his nostrils flare furiously.

"Why is Peter calling you, Ingrid?" He tries to take her phone, but she pulls it away.

"I don't know," she says at a slightly higher octave, feigning ignorance. She keeps the ringing phone close to her chest.

"Answer it then," my dad challenges.

She doesn't. He reaches over and rips the phone from her hand, and she shrieks, "Stop!"

He slides the icon over to answer the call. He doesn't say anything, but Peter starts talking on the other line right away.

"Hey, sorry for calling on this line, but you didn't answer on the other phone. Are you on your way? I'm surprised I still have service honestly. Why'd you get a cabin in the middle of nowhere when—"

My dad presses the end call button so hard I'm surprised it doesn't crack the screen. He rolls down his window and throws her phone out with a furious roar. A car going the other direction on the highway runs it over.

"Have you been sleeping with Peter?" he yells. His head snaps to me in the back and the car swerves slightly. "Do you know anything about this, Elizabeth? Was he at the house?"

Mom's eyes widen at me, begging me not to say anything, and I freeze, caught in the middle. My hesitation must be the only confirmation my dad needs.

"You were meeting him at the cabin, weren't you, that's

why you were pissed I showed up." His voice is low and dark. *"Weren't you?"*

Suddenly my dad jerks the steering wheel, cutting off the car next to us, and taking a sharp U-turn. It's like we're in one of his street races. I always thought being a passenger in those would be a lot more fun.

"What are you doing?" Mom asks with an undertone of fear that mirrors mine. I've never seen this side of my dad.

"We're going to pay the cabin a little visit. He thinks he can make fool out of me?"

"Gunnar, stop!" Mom screeches. "Let's just talk this through!"

My dad doesn't stop the car, doesn't even answer. His jaw ticks as his teeth clench together, eyes shining with fury as he speeds along in the opposite direction of my tournament.

Toward the cabin.

Mom cries.

I'm too hollow to cry. I must have hit some kind of quota for all the crying I've done the last few days, and my tear ducts have now blocked themselves off with bricks.

But all I can think is at least Nikki isn't here to see this. At least she's home where she deserves to be, thinking we have a happy family.

I lose track of how long we're driving as the roads get tighter and the trees get denser. We're further out of the city now. Mom will occasionally have an outburst with some kind of threat or insult at my dad, bang her car door, or she even threatened to throw herself out of the moving vehicle once, but for the most part, she just quietly cries.

He's driving so fast, the thickening trees out my window are blurs of green.

"What the *hell*?" my dad bellows to the rearview, and I

perk up to attention, turning around right away to see what he's looking at.

I could have never guessed what I'd see behind us.

A windowless white van.

Tailing us so closely, I can see the driver as clear as day.

It's him.

Black hat man.

I cry out for my dad in horror. "Dad!"

It speeds up and rams us from behind. I scream. Mom screams.

Dad throws down his window and roars out at it, cursing and waving his arm. "What's your problem?!"

Dad is slowing down to pull off to the side of the road as you do when you get in an accident, trade insurance information, yell at each other a bit, but I shriek at him not to stop. The car lurches with his surprise.

I unbuckle and come up closer to him, starting to panic. "Don't stop the car! They're after me!"

My parents unite on something to look at me in shock.

The van rams us again, throwing me upwards. Mom catches me by the shoulders with a scream. She pushes me back into my seat. "Put your seatbelt back on *now* and explain what is going on!"

"This is all my fault." My hands tremble as I try to buckle up. "I'm so sorry."

Dad speeds up and swerves to the right as the van tries to hit us again. "Lizzy, what did you do?"

"I think it's those Aetherline people, Dad!" I tell him, and if my tear ducts weren't dammed up, I'd cry. "I—I heard you talking to Ava's dad the other night, and I went digging... I found some videos on his computer... they want them back."

"Who?!" Mom cries, but Dad looks like he's seen a ghost.

I've never seen such visible fear on my dad's face, and now I'm more afraid than I've ever been. What have I done?

The road widens into two lanes, and the van speeds up.

"Dad!" I cry as the van pulls up right next to us on the left.

Dad takes a sharp right onto a smaller county road, and the car hits a bump hard. It feels like we're flying before hitting back down with a *thud*.

"Gunnar, what's going on?? Who are these people?"

The van is right next to us again. To my horror, the passenger window rolls down, and the end of a gun points right at me.

"Lizzy!!" My dad swerves again, and I hit my shoulder hard on the door.

I duck my head right in time, flattening into my lower half. My window shatters, glass showering me as a bullet flies through it.

While I'm low, I dig through my backpack at my feet, hardly able to breathe. Another shot shatters the other window. I pull the gun out.

My mom looks at me, eyes widened in horror when she sees it in my hands, but she doesn't have time to question it because the van rams us from the side. I can hardly see through the broken glass of my window. I use the butt of the gun to break it completely, offering me a clearer view to aim and *fire*.

The gun kicks back and hits my cheek hard. I cry out. I don't think I even hit anything.

"Where did you get that?!" Dad thunders, trying to keep control on the narrow road.

The van slows and the passenger is coming right up to my window. They're getting closer, closer. I aim at him with shaking hands. Maybe he'll stop when he sees I'm not defenseless this time.

Closer, closer.

I flex my finger to pull the trigger, but the man leaps at me from his window and shoves the gun as it fires. I scream as an excruciating white-hot pain explodes at my thigh.

There's a ringing in my ears that blocks out all other sound, like I'm underwater. Everything is muffled. Mom and Dad's screams, the roar of the window. Everything except the ringing, ringing, ringing.

I keep my hold on the gun tight as the man tries to rip it away from me. Dad is trying to hit him from his own open window, but he can't quite reach. He swerves and jerks the steering wheel, trying to get him to fall off, but the man is nearly all the way through my window now, only his shins remain in his own car. He grabs hold of my headrest, and pulls his top half in, crushing me. I refuse to let go of the gun, thrashing and pulling with every ounce of strength I can muster.

I can't hear Mom's screams, but she's trying to push him off me. The man finally rips the gun from my hand and time slows as he fires a shot right at her. Her head lolls.

I can't even hear my own screams. Am I screaming? Is the car still moving? Everything feels slow. Her blood is everywhere, my face, my throat.

Before I can even blink, he has fired another shot.

"Dad!!" I think I say, but I can't hear myself. A soundless nightmare. His blood joins Mom's on the windshield. On the ceiling. It's a rainfall of red.

The car swerves off to the right as my dad's head falls onto the steering wheel. The man crushes me, as he scrambles to try to get the rest of the way in to reach the steering wheel. I'm kicking and hammering with my fists, the throbbing pain in my leg spreading up my hip, but he's too strong, too big. I can't get him off me.

Everything jerks forward as we stop with a *crash*. Glass explodes all around us. The man flies forward and hits his head on the passenger back door, instantly crumbling, motionless.

I choke down my sob, forcing it deep down, unable to pause for even a second to even process my parents' unmoving forms because the van ahead is turning around. I rip myself free from under the man's legs, throw open my door, and run.

I run off the road and into where the trees get thicker, where the van can't drive through.

The pain in my leg is blinding. It's throbbing, a pain like I've never felt before. But I push it away. I don't stop. *I can't stop.*

I'm covered in blood. My hands, my face, my clothes. I'm not even sure which is mine and which is my parents'.

My parents.

I don't stop to cry. I just run. I run for a long, long time, far past the time where I'm sure no one is behind me, all the way until my legs crumble under me and force me to stop. I fall into the thicket, catching myself, and my wrist crunches. A branch scrapes my forehead as my head makes contact with the ground.

And here in the leaves, sharp twigs and rocks digging into my entire underside, begging for air from burning lungs, unable to move another inch, a sob finally breaks free, exploding like all that shattering glass. It bursts out as a guttural wail, deep from within me, from a place in my body I've never drawn from before.

"I'm sorry! I'm so sorry!" I scream it again and again and again as if that alone will bring them back.

As if my tears alone could erase what I've done.

I cry for them until my throat is raw.

I sob until everything is empty.

And they're still gone.

A gust of wind brings me back to my body, pulling me from a place I wish I could dissolve into. With effort, muscles quivering, I push myself off the ground to a sitting position. The temperature has dropped. I didn't realize how cold it had gotten. Sniffling, I wipe my face, only to remember the blood on my hands. I try to wipe it off on my pants, but then I'm reminded of the wound in my leg, blood dripping there too.

So much blood.

As the adrenaline slows, a fiery pain takes its place.

Panic roots in my gut like decay, spreading and rotting everything in its path. I don't know what to do.

I don't know what to do.

I dig in my pocket with a glimmer of hope, wincing as a pain in my shoulder manifests itself at this angle.

The phone.

I can barely get my fingers to function, but I manage to unlock it and find the contacts. I make one call and one call only.

"Arrick?" I sob into the phone. "I need your help."

45

NIKKI

A STRANGE HEAVEN CONSTRUCTED JUST FOR US

Present Day

Tears stream down my cheeks by the time Lizzy finishes. We are all in various states of shock. There's a second of dazed silence for a second. Two. Three.

But I break free from it and run across the room to wrap my arms around her tightly. She's tense at first, frozen solid at my touch. Surprised.

"It wasn't your fault, Lizzy," I tell her into her shoulder. I repeat it again. "It wasn't your fault."

Then she breaks, crumpling into my arms. A soul-wrenching sob that has been woven too tightly and shoved down way too deep for way too long bursts out of her. She cries. And I cry.

I'm vaguely aware of Arrick and Ofeliya helping Kieran out of the duct tape as I hold my sister, still not even sure this is real. That I'm hugging my alive sister. Maybe I've actually died too, and this a strange version of heaven constructed just for us. I'm not even sure I'd mind that.

She pulls back and looks at me, eyes red and wet. "I wanted to come back for you, I swear I did, but I hoped they would leave you alone if they assumed I was dead. I didn't want to put you in danger."

Kieran eyes Arrick suspiciously as he massages his sore wrists. "Are we not going to talk about the texts?"

Lizzy doesn't respond. She looks at Arrick with an expectant raised eyebrow, as if he has some explaining to do to her as well.

"And you left Aunt Wren all alone?!" I snivel. Ofeliya stretches to hand me a tissue she got from a tissue box on the coffee table, gives me a flat-lipped smile dripping in pity, and then returns to her spot by Kieran.

"Of course not. Bea is with Wren. She is okay." Arrick is carefully stoic, but he shifts his weight, strong shoulders drooping a fraction. "All those years ago... I picked up Miss Lizzy and brought her here. The house was a family asset of mine I doubted would ever be traced to her. I thought we'd lie low until we figured out what to do. When the investigation dried up and they decided she was dead, we chose to let that be the narrative. We decided it was best for *both girls'* safety if no one ever knew she was here."

My throat tightens, thinking about how scared Lizzy must have been. The guilt, the fear, the loneliness. It's probably been eating her alive all this time. I put my head on her shoulder. She hesitates for a moment before resting her head on top of mine.

Arrick meets our eyes one by one to convey his sincerity when he says, "I vowed on my life I'd never tell anyone she was here, that I would take her secret to the grave. And I mean that, even still." He clears his throat, a sliver of uncomfortableness coming through. "But Lizzy began receiving very threatening messages out of the blue. From someone who suspected she was still alive. The threats were getting more and more persistent, more... *violent*, but she wasn't worried about them. I—I thought if she wouldn't listen to *me*, that maybe Nikki could talk some sense into her if she knew she was alive. If she figured it out herself, I would still be keeping my word. And then Wren got more ill, insurance denied her treatment, Nikki couldn't access the inheritance... it seemed like a solution that could help everyone. So, yes. I sent the texts. Nikki loves listening to those podcasts, I thought she had the skills to figure it out herself. I didn't know she'd bring in Kieran."

Lizzy shakes her head slowly. "I never should've told you about that journal. You should have told me, Arrick. That wasn't your choice to make."

Arrick gives her a steely look as if he regrets nothing. "Keeping you both safe has always ever been my *only* priority."

"Why?" Kieran speaks up from the other side of the room, sitting back in the chair he was once tied to, and Ofeliya is cross-legged on the ground next to him. They've been quiet as everything has unfolded, giving us space to hash this out.

Arrick swallows hard, as if this part of the confession is what he is most nervous to divulge. "My ex-wife and I didn't work out for many reasons. We were very, very young. She was an artist. A dreamer, free spirit. I've always been the opposite, workaholic, too stubborn for my own good. So many arguments that seem so inconsequential now."

"Ex-wife?" I breathe. "I didn't even know you were married. Do you still love her?"

He shuffles a bit in his dress shoes. "I do... but she loves another. She uprooted her whole life to care for this person in a time of need."

I can't bear a tragic love story right now. It hurts too much to think about Arrick being in pain. "I'm so sorry, Arrick."

"I'm not." And to my surprise he smiles. "Because life has a funny way working out, even if it's not the way you planned it. When tragedy struck, life brought her back to me, and life brought you to her."

My breath hitches. "Wait..." I whisper. "Aunt Wren?"

The wrinkles around his gleaming eyes pinch. "Yes. Wren and I were married a very long time ago, but we parted ways as friends. We just wanted different things out of life. Seems like another lifetime now. She's the one who got me this job with your parents all those years ago after our divorce. I'd just left a security guard job that was draining the life out of me. She knew I'd be happy here. And then your parents died, and I clung to you girls like a life raft. I needed your light. And then she came back to care for Nikki, and I suppose after a while, I just began to view you girls as the children we always dreamed of. I'm sorry about the texts." His face crumbles. "I didn't know how else to help everyone. The threats to Lizzy, Wren not being able to get the treatment. I can't stand seeing her like that. All the color and vibrancy stolen from her. I couldn't lose her yet. I felt so helpless."

Lizzy and I are both quick to lend him comfort. We hug and sniffle together.

"I owe you my life," Lizzy tells him, forgiveness shining in her eyes. "I'm indebted to you forever."

"And me too," I add, tears flowing. "You've kept me alive in more ways than one over the years. We love you."

He squeezes us in a tight bear hug. "You girls are my reason for living."

I pull back to give him a knowing look. "You know, I really think she has room in her heart for both of us, Arrick. You have to promise me you'll tell her how you feel when we get her feeling better."

He smiles. "As you wish."

As much as my whole world has just flipped upside down, and I'm totally freaking out, I can't shake off the one thing that still doesn't make sense. It's like a gnawing tug that's keeping me from being fully here in this moment, preventing a full Happy to unfurl. Almost like a ghost with unfinished business, not ready to pass on to the next life.

"Lizzy," I say slowly. "Who did the messages claim to be from?" I share a look with Kieran, hoping her answer is, 'I don't know.'

Lizzy waves it off, still not taking the threats seriously. "Some weird name, Explorer something, I don't know. Probably no one important."

"Ciphered Voyager?" Kieran's suggestion is quiet, hesitant, sharing the same hope that it's not Ciphered, only some other harmless anon.

"Yeah..." Lizzy says slowly, looking back and forth between us. "How did you know that?"

"Let's just say Arrick was right to be worried. Ciphered is dangerous."

Suddenly the air around us explodes.

46

NIKKI

HE'S MONOLOGUE-ING

Shards of glass from the window shatter and fly in all directions. I scream and shrink into Lizzy as we duck together. Kieran pulls Ofeliya away from the window, as pops of bullets come through the shattered window, slicing holes in the curtains that are still drawn.

Arrick picks up Lizzy's shotgun and cocks it, pushing all of us behind the sofa. The front door slams open, and a group of men with guns pointed come streaming in. Arrick doesn't even hesitate before firing. I press my hands over my ears, the blasts from the gun ringing in my ear. There are at least five men on the ground, blood and...insides...everywhere. It coats the whole wall and ground in red. A wave of nausea makes a sweat break out on my forehead, and I try not to gag.

"Now wait, wait, let's be civil here," a voice says from outside. "I think it's time we have a conversation face-to-face since you thought you could just fake your death and ignore me. How about 'Ciphered Voyager' gives you some final motivation?" My pulse abandons me entirely when a slouching figure is shoved in first, stumbling in with his arms tied behind his back.

Hunter.

He looks around the room with wild eyes until he finds mine peeking over the edge of the couch.

"I'm so sorry, Nikki," Hunter cries. "They have my mom, I had no ch—"

A booted leg kicks him behind his knees, cutting him off as he falls into a puddle of blood.

"Hunter!" I move to help him, but Lizzy keeps a firm hand on my arm, keeping me here next to her.

The voice steps into the room and nudges his fallen men out of the way with his boot, stepping on Hunter's back and pushing him further into the blood. "Thanks for showing us the way."

I squint. I can't be seeing this right. *He is Ciphered Voyager??* How? *Why?*

Arrick growls with another cock of the gun, "Michael Montgomery."

"Our lawyer?" Lizzy looks at me with furrowed brows, and I mirror the confusion. *It can't be.*

Kieran springs to action and charges at Michael with a warrior yell. Michael is unconcerned. He simply points the gun at Hunter's head, knowing he has the perfect bargaining chip.

"Kieran, stop!" I rip my arm away from Lizzy's to stop him. I run over and hold Kieran's arm, the feeling of him under my touch unexplainably grounding, that same comforting energy Vinnie exudes, like they both serve the same function to people. Thank goodness Vinnie isn't here.

Hunter looks back and forth between Kieran and me as he manages to get himself off the ground, even with hands behind his back. At first, I squirm a little at the accusation flashing in his eyes, even though I've done nothing wrong, but then I remember that it's his fault we have no evidence, no chance up against Ciphered—*Michael... And he led them here!*

"I have a fleet of vans outside waiting for the go-ahead," Michael says, giving Arrick and Kieran both a side-eye as he lowers the gun, having made his point. "And now that you've led us here, we're prepared to do a little more than just intimidate you, so, let's not be hasty."

"What do you mean 'intimidate us'? Your truck pushed us into a river," Kieran snarls. "We could have died."

A flash of confusion sparks in Michael's eyes. "That wasn't my team. Boy, you sure do like to piss people off, don't you?"

Kieran and I share a look with an unspoken question. If Ciphered wasn't the one in the black truck, who was?

"Truck you say? If I had to guess, that reeks of Moorsebury's style. He's been off the rails, not playing very nice with the rest of us lately. Hemlock too. I assume we have you to thank for that."

The attorney general and police chief tried to kill us?

"You're with Aetherline?" Lizzy materializes by my side and holds my hand.

"You stupid girl, I created Aetherline." Michael looks her up and down in with disdain. "If you hadn't gone meddling into things that weren't any of your business, none of this would have had to happen. You weren't content with getting your parents killed? You had to kill" — he gestures around the room— "*everyone else* in your life too?"

Lizzy tenses.

"Don't listen to him," I whisper to her through clenched teeth. "He's trying to provoke you."

Kieran speaks up, and I sense he's trying to get Michael's attention away from Lizzy. Protecting her. That makes a warmth bloom in my chest. "Why turn on Roger Mackenzie if he was part of Aetherline too?"

"I told Mack and Vanderwaal that their sons were weak all along." He sneers at Hunter in disgust. "Mack knows he's lucky I didn't kill Roger right off the bat for being so careless with our blood vow videos. Letting them get into the hands of a little girl. He's lucky I gave him a second chance after that. But then he crumbled at the very first ounce of scrutiny when your podcast came along and drug up *another* situation we had to clean up eight years ago."

Kieran's eyes turn busy. "Frank Holt was with Aetherline?" He looks at me with widened eyes to mutter softly, "Albert's killer from season two. That video near the middle that the AI program didn't work on, because of the angle his face? Did you and Hunter find a match for him? He was obviously a lot younger, then, but that could be him. Frank Holt."

I cringe. He still doesn't know that all the videos are gone... How am I going to tell him?

"Mack hasn't been exactly happy about the Roger situation, but that's what he gets for having a son with a snowflake for a backbone." Michael waves the gun at Hunter. "At least this one's been cooperative. I'll probably let him live."

"My dad is going to tear you limb from limb," Hunter grits out under his breath.

"Why the games, Michael?" I narrow my eyes, still trying to make sense of this. "Why the texts? Why the ransom, why the threats? Why the day job? The freaking *charcuterie boards* you give me every single year? What's the point?"

Michael's eyes wrinkle at the edges as he smiles, as if he's glad I asked. "Being a lawyer has just always been the perfect way to clean up everyone's untidiness in Aetherline. Without my 'day job', it would have fallen apart decades ago."

He chuckles as he continues, "Annika, did you really think your loving parents would keep your inheritance from you unless you were twenty-one or *married?*" He barks a laugh, and Kieran looks at me, understanding sparking in his eyes, which makes my ears warm. "Your aunt's sickness really was such a perfect coincidence for me. It set everything in motion. The perfect motivation for you to find Elizabeth. Plus, I owed a favor to Vanderwaal, who always thought the best way to get the Sinclair business was by marrying you and Hunter off. Not really my taste, but I planted the seed for Vanderwaal anyway. Three birds, one stone. Find Elizabeth, get the business, and he and I would be square. Well," he chuckles, "we *were* before I threw his wife in a van to blackmail his son to get us here. Oops."

My knees might give out completely. I made it so easy. I played right into his plan the whole time, trusted him so completely. I didn't even request a copy of the will. He could tell me it said I had to tame a unicorn before getting my inheritance, and I'd never know different. I feel so stupid.

"Why the ransom?" I repeat, jerking my head at Kieran, barely able to choke the words out.

"You should be thanking me, Annika. If it weren't for me, Kieran here never would've taken your case at all, and you'd never get to have such a lovely reunion with your sister. What perfect closure."

Closure. I get a sinking feeling at the word. Closure is when something ends. He's going to kill us.

"I sent a team to kill all *four* Sinclairs that day, you know." Michael tucks his hands into his pockets, the picture of casual. As if he's discussing golf or the weather, not his involvement in the murders of a *family*. "It was a solution that would help everyone. Aetherline would absorb the business and use it for our own purposes, and the little nosy know-it-all who stuck her nose where it shouldn't be, would stay quiet forever. It was supposed to be a nice and easy car accident with all of you in it, but it got messy." Michael's demeanor shifts darkly, and he bares his teeth at Lizzy. "You just couldn't let it be easy, could you? You messed everything up that day."

Lizzy and I cling to each other, holding on for dear life because I think we'd both unravel if we didn't.

"I didn't expect you would get away. No one else in Aetherline even knew," Michael continues, probably loving the way he's holding all our attention captive. "But I despise a loose thread. I'd wonder every day when you were going to crawl out of the gutters and expose us, but I couldn't ever find you."

His attention snaps to me, and I want to curl into myself, but I keep my chin high under the weight of his sneer. "And then to top it all off your bitch of an aunt somehow got your name on the TrueNorth board so she could have majority voting power. She'd oppose every time we tried to persuade the board to sell or to get involved in our deals. As much as I wanted to kill you and your aunt and be done with it, it would've raised too much suspicion to have you killed after the fact. It's been very frustrating, as you can imagine. I just waited and planned and waited and planned some more."

Finally he turns to Kieran. "Which brings us to you. After you got Frank arrested in your second season and shed light on the alibi we created for Roger—which was really inconvenient for me, by the way—I knew if anyone could find Elizabeth, it would be you. It was finally time after all the waiting. I knew you wouldn't have the money for the ransom I put over your friend's head, and that you'd get desperate. Throw in a little 'chance encounter' at the country club with a helpless rich princess who was just as desperate, and *bam*. A perfect plan unfolds." Michael sighs proudly. "Man, I'm good."

"You never wanted me to stop the podcast," Kieran growls, and I hold him back gently, squeezing his arm as his hand clenches into a fist. "You killed George, what, just to motivate me?"

Michael beams, his demeanor brightening back up. "I killed George to get you right here where we're standing, and see? You did it, Kieran. All the loose ends are tying up perfectly because of you. I get to take care of all three of you nosy brats all at once!"

Arrick, who has been quiet this whole time takes a step closer, hands tightening on the shotgun. "Alright, Michael. That's enough. You need to leave."

Michael makes a wave of his hand, and a symphony of shutting doors erupts outside. All amusement leaves his face. "You sure you want to get to business to soon, Arrick? I should have killed you years ago." Marching footsteps approach and within seconds, dozens of guns are pointing at us from all directions. Kieran, Lizzy, and I stumble back further into the house, but they're coming in from the back too.

I give Kieran an alarmed look after a quick scan of the room, only mouthing one word to him: *Ofeliya.*

He looks around as discreetly as he can, but the worry floods his eyes. *Where is she?*

In the same millisecond, Arrick and Michael both fire their weapons with an explosive *bang.*

Arrick's pointed at Michael.

Michael's pointed at—

"No!" The shots ring out, and I can't stop my body from acting, an external force of nature thrusting me in front of her.

In front of Lizzy.

47

NIKKI

SHOULD'VE SENT A POSTCARD

A blast of pain erupts in my shoulder, and I collapse at her feet, hitting the ground hard.

On the other side of the room, Michael flies back into the wall at the force of Arrick's hit.

"NIKKI!" Lizzy screams, falling to her knees and pulling me into her lap. "Why would you do that?!" She pats me down wildly, looking for the wound and finding it at my shoulder. She takes off her sweater and ties it around it tightly. Her tears fall over me like rainfall. "Stupid, *stupid.*"

I think the bullet only grazed my shoulder, but it left fire behind regardless. A fire that's spreading angrily.

"You made me believe you were dead for ten years," I groan, pushing myself up to a sit, head spinning dizzily from the pain. "If anyone gets to kill you, it's gonna be me."

She laughs through tears. I pull her in for a tight hug, which is actually excruciating, but I try not to ruin the moment.

"And you saved my life that day you *poisoned me,*" I tell her with a chuckle. "Call it even."

The moment is short-lived as *pops* ring out all around us as Michael's men fight back. Hell rises up and breaks loose, engulfing the entire room in hazy chaos as everything happens all at once. Shots come from outside and inside, glass breaking and bullets ricocheting everywhere.

Kieran drops to his knees in front of me, eyes wild, hands flailing over me searching for the damage. "Are—"

"I'm okay," I finish his sentence with a weak smile, giving him the reassurance to finish what he needs to. Relief loosens his distress ever so slightly, but worry lingers in his eyes.

My vision blackens at the edges, but I force the blackness away. This isn't about me. There's too much left to do.

Kieran pats the ground to grab a gun that has flown loose as a man runs toward us. We scramble to our feet to retreat, bringing stars to my eyes, but Kieran doesn't hesitate. *Bang.* The man flies back.

Kieran is a furious force of nature doling out reckoning to anyone in his path. He roars as he kicks, punches, and shoots, covering Arrick's six as he does the same. It's both terrifying and incredibly attractive.

The *pops* around us multiply, and so do the number of men around. More figures stream in from all directions. Goosebumps ripple across my skin, slimy dread making a permanent home in my gut.

I take Lizzy's hand as the fighting closes in around us. We are surrounded. There's gunfire on all sides, and we have nowhere to go.

How many men did Michael bring? Kieran and Arrick can't hold them off forever.

"We have to do something," I shriek.

Lizzy points. "Wait, look."

They're fighting *each other*. Two groups? Who are these other men? Two men punch each other right in front of us. One stumbles back, and I think it's one of Michael's men, so I trip him. Then the other man shoots him in the head. I gulp as the blood splashes everywhere.

The groups fight all around us. It's an even match, impossible to know who will take the upper hand.

But then the thunder arrives.

A bear-like figure with a huge gun in his hand kicks the door down, with a roar like Kieran's.

My shoulders slump with relief. *His dad.*

The *Pakhan* shouts a battle cry in Russian, and his men echo it like a symphony around us. It's gasoline to their efforts. In only minutes, the tide shifts in their favor.

Ofeliya walks in next, a rifle slung over her shoulder like a school backpack. She winks at me. "Thought we could use some backup."

Kieran's dad squats down to where Michael is slumped against the wall. I can't tell if he's dead or unconscious. Kieran's dad slings him over his shoulder as if he were a sack of potatoes and not a grownup man. He stands, heading toward the door, giving one last command over his shoulder.

"Load up everyone else," he orders. "We can finish our business with these rats at home."

The cleanup crew obeys, Kieran included. They work together to take bodies, both alive and dead, to the trucks and vans outside. Lizzy and I follow, and I try not to stumble from the agonizing pain in my shoulder. Still not about me... So I force myself upright, even though the wildfire pain could consume me at any second, rippling and multiplying.

We step over the wreckage of Arrick's house, Lizzy's home for the past ten years. Bullet holes everywhere, broken windows, shredded sofa, coffee table reduced to slivers, body shaped holes in the drywall. Blood. So much blood.

"Sorry about your house," I tell her with a wince. "But hey, maybe with Michael taken care of, you can come home?" I try to keep the hope out of my tone, but it leaks out anyway.

"Home," Lizzy repeats in a dazed way.

I analyze the flickers of reluctance, sadness, residual paranoia in her eyes, all the things that are opposite of what I'm feeling—hope, excitement, relief.

It stings a little.

She doesn't want to come back with me.

I've never been very good at keeping my exact thoughts and feelings off my face, and she sees everything clear as day. She rushes to reassure me. "I want to! I just—" She looks at the house with a conflicted expression. "I'm not sure where I fit yet."

"We'll take it slow," I tell her. "Let me know what you need."

She looks at me wistfully, reaching for my hand. "You know I would always imagine what you'd be like all grown up, but I never thought I'd get to see it. You look like her."

"You look like him." I sniffle, squeezing her hand back.

She smiles playfully, thankfully taking us away from the edge of grief that would be so easy to catapult off of right now. "Weird seeing you all mature and stuff."

"Mature? Don't be fooled. I'm dying inside trying not to suffocate you with my relentless fear of abandonm—"

I cut off. One of the men carries a thrashing Hunter over his shoulder.

"Wait!" I run over. Kieran and his dad are talking nearby,

but they come closer when they hear me yell, "Kieran, tell him to stop! Not him!"

The man only talks to Kieran's dad, as if I'm not even here. "We found him hiding in the bushes," he explains.

"He's my fiancé," I protest. "Well, *ex*-fiancé."

That gets Kieran's attention.

"Wait, what?" Lizzy asks, but I ignore her. That's a story for another time.

Kieran quirks an eyebrow at me, making a blush spread hotly on my cheeks. And maybe it's just the literal bullet wound on my shoulder, but I'm getting somewhat dizzy at the way those espresso brown eyes are staring at me. And man, do I love espresso. For a second, I tuck myself in them and get lost there, forgetting everyone else for a moment. Then his eyes flick away, and the moment is over, leaving me slightly cold in comparison.

Or maybe that's also the bullet wound. I probably need a hospital. Like now.

Kieran nods at his dad, who barks an order in Russian at the man. He drops Hunter on his butt, and, to my satisfaction, it knocks the air out of him. He coughs uncontrollably as he tries to catch his breath.

Kieran's dad claps his son on his shoulder, a look of unmistakable pride gleaming in his eyes.

"Thanks, Dad," Kieran says, returning the clap on the back.

"мой сын. My son. Call anytime."

And then he loads into the closest truck, and they all take off like a convoy. We shield our eyes as rocks and gravel fling up everywhere.

Hunter has managed to get his hands free from behind his back. He stumbles up to me.

"Thank you, Nikki," he says breathily. "Does this mean you forgive—"

I punch him so hard in the face that he stumbles back, a gush of blood spurting from his nose under appalled and heartbreakingly beautiful eyes. I try not to let it show that my fist feels like it has shattered into a million pieces, but inside I'm screaming.

Lizzy snorts in surprise but tries to hide it under a little cough.

"You're lucky I got shot on my dominant side," I tell Hunter with a flick of my hair.

His eyes say a lot, but his mouth, fortunately, doesn't say anything. Because, I mean, how do you really say, "Sorry for pretending to be your friend your whole life, asking you to marry me so my father could obtain your family's business, destroying all the evidence you've acquired in your family's murder case, and then leading the killer straight to you. My bad."

You can't. So, he does the first smart thing he's done in a while and shuts up.

Kieran tries not to laugh, hiding his smirk behind his hand, but I can see it shining in his eyes. The amusement is going to fade fast when he finds out I lost everything...

"Arrick?" I call out, hoping he's close by. He slams a truck door shut, patting it to send it off, and comes over to me.

His eyes are tired. Deeply tired. But he brightens when he sees Lizzy and I next to each other. "It sure is good to see you together again."

I link my arm in Lizzy's, and she smiles at me, though she looks equally as exhausted as Arrick. I try to remind myself how long she's been in hiding. Her eyes dart around in a paranoid way when she thinks I'm not looking. We *are* out here on full display in her front yard making an incredibly huge scene. How her neighbors haven't called the cops yet is beyond me. Wow, they really do mind their business in this town.

"Arrick, can you do one last favor for me before you take a very long and very mandatory vacation?" I ask.

He chuckles. "How can I help?"

My head flicks toward Hunter. "Can you take him back home and help him make sure his mom is okay?"

Hunter regards Arrick with a respectable amount of fear, I'm sure remembering the way he shot so many dead mere moments ago. But behind the intimidation, is relief. A 'thank you' just for me flickers there for a moment. I'm furious at him, angrier than I've ever been in my life, but I'm also heartbroken to lose the version of him he let me love. For the best friend I lost because he chose to lie. I'm sad wondering how things could have been different if he had chosen honesty instead.

But I'm also sad for him.

Even though my parents made mistakes, at least I know they loved me up to the very end. I feel they love me even now. I believe they're looking down on me, smiling seeing Lizzy and I back together.

I can't imagine being trapped with a father like Hunter's, who will always choose his dangerous business over him. Money will always be more important than his family. Mr. Mackenzie, too, who allowed Aetherline to kill his own son.

Hunter turns and leaves, and I watch him walk away, feeling like a door is closing right in front of me. It'll hurt when I'm not so angry.

Blood is soaking through the DIY tourniquet on my shoulder. My legs quiver and are feeling more like jelly than bones by the minute, but I'm not done yet. I have to take care of one more thing, but I wait until Arrick leaves with Hunter first. I don't know how Kieran will react, and as mad as I am at Hunter, I still don't want him to get hurt.

I gulp, looking up at Kieran and being met with those cozy, deep eyes that I just want to wrap up and fall asleep in. The teasing smirk I have grown fond of. Missed, even. The warmth of him that wraps around me when he's close.

But everything's going to change when I tell him. He'll be another thing I lose today, and my heart prepares itself for the loss. I know my heart won't survive losing Kieran too, it's unimaginable, but he has to know.

I take Lizzy's hand. She needs to hear this too.

"I'm so sorry, both of you." My eyes flicker down, voice no louder than a whisper. "I lost everything. The videos, the journal, the burner phone. Hunter burned it all. We have nothing to use against Aetherline." I force myself to look at Lizzy. "You worked so hard to protect those videos. Now I know why you didn't trust me with any of this. I messed everything up."

Lizzy pulls me closer to tell me sternly, "Never apologize for loving and trusting with your whole heart. Your heart? *That's* what I fought to protect. Not the stupid iPad."

She hugs me tightly, and I don't think I ever would have known how much of me was missing until my other half was close again. It's not a perfect fit. Each half is a little jagged, a little bruised. But they'll find a way to fit together again.

I finally look at Kieran, ashamed and embarrassed. He *told* me not to trust anyone with all of it. If I had listened, we'd still have it. "We have no evidence."

To my surprise, that stupid smirk pulls on his lips, and I'm suddenly doubting if I've grown fond of it after all. "Nikki." The way he says my name, a little teasingly, a little tenderly, it makes my stomach flip upside down. "In my line of work, do you actually think I wouldn't make copies of those videos the second I saw them?"

He wiggles his phone at me with a smile.

"You have them?!" I shriek.

"I have them."

I fly over and throw my good arm around his neck with a near-hysterical cheer, feeling like the very sun has unfurled within me. I jump up and down.

Then I freeze when realize what I've done. Throwing myself at him? Invading his personal bubble, and he probably hates it. Hates *me.* Oh my gosh what have done—

But then he laughs, softening into me, hugging me tightly and picking me up at the waist. He spins around once before setting my feet back down, but he doesn't let go. And neither do I. It's the kind of hug that can change your very soul, your entire chemical make-up. I relax my head onto his chest, and he brings his hand to the back of my head. I sigh out a long breath, feeling the tight pressure coiled deep inside me release.

"Finally," Ofeliya groans, materializing behind us as we pull apart shyly. She turns to Lizzy. "You'd never believe how insufferable they've been. The denied tension has been sickening."

Lizzy chuckles. "I'm sure. Hey nice move with the backup. I'm Lizzy by the way."

Ofeliya grins and juts out her hand to shake hers. "Ofeliya."

"Give it back," Kieran barks, stepping out of the hug to inspect my shoulder. "Now."

Ofeliya laughs in that unapologetic sing-songy way she

does. "You guys are no fun." Then she holds out Lizzy's watch.

Lizzy takes it back in wordless shock, but an impressed glint flashes in her eyes.

Ofeliya puts her hands on her hips, straightening to get back to business. "So, what's the plan? What are we going to do about Aetherline?"

"Hospital first," Kieran answers, eyebrow raised at me pointedly. "And then?"

The four of us share a look full of devious hope.

"Take the bastards down?" I suggest sweetly.

Kieran puts his hand out like we're in a football huddle. We all join in, even Lizzy, layering our hands together, like a real team. "Take the bastards down on three!"

PODCAST TRANSCRIPT
Secrets in Ice **Season 3, Episode 6: The Truth, Finale**

[Secrets in Ice opening theme music plays]

KIERAN BERGSTROM:

Hey, Icers, surprise! I'm alive. And boy do I have so much to catch you up on. I want to apologize for making you all think I was dead. Would you forgive me if I said I had a really good reason? Joining me for this special finale episode is the one and only Nikki Sinclair herself.

NIKKI SINCLAIR:

Thank you for having me, Kieran. And I'd also like to personally thank every person who has sent in tips, ideas, encouraging messages, and just overall support while we've been working this case. We have miraculously been able to uncover evidence that we believe will bring my family's killers to justice.

KIERAN BERGSTROM:

Before we tell you everything we've learned about the Sinclair case, and believe me it's shocking, head over to my channel and check out the recent video that just dropped this morning. It's recommended to only view if you are over the age of 18, and please be advised this compilation of videos may be hard to watch, and honestly will probably be reported *a lot*. Nathaniel Moorsebury, the attorney general, and Chief of Police Timothy Hemlock will be especially motivated to get it taken down. And last time I mentioned them on this podcast they sent a hit crew after me to push my van into a river. Who knows what they'll try this time? So watch and reshare quick before they get it taken it down or try to have me killed again. Nikki, care to explain?

NIKKI SINCLAIR:

In our investigating, we uncovered a secret criminal organization that calls themselves Aetherline. It's a network of twenty-two—that we know of—high profile individuals, who use each other's careers to engage in illegal activity here and in British Columbia. So far, we've found evidence of international drug and weapon trafficking funneled through at least twenty different businesses.

KIERAN BERGSTROM:

We think the videos were some kind of initiation or blackmail assurance for these individuals. They each had to submit a reputation-ending video that bound them together. If you betrayed the organization, they could all collectively end you.

NIKKI SINCLAIR:

My father's company does a lot of crossing the Canadian border for oil transports, so the organization really wanted him in to make the cross-border smuggling of their goods easier. He refused. Unfortunately, that would be the cause of his death. When he uncovered these videos, it put a target on his back and my mother and sister were collateral damage. Aetherline killed my family.

KIERAN BERGSTROM:

Conveniently, because Chief Hemlock is one of these individuals, the Portland City Police Department hasn't been very cooperative. They weren't interested in hearing about this organization. So—media, viewers, listeners, we need your help. These men are the scum of the earth. They live in the shadows all among us, parading as run-of-the-mill business owners— and their crimes and secrets need to be brought to light. Who knows how many other families have been hurt by Aetherline? They need to be stopped.

NIKKI SINCLAIR:

We also are asking the community to help us put pressure on the officials in Thurston County to dredge Deep Lake in Olympia, Washington, where we believe they will find the remains of my parents and sister, so they can finally rest in peace.

KIERAN BERGSTROM:

Nikki, thank you so much for being here today. I know your family would be so proud of you for finally finding answers, both for them and yourself. What's your plan now that you can start to see that closure coming together?

NIKKI SINCLAIR:

Thanks. My guardian is in recovery right now from her lung surgery but when she's feeling better, we've decided to turn my parents' estate into a group home for foster youth. It's too big for just her and I, and we want it to be put to good use. To mean something. I think my family would like that.

KIERAN BERGSTROM:

Any college plans? I mean, the *listeners* may be curious if you're planning to stay around.

NIKKI SINCLAIR:

Well, I've always heard the van life can be pretty fulfilling. Maybe I'll give that a try for a while. I happen to know someone who's really good at that. Even has a brand-new van with all the upgrades. Maybe he'd let me help him put it all together. Tag along, I don't know, travel a bit? See the sights I couldn't ever see before? Who knows?

KIERAN BERGSTROM:

Van life does get pretty lonely sometimes. I'm sure he'd be grateful for a travel companion.

NIKKI SINCLAIR:

Oh, here is my friend now. Vinnie, what do you say? Can I tag along with you? See the sights?

[bark]

KIERAN BERGSTROM:

Well, I guess that's settled then, Heiress.

THE END

EPILOGUE | NIKKI
HAPPILY EVER AFTER (TERMS AND CONDITIONS APPLY)

4 Months Later

"Kieran? Help?" I squeak in distress as a slight breeze picks up the other end of the plastic tablecloth that I'm trying to spread out and smacks me in the face. I'm trying to hit it away, but it surrounds me, and it's suffocating me now? What vendetta does this tablecloth have on my life?

Kieran laughs and helps me untangle myself. I thank him breathlessly, and even though I'm now safe from the vengeful tablecloth, he doesn't step away. If anything, he has stepped closer. "My hero," I say playfully.

He straightens importantly. "All in a day's work, ma'am."

"How can I ever repay you?" I tease.

He leans in and brushes a soft kiss on my lips, making my stomach flip. "This will do," he says the words on my mouth.

I return the kiss, forgetting the entire world, still in awe of how easily everything melts away when he's close.

He kissed me for the first time on my birthday a couple weeks ago. He was so shy about it, and I found it absolutely adorable. Asked permission like a complete gentleman. To my delight, he hasn't stopped since. A tiny piece of my broken heart tapes itself back together every time he puts his lips on mine, healing itself little by little, slice by slice. And it might not ever be the same, my heart. But I might like it better this way. A little bruised, a little sore, but fuller than it's ever been.

The last few months have been a perfect mix of work and play, loss and hope, grief and healing. Everything blended up together in a beautiful and painful and *real* way.

Thanks to pressure from fans of the podcast and the media, all twenty-two Aetherline men have been arrested, apart from Frank Holt, who was already in custody for Albert's murder. Luckily, his involvement in this organization gives Albert's defense more legs to stand on. Albert's family is closer to justice than ever.

The Aetherline men, including Hunter's dad, the attorney general, and chief of police have all been charged with a grocery list of crimes. Conspiracy, aiding and abetting a murder, solicitation of minors, statutory rape, drug possession, drug use, drug and weapons trafficking, money laundering, and so much more. Police don't know Michael crossed the wrong people and was served final justice another way, but he is wanted for four counts of first-degree murder, thanks to his confession of killing George and the Sinclairs caught on a security camera inside Arrick's house (though carefully spliced to avoid any mention or sightings of Lizzy).

Through Kieran's family and their terrifying, but albeit useful collected talents, knowhow, and resources, they were able to acquisition a medical cadaver body around the same size Lizzy would have been. Having access to her teeth and other DNA, some knowledge that Pavel (which Kieran's dad insists I call him, though *sir* seems much more fitting) was alarmingly familiar with, about speeding up the decomposition process, we were able to plant a third body in Deep Lake for divers to come across when they eventually did dredge the lake.

Three bodies. Three deaths. Case closed.

We were finally able to have our parents buried in their vault at the local cemetery that has been there in their honor all this time, marble and haunting, but has sat empty until now. Arrick, Bea, Kieran, Vinnie, and I said a few words, cried a bit, and that was that. I never visited it before, but I do now occasionally. When I need a good cry. Despite their mistakes, Mom's especially, I miss them. But I'm learning how to accept their deaths again little by little.

I argued with Lizzy for a long time about her choice to remain dead, and honestly it still hurts sometimes. Even with the videos out in the open, Aetherline and Michael gone, nothing left to fear, ultimately, she still chose to stay dead. I lost my sister after all, but I gained a friend. The other half of a broken family that is healing and mending back together, even if it looks different than I thought it would.

Kieran's family was able to get her a new name and identity, so she doesn't have to hide anymore. She just has to be someone else. I'm happy for her that she gets to decide who to be now. It's a fresh start not many get to have.

To start, she's the proud new official owner of Arrick's place and has been fixing it up and making some upgrades to it. She has also enrolled at an online university and wants to study architecture. It turns out she has a knack for creating things.

She's taking her new life one slow step at a time, and I'm trying to give her time to adjust. I don't mind slow steps. I'm just glad to have my sister back in whatever capacity. The nightly FaceTime and occasional game night with Kieran's family is non-negotiable, however.

Aunt Wren's pneumonectomy went perfectly, and she's making a full recovery. It may have only given her a few more years, but they are years that I will treasure for my entire life.

And speak of the devil, Arrick is wheeling her out now onto the patio I've been decorating. Aunt Wren immediately begins fussing over the red, white, and blue centerpieces that have blown over in the breeze. I forced Arrick and Aunt Wren to have a long, long, *long* talk. The steps there are slow too, but I see the way they look at each other. Once we get past the pride, the stubbornness, the pain for old wounds, I know they'll be able to dust off the love that never really left and create something new together. What matters is they both want to, and now they've finally admitted it. I'm trying to play it cool, but I'm so happy for them I could die.

Kieran jumps over to help Aunt Wren, and she beams at him, mumbling something affectionately at him as she pats his hand. Luckily, she already knew him as my 'boyfriend,' so we skipped over the explanation and rolled with it. She adores him. So much so that they often team up against me, taunting me or whispering about me. I wouldn't be surprised if she loves him more than me. But I love it.

Aunt Wren is even coming around to Vinnie, too, but at a distance. He waits at the other side of the patio next to the sizzling grill, awaiting the promise of unrestricted hotdog access in just a few minutes, tongue lolling happily.

After some back and forth, Kieran agreed to let me make a social media account for Vinnie with the purpose of spreading awareness about service dogs for people with Type 1 Diabetes. The account went viral almost immediately, and now Vinnie has more followers than any of us combined, receiving comments and DMs by the minute about how much comfort he's brought someone who was recently diagnosed, or the smile and hope he gave a child learning how to manage their T1D. You can see the pride in his countenance, glowing in his fur, in his eyes, somehow knowing that he's doing even more good. Such a good boy.

With full access to my inheritance without Michael blocking it, as well as the (appalling) proceeds of selling my father's company, I replaced Kieran's van, as promised. I could have kept my father's business running, but part of me felt like he wouldn't want me to be tied down by it. I felt like he'd want me to have a fresh start, like Lizzy. To get to decide the person I want to be. So I sold the company and bought a van that matches Kieran's for me too. Ofeliya and I will share it, and I'm so excited to have a roommate. When we realized Kieran was a grouch in the mornings, a coffee snob, and has an old man decorating aesthetic, we decided we needed our own. We have so many fun and girly plans for it, involving lots of plants and a despicable amount of the color pink.

When the van renovations are all done, season four of the podcast will be in full swing. I'll be doing background work—scheduling calls with witnesses and leads, answering emails, running social media, things like that, and Ofeliya and Kieran will host. I like it better that way, out of the spotlight. Mostly, I'm excited to help people. Other people like me who thought they'd never get the answers they begged for. That no one cared anymore because it had been so long. Helping them have hope again. I can't wait.

"Dinner's ready!" George's wife Tina and Bea come out the backdoor, hands full of casserole dishes and mixing bowls. They help Aunt Wren arrange them on the table, which is already full of barbecue ribs, fruit, salads of every variation, giggling together like teen girls at a slumber party. Arrick rushes over to help, and the women all dote on him and fuss over him. He pretends to be embarrassed, but he secretly loves it.

Tina, it turns out, once lived in a group home and has since had a lifelong dream of helping foster youth. After some gentle pressure and reassurance that she is far from an imposition, we convinced her to move in and help Arrick, Bea, and Aunt Wren get the group home up and running. She's the kindest person I've ever met. She's going to make such a difference with these kids.

"They're here!" I sing as Ofeliya and Lizzy finally walk onto the patio. "Everyone, these are Kieran's cousins! Ofeliya and Beth."

All the women crowd and gush over them even though they're both fully grown adults, cooing affectionately and pinching their cheeks in that way all old ladies collectively can't help but doing. I hold my breath as I wait to see if any of them will mention that Lizzy looks vaguely familiar, but luckily no one does.

Eventually Lizzy wants to tell Bea the truth—she was such a huge part of her childhood, after all—but she's letting things die down first and lying low until the trials are all done, just to be safe. The less people who know her real identity right now the better. Eventually I hope she tells

Aunt Wren, too. Even though Aunt Wren and Lizzy never knew each other well, I think they'd absolutely love each other.

After some time, the ladies go back to fixing up the food table and Lizzy steps over to Arrick at the grill. With a knowing smile, he stretches out his hand to shake hers. "Beth, nice to meet you."

"You too," Lizzy replies, and I swear I see a little sparkle come back to her eyes.

She sacrificed so much back then to protect my sparkle, my innocence. She gave up the rest of her childhood, and grew up sooner than any child should have to, so I could live out the rest of mine. She lived alone in fear every day, so I could sleep peacefully every night. I'll be indebted to her forever. She deserves to sparkle too, and I'll never stop helping her find her own light again.

I smother her with a hug I don't let her escape from for at least a minute. "Ready for fireworks?" I ask her excitedly.

She looks longingly at the table of food. "Sure, fireworks are great, but I've really missed Bea's Jell-O salad. That's first on my list."

I pull back and regard her with a long look, whispering, "Welcome back home."

Her eyes flick around familiarly. "It's good to be back. I feel them here. It's nice."

We share a smile with a million layers. Complicated layers of hope, pain, healing, grief. It's different than I pictured. But we're together. And that's all I've ever wanted and more.

THANK YOU READER!

First and foremost I want to thank you for taking the time to read my book! Having people read my books is my biggest dream come true, and I'm so grateful that out of everything on your TBR, you chose this!

Secrets in Ice was my first go at this genre, and I had so much fun with it. Reimagining my favorite fairytale characters in a murder mystery was a blast!

If you enjoyed it, it would mean so much to me if you take the time to leave a review on Goodreads and Amazon, so I can get connected with other readers like you.

You can also subscribe to my newsletter to receive updates about future releases, giveaways, and updates at kennedyplumb.com I promise not to spam!

Grateful for your support!

<3 Kennedy

ACKNOWLEDGMENTS

To the friends and family who are always the FIRST to pre-order when I announce a new book: thank you, thank you, thank you for being my biggest cheerleaders. You know who you are, and I'm so grateful for you.

I couldn't have done it without my amazing beta team: Katie N., Emma, Morgan, Chelsea, Capri, Ashley G., Ana, Judith, Melissa, and Skylar. We can just pretend like those plot holes never even happened ;)

Morgan - Thank you for your special set of skills. Glad we could put your criminal justice degree to use :D

Katie N. - I value your advice and feedback so much. Grateful for you.

Melissa with Desert Rose Edits - Thank you so much for the early developmental advice when I was feeling stuck. You gave me the encouragement to finish this!

A huge thanks to my editor, Mallory Day. Thank you for not judging my exorbitant use of "just" and "like", and for bringing my baby to her final form.

To my cover illustrator Melody with "Whim and Joy", you are absolutely incredible. The cover of my DREAMS.

Thank you to my incredible podcast team - Phillip Church and Rebecca Brokaw-Sands. Thank you for bringing the *Secrets* podcast to life!

Thank you ARC readers for the reviews, both glowing and constructive. I appreciate you taking the time to read my book! Your reviews mean everything.

And thank you to my husband, Aaron, for being my biggest fan since we were teens with big dreams and hearts in our eyes. I love you always!

ABOUT THE AUTHOR

Kennedy is a former middle school teacher, who began writing her debut novel *Buried* in the hopes of giving her resistant readers something they might actually read!

She now resides in Arizona with her high school sweetheart, Aaron, their 5 human children and their fur-daughters Granger and Bellatrix (Trixie). At any given moment she is either moving a hundred miles-an-hour on a new project, or scrolling mindlessly for hours on BookTok. There is no in between.

She welcomes you to follow her on Instagram @kenn_plumb and TikTok @plumbpages or @bookishkenn for book and family content.

ALSO BY KENNEDY PLUMB

Lightkeepers: A Modern Tangled Retelling

Buried (The Underground Series #1)

Royale (The Underground Series #2)

Love and Other Dangers (A Dystopian Romance Anthology)